"WELL, THIS ROOM'S SE...

It was until you wa... ...e took off his jacket an... ...e leather chair. Over hi... gun in a shoulder hols...

"Do you have a lice... ...d at it.

"Of course." He loo... at me slant-eyed. "Why do you ask?"

"They make me nervous, guns."

"Oh? It's a deadly business we're in. You should carry protection of some sort."

"I can take care of myself. I've got a license to ensorcell. There's only four of us in the entire Agency who do," I went on. "It's not a skill we use lightly. I hope you feel the same way about that gun."

I picked up the two drawings I'd just done, and waved them at him.

"Anyway, your target's in San Francisco, all right, or he was ten minutes ago. He was at the Cliff House out on Ocean Beach. He's driving a blue late-model four-door sedan, but I couldn't see where he was headed."

He took the drawings, looked at them, laid them down, then picked up the white envelope. "You haven't even opened this."

"I didn't need to open it. That's not how Long Distance Remote Sensing works."

The words seemed to burst out of him. "I cannot tell you how much I hate this kind of—of—this psychic bilge."

"Then what are you doing here?"

"Following the orders my superior gave me." He threw the envelope into my lap. "Open it, will you? At least do that much. Pander to my sense of reality."

"If you're not going to believe a word I say, why should I do anything you want?"

He started to retort, stopped himself, then shrugged. "You've got a point," he said. "Very well, would you please open the sodding envelope?"

KATHARINE KERR

LICENSE TO ENSORCELL

A Nola O'Grady Novel

DAW BOOKS, INC.

DONALD A. WOLLHEIM, FOUNDER

375 Hudson Street, New York, NY 10014

ELIZABETH R. WOLLHEIM
SHEILA E. GILBERT
PUBLISHERS

www.dawbooks.com

First Printing, February 2011
1 2 3 4 5 6 7 8 9

DAW TRADEMARK REGISTERED
U.S. PAT. AND TM. OFF. AND FOREIGN COUNTRIES
—MARCA REGISTRADA
HECHO EN U.S.A.

PRINTED IN THE U.S.A.

FOR ALIS

Who understands family

Acknowledgments

Many thanks to Kate Elliott and Amanda Weinstein, who gave me the kind of information about Israel one doesn't get from gazetteers—to say nothing of their emotional support. Also, many thanks to Christian Stubø for the data about the sniper's rifle that appears in the text.

Chapter I

I HAD JUST STEPPED OUT OF THE SHOWER when the angel appeared. It stood in the bathroom door and scratched its etheric butt through its billowing white robes.

"Yeah?" I said. "I'm dripping wet, so hurry it up."

"Joseph had a coat of many colors." Its hollow voice echoed through my apartment, although the angel itself turned transparent and vanished.

As I dressed in a tan corduroy skirt and an indigo and white print blouse, I asked myself if real angels itched. It seemed unlikely. Yet I doubted that demons suffered from skin problems either. Heat rash, maybe. Itching butts—improbable. So, the question became: which side was this apparition on in the eternal battle between Harmony and Chaos?

My name is Nola O'Grady. I can't tell you the name of my agency. You wouldn't believe it if I did. Let's just say it dates back to the Cold War, when certain higher-ups became convinced that the Soviets were using psi powers against us. The Soviets thought the same thing about us. Neither side had it right, but the paranoia turned out to be useful. Other people—if you can call them people—have given the Agency plenty of business over the years, which, incidentally, gives me a job. I had come home to San Francisco as an Agency operative, investigating a Chaos breach.

I grabbed an apple for breakfast and ate it while I waited for the N Judah streetcar. I stood on the concrete platform with a small mob of bleary-eyed office workers and college students, the majority of whom were drinking coffee from those fancy insulated paper cups. In a gloomy Tuesday mood, still a long way away from the weekend, most aimlessly watched the cars whizzing past us on the street. A few, like me, studied the weather. The night's fog was just beginning to pull back from a sky that promised to be sunny later. Although I kept a lookout, I saw no more angels in the silvery mist.

When the streetcar finally arrived, however, St. Joseph di Copertino was holding a seat for me next to a nice-looking blond guy in jeans and a leather jacket. To be precise, the saint was floating with his legs crossed under him above the seat. Although no one else seemed to see him, the other boarding passengers walked right past the empty seat, most likely for no reason they could have voiced. When I sat down, St. Joe obligingly floated higher and hovered over the back of the seat in front of me. The good-looking guy next to me smiled a little and looked at me sideways, waiting for me to break the ice, but saints always come first.

"What are you doing here?" I said. "I'm not an astronaut."

St. Joseph of Copertino smiled his trademark gape-mouthed grin and disappeared. The streetcar started up with its usual jerk and whine. It's gonna be one of those days, I thought. The guy next to me had stopped smiling. He was trying to merge with the wall.

"Sorry," I said. "I see saints now and then. This one happened to be the patron of astronauts, and so I wondered—"

He gave me the blank stare that people cultivate in a

city known for its crazies and weirdos. Scratch this one, I thought. I'd learned, over the years, that I needed to let prospective friends and especially interested guys know what I'm like right off the bat. It saved hysterics later. Still, I wondered why St. Joseph di Copertino had appeared just then, until I remembered he's also the patron saint of fools. Maybe he was making a general comment on my current love life, though the patron saint of zero, nothing, nada would have been more appropriate.

My cover story office, Morrison Marketing and Research, sat on the top floor of a 1930s building south of Market Street, a believable location for a low-level business, and pure WPA—the clunky stone contruction, the neoclassical pilasters, the dark wood interiors. I chose that office partly because the other suites on that floor stood empty, probably because of the view, or its lack thereof. The windows gave you a good look at the on-ramps to the freeway leading to the Bay Bridge.

Still, it offered advantages—its age for one. In my small suite the wood-framed windows opened to let in the outside air and the vibrations the air carries. I had a wood desk and a wood file cabinet, plus a couple of chairs for the nonexistent customers and a big potted plant. The expensive furniture the Agency had provided had gone into the office behind mine, the one for my nonexistent boss.

I wrote up the morning's two sightings and sent them off to the Agency via e-mail using the Agency site, the heavily encrypted TranceWeb, then took my standard morning walk. I was on Chaos Watch, which means you do a lot of looking around, preferably in as random a manner as possible. Chaos eruptions follow no schedules, no reasons, no logical connections—if they did, they wouldn't be chaotic, would they?

I used a procedure the Agency calls Random Synchronistic Linkage to determine my route. In

laymen's terms, I threw dice. You take a map of the
city and pinpoint where you are, then assign the numbers two through twelve to the surrounding directions.
Throw the dice and follow their lead, just so long as the
chosen direction doesn't take you into the bay or onto a
freeway without a car.

I set out on foot into a day turned bright and sunny,
though still cool from the halo of a winter fog wrapping
the horizon. Up the concrete canyon of Montgomery
Street, past the new glass and steel towers and the old
marble fronts where bankers work their legal mayhem
on the body politic, out again into the sunlight. At the
corner where Montgomery heads up a steep slope toward Russian Hill, a gray-haired woman stood waiting
for me. I recognized her pink and black tweed Chanel
suit first—vintage Fifties—with the pointy-toed black
patent shoes and matching handbag. She waved.

"Aunt Eileen," I said. "Fancy running into you! I take
it you saw me here in one of your dreams."

"Of course, so I came down to meet you." She wagged
a finger at me. "Really, Nola darling, it was awfully mean
of you to come home and never call."

"I don't want Mother to know—"

"Not one word. I promise."

She smiled. I smiled.

"And the rest of the family?" I said.

"Doing well, most of them—" She let the words trail
off.

"How's my little brother?" I could guess at the reason behind her reluctance.

"Still trying to transform himself." Aunt Eileen rolled
her eyes heavenward. "I do not have the slightest idea,
not the very slightest, why Michael wants to be a werewolf, but he does."

"I was afraid of that."

"After what happened to Patrick, you'd think he'd have learned, but no."

"Let's not talk about Patrick. I don't want to cry in public."

"I understand, dear." Aunt Eileen paused, glancing around her. "I don't think anyone can overhear us."

Traffic was rushing by, the wind was sighing through the concrete canyon behind us. I let my mind go to Search Mode: Danger and felt nothing.

"I don't think so, either," I said. "Why the secrecy?"

"Well, I've been having a really awful dream about you, and you never know who's where." She glanced around for a second time. "In the dream someone wants to kill you."

When she comes out with statements like that, I've never known her to be wrong. "Uh, where is this supposed to happen?" I said.

"Somewhere in San Francisco." She lifted one Chanel-clad shoulder in a nervous shrug. "I certainly hope I'm wrong this time. It's all been very distressing, especially once I realized you'd come home."

"Can you see what he looks like?"

"No, which is so annoying! He dresses like Sam Spade. He's in black and white even when the rest of the dream's in color. Very shadowy. Very Thirties." She gave me a sad look. "If you'd called me when you got in, I would have told you earlier."

"I'm sorry now I didn't. Can I buy you lunch to make up for it?"

"Some other day, I'd love that, but I have to go to the dentist." She wrinkled her nose. "How I hate it, but then, everyone does. I really must run, but I saw you here when I was waking up this morning, and so I thought I'd just catch up with you. You should go to the police about this person."

"And what am I going to tell them? My aunt had a dream?"

"Um, I suppose they wouldn't take it very seriously. I do wish you'd get a regular job, Nola. Something safe."

"It would bore me to tears."

I had never wanted her to know about my real work, but no one in the family can hide anything from Eileen. If one of her blood relations has a secret, sooner or later she'll dream out the truth, even when she'd rather not know.

"You always were a difficult child, and in our family, I'm afraid that's saying a lot." She rolled her eyes. "Now, you call me when you're free. Ah, here's my cab."

An empty cab was gliding up to the curb. She had luck that way, if you can call it luck. I waved good-bye, then stepped into a doorway to consider. Did I want to continue the dice walk so soon after hearing about this would-be assassin? Possibly my knowing about him had made a synchronistic connection that would lead me right to him, to the detriment of my health.

I turned around and went back to the office.

The answering machine on my desk was blinking when I came in. I kicked off the cheap high heels I was wearing as part of my cover persona, then punched the button on the machine to retrieve a message from Y's secretary. (That's the only name I have for him, Y, even though he's been my handler for years.) She told me that her boss wanted to know how the ad campaign for his company's new dog food was going. Dog food. With an assassin looking for me, that particular bit of code sounded entirely too appropriate.

The Agency loves code. It's heavy on the secrecy in general, mostly because the higher-ups are afraid that Congress would cut our funding if it ever found out what we do. I don't even know how large the Agency is or how many other agents work for it, though whenever

I've needed help, I've always gotten it. Code words and handles may keep us separate, but our skills unite us at a deep level and get the work done.

I found a notepad and a ballpoint pen, then went into the supposed boss' office, which I'd done up with blue wall-to-wall carpet, a big oak desk, and a black leather executive chair. I sat down in the secretary's chair next to the desk and went into trance. In a few minutes Y's image materialized in the leather chair. I can't tell you what he really looks like. The image he used back then for these trance-chats radiated pure movie star, the tousled blond hair, the crinkly smile, the blue eyes.

"So what is all this?" I said.

"I have a job for you," he said. "But you probably knew that already."

"Why else would you call me?"

"To talk about this alleged angel, for one thing. Seen any more of them?"

"None. They're probably just the usual visual projections." I tend to see clues, and I do mean *see* them.

"That's the safest assumption, but in our line of work you never know."

Ambiguity, the bane of my profession—having psychic talents makes the job sound easy. People think that clues should just drop into your lap, but on the rare occasions when they do, they usually mean two or three things at once.

"Any other Chaos manifestations?" Y continued.

I considered telling him about the assassin, but he'd want to know how I knew. I wanted to keep the family out of official business. Sooner or later, the guy from the Thirties movie would make a move or leave a track for me to follow, something I could report to Y as standard information.

"No, none yet," I said.

"Good. Now, about this job. It concerns an agent from Israel."

"Holy cripes! Mossad?"

"No, some group we're not supposed to know about. Now, technically he works for Interpol. Technically. This is all very hush-hush, but State called me in." He paused for a smug smile. "Called me in personally, that is. You know that State doesn't like asking for our help, but they've got good reasons to, this time."

"Any you can tell me?"

"Sure. This agent is hunting down someone wanted for a couple of murders back in Israel. One of the victims was an American citizen, working for the consular office over there." He leaned forward and lowered his voice, just as if someone could actually overhear us. "There were circumstances, our kind of circumstances. The agent will fill you in when he arrives."

"Now wait a minute! I already have a job on hand. Our stringers sent us evidence of a Chaos eruption. Why are you saddling me with some kind of secret agent?"

"Nola." His image looked at me sorrowfully. "In the service of the Great Balance, everything serves to further. Melodies appear, sing, and twine together. I don't know why this fellow is appearing at the moment, but he too is a thread in the great web of sapient life, a thread that has crossed our threads. Is it ours to question?"

When Y starts spouting philosophy, arguing gets me nowhere. I did allow myself a vexed sigh, which materialized as a rat skittering around between our chairs. Y never noticed it, and a good thing, too.

"All right." I surrendered. "How am I going to contact this guy?"

"Openly. He's going to come to your office on the pretext of hiring the marketing firm. His words to you are 'prayer shawls.' Yours are 'four-thirty appointment.' Got that?"

I could feel my hand writing of its own will. "Got it."

"Ask him who recommended Morrison Research to him. The right answer is Jake Levi of Sheboygan."

"Sheboygan? Why Sheboygan?"

"It's not the kind of name a foreigner could just pull out of the air."

"That's for sure. Okay, I've got that, too."

"Good. He has an odd kind of British accent. If the person who contacts you doesn't, you know what to do with him."

"Sure do, but I thought you said he was Israeli."

"He is. His parents emigrated from Britain right before he was born. They must have spoken English at home."

"Ah. That makes sense."

He leaned back in the chair a little too far. The line of his image sank into the leather. "Now, be careful with Mr. Ari Nathan. He's very high up, very well connected, been around a long time, knows everyone."

I immediately imaged him as a middle-aged, utterly earnest guy who wore glasses and was losing his hair. Probably paunchy, too, and wearing a rumpled white shirt and a gray suit. Y leaned forward in his chair and considered the extruded image.

"I don't know what he looks like," he said. "I've never seen a picture of him, and that's probably significant."

"All right, don't worry. I'll use my Company manners."

Y laughed at the pun, then withdrew his projection. I banished the image and woke from the trance.

Ari Nathan called early the next morning. He was an Israeli importer, he said, with a line of prayer shawls woven in the Holy Land that he wanted to place in California shops. He had a smooth middle-range voice that did indeed sound British.

"Mr. Morrison has an appointment open today at four-thirty," I said.

"Fine. I'll take that."

"May I ask you who recommended us to you?"

"Certainly. Jake Levi of Sheboygan."

All nicely in place and accurate.

Right on time Nathan arrived. The only thing about him that matched my extruded image was his clothing. Even in his cheap gray suit you could see that he had the kind of body you only get by working out regularly. His hair was dark, thick, and loosely curly—but his eyes caught my attention most of all, large and jet black, with a straight ahead stare under high arched brows. He looked like someone in a Byzantine icon. Yeah, I know that's the wrong religion, but the image fits. I put his age at about thirty, three or four years older than me, anyway. He looked at me, took a step back, then another forward again. Apparently I didn't fit his expectations either.

"Mr. Nathan?" I said.

"Yes." He hefted the tan leather sample case he was carrying. "I came about the prayer shawls."

"Yes, the four-thirty appointment."

"Sheboygan." He smiled with a slight twitch of his mouth. "Where might Sheboygan be, anyway?"

"I've got no idea. I could look it up for you on the Internet."

"No need to bother." He set the sample case down on the floor. "I was expecting some old granny. I must say you're quite a surprise."

"Same to you."

He smiled again, a little more broadly this time.

"I'm Nola O'Grady," I said. "Welcome to California."

"Thank you."

He leaned over the desk, and we shook hands. I liked his grip, firm without being bone-crushing, though he held onto my hand a little too long. I pulled it away as gracefully as I could. He straightened up and arranged a more businesslike expression.

"How can I help you?" I said.

He reached inside his jacket and pulled out a white business envelope. "I've been told you might be able to tell me something about this person. He was last seen in your city. I need to know if he's still on the premises."

"What's in that?"

"A set of pictures—his passport photo, some stills taken from security cameras."

He started to open the envelope.

"Don't," I said. "Just hand it to me sealed."

With a shrug he dropped it on my desk. I opened a side drawer and got out a big pad of paper and a box of crayons. I always use crayons to capture impressions. They're fast, they don't spill water all over, and you get sixty-four colors for cheap. He was staring at the box as if he expected a spider to crawl out of it.

"Is something wrong?" I said.

"Crayons? Children's crayons?"

I sighed. "Mr. Morrison will see you now, sir." I waved a thumb at the door to the inner office. "Go right in."

He started to speak, shrugged again, then picked up his sample case and followed orders. With him gone I could concentrate. Although the Agency calls this procedure Long Distance Remote Sensing, the old name offers more poetry: farseeing.

I laid the envelope of photos to one side of my drawing pad, put my left hand on it, and waited. I can't tell you what I think of when I begin an LDRS because there's nothing to tell. I get a jumble of thoughts, a twitch of the mind, and then all at once images start to develop. In this case I saw the ocean. I grabbed a blue-green crayon and began. Ocean—rocks, big rock—cliff—some yellow smears that might have been taxi cabs. I saw red in the shape of a long box with wheels, a tourist bus.

Everything changed. New sheet of paper, gravel on the ground, a blue car, the bright green of trees, a weird gray shape, a black smudge—nothing. Whoever he was, he was moving too fast for me to reach him, probably driving the blue car. That much the rational part of my mind could tell me. I leaned back in my chair and considered the scribbles on the two sheets of paper. An LDRS never produces fine art. Interpretation's everything.

I looked away, got up, stretched, then sat back down and looked at the scribbles again. One thing jumped out: the weird gray shape formed a trench coat. I'd even drawn in the belt. The black smudge defined a hat shape, floating over the coat. Sam Spade in black and white, when everything else in the picture had showed up in Technicolor. My hands started to shake. I made them stop. The entire experience left behind a feeling like the lingering stench of old kitchen garbage.

I tore the two sheets off the pad, got up, and went into the inner office. Nathan had closed the windows and the venetian blinds. He held a black gadget that looked like a light meter or a stud finder. As I watched he drew the gadget along the far wall in short, controlled passes.

"Looking for bugs?" I said.

"Yes." He continued working while he talked. "I've got an interference generator in that sample case, too."

The sense of danger struck me in a long chilly frisson. I sat down in the secretary's chair and laid the two drawings on the executive desk. Even though the room had become hot and stuffy with the window closed, my hands ached with cold. The danger flowed out of Ari Nathan, it seemed to me, far deeper than the Sam Spade scribble or Aunt Eileen's warning, danger he'd brought in that sample case, maybe, with the job he needed done.

He finished scanning the window and slipped the device into his pants pocket. "Hot in here," he said.

"It is, yeah." My voice stayed steady, fortunately. "That's because we're right under the roof. I didn't want

anyone moving in above me who might want to eaves-
drop."

"Good idea. Well, this room's secure."

It was until you walked into it, anyway, I thought. He
took off the jacket and draped it over the back of the
leather chair. Over his pale blue shirt he was wearing a
gun in a shoulder holster. I hate guns, partly because of
what happened to Patrick, partly for all kinds of rational
reasons beyond that.

"Do you have a license for that thing?" I pointed at it.

"Of course." He looked at me slant-eyed. "Why do
you ask?"

"They make me nervous, guns."

"Oh? It's a deadly business we're in. You should carry
protection of some sort."

"I can take care of myself. I've got a license to ensorcell."

He blinked at me with those gorgeous Byzantine eyes.

"There's only four of us in the entire Agency who
do," I went on. "It's not a skill we use lightly. I hope you
feel the same way about that gun."

I thought he was about to sneer, but he kept his face
expressionless. I picked up the two drawings and waved
them at him.

"Anyway, your target's in San Francisco, all right, or
he was ten minutes ago. He was at the Cliff House out
on Ocean Beach. He's driving a blue late-model four-
door sedan, but I couldn't see where he was headed."

He took the drawings, looked at them, laid them
down, then picked up the white envelope. "You haven't
even opened this."

"I didn't need to open it. That's not how Long
Distance Remote Sensing works."

The words seemed to burst out of him. "I cannot tell
you how much I hate this kind of—of—this psychic
bilge."

"Then what are you doing here?"

"Following the orders my superior gave me." He threw the envelope into my lap. "Open it, will you? At least do that much. Pander to my sense of reality."

"If you're not going to believe a word I say, why should I do anything you want?"

He started to retort, stopped himself, then shrugged. "You've got a point," he said. "Very well, would you please open the sodding envelope?"

I tore it open and shook out the photographs. On top lay a fuzzy snap from a security camera. Although I couldn't discern the perp's features, I could tell he was wearing a Dodgers cap. It figured. The passport photo clearly showed me a skinny white man, nearly bald, light-colored eyes, thin lips, wearing a plaid sports shirt, a very ordinary American face, except it belonged to a man who wanted to kill me.

"Do you know that fellow?" Nathan said. "The name we have for him is William Johnson."

"No. Never seen him before."

He cocked his head to one side and gave me a cold look. "You're hiding something, aren't you?"

"How can you tell? I thought you didn't believe in all this psychic bilge."

"I said I hated it. There's a difference. I wouldn't be in the line of work I'm in if I couldn't tell when someone was lying, and that's training, not psychism."

His tone of voice made me feel like slapping him. Instead, I said, "All right, I've been warned that someone wants to kill me. I think it's this guy, but I can't be sure."

"What? Who warned you?"

Since I had to work with this guy no matter what, I saw no point in telling him the truth, especially with a dodge so close at hand.

"Psychic intuition," I said. "The Agency calls this phenomenon Semi-Automatic Warning Mechanism."

He stared at me.

"That's why you're here, isn't it?" I said. "Because I have psychic skills?"

"Unfortunately, yes." He leaned back in the chair with a long sigh. "I should have taken my father's advice. I should have been an insurance adjustor. But did I listen to him?"

"Your father was in the insurance business?"

"Eventually. Before that he was a nutter."

"Say what?"

He ignored the question and continued staring at the opposite wall. From the slack jaw as well as his general vibe—what the Agency calls the Subliminal Psychological Profile—I could tell that he felt personally betrayed by something. Life, probably. After a couple of minutes he roused himself.

"My contact at your State Department told me I could use this office as my temporary work arrangement."

"Oh, did they? It's the first I've ever heard of it."

"You're supposed to contact your handler about it."

"Oh, am I? That's pretty high handed of them! What do you propose for a cover story?"

"Simple." He gave me a crooked smile. "I'm going to be Mr. Morrison."

I let fly with some words that weren't ladylike. He winced and stood up, then picked up his sample case to take with him.

"Oh, for God's sake, wipe that sneer off your face, will you?" he said. "If someone's out to kill you, you need the kind of protection I can offer. Well, don't you?"

He had me there. Of course I did.

"You haven't told me why you're looking for this guy," I said as pleasantly as I could manage.

"I'll do that tomorrow." He took his jacket from the back of the chair. "I've got another appointment. Something personal."

He put the jacket on and walked out of the office. I followed just in case he decided to steal something from my desk, which he didn't. As soon as he'd well and truly left, I went back into the new Mr. Morrison's room, sat down in the secretary's chair, and tranced a sharp message to Y. Even though it was eight in the evening, D.C. time, he answered promptly, a little too fast, maybe, because his image had dark eyes instead of the usual blue.

"I take it you don't like Mr. Nathan much, either," Y said.

"You've met him? You told me you hadn't."

"I haven't. Our contact at the State Department has. He warned me this morning. He was close to frothing at the mouth."

"So am I. What's this garbage about Nathan taking over my office?"

"Well, State wants him to have a base to work out of. There's nothing I can do about it, Nola. I'm sorry."

Y sounded so genuine that I calmed down.

"Look, if he gets too obnoxious," Y continued, "tell him that you're his handler now. State will back you. I'll make sure of that."

"Oh, thank you very much! He's going to really like that. Take it just like a little lamb."

"Spare me the sarcasm. I've sent you an encrypted file on Nathan's background to the other location."

"I'm surprised their secret service told you anything about him."

"They didn't. This is what our operatives could find out." He paused. "Look, I've got to go. Dinner's on the table."

Y vanished. Was he married, I wondered?

I took the two pieces of scribble art and went back to my own desk where I could sit in comfort to think. So Aunt Eileen's Thirties movie villain had appeared in my remote sensing pictures. I had a name for him now, even though it sounded fake. I considered trying to sense him again, then shelved the idea.

Johnson's black and white Shield Persona, as the Agency terms these false images, told me that he had talents of his own. So far both Aunt Eileen and I had partially overridden them. Still, challenging him at this stage of the game struck me as too risky. I liked the idea of giving him a link back to me even less. I therefore needed to get my mind off him. As a symbolic action, what the Agency calls Conscious Evasion Procedure, I sent the scribbles through my cross-cut shredder.

Night came early this time of year. Even though I twitched at the thought of Johnson hunting me on dark streets, I refused to spend the night sleeping on the office floor. I locked up the suite, then took the N Judah streetcar home. Safety in numbers—as always at rush hour, commuters crammed the car. I stood all the way to Ninth Avenue, my stop, did a little grocery shopping, then hurried up the stairs to my apartment before my landlady realized I'd come home. Mrs. Zukovski loved long conversations on the stairs, or to be precise, long monologues, usually about her cats.

Before I locked the door behind me, I did a quick mental scan of the apartment: all clear. Nathan had his ways of securing a place. I had mine. Glare from the streetlight outside fell through the bay window onto my saggy blue couch and the book-littered coffee table. I switched on the overhead light. From the door I could see into the tiny kitchen with its black and white tile; it lay in shadow, but the shadow came through the side window from the building next door, not occult forces, or as the Agency prefers to call them, Unexploited Personnel Capabilities. I put the salad fixings away, then decided to wait for dinner.

My home computer connected to a scrambled DSL line, not a business wireless setup like we had in the office. On top of the scrambler, the Agency double-encrypts all files with a private system. We call our site TranceWeb because you need to go into trance to read it, which effectively limits snoopers. I logged on, grabbed the Nathan file, and let myself drift into the proper frame of mind.

What I read made a lot of things clear. His parents were middle-class Jews in London who came under the influence of a New-Age type "spiritual practices rabbi." Although no one seemed to know exactly which powers this "New Ezekiel" had, he must have developed the ability to talk people out of their hard-earned money. This supposed spiritual leader acquired a lot of land in Israel in the 1970s and decided to found a kibbutz. He told his followers that he wanted to revive the old Zionist days before Palestine became Israel, a time of hard work and simple living, but also of pure communal goals and ideals, a collective farm in the best sense.

Unfortunately, he was somewhat less than sane. His actual goal turned out to be a kibbutz dedicated as a training center for Armageddon. The men studied weaponry, ready to fight on the side of the Messiah, while the women went off into the desert to have visions. They were hoping to learn who this Messiah was and when they should get dinner ready for his arrival.

After seven years Nathan's mother had had a vision. She'd seen that she'd married the wrong man. After the divorce, she headed back to London with a new lover. Every summer Nathan visited his mother in the U.K. for six weeks, which explained his good but oddly formal English. Nathan's father stuck it out on the kibbutz for a year, then took his son and went to Tel Aviv and that job in the insurance business.

In Tel Aviv Nathan had a normal life, if you can consider a ten-year-old boy who knows how to clean, load, and fire every handheld weapon known to modern man normal. He'd done very well during his compulsory stint in the army. Way ahead of his class, I figured, judging from the number of sharpshooter medals that studded his public record.

When he left the army, Interpol recruited him because, according to the file, he had an unusual flair for languages as well as guns. Yet he left there after two years, apparently or maybe. They no longer listed him on any official public documents, but a year later he showed up working for them again. His life fell into a pattern of disappearances followed by a return to respectable police work. None of our operatives could find out why. No one knew where he went in between his Interpol stints, though we could assume that he was working for his deep cover agency. About his personal life, nothing except for a brief mention that he'd never married.

And one detail that struck me as oddly humorous— his actual name: Ariel. Yes, I know about Ariel Sharon, who had more in common with fire and brimstone than magical spirits, but my education had pounded Shakespeare into my brain. No wonder, I thought, Nathan went by Ari.

I logged off and shut down. When I came out of trance, I heard a slice of cold pizza calling to me from the refrigerator, a lot louder than all the healthy salad stuff I'd bought at the grocery store. After I ate, I considered turning on the TV, but my mind kept revolving around the problem of Ari Nathan. Tell him I was his handler— sure, easy enough to tell him, but would he listen? The way he'd run out for his "something personal" appointment without even giving me a full briefing made me doubt it. And where was he, anyway? Probably with some unfortunate woman, I figured, and good luck to her!

Eventually, of course, curiosity got the better of me.

Hey, it's one of my job qualifications. I took out the pad
of paper and box of crayons that I keep at home.

The LDRS gave me three drawings, all of them less
scribbly than usual. The first two puzzled me. I wondered if I were looking at a crime scene, because pale
white bodies lay on the ground behind barbed wire.
They all wore white clothing, as shapeless as pajamas.
What had Nathan done, gone off the deep end and shot
a lot of people? The third drawing showed two standing
figures: a flesh and blood elderly man wearing a heavy
gray sweater, black pants, and a yarmulke. He was looking at a white ghost—no, at a plaster sculpture.

All of a sudden I realized what I was seeing: the
Holocaust memorial out at the Legion of Honor art museum. I caught a glimpse of Nathan himself, also wearing a yarmulke, standing and staring at those symbols of
remembered murder lying on the ground. I broke the
trance. I was ashamed of myself, spying on him at such a
moment, but the shame didn't last, because the sense of
danger came with the glimpse.

I had a hard time breathing for a moment, just because of the danger-sense, or the Semi-Automatic
Warning Mechanism. Outside the sunlight had faded.
The purple neon sign on the Persian restaurant across
the street lit up and began to blink. I drew the curtains
and switched on both of the lamps in the living room,
turned on the one in the bathroom, too, just because.
Was he really an Israeli agent, I wondered, or was that
a pretense? Was he working with Johnson instead of
tracking him down, a double agent, a traitor? I decided
to try to find out.

At my kitchen table I did a tarot spread, something
the Agency doesn't have a name for, but it's always
worked for me, provided I use the old Marseilles deck
and do a full layout. I took my pack out of its silk-lined
sandalwood box. The scent from the wood soothed me

and put me in the right mind for a reading. As I shuffled the cards, I focused on the sense of danger Nathan brought with him. Some guys smell of sweat; this guy smelled of danger.

When I began turning them over, I expected to see a good many swords and maybe even the Death card or the Broken Tower. Instead, a spread heavy on cups lay in front of me, with the ace prominently displayed beside the Sun. In the middle, covering my significator, sat the Knight of Cups himself. The Empress leered at him from several cards away. The danger Nathan represented appeared obvious.

"No," I said aloud. "Not for all the cold cash in the world am I going to fall in love with this guy, or with any guy, but especially not this guy. And that's that."

It had taken me years to reconcile myself to my talents and find some kind of mental equilibrium. Having the family I do didn't make it any easier. Falling in love with a difficult guy would take more energy than I could spare. I gathered up the cards and shoved them back into their box, slapped down the lid, and wrapped the entire thing up in a scarf to block the vibrations.

I wandered back into the living room and flopped down on the couch. I was going to watch the nightly news—in my business you have to be a news junkie, no matter what the source—but what did I see onscreen but another lousy angel. It waved, then morphed into the face of the usual anchor, babbling about the state budget.

Joseph and the coat of many colors. Lean years, then fat years? Sold into slavery in Egypt? I grabbed the remote and flipped channels until I found some ancient Looney Tunes, a fitting end to the day.

CHAPTER 2

THE NEWLY CREATED Mr. Morrison strolled into the office around ten in the morning. Nathan had upgraded his suit to a navy blue pinstripe, a little too broad in the lapels, set off by a yellow and red silk tie, giving him just the right air of a small businessman trying to look like a big businessman.

"Good morning," I said brightly. "Sir."

He stopped in front of my desk, shoved his hands in his jacket pockets, and scowled at me. "I heard from your State Department this morning," he said.

"Good. Then you know I'm your handler."

"I know that they told me you were. There's a difference. Listen, I don't want interference."

"Then you don't want my help. You can call me your liaison if that makes you feel better."

He snarled on past and slammed into the inner office. I let him brood while I called Aunt Eileen. I reached her answering machine, left a message about lunch, and hung up just as Nathan slammed out again. He'd taken off his suit jacket and the gun harness.

"Yeah?" I said.

"Come into my office, and I'll finish briefing you."

I left the door between our offices open so I could

hear the phone if Aunt Eileen returned my call, then followed him in. The gun lay on his desk in plain sight.

"Can't you put that thing away?" I said.

He scowled, but he did shove the gun into a desk drawer.

"This fellow, William Johnson," he began, "we know him as an American who came to Israel to buy land for a Christian kibbutz."

"Christian? Does your government let Christians buy land?"

"Why not? They're a lot less obnoxious than the black hats."

"The who?"

"Sorry. The *haredi*, the ultraorthodox. The ones who don't want the streetcars to run on the Sabbath and think everyone should keep kosher and the like. The men all wear black hats. Hence the name, though it's old-fashioned. Most people at home just call them 'the blacks' now, but that name won't do here in America."

"No, it sure won't." I assumed then that life in the spiritual practices kibbutz had formed his opinion, but later I found out that a lot of Israelis felt as he did. "So Johnson had a legit reason to be there."

"No, as it turned out. The group he claimed to belong to doesn't exist. We didn't find that out until too late. The government doesn't investigate every tourist who comes through. By all accounts he seemed like an ordinary sort of pilgrim, except he had a lot of money to flash around. We get them all the time, tour buses full of Americans babbling about Bethlehem and the footsteps of Jesus."

"Yeah, I know the type." Most of my relatives, I thought.

"So," Nathan continued. "As far as the police can tell, he was using the land buy to give him an excuse to

look for someone or something beyond the usual tourist routes. He may have found it—a young woman who
worked for an estate agent who turned up dead two
days after meeting him."

"May have?"

"There was a lot of muddled evidence pointing to
Johnson, but no motive and nothing that would have
stood up in a court of law. Still, the police kept an eye
on him as he moved on. The next victim was a member
of the American consul's staff. The secretary told me
that Johnson came in to ask about handling the police.
He knew they suspected him for the murder of Miriam
Greenbaum."

"Miriam was the realtor?"

Nathan looked briefly puzzled. "You mean the murdered estate agent. Yes, she was."

"That name's familiar, but damned if I can remember
why."

"Well, try, will you?" His voice echoed sneers. "She
was a recent immigrant, if that helps."

The man had a genius for driving thoughts out of
people's heads. Who can remember names they heard
once, maybe, when they're furious?

"Anyway," Nathan continued, "during his interview
with the consular officer, the receptionist heard them
arguing, though she couldn't understand what they were
saying. The officer only told her that Johnson was an
idiot with too much money who should go to the police
and tell them what he knew. Two days later the officer
was found dead in his apartment."

"I was told there were odd circumstances around that
murder, the sort of thing my agency specializes in."

"Oh, yes. Both victims were killed with silver bullets.
That's what linked them."

"Were both bodies found naked?"

"Yes."

"And both happened around the time of the full moon?"

"How did you know that?"

"This gets us somewhere, Nathan. Both of these victims must have been werewolves."

He winced. "That's absurd."

"No," I said, "it's logical."

"Logical? You know, if you start with an absurd premise, you can be as logical as you like and still reach an absurd conclusion."

"Oh, all right! It appears, it may be, it could be, that Johnson thought these people were werewolves. Is that better?"

"Yes, actually. Thank you." An adolescent sarcasm poisoned every word.

"Listen, Nathan," I said. "Neither of us likes this arrangement. But you don't have the psychic skills to track this guy down, and I don't have the brawn to bring him in once I do." I braced myself for an explosion. "So we have to work together. Can we try to do it pleasantly?"

The explosion never came. He spent a minute or two looking at me. He lowered his hands and sat up straighter in his chair. When he spoke, his voice sounded level. "Quite so. We're both stuck with each other, I suppose, as you Americans say."

"Yeah, we are."

All at once he grinned, a warm smile, boyish and seductive both. "Very few people stand up to me," he said. "You do it quite well."

"Yeah? Good. Get used to it."

I had no more attention to waste on him at the moment. I needed to get control of my own rage. My brother Patrick had been shot and killed with an ordinary bullet, which had left his corpse in wolf form. The family never could go to the police, never get justice for his murder. This Johnson had at least done the honorable thing—

all at once the hair rose on the back of my neck. Could Johnson have been the killer?

"What's wrong?" Nathan said.

"Just evil thoughts. Johnson's running around loose in my hometown. I'm wondering what brought him here."

"So am I. He's quite obviously deranged if he thinks innocent people are werewolves, which means one of two things. Either he's a psychotic serial killer, or the two victims weren't the innocents they seem. I tend to the latter, because he fled Israel to Syria. There's also a semi-reliable report placing him in northeastern Iran."

"Only semi-reliable?"

"Yes." He paused, considering me. "You can't blindly trust any information from that part of the world, the Hindu Kush, that is. Even, at times, if you've gathered it yourself."

Something lurked behind this reasonable statement. I marked it in my mind.

"At any rate," Nathan continued, "it was impossible to trace him beyond that until he reappeared in San Francisco."

"Your people think there might be an Al Qaeda connection?"

"That's the reason I'm here and not an ordinary Interpol officer."

I could guess that his background in that peculiar excuse for a kibbutz had something to do with the assignment, but I couldn't blame him for not wanting to dwell on that.

"If he's Al Qaeda," I said, "what was he doing in Shia Iran?"

"A very good question. I asked it myself, but my superior couldn't answer it. He told me that finding out was my job."

"Your superior sounds like mine. You have my sympathy."

Again that boyish grin, and his eyes looked less Byzantine, suddenly, and a lot warmer. I suppressed an urge to call him by his first name.

"I can give you the dossier on the murders," Nathan said eventually. "It's not terribly detailed, I'm afraid, but—" He stopped and held up his hand for silence.

I heard the footsteps, too. Someone was in the corridor outside our office. Since the other suites stood empty, whoever it was concerned us. Nathan got up, slid the drawer open, and picked up his gun, all smoothly, utterly silently. In a few long strides he crossed into the outer office. I slipped off my noisy high heels and followed. Pebbled green glass filled the window in the door that led into the corridor. I could see the silhouette of a person standing just outside and hear the noise of the handle turning, clicking against the lock.

"Nola? Are you in there?"

"Aunt Eileen!" I called out. "Just a minute. The lock's stuck."

Nathan trotted back into his office while I pretended to fiddle with the door. I finally opened it with a flourish.

"You must have gotten my call," I said.

"I did, dear, and thank you." Eileen came bustling in, swinging a brown paper shopping bag. "I have a cell phone now, and Brian showed me how to get messages by relay or remotely or whatever they call that. I was downtown at the big Goodwill store over on Eleventh." She held up the shopping bag. "And so I thought I'd just stop by since it's almost lunchtime. I hope your boss doesn't mind." She spoke the word boss with invisible quotes around it, playing along with the cover story.

In the doorway between the two rooms, Nathan stood frozen, staring at her. She was wearing one of her usual outfits, a white blouse complete with a peter pan collar, and a red felt circle skirt with a fuzzy appliqué of a poodle near the hem. She'd cinched in both with a wide black belt, the kind shaped in back to hug your waist.

"Well, young man," she said, "do you mind?"

"Not at all," he said. "Take a little extra time if you'd like, Nola."

"Thank you, Mr. Morrison. This is my aunt, Eileen Houlihan."

Nathan nodded to acknowledge the introduction. Aunt Eileen glanced at my bare feet. "Where are your shoes, darling?"

"In my office, I should think." Nathan struggled to suppress a grin but failed. "I'll just get them for you." He hurried back into his inner sanctum.

"Nola!" Aunt Eileen hissed. "Honestly!"

Lunch came with an extra helping of Aunt Eileen's religious views on womanly behavior. Like her clothes, they date to the 1950s.

"He *is* awfully good-looking," she said, "but honestly! I hope you weren't sitting in his lap."

"Say what?" I said. "This pair of shoes hurts, and I'd just slipped them off for a minute when you arrived."

She glared at me over her coffee cup.

"Really," I went on. "Nothing's going on. I hardly know the man."

"That's my point. You shouldn't be necking with someone you hardly know."

"I wasn't doing anything like that at all."

"And if you wore stockings, your shoes wouldn't hurt."

"That reminds me," I said, "what did you get at the Goodwill?"

"A perfectly lovely baby blue twin set. It must have been lying in storage for years. But don't you try to distract me. I sincerely hope your Mr. Morrison isn't a Protestant."

"No, he's certainly not! And he's not mine. He's just my boss." I lowered my voice. "A coworker, really."

She gave me the stare that her daughter, Clarice, calls

the "gimlet eye." "Well, you should keep your shoes on in his office. What if he's a foot fetishist?"

I blinked several times. "You know," I said at last, "that idea never occurred to me."

"That's why girls have aunts. To warn them about the possibilities."

At that point, fortunately, she allowed me to change the subject.

Once I'd caught up on all the family gossip, I returned to my office. I found Nathan standing at one side of the window and looking out at an angle.

"See anything interesting?" I said.

"No. Just checking the lines of sight." He turned back into the room. "We need to move your desk. A sniper on that motorway overpass with the right sort of rifle could take your head off."

"I'd call that very interesting." For more reasons than one—why wasn't I more afraid of this possible assassin? Although I suspected that he'd left town, I couldn't depend on a suspicion, especially since he might come back at any time.

I shut down the computer and began clearing the clutter off the desk. Once we had the furniture rearranged, I left for the day, but work followed me. In the lobby of the office building, tiled in dirty green, what light there was came from a pair of bulbs in a dust-clogged overhead fixture. In late spring and summer, glare from the street did seep through the glass doors. In winter, only the streetlights outside got through and produced interesting shadows.

When I stepped out of the elevator I saw movement in one of the shadowed corners. I took a few steps closer to investigate and heard a hiss, more like a cat than a snake. The creature I saw, however, looked reptilian— scaly blue skin, wedge-shaped head—as it rose onto its hind legs like a meerkat. It stood perhaps two feet tall and had shiny yellow claws that looked like they could give its prey a good rip and tear. About this apparition I had no doubts at all. I shifted my bag to my left hand and with the right sketched out a Chaos ward. The creature popped like a balloon. A shriveled skin fell to the floor, then disappeared.

The forces of Chaos had found my office and sent one of their spies, constructs modeled on some creature from one of the nastier places in the universe. I could see two possibilities: the Chaos masters wanted to kill me specifically, or they merely knew that an agent of Harmony had appeared in their territory and wanted to kill whomever it was. I disliked both options and got the hell out into the open air.

Back home I took the salad out of the fridge and turned on the TV news to get a quick look at the day before I began working the Internet. The lead story nearly made me choke on my arugula. Another murder that pointed straight to Johnson: a young woman's body found naked in a deserted area of the Presidio. The news anchor got lurid over the silver bullet that had killed her, and the phase of the moon, just past full, but for a change lurid rang true. It did point to the killer thinking she was a werewolf—or to her actually being one.

The police, damn them, were keeping her name to themselves, pending notification of her next of kin, nor did the news show a picture of her face. They did say that she'd been dead just under twenty-four hours. When I'd Remote Sensed Johnson leaving the Cliff House, he could have been heading to the Presidio to lie in wait for his kill. Maybe he'd already fled the Bay Area or maybe he was hanging around for me.

Suddenly I didn't feel like eating. I'd just put the remains of the salad back in the fridge when the landline rang. I hurried to the machine and saw that the caller ID had been overridden. I picked up the receiver.

"Nathan?" I said. "What's up?"

"How did you know it was me?"

"How do you think?"

He made a noise halfway between a growl and a word, then spoke normally. "Did you see the news?"

"Sure did."

"We need to talk about this. I'll be right over."

"How did you get my number?"

"How do you think?" He made a sound that was probably meant to be a laugh. "I know where you live, too." And the bastard hung up before I could say a word more.

Nathan appeared at my door so fast that I realized he'd been phoning from nearby. I'd only ever seen him in a business suit. The way he looked in a pair of good-fitting jeans, a white shirt, and a brown leather bomber jacket made the danger warning swirl around me like a San Francisco fog, but when he took the jacket off, I saw that damned gun again. I made him wait by the door while I shut the curtains over the bay windows.

"So, this murdered girl," he said. "She fits Johnson's way of working."

"Yeah, she sure does. I wish they'd release her name and picture."

Nathan tossed the jacket onto the arm of the couch, then flopped down on the middle cushion. I turned my computer chair around and sat down facing him. He looked disappointed, just for a moment, but long enough for the warning to double.

"When's the next newscast?" he said.

"Nine o'clock, but I can get the news faster from the Net."

"Assuming your Net news has a reporter down at the police station."

"Well, true. The TV people will."

He glanced at his watch. "Only seven now. That chair doesn't look comfortable enough for a two hour wait."

"It's fine, thanks."

He grinned at me, a warm smile that made me feel like melting. Fortunately, I remained solid. I was just thinking up a suitably cold remark when my cell phone rang. I took it out of the pocket of my jeans and flipped it open. Aunt Eileen.

I got up and went into the kitchen to take the call. I looked back through the open door in case Nathan had gotten up to snoop, but he kept his nice little behind on the couch. I moved away into the kitchen as far as I could get and kept my voice soft.

"Hi," I said. "Did you see the news?"

"I certainly did." Aunt Eileen's voice ached with worry. "Michael's just sick about it."

"Did he know that girl?"

"I doubt it. He's terrified that the same thing could happen to him."

"Don't tell me he's managed to transform!"

"Not yet, but the stubborn little darling doesn't want to stop trying. He really needs you to talk him out of it, but I haven't even told him you're back."

"I'd call him, but I don't want Mother—"

"I understand that. He's living here again. The same old problem, and it really seemed like the only way he was going to stay in school and not run off somewhere was to get him out of that house."

"My dear mother. Dear, dear Mother."

"Well, yes. Heaven knows I've tried to talk to her, and Father Keith has tried, but—well."

"Is he still at Riordan? Michael, I mean, not Father Keith."

"No, I've put him in public school. For someone in our family, I think it's healthier to be around a good mix of people."

"Yeah, I agree." An idea struck me, a good way to

avoid the temptation to cuddle up to Nathan on my couch for a couple of hours. "Hang on."

As I walked back into the living room, Nathan slipped something into his shirt pocket. I suspected the worst.

"Do you have a car?" I said.

"Yes."

"Okay, can you do me a favor? I need to get over to my aunt's house." I paused, struck by one of those thoughts that come out of nowhere, or the Collective Data Stream, as the Agency calls it. "Someone there has something that relates to our job. I don't know what it is yet, but it's waiting at my aunt's."

Nathan rolled his eyes, but he spoke in an ordinary tone of voice. "I can drive you, certainly."

"I was thinking about just borrowing the car."

"You're not on the insurance I got from the rental agency." He smiled, more than a little smugly. "Sorry."

"Aunt Eileen?" I spoke into the phone. "I'll be right over. I'm bringing a friend—well, it's Morrison, actually. He's here and has a car."

"Nola! Honestly!"

I switched off the phone. I didn't need to be psychic to know what she was going to say next. Nathan got up and grabbed his jacket from the arm of the couch. As he shrugged into it, the white shirt stretched tight against his chest, just enough for me to see the suspicious shape in his shirt pocket.

"You were listening in, weren't you?" I said.

"Oh, yes. It's my job." He grinned at me. "I just can't help myself sometimes."

"Self-control is a wonderful thing. I recommend it."

He opened his mouth, then shut it again. I hurried into the bedroom to get a jacket before he could think of anything to say.

Driving with Nathan took my breath away, and I

don't mean from the beauty of the view. As long as we picked our way through the traffic around the Ninth and Judah neighborhood, I noticed nothing unusual, but our route took us to Seventh Avenue and up over Twin Peaks, a four-lane road through trees and what almost appears to be open country around the city reservoir. Nathan hit the accelerator and drove like a fiend out of hell, or at least, what a fiend would drive like if a necromancer were stupid enough to let one take the wheel.

I yelled at him, I begged him, but we swerved around cars, changed lanes at top speed, and generally screeched along uphill and down, with me screaming directions and curses alternately. How we avoided being stopped by cops or mangled in the cross traffic by Laguna Honda, I do not know. All the way down O'Shaughnessy like an out-of-control bobsled—but we lived. Maybe Father Keith is right about guardian angels.

Aunt Eileen lives in the Excelsior district, which rises from outer Mission Street on a long sweep of hillside, terraced over the years into city streets and crammed with modest houses. About halfway up the hill toward McLaren Park, she and her husband have a rambling old house that started life as a cottage on a double lot around 1910. Generations of Houlihans built onto it, sometimes according to a plan, usually not. By the time Eileen married into the family and went to live in it, it contained ten bedrooms and a collection of odd hallways and corners as well as the usual living arrangements, all piled together, two stories high in some places, three in another, and only one in the middle, which gave it the look of a couple of houses shuffled like cards and then fanned onto a table.

Nathan parked his rented gray Audi across the street, a modestly nice little car, suitable for his cover persona, utterly wrong for his real nature.

"Next time," I gasped, "I'm driving."

"Why? What's wrong?"

"Don't tempt me! Listing what's wrong could take hours. And would you lock that damned gun away? Like in the glove compartment? My aunt always keeps her house really warm. You'll roast if you have to leave that jacket on."

Nathan turned toward me, his eyes narrow, his mouth set. He started to speak, then shrugged. "All right," he said. "I don't believe in carrying a gun around children, anyway. I take it that your brother qualifies as a child."

"I'd say so, but never tell him that."

We hiked up the steep brick stairs that led to the front porch. Aunt Eileen opened the door before I could ring the bell. She was wearing a leopard print blouse, a pair of turquoise blue capri pants, and fuzzy pink slippers. Nathan did his best not to stare. He smiled pleasantly even when she fixed him with the gimlet eye.

"Good evening, Mr. Morrison," she said. "Do come in."

Aunt Eileen's house always smells of scented chemicals: room freshener, dishwasher soap, rug cleaner, with a tang of ammonia from the windows under it all. Her front door opens into the middle of the big white living room, which runs across the entire front of the house. To the left as you step in she has a matching pair of chairs and a curved sectional sofa, all covered in pale gold brocade. I don't remember anyone ever sitting on any of them. Over the fireplace on the end wall hangs a portrait of Father Keith O'Brien, her oldest brother (and my mother's, too, of course) in his Franciscan robes.

Eileen steered us toward the other end of the room, the one with the collection of sagging armchairs that people actually use. Tattered Navajo rugs covered that section of white wall-to-wall carpet to guard against soft drinks and snacks.

"Boys?" she said. "Turn that thing off, will you? We've got company."

Eileen's youngest, Brian, and my brother Michael
sat on the floor in front of the enormous flat-screen TV,
but rather than watching a show, they were playing a
video game. They looked enough alike to be brothers,
not cousins—skinny sixteen-year-olds with dark hair
and blue eyes, both of them with thin straight noses and
thin mouths, though Brian was a head taller. Michael's
hair fell just above his shoulders, while Brian kept his
short. The family inbreeding runs deep, though some
of us, like me, have hazel eyes—witch eyes, as we call
them—to go with the wavy black hair. They both wore
jeans and black T-shirts, though each did have a different rock band logo across the chest.

Brian muttered something that sounded like "hello"
and went on clicking away at the game. I got a glimpse
of what seemed to be zombies staggering around a room
before Michael grabbed the controller from his cousin
and pressed a couple of buttons. The game disappeared.
Michael scrambled up and ran over to throw his arms
around me. I caught the scent of cheap marijuana.

"Boy, am I glad to see you," he said.

"You look pretty good yourself." I returned the hug.
"I guess things have been kind of hairy at home."

"Yeah, like, you know." He let me go. "Are you really
back?"

"For the foreseeable future."

Everyone laughed at the family joke but Nathan, who
manfully continued smiling.

"There's some cookies in the kitchen," Aunt Eileen
said. "Why don't you two go get them? Put them on a
plate, will you, Nola?"

"Sure," I said. "C'mon, Mike."

We went down the long hallway, which bent at an odd
angle, probably about sixty degrees off straight, before it
reached the kitchen. When I was a child, visiting my aunt
and uncle, turning into that angle had always given me

an odd sensation, not quite fear, but close, and I could never figure out why. My brother Sean, who's about eighteen months older than I, always called that portion of the hall the ghostwalk, because he claimed he heard people talking when no one was nearby.

The kitchen itself, a wedge-shaped room crammed at the very back of the house, had never struck any of us as creepy, probably because my aunt loved to cook fancy desserts. That night, a big platter of chocolate chip cookies sat on the beige Formica counter near the sink. Eileen had planned ahead to let Michael and me spend a few minutes alone.

"What did you think of the news?" I said.

"It scared the shit out of me."

"It should. I'm wondering if the murderer is the same guy who killed Patrick."

Michael winced, then walked over to the round maple table and slumped down into a captain's chair. I followed and perched near him.

"Mike, tell me, tell your poor aged sister why you want to be a werewolf. Please?"

He squirmed in his chair, looked up at the ceiling, groaned a couple of times, squirmed some more, then came out with it. "Well, there's this girl at school," he said. "She's always reading these emo sticky books about vampires and werewolves. And she's always saying she wants to meet someone like that, and she's really hot, and well y'know."

"You want to impress her."

He nodded at the kitchen table. "Mom says there's no such thing as vampires."

"There certainly aren't any like the ones in those books. For a change Mom is right about something."

"So that leaves werewolves. I know that's possible."

"Yeah, sure, but what makes you think you can turn yourself into one? It takes more than just wanting to."

"Yeah, I know." He looked up. "I've got Pat's journals. He like writes about it a lot."

I nearly choked on my own breath. The Collective Data Stream had scored a hit.

"I thought Mom burned those," I said.

"She thought she did." He looked up with a grin. "I gave her a pile of my old school papers from Latin class. She never even looked at them. Just threw them in the fire."

It never occurs to our mother that anyone would disobey her, an annoying trait but at times useful.

"Good for you," I said. "Mike, you've got to give those journals to me."

"I don't want to."

"There are better ways to impress pretty girls than turning yourself into a werewolf."

"But she—"

"Do you want to end up like that poor girl on the news?"

He shook his head no and returned to staring at the kitchen table.

"I'll bet they're in your room," I said. "I'll bet I can find them."

"You wouldn't dare!" He shoved his chair back. "I won't let you."

"Oh, yeah?" Being his older sister was the only psychic ability I needed at that point. "What else do you have stashed up there? Something you don't want Aunt Eileen to know about, I bet. Something green and flakey—"

"Oh, shut up! You can have the damn journals!"

"Thank you," I said. "Go get them."

Michael got up and started for the door on the opposite side of the kitchen, which led to the rear stairway up to the second floor.

"All of them," I called after him. "I know how Pat

numbered them, and I'll be able to tell if some are missing. Unlike our dear mother, I'll look at them."

"Oh, shut up!" He slammed out of the room.

I heard his footsteps pounding up the stairs. I figured I was in for more charming conversation, but when Michael came back, he looked reasonably unsullen. He handed me a dirty green book bag bulging with sharp corners. I opened it and looked inside: twelve spiral-bound school notebooks, all well-used. I pulled out one at random and flipped it open: Pat's tiny scrawl, sure enough.

"Thanks." I put the notebook back in the bag. "You've done the right thing."

He spent a minute staring at the floor.

"You know what?" He looked up. "I'm kind of glad to get rid of them."

"I kind of thought you would be. Mike, consider your place on the family tree. You don't need to force a talent on yourself. Yours is bound to come along any day now, and it's going to be really strong when it does."

"Yeah?"

"Yeah. You're the seventh child of a seventh child, aren't you? Well, there you are. In the meantime, do you want to know how to impress that girl? Read one of those books she likes and then talk to her about it."

He gave me a Christmas present of a grin. "Jeez," he said. "I never thought of that! I bet it would work."

"Yeah, so do I."

"And you won't tell Aunt Eileen about—well, like, y'know?

"Of course not. But if you don't wash your hair every day, she'll figure it out on her own."

"You mean—" He gaped at me. "Shit! I thought you sensed it."

"I did. With my nose."

He blushed a full scarlet.

"And your language these days is awful," I said.

"All the guys talk like that."

"Yeah? But I'm not a guy." I pointed at the plate. "Grab those cookies. I need to go rescue Morrison from our aunt."

"Yeah, we better." The blush receded. "So you've got a boyfriend now, huh?"

"No. He's my boss, and he kindly gave me a lift over here."

"Oh, yeah, sure." He smirked at me. "I saw the way he looks at you."

"That's his problem, not mine. Now go get the cookies."

We carried the platter in procession back to the living room. Brian had returned to his game, but mercifully he'd shut off the sound. Nathan was sitting on the edge of the brown armchair with a thick family photo album in his lap, while Aunt Eileen hovered behind, leaning over now and then to point something out as he turned the pages. I expected Nathan to be bored one degree away from rigor mortis, but damned if he didn't seem interested.

"Now, who's that?" he was saying. "The man in the gray suit."

"That's Nola's dad," Eileen said. "Right after he married my sister, poor fellow."

"There's quite a story in that," I said, as firmly as I could. "But it's not one for right now."

"Well, of course not!" Eileen reached over and retrieved the album. "Brian, please, turn that awful thing off!"

Brian had just finished splattering three zombies against a wall with a ray gun. He started to protest the order, then saw the cookies. The game went off. Nathan glanced at the book bag and raised an eyebrow.

"Some things that belonged to my brother Patrick," I said and nodded a slight yes. "Michael saved them for me."

"Ah," Nathan said. "Nice of him." He stood up. "I'm sorry, Mrs. Houlihan, but we've really got to leave. There are things I need to do after I drop Nola off at her place."

Aunt Eileen fixed him with the gimlet eye. "Drop her off?" she said. "I should hope so!"

The weapons expert looked briefly terrified. I said good night all around and got us out of there before the lecture began.

The sky was darkening to twilight as we hurried across the street. He unlocked the passenger side of the car and opened the door for me. I stood my ground and held out a hand.

"The keys, Nathan," I said. "If I do the driving, you won't need to use that insurance policy from the rental agency. If you drive, we will."

"I've noticed," he said stiffly, "that California drivers do seem to be timid souls."

"We happen to love life, that's why. Give me the keys."

"You know, you remind me of your aunt at the moment."

"Good. If you don't give them to me, I'll take the bus home, and you can damn well find your own way to either my apartment or a premature death. I put the odds at fifty-fifty."

He sighed and handed over the keys. As soon as we'd gotten back into the car, he retrieved his gun in its shoulder holster and strapped it on.

"By the way," I said, "I'm sorry about the family photos."

"What? Why?"

"You weren't bored?"

"Only a little confused. You certainly come from a large enough clan."

"You could say that, yeah. My grandfather—Eileen and Mother's dad—was the seventh child of a seventh child. Then Grandpa had seven kids, too. Those are the O'Briens. Father Keith is the third O'Brien, Eileen's the sixth, and my mother hit the jackpot—she's the seventh of them. She married Flann O'Grady, and they had seven kids. Michael's the seventh in our batch."

"Isn't there a superstition about that? All those sevenths, I mean."

"If you want to call it that, yeah. There sure is."

Nathan turned and looked out the windshield. In the cold glare of the streetlight, he looked exhausted. "The vast majority of my grandparents' families died in the Holocaust—their parents, brothers, sisters— anyone still in Europe when the war started. Well, except for one brother who was an infant at the time—my great-uncle. A Dutch family took him and risked everything by pretending he was theirs." He shrugged as if tossing the grief away. "But I don't have much of a family."

"Uh, God! I'm so sorry."

"So am I." He began fiddling with the safety harness on his side of the car. "Let's go, shall we? I want to get back to your place in time for the news."

So did I, but when we watched it, him on the couch, me on my computer chair, the news had nothing to add to the murder story. Apparently the police had yet to notify the next of kin.

"Next broadcast?" Nathan said.

"Eleven." I paused to yawn. "Can't you just hack into something and find out who she was?"

"I can contact the police, and I suppose I'd better. I'm working for Interpol again."

"What? You mean you can just go ask? Why are you sitting around my apartment waiting for the news, then?"

He gave me a look full of sorrow, as if he couldn't believe my lack of brain.

"No," I said, "and you know what I mean by no. It's time for you to leave, by the way."

"What about those journals? Do you think there's something in there for our job?"

"I don't know yet. I do know I need to read them."

"Spying on your brother's love life?" He grinned at me.

I realized I'd never told him about Patrick. "No," I said. "I'm afraid he's dead."

The grin disappeared, and he winced. "I'm so sorry," he said. "I didn't realize—"

"I know. It's okay." I hesitated, then decided the truth about his murder could wait. "He had a lot of psychic talent. There may be something for our job in these notebooks, something he noticed or wondered about."

"I see. I'd like a look at them."

"Sure."

I'd piled the journals up next to my computer. I scooted the chair around, took the top one from the stack, and handed it to Nathan. He flipped it open and swore.

"What's wrong?" I said. "Can't you read Latin?"

"No. I take it you can."

"I endured twelve years of Catholic school. Damn right I can."

"Why did your brother choose to write these in Latin?"

"That's kind of the family code. He went to Catholic school, too. Hey, it could be worse. He also knew classical Greek, and I don't."

Nathan snarled like an angry dog.

"But don't worry," I said. "I'm planning on reading every word. I'll give you a full report if I find anything of interest."

And with that I shooed him out.

CHAPTER 3

EVERYONE IN THE FAMILY KNEW that Patrick wanted to become a priest, but until I read his journals, I never realized just how desperately he longed for a refuge within the church. When our dad went missing, Patrick was five years old. He turned to his uncle, Father Keith, who took over the role with his usual understanding. Unlike me and most of my siblings, Patrick kept up his belief in God and the specifically Catholic doctrines at least partly because Keith believed them. Fortunately for Keith, his share of the family talents fit into his priestly vocation: a heightened empathy, psychic insights, warnings of danger, spiritual revelations, all the phenomena that supposedly derive from the God of the Christians. Unfortunately for Patrick, hiding lycanthropy in a seminary would have taken godly powers.

He started keeping journals when he was living at home and attending classes at the local Catholic university. I found the first volume hard reading. Pat's grief, loneliness, rage at the talent the family genes had devolved upon him, thoughts of suicide restrained only by his knowledge that Keith would be shattered—I kept thinking, why didn't he tell me all this? Why didn't he let it out? I reached the conclusion that he didn't know why. Through the entire notebook ran the festivals of the church. He recorded each saint's day, each feast, in different colors of ink to match the appropriate liturgical garments. And every month, around the full moon, for three days he wrote nothing at all.

When I finished the first journal, I realized it was two in the morning. Going to bed struck me as a great idea. I laid the journal down on the couch beside me, yawned, stretched, and opened my eyes to find the angel standing in the middle of the living room, between me and the TV. He seemed to be studying the pattern on the faded Persian carpet I keep under the coffee table.

"Uh, is there something you want to tell me?" I said.

"Coat of many colors." He pointed at the carpet with an urgent forefinger. "Many many colors."

"Uh, yeah, but why is that important?"

"Read the next book."

He vanished before I could test him for Chaos affiliation.

Still, I picked up the second journal and started leafing through more grief, rage, and loneliness. Just when I was ready to hang it up, angel or no angel, a pattern began to develop. I found only hints at first, references to odd e-mails that Pat was afraid to hope meant what he thought they meant—not that he'd deigned to copy any of them into the journal, the annoying little brat! Slowly though the hints added up to possibilities. What if there was a place where he could serve God as he was, wolf nights and all?

At last, with only ten pages to go in that notebook, whoever sent those e-mails contacted him outright. They had smelled Pat running at the full moon, then seen him from a distance right after the wolf-form left him. They had decided to take the chance and approach him. On the second to the last page, Pat sent an e-mail in answer. On the last page, in big letters, he'd printed, "*Fr. LG respondit!*"

By then my eyes were watering, my back ached, and I was beginning to think in Latin. I checked the time: five A.M. Going in to my fake job had become impossible. I could phone in using the landline and leave a message for Mr. Morrison, then go to bed—but damn it, I had to find out who this mysterious "they" were. First, coffee! I stood up, creaking in every joint, and staggered into the kitchen.

I had just poured myself a cup when the landline rang. I drank a couple of mouthfuls and picked up the receiver on the sixth ring.

"Bona matutina," I said. "I mean, morning, Nathan."

"Morning," Nathan said. "I'm glad you're safe. I just drove by your place and saw the light on in the window, and I wondered why you hadn't turned it off. I'll be right up. We can go out for breakfast."

"No, we can't!"

But he'd already hung up on me.

I put the receiver back and stood fuming beside the phone just long enough for his meaning to soak in. "I'm glad you're safe." With the light still burning in my window, I could have been lying on the floor dead, murdered by William Johnson in one of his bad moods. Once again I'd forgotten about him.

I began to wonder if he was meddling with my mind, making me forget so he could have an easier shot at me. I tried a Search Mode: Individual scan, just a quick cast into nowhere in particular. I picked up nothing, absolutely nothing. Johnson could have been dead or heading to Mars on a spaceship for all I could find.

Still, I took the warning to heart. When Nathan knocked on my door, I made him repeat our passwords before I opened up. He strode in, freshly shaved, smelling of witch hazel, wearing a blue shirt, and waving a manila folder.

"The police report on the Presidio murder." Nathan

tossed the folder onto my coffee table. "Where do you want to go for breakfast?"

"I don't," I said. "I never eat a real breakfast, and I've been up all night reading."

"Ah. That's why you look like something the cat dragged in."

I refrained from throwing my coffee into his face only because I probably did.

"You go out to breakfast if you want," I said. "I need to keep reading Pat's journals."

"Find anything in them?"

"Maybe. I'm not sure yet."

Nathan walked over to the couch and leaned over it to pull the curtains open a few inches. The cold gray light of a foggy dawn sliced into the room. He stood there looking out for a minute or two, then switched off the floor lamp.

"I'll go out for breakfast alone," he said, "if you'll do your reading somewhere else. Sitting in a window with the light on! Do you want to get your head blown off?"

"It's not high on my list of priorities, no." I began to feel like a fool. "I'll find a nice safe spot."

When he left, I shut the door, locked it, slid on the deadbolt, and put on the safety chain for good measure. I took the third journal into the bedroom. The only window there opened onto a narrow air shaft. I put a Chaos ward on the glass and pulled the curtain shut. Since the ward only worked against dedicated followers of Chaos, and I didn't know yet if Johnson followed that path, I moved my floor lamp and pulled a chair around so I could sit away from the window rather than sprawling on the bed to read as I usually did. I got myself another cup of coffee and opened the third notebook.

This mysterious Fr. LG—I assumed the Fr. meant *frater,* a brother as in some kind of Catholic order, and that LG were his initials—had a lot to say to Patrick over the next few weeks, all of which Pat recorded in the journal. At first LG dropped only hints, a few leading questions, a sliver of information here, a morsel more there. Pat sounded dubious himself, afraid to believe rather than openly skeptical. "The next full moon will prove the test," he remarked at one point.

A few days before, he met LG for coffee, as casually as you can get at a doughnut shop near campus. LG brought along a Sr. MR, a sister, which ruled out any kind of official religious order in my mind. I considered the possibility of a magical lodge, a kind of anti-Masons, maybe, since Pat would never have had anything to do with the actual Masons or their offshoots. He liked both the *frater* and the *soror* and left the meeting inclined to trust them, though, of course, they'd only chatted about trivial matters in public. He agreed to meet them at Land's End at the full moon.

I was reading as fast as I could, scanning pages and leaving the details for later. As usual, he'd made no entries on the three days of the full moon's influence.

The fourth day, he wrote in big shaky letters: *verum!* It's true. And for the first time I saw the words the Hounds of Heaven. Frater LG, Lupus Gubbionis—his name came from the wolf of Gubbio, the giant wolf who terrorized an entire medieval village until St. Francis tamed it—headed up a small group of lycanthropes dedicated to serving the Good in their own way rather than giving in to the forces of Chaos that always threatened them from within. Soror MR, aka Mater Remi and LG's fiancée, had taken for her name the wolf mother of the brother who hadn't founded Rome. An interesting touch, I thought, to identify with the outsider.

By then I was so tired, and my eyes ached so badly, that tears were running down my face, partly for Pat, too, of course, who at last had found the friends and the place in life he'd always wanted, only to die a year later.

Well, all right, mostly for Pat. I got up and grabbed a box of tissues.

After I got control of myself, I washed my face, then went back out into the living room for a look at the copy of the police report Nathan had brought by. I was beginning to form a theory about why Johnson had come to the Bay Area. I hoped the young woman found dead in the Presidio had nothing to do with the Hounds, but I worried.

I had just picked up the folder when I heard a sound at the door, a little click, a scrape of metal on metal, another click. The doorknob quivered. I put the folder down on the coffee table and stepped back. Tired though I was, I could still summon plenty of Qi. If Johnson opened that door, he was in for a blast of it.

The door moved inward, then slammed against the safety chain. Through a crack about an inch wide I could see the pale yellow glow of the light above the stairs. I raised my hands and breathed slowly, regularly, feeling the Qi ascend with every breath. I stripped Qi from the air to match what I was summoning from within. The energies twined themselves into a ball of fire between my hands. I waited, ready to let it go as soon as I had a target.

"Brilliant!" Nathan called out. "Nola, you can open it now. You've got the right kind of chain in place. I'm glad to see it."

I was tempted to blast the bastard anyway, but I'd signed a contract restricting ensorcellment to life and death situations. He shut the door again to allow the chain to sag back to normal. I let the Qi spill and dissipate harmlessly as I walked across the room.

"Where does Jake live?" I said.

"Sheboygan," he said. "Which is in Wisconsin, by the way. I looked it up on the Internet last night."

I opened the door to find him smiling, a lockpick in

one hand, an object wrapped in a paper napkin in the other.

"I brought you an English muffin," he said. "With butter."

"Thanks," I said. "Come in. I've got something to tell you about my brother Pat."

I locked and chained the door behind him, then took the muffin. Coffee on an empty stomach after a long night is never a good idea. I ate the muffin fast to keep it company. Nathan stood beside the window, pushed back one curtain a bare crack, and peered out at the street below.

"One quick question," I said. "The murdered consular official?"

"What about him?"

"Was he from the Bay Area?"

"Yes, from San Francisco, in fact." Nathan let the curtain fall and turned back into the room.

"Did Greenbaum have a Bay Area connection?"

"Is Fresno in the Bay Area?" He pronounced it "freez-no."

"No, thank God! But it is in California."

"She was born there. Her parents didn't emigrate until she was a teenager."

"So I'll bet they came to San Francisco now and then to see the sights. Huh, everything fits."

"Fits what?"

"The pattern that's emerging. Look, there's no subtle way for me to say this. My brother was a werewolf, and I'm beginning to think that Johnson may have murdered him, too."

Nathan opened his mouth and shut it again, several times.

"You're a nutter, aren't you?" he said at last. "Beautiful but stark raving, and I'm supposed to work with you."

I had expected no less. "No, I'm the sane one in my family."

"That I can believe, having met some of them."

"Oh, come on, Nathan! There are more things in heaven and earth than are dreamt of in whatever that was. That's why you're here, isn't it? What happened back in your home territory was so weird that my agency is about the only thing that could help you. Your higher-ups must have known that." I gave him my version of the gimlet eye. "Either they're holding out on you, or you're holding out on me. Why were you given this assignment? A pair of murders by a non-national is a fairly routine Interpol matter. Why bring you and your deep cover connections into it?"

Nathan considered me for a long moment. "You're sharper than you let on," he said eventually. "Johnson's itinerary sounded suspicious, Syria, Iran, and so on."

"Yeah, but is that all? Why were you put in touch with my agency?"

"I've wondered that myself. Your lot apparently have nothing to do with counterterrorism."

"I have connections with one unit, but that's in case something comes my way by accident. Any hint of organized Islamist activity, and I turn it over to them."

"Well, there we are." He made a fist with his right hand and punched it into his left palm. "That's really all I can tell you."

"I don't like working in the dark. I'll contact my handler and tell him to end our involvement."

Again the stare. His Subliminal Psychological Profile registered the highest level of stunned disbelief I'd ever run across.

"I mean it," I said.

"I can see that." He hesitated, glanced at the door, glanced back at me. "Oh, very well! It's because of the gaps in the itinerary. We have no idea of how he got from Israel to Syria, from Syria to Iran, and from Iran to here. For all we know he could have made ten other stops in between, and none of our stringers or operatives saw him—or so they say."

I could recognize that signal and link it to a remark he'd made during the briefing. His superiors suspected that traitors or moles in their network were suppressing information or supplying disinformation or maybe both. Nathan had been assigned to do an end run around them by working backward from San Francisco.

"I think we're touching on something that's none of my business," I said.

Nathan nodded and sighed in a brief puff of relief.

"Except for one last thing," I said.

He winced.

"Why my agency?"

"I honestly don't know. I asked my immediate superior about that last night. He hemmed and hawed and talked all around the point." Once again he slammed his fist into the palm of the other hand. "I had the distinct impression that he wasn't completely sure himself. The higher-ups suspect something peculiar is at work, but they don't know what." For a brief moment he looked furious. "I'm the one who's working in the dark, actually."

His SPP indicated these doubts were genuine.

"As to why I'm here personally," he went on, "and not some other agent, my language skills may have had something to do with the assignment. I can get by in a number of foreign languages besides English. It allows me to work for Interpol, which I quite legitimately do. Interpol keeps its eyes on terrorism, you know, and I've some experience with that."

Since this matched what our contacts had reported, I believed him there as well.

"Lucky old you." I gestured at the couch. "Have a seat."

Nathan sat down on the couch. I pulled the computer chair around to face him across the coffee table.

"About this werewolf business," he began.

"Let me start with Pat's friends," I said. "He belonged to a group of werewolves, a pack, I'd guess you'd call it. That's one thing I've learned from his journals. Let me check something here."

The printout of the police report still lay where I'd dropped it. I felt my stomach twist as I picked up the folder and opened it. The victim was Mary Rose Romero, a student at the local Catholic college.

"And I bet that this poor girl," I said, "belonged to it, too. Someone's on the prowl for werewolves, and just maybe my brother was the first to die."

Nathan crossed his arms over his chest and glared at me.

"Let me tell you what I know." I set the report back down. "I was out of town at the time, unfortunately. Every month when the moon started to get full, Pat would get this urge to run through wild country. It got stronger and stronger as the change came on. So he'd go to some wilderness area for the big night itself. Luckily there's a lot of open country around here."

"I noticed that, yes, when my plane was circling to land."

"So that particular month, he was visiting one of my sisters out in Marin County. He went out for the full moon night and never came back. When she went to look for him, she found a dead wolf. He'd been shot a couple of times, but with ordinary bullets, so he didn't change back."

Nathan held up one hand in the stop position. "For the sake of argument, let's assume that you and your sister aren't nutters or liars," he said. "Why was she so sure the corpse was your brother?"

"Because there aren't any real wolves within hundreds of miles of Marin County."

"Oh. Did she call the police?"

"Of course not! Do you think they'd have listened? They would have reacted just like you're doing. The only thing she could do was call the SPCA."

"You're having a joke on me, aren't you." It wasn't a question.

"No, I'm not." I was wiped out as well as grieving all over again, and tact lay beyond me. "Listen, you stubborn bastard, do you know how insulting you're being?"

At that he had the decency to wince.

"The SPCA did try to find out who was shooting at wildlife out of season. The shooter couldn't have had a permit, either."

"You'd need a permit?"

"Of course. California wolves are an endangered species, and because of that, some animal rights groups took up the case. They assumed, of course, that Pat was a real wolf, one that escaped from a zoo or something, but they never found any missing wolf reports. They figured someone must have been keeping him as an illegal pet, a dope dealer or someone like that."

Nathan leaned back and rested his head on the back of the couch so he could stare at the ceiling.

"Now what's wrong?" I snapped.

"I'm trying to believe you." He sounded personally affronted. "Missing wolf reports!"

"Okay, Mr. Smartass. Let me show you something. My brother Sean put this together for me. He knew I'd want to know the details."

I'd kept the album Sean had made about Patrick's death in the hopes of one day finding out what had really happened to him. It occurred to me, as I dug through my underwear drawer, that the day might have finally come. I retrieved the black album from under a pile of bras and stood up to find Nathan in the doorway, lounging against a doorjamb and watching.

"Nice bedroom," he said.

"Just get back in the living room, will you?" I shoved the album into his hands. I was tempted to shove him, as well, but fortunately he grinned at me and left to sit down on the couch like a good boy.

I enjoyed watching his face when he opened the album. The first thing in it was a page from the *Independent Journal,* a local Marin newspaper, with pictures of my dead brother and the headline "GIANT WOLF SLAIN NEAR SAN ANSELMO." Lycanthropy doesn't produce instant weight loss. The wolf had weighed the same as Patrick, 150 pounds, and it stretched 5'9" from nose to tail, dimensions that shocked local wildlife experts. Because of that angle, the whole ghastly affair had gotten a lot of coverage in the San Francisco papers. Sean had clipped every article and pasted them in, weeping the entire time, or so he'd told me.

Nathan turned the pages slowly, carefully, reading every single yellowing page. Besides the information about the wolf, the album contained a couple of small articles about the missing persons report my mother had filed on Patrick in human form. She'd stayed in denial for months over his death. When Nathan reached the end, he shut the album with a snap and stared at me.

"Well?" I said.

"I'm trying to figure out," he said, "how anyone could have worked this up for a hoax, and why they'd bother."

"You stinking—"

"No, wait!" He held up a hand again. "My conclusion is that no one could have done that. I hate to admit this, but I'm starting to believe you. Look, I didn't mean to sound so callous about your brother's death. I just had my doubts about the werewolf business, that's all."

His SPP told me that he was apologizing as much as it was possible for him to apologize, but I had no intention of forgiving him. Apparently he hadn't expected me to.

"These animal rights groups." Nathan vaguely waved the album in my direction. "They wanted the police to find the shooter. I take it the police refused."

"The Marin sheriff asked around. He agreed that shooting anything out of season was some sort of misdemeanor, but that's all he saw it as. Who could blame him?"

"You've got a point." He laid the album down beside him on the couch. "You said your sister found the body. I'd like to talk with her. Is that possible?"

"I suppose so. Why?"

"Because you might be right about Johnson being the shooter. Local law enforcement's treating him as a serial killer because the MO of the Romero murder matches the two Israeli cases. I have to agree. It could be that he's got some sort of psychosis and thinks he sees werewolves everywhere."

"It could be that he does see them."

"I'll take that under advisement."

Another concession, and I wondered if anyone else had ever gotten two from him in the same day. "If I weren't so tired," I said, "I'd drive you out to Kathleen's right now."

"Well, you can sleep in the car, and I'll drive—"

"No, you won't. I don't want to wake up dead. If you'll just go away till, say, one o'clock, I'll take a nap, and then I'll drive you out."

"Oh, very well." He stood up. "I've got to go confer with the local police, anyway. Interpol has its protocols, and I need to keep up my cover. One o'clock it is."

As soon as I'd gotten him out of my apartment, I

went to bed. The coffee had no effect on me. I slept, and if I dreamed anything significant, I forgot it when the alarm went off. I staggered into the shower and finished waking up in the water, then combed out my wet hair and got dressed—in a denim pencil skirt and a striped blouse—before calling my sister.

We'd had to share a room when we were growing up, Kathleen and I, and we hated it and each other. We fought over space, plush toys, doll paraphernalia, books—anything and everything. She used to borrow my clothes without telling me, too. At one point I even put down a stripe of masking tape to divide the room into halves and dared her to step over the line. She did, of course. It took both of our older brothers to break up the resulting fight.

Looking back, I'm amazed that we both lived to grow up. But we did, and the old feud died somewhere around the time she asked me to be maid of honor at her wedding.

When I punched in her number, Kathleen answered immediately.

"Hi, Nola," she said. "Aunt Eileen told me you were back."

"I figured she would have."

"You might have called me before this."

"Well, I'm sorry about that. I was working into a new job and finding a place to live and all that stuff. Look, are you going to be home this afternoon? Something important's happened."

"Yeah, I will be. Important how?"

"I've been contacted by Interpol—that's the international police agency, you know? They're looking into Pat's murder."

I could hear her gasp, then a long silence before she answered in a shaky voice. "After all this time?"

"Yeah. There were two similar cases in Israel, is why.

The cop in charge of the investigation wants to interview you."

"Okay, bring him over. Just make sure you don't let
any of the cats out when I buzz you in."

"I'll be extra careful. Promise."

There was a time when Marin County was a place of
dairy farms and fishing villages and little country towns
with quaint wooden houses and truck gardens, but no
more. To buy in there now you need serious money,
despite the shabby genteel *optique* that many wealthy
Marinites favor. Kathleen had married very well indeed.
Although their house, in San Anselmo a couple of miles
behind Red Hill, had started life as a Victorian farm-
house, over the years it had sprawled out into something
much grander. It sat on four landscaped acres, with a
pool and various outbuildings, all surrounded by a
eighteen-foot-high chain-link fence.

When we got out of the car, Nathan retrieved his gray
suit jacket from the back seat. As he shrugged into it, he
noticed the fence. "Is there a reason for that?"

"Several." I pressed the electric buzzer on the fence
lock. "You'll see."

One reason greeted us at the gate in the form of six
dogs, all rescued mutts, barking and leaping. Over the
bobbing canine heads and flapping ears I could see up
the flagstone path between the rhododendron bushes to
the big white house. The front door eventually opened
and Kathleen wandered out, dressed in her usual dirty
jeans and a white shirt that, judging from the perfect cut
and the way it fit, must have come from a name designer.
She stood on the steps and yelled over the dog noise.

"Nola, is that you?"

"Yeah," I called back. "With the police officer I told
you about."

"Okay." She whistled to the dogs, who immediately
canned the cacophony and raced back up the path.

"At least they're well trained," Nathan muttered.

"Uh, well, yeah," I said. "Sort of."

Kathleen pressed the electronic gizmo she was holding. The gate lock buzzed, and I opened the wire panel.

"Hurry!" I said to Nathan. "Get in before any of the cats get out."

He obligingly darted inside, and I followed. I shut the gate fast and pulled till I heard the lock click. As we started up the path, I kept an eye out for more dogs, but Kath had sent her pack around the house to the garden. It's not that she can talk with animals like Dr. Doolittle, rather that she communes with them, or so she describes it. She understands them, they understand her, and they do what she wants. When the wolf-form took Pat over, she was the only family member who could reach his actual mind within the wolf-mind.

"How many cats does she have?" Nathan said.

"Don't ask," I said. "I hope you're not phobic or anything."

"No. Just curious."

On the way up to the porch I spotted a couple of feline faces among the shrubbery, plus one tabby lounging on the sunlit walk, who fled at the first sight of us. An elderly gray Persian sat on the porch and sneered as we climbed the steps.

"That's four," Nathan said.

Kathleen greeted me with a hug. Although all the O'Gradys are good-looking, Kath is one of the two beauties of the lot of us, with wide dark blue eyes and perfectly straight black hair that falls to her always slender waist. When we were teenagers, I had an additional reason to hate her beyond our having to share a room. All the boys flocked around her and never noticed me, or so I thought at the time.

"This is Inspector Ari Nathan," I said. "From Interpol."

"Cool." Kath glanced his way. "Hi."

"How do you do?" Nathan said.

She ignored him and led the way into the house. After the bright sunshine outside, the wood-paneled hallway was dark enough to make me blink. I nearly stumbled into the Louis Quinze writing desk that stood by the door into the living room. Kath switched on the Tiffany desk lamp. By its light I noticed that some feline vandal had ignored the forest of scratching posts in the hall and clawed one of the desk's legs nearly through.

Cats scattered ahead of us or raced up the staircase beyond the living room. Nathan counted under his breath but stopped when he reached fifteen. I could catch the whiff of cat boxes on the air.

Despite its white walls, the living room lay in semi-darkness, thanks to the trees right outside the windows and the dark blue velvet furniture. Kath gestured at a couch, and I sat down at one end. Nathan paused to look at the Childe Hassam winter landscape—an original, of course—hanging over the mantel of the natural stone fireplace. He started to sit down on the middle cushion of the couch, but just as he was about to lower his seat onto the seat, something yowled and he yelped. He stood up fast as a gray and black striped cat shot off the sofa.

"Archie!" Kath intoned the name like a priestess in some ancient rite. "You know you're not supposed to sit on the furniture in here. Go to your room!"

The cat stalked out, tail held up, a flag of defiance.

"Uh, sorry," Kath said. "I hope he didn't claw you."

"No, no," Nathan said. "It's quite all right."

"You're a Brit?" Kath gave him a stiff smile. "At least they like animals." She turned away before he could answer and glanced around the living room. "I guess the rest of the guys are somewhere else. Jack hates it when he sits on a lot of cat hair."

"Especially when it's still attached to the cat," I said.

She grinned at me and flopped down into an over-stuffed armchair opposite the sofa. "I'd offer you drinks," she said, "but the police aren't supposed to have them, are they? When they're on duty, I mean."

"Quite so." Nathan reached inside his sports coat and brought out a small black box. "Now, Mrs. Donovan, is it?"

"That's right."

"This is a tape recorder. Do you mind if I record your answers?"

"Not at all. I'm just glad someone's taking my brother's murder seriously."

"You're sure it was murder?" Nathan clicked the recorder on. "And not accidental?"

"Nobody puts three bullets into an animal by accident." Kath's beautiful eyes filled with tears. "Sorry." She wiped them away on the sleeve of her shirt. "It's been a year, but just thinking about it—I get so mad—and the stupid sheriff wouldn't do anything." She glanced at me. "He knows about the lycanthropy, right?"

"Of course," I said, "or we wouldn't be here."

"I'm sorry to make you relive the painful memory." Nathan put on a professional sort of voice, calm, a little clipped. "But since the local law enforcement refused to file a detailed report, I'm relying on the newspaper accounts, and they're never as accurate as they should be. I understand that you found the body out in the hills. May I ask how you knew where to find it?"

"Whoever shot him didn't make a clean kill. Pat almost made it back to our meeting place. He used to come out here a lot for the full moons. I'd drive him up to the park and let him out of the car at the turnout, and then I'd go back and get him a couple of days later."

"No one noticed the wolf when you did this?"

"I'd drive him out at night. I've got a dog grate in the

back of the SUV, and if anyone saw us, they'd just think he was a German shepherd or something."

"Did anyone search the area around the body?"

"Jack did with a couple of his guy friends."

"Your husband knew about the lycanthropy?"

"Of course. I wouldn't have married him without telling him about my family. I thought for sure he'd break off the engagement, but when he didn't, I knew I'd found the right man." She sighed and looked away. "Finally."

"So, then," Nathan picked up the thread again. "Someone did search the area."

"Yeah, and they found blood drips from Pat's wounds, and they led to a place where the grass was all matted down, like someone had been sitting there. I don't know if it was the killer or Pat. Jack said there wasn't any fur that he could see."

"I don't suppose anyone took photos or searched that place for further evidence."

"No. Stupid sheriff!"

"What about dropped shells? Spent bullets, that would be."

"Jack found a couple near the squashed-down grass. He told me the shooter must have used a really high-powered rifle, a military sniper's rifle, he called it, some kind of foreign gun. The SPCA guy told us that he could have been a long way away from the wolf when he . . ." Kath let her voice trail away. A single tear trickled down her cheek. She wiped it off on her sleeve, leaving a smear of cat hair on her face.

"Your husband knows something about guns?"

Kath sat up straight and stared at him wide-eyed. "Yeah," she said at last. "He used to hunt before he married me. I told him I'd leave him if he ever killed another animal. Now he, uh, does target shooting. Paper stuff, you know."

"Yes, a pleasant enough hobby." Nathan clicked off the recorder and stood up.

I joined him and after a moment, so did Kathleen. "Thank you for your time," Nathan said. "This case does have parallels with three others that I'm investigating."

"Like that poor girl they found the other night?" Kath said.

"Yes, exactly." Nathan paused as if he'd just thought of something. "This is a long shot, but I don't suppose you know a young woman by the name of Miriam Greenbaum? She came from Fresno originally."

"Oh, for sure I do! I mean, I don't know her, but she's the girl Pat bit." She looked my way again. "Don't you remember that? He didn't mean to, but jeez, were her parents frosted!"

"I do remember now," I said. "The summer when the grandparents took us camping in Yosemite."

"Right, and you kept sneaking off with that young ranger, the cute one. I'm not surprised you don't remember Miriam."

I refused to look Nathan's way. "The suspicions about that relationship were totally unfounded," I said in a steely cold voice. "But didn't the biting incident happen the first time Pat changed?"

"The second. We just pretended he was our family dog," Kathleen said to Nathan. "He was only thirteen then, so the wolf was just dog-sized. But her parents threatened to sue, so Grandpa had to pay all the medical bills and stuff. If the rangers had impounded Pat— God, who knows what would have happened when he changed back." She glanced my way. "So it was a good thing you and that ranger were—"

"He was just being kind to the family," I said, again in the steely voice. "Out of respect for our grandparents' age."

"Oh, yeah sure, Nola! But anyway, Miriam was so

dumb! You should never just go up to a strange dog and
try to pet it."

"So my father used to tell me." Nathan forced out a
smile. "Well, thank you again."

We all walked out onto the porch so Kathleen could
unlock the gate with her electronic device. Since I'd left
my sunglasses in the car, I stood blinking at the green of
the garden to let my eyes adjust to the light.

"The rhododendrons are doing well this year, huh?"
I said.

"Yeah, but there aren't as many hummingbirds as
there used to be." She sighed with a shake of her head.
"It's all the damn chemicals people use."

"You sure it doesn't have something to do with your
surfeit of cats?"

"Nola!" She rolled her eyes heavenward. "They don't
eat the birds. I told them not to."

When we got back to the car, Nathan stripped off his
jacket and laid it in the backseat. Kathleen kept the heat
up so high in her house that he'd been sweating. Normally
the very idea of a sweaty guy would have turned me off
by itself, but on him it smelled oddly good, acrid, yes, but
at the same time, intensely male. I put my reaction down
to spending time in my sister's menagerie, an uprush of
animal instincts in answer to the pheromones. I rolled
down the car windows to let them escape.

"Your sister," Nathan said abruptly. "She's not quite
right in the head, is she?"

"Say what?" I snapped.

"Not quite all there." He frowned at me. "I'm trying
to be tactful."

"You're not succeeding."

"Very well, then. She's stupid, isn't she?"

I wanted to shove him out of the car and drive off, but
since it *was* his car, and he *was* a cop, I decided against it.

"I wouldn't call her that." I tried not to snarl. "She's

just never had to depend on her intelligence to get what she wants in life."

"Not with looks like that, no. Pity."

Rather than get into a nasty argument, I started the car. As we headed back to the city, Nathan sat silently, staring out the car window at the random suburbia of San Anselmo. Once we were back on Highway 101, I headed for the Golden Gate Bridge. Nathan watched the green hills roll by until we passed Mill Valley.

"If I remember correctly," he said then, "lycanthropy's supposed to be spread through werewolf bites. In the superstitions about it, that is."

"Yeah, I've heard those, too. One theory is that it's a virus carried in saliva. Pat, though, just inherited it somehow from some ancestor. Maybe the virus installed itself in the family genes or something. I guess that can happen. I'm no geneticist."

"Obviously not." He continued to stare out the window. "Have you read that police report yet?"

"I haven't, no, just glanced at it. I got hung up in Pat's journals."

"Well, the Romero girl fought back. When he shot her, the killer must have been at point-blank range, judging from the wound analysis. She got her claws into him at some point. The technicians managed to extract some blood and a trace of skin from under her fingernails and from a smear on her back that was too far from the wounds to be her own blood."

"DNA evidence! When will you find out the results?"

"In a couple of weeks."

"Weeks?"

"Nola, it's not like the shows on television." His voice dripped scorn. "These things take time, particularly with a small sample like this. Still, I have hopes it'll match another sample we have, from the consular official's apartment."

"I hope it doesn't turn out that the official's someone else that Pat bit. That's a joke, by the way. As far as I know, the only person that Pat ever snapped at was the Greenbaum girl. He was too young then to control himself when she startled him."

"I see. I hate to admit this, but a pattern's beginning to emerge here, if, that is, there really is such a thing as werewolves."

"Oh, come on, Nathan! Do you really doubt it?"

"No, I don't, not anymore. I just don't like believing it."

Three concessions in one day. Somewhere a celestial slot machine was ringing "jackpot!"

"If Mary Rose bit Johnson," I said, "things could get real interesting for him."

Nathan did the last thing I would have expected from him. He laughed, a real honest laugh instead of his usual morbid chuckle. Since I was busy dodging traffic on the freeway, I had to keep my eyes on the road. When the traffic began to slow down and thicken on the Waldo Grade, I risked a glance at him. That grin of his—I reminded myself to keep from melting and concentrated on the traffic.

The flow of cars stayed slow all the way through the rainbow tunnel. As soon as we hit the cooler air at the western exit, the traffic began to crawl. Since we had a couple of hours till the evening rush, I wondered if we had an accident ahead, but the electronic "CAUTION" sign on the approach to the Golden Gate Bridge stayed dark.

"What is *that*?" Nathan said suddenly. "Out to sea, up about forty-five degrees from the horizon, in the fog bank."

By then we were making five miles an hour because every driver on the highway was gawking at the sky. I could safely look and see a thick gray wave of fog oozing toward the bridge, a perfectly normal phenomenon except for the pair of bright green lights dancing inside it. They behaved in the classic manner of UFOs: flying too fast for normal aircraft, changing direction abruptly, glowing and flashing as if they signaled to someone on the ground.

"I've never seen them in daylight before." I turned my attention back to the sea of crawling cars ahead. "The fog gives them just enough of a dark background to be visible."

"Yes, but what are they?"

"Chaos lights. I'll bet the flying saucer people are going to have a field day over them, though. They want to believe in spaceships so badly."

Nathan made a strangled noise deep in his throat. I risked a quick glance at him and found the grin replaced by the reproachful stare.

"I don't know exactly what they are," I went on. "No one does, except they're manifestations of the Chaos principle. What we call matter is mostly empty space, you know. All kinds of things can slip through the cracks."

"Is that your idea of an explanation?"

"As much of one as I can give you and still drive. Weren't you briefed about my agency's mission?"

"Yes, but I didn't believe it. I suppose I'd better try."

The pair of lights whipped around one another, then raced off, heading out to sea. After a few seconds they disappeared in a white flash that turned the fog around them silver.

CHAPTER 4

A S SOON AS THE CHAOS LIGHTS SHUT themselves off, the traffic picked up speed and began to
spread out. I managed to get into the far right lane at
last. Just past the toll booth I made the quick turn that
leads onto the back road to the Palace of the Legion of
Honor and from there to a crosstown route. Instead of
choking on the traffic fumes along Park Presidio, you
travel through trees and get a nice view of the Pacific
Ocean puddling at the foot of the cliffs. We'd gone about
halfway up when Nathan asked me to stop.

"We need to discuss something," he said.

I pulled over and parked in a shady spot on the
gravel shoulder. Down below the ocean stretched out,
shrouded in the gray of approaching fog. Nathan turned
toward me, but in the bucket seats he could get no closer,
particularly with the gear shift threatening to make se-
ducing me a moot point. I figured he wanted to ask more
about the Chaos lights, but instead he brought up the
most recent murder.

"The Romero girl's body is going back to her family tomorrow," Nathan said. "Serial killers have been
known to attend the funerals of their victims. They keep
a good distance away, of course, at the cemetery, but
the bastards like to watch the families mourn. I don't

know when they'll schedule the funeral, but I thought we should go and keep an eye out."

"Good idea. I might be able to make contact with the Hounds that way."

"With what?"

"The Hounds of Heaven. The pack my brother belonged to, good Catholic werewolves all."

Nathan muttered something under his breath. "Just when I think I'm used to all of this," he said eventually, "you come up with some sodding tidbit like that."

"I didn't come up with it. That's what they're called in Pat's journals."

Nathan opened the car door and slid out. I had a brief moment of wondering if he was going to throw himself off the cliff in despair, but instead he merely opened the back door and got out his suit jacket. With the fog racing in, the wind had turned cold. He took his holstered handgun out of the glove compartment and strapped it on before he put on the jacket, then got back in the car.

"I've got Agency business to tend to tonight," I said. "I'll drop myself off at my place."

"Nola, aren't you forgetting something?"

"What?"

"That someone wants to kill you. You're living in an apartment overlooking a busy street, with big windows where you insist on sitting, a perfect target. Now you're planning on going back there alone." He paused for effect. "At night."

The wind seemed to have gotten into my blood and chilled my bones. I thought of the creature I'd caught spying in the lobby of the office building and shivered.

"Actually, it's even worse than that," I said. "I was planning on going out alone to talk to a couple of Agency stringers. One of them works in the Tenderloin. Know what that is?"

"Oh, yes. Your police made a point of telling me."

He crossed his arms over his chest like an angry school-teacher.

Which may be why Sister Peter Mary appeared on the hood of the car, about half life-size. When I went to high school, most of the teachers were laypeople, thanks to the emptying of the convents in the '70s and '80s, but for religion class we had a nun, black habit, bobbing white wimple, and all. I'd heard that some years previously she'd gone to her reward in heaven. Now she dropped back down to point her ruler at me like the weapon it had always been in her hands.

"Lust," she said, "can kill. Remember Bathsheba."

As visitations went, this one lacked all justice. Wasn't I trying to avoid emulating Bathsheba despite Nathan's obvious qualifications to be one hell of a David? Sister Peter Mary slowly dematerialized, ascending back into heaven, I assumed.

"Thanks for the warning," I said.

"You're welcome," Nathan said, "though I have the distinct feeling you weren't talking to me."

"I wasn't, actually. Sorry." I managed a smile. "Just one of my—uh—visions, I guess you'd have to call them."

He sighed and uncrossed his arms, then turned in his seat to look straight ahead.

"What gets me," I went on, "is this crop all seem to have religious content. That's probably because of the Hounds."

Nathan continued staring out the windshield. I remembered St. Joseph di Copertino and let the subject drop. Still, Nathan had spoken the truth about my putting myself in danger. If danger existed—I'd not received a single warning since the day Aunt Eileen first met me on the street, not about assassins, at any rate, only about Nathan himself.

Sometimes I'm slow. The tarot reading finally fell

into place along with the latest vision. Lust kills. Sister Peter Mary had been right, though not quite in the way she'd meant. What most people would call sexual desire comes from the Qi flowing between two people. What summons the flow depends on the desiring person's psychology, whatever they find sexually attractive for whatever reason. Nathan and I attracted each other enough to pour out Qi, surrounding both of us in what amounted to a thick psychic fog. While it was physically uncomfortable for him, it made my talents impossible to control.

"Tell you something," I said. "I'd be safer if you weren't around."

"No, you wouldn't." He slewed around to face me.

"You told me that first day that you prefer to work alone."

"Yes, well. That was before."

"Before what?"

"Before I realized you have suicidal tendencies. Why do you think you'd be safer alone?"

"I'm good at avoiding being noticed. You're not."

"Don't lie."

"Bastard!"

We both began staring out the windshield. I could either tell him the truth or just put up with him acting like a bodyguard, even though my raw physical feeling for him was causing nothing but problems. I could see a third option, allowing us to balance out the Qi in the usual way, but that would bring problems of its own.

"You *were* lying," he said eventually.

"Yeah, so what?"

"I'm not going to apologize."

"What makes you think I wanted you to?" At that point, I realized that our conversation had sunk to the level of thirteen year olds, and for reasons appropriate to that age. I thought up a half-truth as a cover story.

"Nathan, look, I'm sorry. I'm all to pieces, thinking about Pat."

"Well, yes, you must be." He turned toward me again. His Byzantine eyes radiated genuine sympathy. "I just don't want you to join him."

"I'm not real keen on leaving this wicked world the same way he did, no. All right, I won't go down to the Tenderloin alone."

"Fine. With me along you'll be a lot safer."

"You can't stay with me twenty-four hours a day."

"Why not? I've got my suitcases in the boot."

"No. You're not moving in."

"I was planning on sleeping on the floor of your lounge."

Oh, yeah? I thought. For how long? Five minutes? Aloud, I said, "I can protect myself. I know you don't believe in things like ensorcellment, but they work."

"Against a military sniper's rifle fired from a hundred meters away?"

"How is your body on my floor going to protect me from that?"

"It won't, of course, but if someone tried to break in, they'd have a surprise waiting for them. Nola, why aren't you taking this threat seriously?"

"I've wondered that myself."

"Look." He made a fist with his right hand and punched it into his left palm. "My superiors must have believed that the kind of talents your Agency offers are essential to this case. I scoffed at first, but I'm coming around to their way of thinking. I need your help, so damned if I'm going to lose you to the psychopath we're hunting."

I considered the offer on its merits. Beyond the problem of the superfluous Qi that Nathan and I were generating, I suspected that Johnson had talents of his own that allowed him to interfere with my extra senses.

If I had a bodyguard, I could take the risk of scanning for him. If he physically followed the scan back to me, Nathan would be waiting to surprise him.

"All right, Nathan. That makes sense."

"Brilliant." He hesitated briefly. "Why won't you call me by my first name?"

"Because," I said and started the car.

I drove back to the apartment in a foul mood. I knew the route well enough to drive with half a mind and think with the other half, more than I'd been using recently. I needed to figure out a way to keep my animal instincts from blocking my mental talents.

Parking, as always, took far too long, but eventually I found a spot on a side street uphill from Judah. By then the fog had covered the entire sky and turned to a drizzle. In the midst of a canyon of art deco apartment buildings the passersby hurried along; some held newspapers over their heads; others had pulled up the hoods of their sweatshirts or parkas. Nathan took his suitcases from the trunk and shot the sky a baleful glance. I put on a jeans jacket over my cotton shirt.

"You must be cold," Nathan said. "You should dress better."

"I'm used to this weather."

He snorted in a particularly unpleasant way. Under the cover of the rattle and rumble of a passing streetcar, I refused to answer. As we walked around the corner, I glanced at the row of newspaper racks cluttering up the curb. In one box a couple of morning editions of the *Chronicle* sagged, unbought and forlorn. A secondary headline caught my eye.

"Wait a minute," I said.

I fished in my pocket, found a couple of quarters for the automatic mechanism, and bought a paper. Nathan glanced over my shoulder as I read, "Another Zodiac?"

"Astrology?" Nathan said.

"No, a serial killer that the San Francisco police never caught. That was back around 1968." I glanced at the story under the header. "Our Johnson seems to have sent a letter to the paper, just like the Zodiac used to do."

Nathan swore under his breath in some language that I took to be Hebrew. As we walked back to my building, I read the article aloud while he steered me around pedestrians and other obstacles. The killer of Mary Rose Romero had written a letter to the editor that spoke of ridding the city of an ancient Native American curse by blood sacrifice of those who engaged in unclean practices—whatever the writer meant by that. The reporter remarked that the letter's garbled prose made very little sense.

Although the paper had followed the police request to refrain from printing a complete facsimile, the reporter did state that the writer had filled the margins with occult symbols that "harked back," as he put it, to the Zodiac letters.

"The question remains," the article finished up, "whether the letter is genuine or a hoax. The police are running a battery of forensic tests in an attempt to answer this question."

I folded the paper and glanced at Nathan for comments.

"The Israeli papers received a similar letter about Greenbaum," Nathan said, "though not about the consular official. The curse in our letter was attributed to 'Arab occult magic,' not Native Americans, of course."

"Then this one's likely to be genuine. Do our police know about the previous letter?"

"They have the full dossier, yes," Nathan went on. "I'll inquire if they've read it. You need to read the police report on the Romero murder. I included a translation of the original dossier on Johnson for you, too. A copy of the letter's there as well."

A translation. Of course, the original dossier had to be in Hebrew. Somehow with his classy accent and his perfect English, I kept forgetting just how foreign he was, a man who'd lived his entire life in a country surrounded by enemies. No wonder he carried a gun. O'Grady, I told myself, you're melting. Stop it!

"I will," I said. "Maybe the gruesome details will wake up my SAWM."

"Your what?"

"Semi-Automatic Warning Mechanism. Sorry. Agency slang."

The door to the stairway leading to my apartment stood between a used clothing shop and a laundromat. I opened the door, but Nathan insisted on going in first, just in case a sniper lurked on the landing.

"This door should be kept locked," he said.

"It is at night."

"Murders have been known to happen during the day, too."

Since nobody shot at us, we climbed the first flight of stairs. At the landing I could hear Mrs. Zukovski's TV blaring *Oprah,* her favorite show, or so she'd told me often enough. At my landing Nathan stopped, motioned me back a step, set the suitcases down, and drew his gun.

I could sense no one inside. I let my mind range around, visualized every room—I even pictured the dust bunnies under the bed—not one trace of danger could I pick up. As quietly as I could, I mouthed the words "should be okay." Nathan nodded, but he stood to one side when he put the keys in the lock and turned. The lock clicked loudly, nothing else.

"Were you expecting a bomb to go off?" I said.

"That's not funny, considering where I come from."

"Sorry." I winced.

No assassins lurked in the apartment. Nathan put his suitcases down by the door, then double-locked and chained it. I headed straight for the thermostat to turn on the wall heater.

"Coffee?" he said. "I'll make it if you've got some."

"Always. There's the kitchen, and I've got one of those drip systems."

"Milk? Sugar?"

"No, just black, thanks."

I picked up the police report and sat down on the computer chair to read. The description of wounds and a tentative reconstruction of the fight Mary Rose put up would have awakened survival sense in a zombie. Apparently she'd seen or smelled him stalking her, then lain in wait and jumped him from behind. He'd rolled and managed to squirm and face her, then shoved his gun under her chin and—well, let's just say it was going to be a closed casket funeral. I felt my talents beginning to stir, only to lie down again when Nathan returned carrying two mugs of coffee. He'd taken off his jacket and the gun, making it obvious how well that blue shirt fit him.

"There's nothing to eat in your refrigerator," he said, "except black lettuce."

"That's arugula. It's perfectly fresh."

"It's still not enough for a meal."

"I don't eat much, usually." I took the proffered coffee from him.

"Ah. That's why you're too thin." He paused for a sip from his mug, then sat down at one end of the couch.

I felt a brief urge to swat him with the police report. All the suffering I endured to stay fashionable, only to be told I was too thin! He was grinning at me as if he knew damn well how annoyed I was. I spun the chair around to set my mug down next to the computer. I kept my back to him while I finished reading.

Even in a photocopy, Johnson's letter to the Tel Aviv media brought me the smell of insanity. He rambled about dangers of the night, ancient curses, the rise of avengers to purify the human race—a particularly unfortunate turn of phrase, I thought, to use in a Jewish nation. In the margins he'd drawn an assortment of occult signs, the astrological symbol for Saturn, the alchemical shorthand for sulfur and phosphorus, and others that I couldn't identify. It seemed that he was using them to creep people out rather than convey a message, but I decided to keep an open mind about that.

"Can I send a scan of this letter to my agency?" I said. "We've got a code expert who should take a look at these symbols."

"Please do, but ours couldn't find any meaning in them."

"Your expert is probably used to dealing with rational human beings. Ours has a wider range."

Nathan smiled at that. I returned to reading.

The various dossiers themselves told me little more than I could figure out for myself, except for a few details about Miriam Greenbaum. Her parents had chosen to emigrate to Israel under the right of return when she turned fourteen. After she'd been killed, they told the Israeli police that they'd emigrated because she was having difficulties in school in the "oppressive and conformist" United States.

"Nathan?" I said. "Suppose the Greenbaum girl started making the full moon changes just before her parents decided to leave the States. Would it have been easier to hide her condition in Israel?"

"I don't know for certain, but it's easy to get a license to home school a child if the parents plead orthodoxy, particularly for a girl. The black hats, again. The Greenbaums lived on the edge of the desert, too, not all that far from Qumran, if you know where that is."

"I do. The ruins there loomed large in the legends we got told in school."

I swiveled the chair around to ask him another question, only to have it go right out of my mind. He was holding his coffee mug in both hands and watching me over the rim with a real longing. I had the sudden urge to take the mug away and rub my face on his sweaty shirt. I thought of Sister Peter Mary, the real one, not just the visitation, and remembered the question.

"These silver bullets," I said. "Do you agree that he must be making them himself?"

"Yes. The Tel Aviv police tried to track Johnson's movements. They were looking for a jeweler who might have done some custom casting, but they didn't find one. The conclusion was that he'd brought them with him. Something that small—he could have hidden the slugs in a box with cufflinks or something of that sort. They would have scanned as jewelry."

"How could he get a gun into the country?"

"He couldn't have. Someone there had to have supplied him with one. He carried plenty of currency. With the proper connections he could have bought one from a Palestinian group that deals in smuggled small arms."

"And since he turned up in Syria, it's likely he had those connections."

"Exactly. The San Francisco police are looking for a jeweler now, but I'm fairly sure that you're right, and he must be doing his own casting."

"He's got to have some kind of base of operations, then. You can't go smelting metal in a hotel room or the backseat of a car."

"Of course not."

I let the image from my first remote sensing rise into my memory, the black hat, the gray trench coat. The hat gave me a frisson as I thought of implications beyond

Sam Spade. "Is it possible that this Johnson is one of the orthodox?"

"He couldn't be, if he's our killer. He shot Greenbaum on a Saturday."

"Okay. I can't imagine one of the people you describe professing faith in Jesus even as a cover story, anyway. It was just a thought." And not a very good one, I told myself. "Do you think he's working alone?"

Nathan gulped coffee while he considered the question. "I don't," he said at last. "He disappears too easily. Someone's got to be sheltering him or at the least providing him with a safe house. He must have had such a connection in Israel and one in Syria and Iran, too."

"Which leaves out the psychotic serial killer."

"Unfortunately, I can't disagree with that. Neither, really, can the local police. They can see the possible political implications as easily as you and I can. They're afraid that the CIA will come barging in."

"It's a good bet." I Frisbeed the manila folder back onto the coffee table. "To be honest, I'd be glad to turn the whole mess over to the CIA or FBI or any agency that wants it. I signed on to keep Chaos within necessary bounds, not to deal with spies and serial killers."

"Which reminds me. If you've finished reading, I've a few questions for you. What do you mean, Chaos lights?"

"Basically what I told you on the bridge. The Agency calls them Manifested Indicators."

"Indicators of what?"

"Chaos forces, of course. No one really knows what they're composed of. The Agency has a research project going forward to find out. Some sort of radiation would be my guess."

"That sounds logical. Is there any evidence for it?"

"No. Only the process of elimination. What else could they be?"

Nathan scowled at me.

"Sorry, but I can't tell you what no one knows," I continued. "We do know that they only appear when the forces of Chaos are threatening the balance point to a dangerous degree. They showed up in America and Russia for the first time in the 1950s, when the U.S. and the Soviets were building atom bombs like crazy."

"The balance point?"

"Between Chaos and Order. We live in Chaotic times, and so most people would think of me as an agent of anti-Chaos or Order. But really, I serve the balance, not either side, which makes me an agent for Harmony."

"Harmony is different from Order?"

"It's the product of Order and Chaos in balance."

I could tell that Nathan was actually thinking about what I was saying instead of searching for counterarguments, a trend I wanted to encourage.

"Well, look," I continued, "Too much Chaos, and things fall apart, like the poet said."

"'The falcon cannot hear the falconer.' That one?"

"Yeah." I was impressed despite myself. "But too much Order, and things stagnate like a silted river between narrow banks."

"I don't know that poem."

"That's because I just made that up."

"Not bad." Nathan paused to consider something. "When I was put in contact with your agency, I was given a briefing about it, a very strange, very short briefing. I gather, though, that your Congress founded it back in the Fifties. Was that because of the flying saucer hysteria?"

"That was part of the reason, yeah." I wondered how much he'd been told. I didn't want to give anything away. "The Air Force set up the first project, down in Palo Alto. That's just south of here."

"And it grew from there?"

"You could say that."

I smiled, he waited. Finally he looked into his mug, frowned, and set it down empty on the coffee table. "I'm really quite hungry. Do you think you might actually eat something if I pay for it?"

"That has to be the worst dinner invitation I've ever gotten, but yeah, I'm hungry, too. One thing, though. Those pictures of Johnson. Are they here or in the office?"

"Here, of course. I don't leave things like that lying around."

"Bring them along. I want to show them to the stringer."

We ate at a local Chinese place decorated by someone who believed in a daily hosing down with Lysol—bare pale green walls, white tiled floor with an obvious drain in the middle, vinyl-covered chairs, Formica tables. They had at least covered the bare light bulbs with silk lanterns that dangled red tassels for a spot of color. The food, however, I'd always found to be first-rate. Whenever I took anyone there, I'd order a number of different dishes and then just sample them while the guests did the serious eating.

When we walked in, Nathan stood looking narrow-eyed around the room. When a waiter tried to show us to a table in the middle of the room, he shook his head no.

"Sorry," Nathan said. "I'd like that table over there in the corner." He gave me an apologetic smile. "I'm never comfortable unless I can keep my back toward the wall."

With a shrug the waiter led us to the chosen perch. He took my order, then trotted off to fetch the usual pot of tea.

Nathan had never used chopsticks before, and he set himself to be charming when I tried to teach him over an order of tiger prawns. We laughed a lot, but when the waiter brought the lo mein, he also brought Nathan a fork. Nobody in the room wanted to see him covered in noodles and sauce, not while they were trying to eat. He'd kept his jacket on during the meal, too. It didn't look washable.

By the time we left the restaurant, the sun was setting off to the west, an orange glare behind the encroaching fog. Streetlights glimmered, waiting for full darkness. Shop windows and neon signs lit up in splashes of red and purple, glittering on the sidewalks damp from the fog. I love night in the city, cool, mysterious, jeweled with lights—I always feel that some magical thing waits for me, maybe around the next corner, maybe in some strange little shop still open when its neighbors have all gone dark.

Nathan, however, shivered and buttoned up his jacket with a small growl.

"I suppose you keep that coat on to hide the gun," I said.

"Yes, but it's the damp weather, too. I've been cold ever since I got here."

"I hope you brought a raincoat. It *is* winter."

We were walking side by side down the sidewalk. Without looking my way he reached for my hand. I almost let him take it, but just in time I pulled it away. I tucked both hands into my jacket pockets for safe keeping.

"We'd better not take the car," I said. "The parking downtown is really lousy."

"As far as I can tell, the parking all over San Francisco is lousy." Nathan paused to look up and down the street. "This doesn't look like a good district to find a cab."

"There's this thing called streetcars. We can't pull up at Jerry's corner in a cab, anyway."

"Jerry is the stringer?"

"Yeah, and a hustler."

"A what?"

"A male prostitute."

"Um." Nathan seemed unfazed by the revelation. "Is he reliable?"

"Very. He's always had a good eye for Chaos."

By the time we got downtown, night had fallen, close and silver in the fog. As we climbed out of the underground Muni Metro station, Nathan took a good look around at the scrappy shops, the drunks sitting on the sidewalk, the general disorder of Market Street once you get past Sixth and leave the big touristy department stores behind. Our route ahead on the side street lay between high stone buildings, dimly lit by streetlights alone, a shadowed canyon into the night.

"I don't like this situation," he said. "Let's get in and out as fast as we can."

"All right. I'll give Jerry a call."

Since Jerry's fairly successful at his chosen line of work, he has a cell phone. He was standing, he told me, on a "good" corner on Ellis Street, a couple of blocks behind but not too near the big hotels around Union Square. With the economy so bad, the doormen were getting too greedy about kickbacks, or so he said, for him to sit inside. As we walked up, I saw him hovering by the lighted windows of a bar in his work clothes: a tight short skirt, sleeveless red blouse, black stockings, and very high heels. Thanks to the cold he'd added a ratty black fur coat to this mess. He wore his bleached hair—all his own, though—in that odd poufy style favored by drag queens, very Fifties with tons of hair spray.

"He's not here?" Nathan said to me.

At that point Jerry waved and came flouncing over.

"Nola, darling," he said in his baritone voice. "Have you brought me a john or is this one yours?"

This time Nathan did look fazed, but only briefly. "Definitely hers," he said. "Sorry."

"I'm not having any luck tonight at all," Jerry said. "Unless Nola's brought me some charity."

I took the four hundred-dollar bills of Agency money out of my jeans and held them out between my thumb and forefinger. Although Jerry didn't appear to snatch them, they disappeared smoothly and suddenly into his taped-up cleavage.

"That's your quarterly accounting," I said, "and the pay for the latest job. Your requisition for expenses still hasn't come in yet."

"Why am I not surprised? This will come in handy, though."

"Try not to shoot it all at once. You're too valuable to lose."

"You *are* sweet, but I don't do needles, darling. My kind of customer doesn't like tracks on the merchandise."

"Then don't snort it all at once."

"I'll restrain myself just for you. Did you see the lights today?"

"I did, yeah. I'm surprised you could see them from downtown."

"I wasn't downtown, is why. Every now and then I get this mad craving for sunshine, and I went to the park." Jerry frowned down at the sidewalk. "You know I see things, and it's not the drugs."

"Yeah. You've always been accurate."

"There was someone down by the windmill in the park." He glanced at Nathan. "That's Golden Gate Park, down at the west end, almost at the beach. A very well-dressed fellow, Armani slacks, D and G shirt, very pricey-looking camera. He was taking pictures of the windmill. Tourists do that all the time. But he gave me the creeps. I don't know why. He just did, and I thought, that's who the lights came for. I don't know why. I just did."

"Oh, really?" I touched Nathan's arm. "Can I have those photos?"

Nathan brought the envelope out of the inner pocket of his jacket. Jerry's eyes went very wide at a glimpse of the gun.

"Why are you packing?" he said. "Nola, is this guy a cop?"

"Yeah, but he's not interested in local regulations. Don't worry about it. Is this the guy you saw by the windmill?"

In the yellow glare of the streetlight, Jerry looked through the photos. "No," he said eventually. "The guy I saw was much younger. Brown hair, darker than this guy's." He flapped the envelope, and Nathan took it back.

"Well, remember the face in the photo anyway," I said. "He's dangerous."

"I noticed he was a Dodger fan. It figures."

"If he comes by pretending to be a john, don't go with him. Okay?"

"I'll mention that I've just come from the AIDS clinic," Jerry said, grinning. "That turns the smart ones off. Very well, darling, if you say so. He doesn't look like a big spender anyway."

I took one of Jerry's hands in both of mine. "Think about that guy you saw," I said.

Jerry obligingly thought. I soaked up a vibe, not a clear image, nothing so useful, but a vibe, and an impression of a small room with wood paneling—better than nothing, but not very good. I let Jerry's hand go.

"That'll give me a start," I said. "Thanks."

As we walked down Ellis Street toward Market, we saw an empty cab coming our way, probably after dropping a fare off at one of the big hotels. Just as Nathan hailed it, I had the odd thought that Aunt Eileen was watching us. We'd gotten into the backseat, and Nathan had told the driver our destination, when my cell phone rang. I took it out of my shoulder bag and flipped it open.

"Nola, is that you?" A dark male voice, with the deep growl of a heavy drinker.

"Uncle Jim! What's wrong? You sound like something is."

"We've just been burgled, that's what. Jeezus H, I can't believe the damn bad luck."

As the cab started off, Nathan slid over next to me to listen. I was too worried to care one way or the other.

"Burgled? How bad is it?"

"Damnedest thing. Eileen and I took the boys out for an early movie and a pizza. When we came back, we found the front door wide open. The new TV was gone, and that brand-new game system, but they didn't take my laptop. They trashed the boys' rooms, though, turned everything upside down, threw stuff around. I don't know what in hell they were looking for up there."

"Have you called the police?"

"Jeezus H, of course I did. They're here now, not that they can do much about it."

"Didn't they ask the neighbors if they saw anything? It still must have been light."

"Hell, yes, and here's the thing that really gripes me. The crooks—they drove up in a TV repair truck. Stolen, of course. So when Mrs. G across the street saw them carrying the TV out, she didn't think anything about it."

"Oh, for crying out loud!"

"Smart cookies, huh? Next I'm going to call the insurance agent, but Eileen had the idea that you'd want to know." Jim paused, and in the background I heard her voice. "She wants to know if you got the cab she sensed."

"Tell her yes, and thanks. Do you want me to come over?"

Again the pause, and Aunt Eileen's voice, sounding weary.

"Naw," Uncle Jim said. "There's nothing you can do, either. She just thought you'd want to know."

"I do, and tell her I'll call her when I get home."

"Good. Do that. Here's the damn useless cop again."

I clicked off and put the phone back in my bag, then scowled at Nathan until he returned to his side of the cab. By then we were driving up McAllister past the housing projects, heading for Stanyan, I assumed, to cross over to the inner Sunset district.

"Your aunt sent this cab?" Nathan said.

"No, she sensed it. She does that with cabs. It's an urban evolutionary adaptation."

"You're joking."

"About the evolution bit, yeah. But she does sense cabs."

Nathan spent the rest of the ride scowling out the window. I spent it worrying about Pat's notebooks—would they still be in my apartment when we got back?

When we arrived, Nathan insisted on going up the stairs first, gun in hand, but again, the only thing we saw or heard was Mrs. Z's TV. Nothing in the apartment looked the least bit disturbed, either. I went straight to the bathroom and took the Chaos ward off the clothes hamper by the shower. The green book bag still sat inside under some dirty towels. I pulled it out and checked. None of the notebooks had gone missing.

I took them back out into the living room, where Nathan was slouched down on the couch. He'd tossed his jacket over the coffee table.

"You look angry about something," Nathan said.

"I never wanted my work to touch my family. Damn right I'm angry."

"You're assuming Johnson had something to do with the burglary?"

"Yeah, and that he wanted these." I patted the book bag.

"Would he have known about them?"

"Good question. What I'm hoping is that it's local

teenagers who knew about the new TV and the dope that Michael keeps in his room."

"Dope?"

"Marijuana. Sorry. I'm old-fashioned sometimes."

"He smokes? You should put a stop to that."

"I've tried. It's probably only a lid, if that."

"What?"

"An ounce. An archaic term for how much dope will fit into a plastic coffee can lid."

"You seem to know a lot of odd information and a lot of odd people, I must say."

"I haven't led a quiet life. Have you?"

"No. Sorry. I can see why you'd want to keep your family well clear of all this. I take it that this is a new assignment for you."

"Yeah, I usually work out of town. My superior cast the I Ching and decided it was time for me to come home."

"He cast the—wait, that's a fortune-telling device, isn't it?"

"A very old one. Bronze Age, in fact. Sometimes I think he's nearly as old, but more likely he just dates from the Sixties."

"Maybe I should stop complaining about my superiors."

"You may be lucky, yeah. Look, I want to call my aunt, but I'm going to do an LDRS for Johnson first."

I put the book bag down on the coffee table, then got out my crayons and pad of paper. I went into the kitchen to work at the table. When I let my mind range out to Johnson, my hand started drawing immediately. The blue car, trees, dark sky, waning moon, a structure of some kind off to one side—the information began flowing in fast. I tore off the first sheet and started on a second. The structure was a couple of columns and a lintel by a lake, more trees—

As fast and sharp as a slap to the face, the flow turned into a shudder of pain. I felt my body jerk around in the kitchen chair. My hand spasmed and snapped the crayon I held. Although I couldn't hear myself, I must have made some kind of noise, because Nathan came barreling into the kitchen.

"What's wrong?" he said.

I held up one hand as a signal for him to wait. I took a deep breath and sealed off my mind by reciting the alphabet backward. When I made it to A, I let out my breath in a long sigh. My hand dropped the pieces of crayon.

"What happened?" Nathan said.

"I ran into Johnson," I said. "He's got talent, this guy. I've never touched an electric fence, but I bet it's lot like what just happened to me."

"Are you all right?"

"Yeah. Just tired."

"Very well, then." He picked up the drawings and began to study them.

I realized that he wasn't going to cluck and fuss, that he'd simply believed me when I told him I'd survived okay. I began to see formerly hidden qualities in the man. I saw something else, too: I was glad he was there, gun and all. That's the edge of the slippery slope to meltdown, O'Grady, I told myself. Keep your mind on business.

"He was obviously outside somewhere," Nathan said.

"I'd say Golden Gate Park. There's a shallow lake there with this odd doorway to nowhere standing beside it. The story runs that it was part of a Nob Hill mansion that the 1906 earthquake and fire leveled. The only thing left of it was that marble lintel and the columns, so the guy who owned it gave it to the city. I don't know why they set it up in the park."

"Do you think Johnson might still be there?"

"No. He knows I caught up with him."

I was expecting Nathan to argue, but he merely nodded and went on studying the scribbles. I wanted to sit for a few minutes and think about my next move before calling Aunt Eileen. Although I'd suspected that Johnson had psychic talents himself, now I knew, in a very immediate way. I was going to have to proceed carefully if I did a full scan for him.

"Tell me something." Nathan laid the papers back down on the table. "Why do think he's hunting you? I've got the distinct feeling you didn't tell me when I asked before."

"I didn't, no, and I'm not going to now. For one thing, I don't know if it's me as me that he's after, or if he just knows that someone from the Agency is after him. It could be either."

"Well, why won't you tell me the truth? Or are you protecting someone in your family?"

"Protecting them? No. Keeping them out of this, yeah. There's a difference. Which one were you thinking of?"

"The latter, actually. Why are you so touchy?"

"Because you're so damned rude."

The squabble of thirteen year olds again. Apparently he felt it too.

"I'm sorry," he said. "I just wanted to know if the information came from someone in your family. I'm not accusing anyone of anything."

"Oh, okay. Yes, it did. What made you think so?"

"They all seem to be as odd as you."

I reminded myself that "odd" did in fact describe my family and bit back a nasty retort.

"Your aunt's an O'Brien, right?" Nathan went on. "What about the Houlihans, the family she married into? Do they have these talents too?"

"Some of them. That's one reason Eileen married

Jim, because she knew he'd understand about her and her family. Kathleen's husband is just an ordinary guy— well, an ordinary very rich guy—but she's incredibly beautiful, and he would have accepted Godzilla as a brother-in-law if he'd had to."

Nathan's mouth twitched at the joke. "But Eileen didn't have the requisite seven children, did she?"

"No, just three, James Junior, Clarice, and Brian."

Very carefully I pushed back my chair and stood up. He started to reach out to steady me, then drew his hand back.

"I'm going to call my aunt," I said, "and then read some more of Pat's journals."

"Good. I want to know what's in them."

"So do I, but before I start, I'm going to wrap a barrier around me. I don't want Johnson reading over my shoulder."

"Do you think he knows Latin?"

"If he's reading the information from my mind, he wouldn't have to."

Nathan looked puzzled.

"Some thought is preverbal," I said. "Especially the telepathic kind, because it's apparently more primitive than actual language."

"What? Explain."

"Can't. You'll have to take my word for it, because I don't know how it works, either. It's got to do with deep mental structures, though. Ask Noam Chomsky."

Nathan stiffened like one of Kathleen's cats when a dog sniffs it. "What do you mean by that?" His voice hovered just above an animal growl.

"Huh? What's so wrong? He's a linguist, the one who invented the concept of deep mental structures, is all."

"Not all." His voice returned to normal. "You don't really know what you've just said, do you?"

"No, I sure don't."

"He defends the PLO and Hamas. Drums up a lot of support for them in America."

"Oh, my God! I'm sorry. That's news to me. I only knew about his linguistic theories."

Nathan shook his head. "You *are* amazing," he said. "You live in a different world than the rest of us, don't you?"

"Just what do you mean by that?"

"I hardly know myself."

Nathan walked out of the kitchen. I sat back down and stared at the two LDRS drawings. They'd gone so dead that I knew Johnson had left the location for somewhere far, far away.

CHAPTER 5

BEFORE I PHONED AUNT EILEEN, I asked Nathan to refrain from bugging the call. He solemnly promised me he would. He was turning on the TV as I went into the bathroom, as far away from him as I could get in the apartment, so I could hope he'd keep his promise. When I reached my aunt, she sounded reasonably calm, though I could hear Uncle Jim storming around in the background, yelling at Brian and Michael.

"I don't know why he's blaming the boys," Eileen told me. "He thinks they may have bragged about the new TV at school, where some gang members overheard them. Even if that did happen, it wouldn't be our boys' fault it was stolen."

"That's very true," I said. "He's just mad and needs to vent, I guess."

"He usually does. It's nice of you to call, though really there's not much you can do."

"Well, if you think of anything, let me know. And if Michael needs to talk to me, he can call, too."

"That's a very good thought. I'll make sure he has the number of your cell phone."

"Thanks. There's something I wanted to ask you. Have you had any more dreams about that Sam Spade character, the one who wanted to kill me?"

"No, I'm glad to say. I did have one rather worrisome dream about you and that good-looking Mr. Morrison, though."

I should have known. I may have groaned aloud.

"About Sam Spade," I said as fast as I could. "Did you get the feeling that he knew specifically who I am? Or could he have been worried about my job? In general, you know."

"That's a very good question." She was silent for a long time. "He was such a vague figure that I think it might just be your job. He was going to kill someone who might cause him trouble. But still, in the dream, that someone was you. Of course, I know you even if he doesn't. You know how ambiguous these things are."

"I'm afraid I do, yeah."

"Well, if I get anything more, I'll call you right away. I'd better go now before Jim pours himself another shot. He's had quite enough."

I returned to the living room to find Nathan slouched on the couch and watching the news, or to be precise, a commercial with the sound off.

"What about your other stringer?" he said. "You implied that there was more than one."

"That's true." I glanced at the clock. "She'll be asleep by now, and I don't want to risk leading Johnson to her, either. She's elderly and couldn't defend herself. In the morning I'll see how things are and then give her a call. What I want to do now is read more of Pat's journals."

"Good idea."

The commercial break ended, and Nathan clicked on the sound again. I started to go into my bedroom to read but stopped when I heard "breaking news" and turned to watch. What I saw sickened me. The police had found the stolen TV repair truck with the driver dead inside.

"An execution style murder," the anchorman was saying. "He was bound hand and foot and killed with one shot to the back of the head. Police suspect links to recent gang activities in the Mission district. The truck was otherwise empty, although it was apparently used in a burglary earlier this evening."

Nathan clicked off the sound again as the anchor began another story.

"Does this sound like teenage gangs to you?" I said.

"No. The police have to give the media something, I suppose. I'll call in tomorrow morning and see what kind of bullet they've retrieved."

That simple word, "retrieved," made my stomach clench when I realized exactly where they'd be retrieving it from.

"I doubt, though," Nathan went on, "if it's going to be a silver bullet, even if Johnson is involved. You don't use a long gun to execute someone."

"He wouldn't use the silver bullets in a handgun?"

"If it's a modern handgun, it wouldn't fire properly with that kind of ammunition." He paused to cover a yawn with the back of one hand. "You know, tomorrow we should drop in at the office if we're going to keep our cover."

I remembered the creature I'd seen in the lobby. A part of my mind had been keeping me away from the place, I realized. Smart or cowardly? I wasn't sure.

"That's true," I said. "I need to file a report to the Agency. I'm assuming you've got your own ways of keeping in touch."

"Through the local police and Interpol, yes." He yawned again and shook his head. "Sorry. I don't think I'm completely over the time change. Jet lag and all that."

I was expecting a hassle over the sleeping arrangements, but Nathan kept his word, though he decided to try sleeping on the couch instead of the floor. I had an extra pillow and blanket for guests, and then I gave him one of my blankets, too, because I can stay warm by stockpiling my energy in what the Agency calls Mental Thermal Regulation. The bathroom had two doors, so I could lock the one that led into my bedroom and let him use the other.

Once Nathan was settled, I took the book bag into my bedroom and picked up journal number four. I ended up flipping through it, scanning rather than reading, because it mostly contained a collection of special prayers for the Hounds to use during their meetings. Some touched me deeply, others I found unsettling, full of imagery that would, I suppose, make a lot of sense to wolves. I could understand the theme of not slaughtering Jesus' sheep, but marking God's territory in your heart? I knew what he meant, but I decided not to dwell on the details.

The fifth journal brought more information about the Hounds, though nothing so concrete as where they met or their human names. Apparently they had organized themselves like a real wolf pack. As the alpha pair, Fr. LG and Sr. MR were planning on marrying and having cubs. Pat, as the newest member of the club, was the omega wolf. In the wild, he would have eaten last and acted in general like a puppy, starting wolfish games such as tag and mock tussles over sticks. In this version of wolf society, he took on the role of deacon, hence the book of prayers he'd written. He also supplied the refreshments—raw legs of lamb and the like—for their wolf-night meetings. Although it all made great sense to them, I'll admit I found it disturbing.

Although I did manage to finish journal five, I was yawning compulsively by the end. I put it back in the bag, put the bag back in the hamper, sealed it with a Chaos ward, and went to bed.

I woke in the morning to the sounds of Nathan shaving in the bathroom. Although it had been a while since

I'd had a live-in boyfriend, I recognized the dabbling of the razor in the basin, the slapping sound of applying aftershave, the gurgle of the filthy water—

"Nathan!" I called out. "Make sure you rinse the sink, will you?"

He laughed and called back that he would.

I got out of bed and craned my neck to look up the airshaft: steel gray sky. When Nathan finished, I showered and dressed in a pair of gray glen plaid slacks, warmer than jeans, and a dark green cotton top with long sleeves. No angels appeared during the process. I assumed that they'd delivered their one important message about Joseph's coat and now had nothing more to tell me.

I came out into the living room to find that Nathan had folded the blankets into a precise cube at one end of the couch. He'd made coffee, too. Without a word he handed me a mug, then looked me over.

"Don't you ever wear dresses?" he said.

"When there's an occasion," I said. "This isn't one."

"I don't suppose I can talk you into eating breakfast."

"That's right. You can't."

He shrugged the problem away. "I just heard from the police. They've been in touch with Interpol, and they've run a check on their own records. We have another impossibility on our hands."

"Say what?"

"William Johnson, a man who looks exactly like the pictures I have from the Israeli cases, is in prison in California for aggravated assault. He's been there for four years now."

"Well, William Johnson is a real common name, and the guy in those photos looks like a basic American type."

"Yes, but their fingerprints match."

I stared. My mouth would have dropped open like

in the cartoons if I hadn't kept it firmly shut. Nathan allowed himself a brief smile at the effect he'd produced.

"The Israeli police found fingerprints in the consular official's flat," Nathan went on. "The local police have a clear print and a couple of partials from Romero's body. Johnson had her blood on his hands, apparently, when he shoved the corpse away."

"And they all match this guy who's been in prison for the past four years?"

"Yes. Identical twins, by the way, have different fingerprints."

"So much for the last rational explanation."

"Just so. Now, look, I want you to stay inside till I get back. Keep the curtains drawn and avoid the windows as much as possible."

"Okay, but for God's sake, will you watch the traffic? If you cause a multiple fatality, you'll spoil your good relationship with the local cops."

"There's nothing wrong with my driving."

"The hell there isn't."

He scowled but let the subject drop.

After Nathan left, I logged onto TranceWeb and posted the news about Johnson's apparent double on our open board—open to agents, that is. I was hoping that someone would have an explanation or at least a theory about doppelgängers to offer me. When I finished, I logged off and continued with Pat's journals, scanning more than reading, until I reached the second to last notebook. It began with a few pages of his usual mix of spiritual meditations, family gossip, and chatter about the doings of the Hounds. Soon, though, his prose turned cryptic, echoing the style of those pages written when Fr. LG had first contacted him. I could pick up, however, that someone had approached the Hounds and wanted to join them. The pack scented trouble. How had this person even known they existed?

Pat believed that the alpha Hounds suspected him of letting the secret out, even though they denied it. He went on to write a lot about how grieved and hurt he was and nowhere near enough about this mysterious person. I was ready to bite him myself by the time he finally divulged that this man, whom he called DD, had been hinting that he could put the Hounds in touch with something very "big and important," something hidden from the *vulgus,* the common herd. DD often expounded on his scorn for the *vulgus.*

I had just turned the page when I heard a key slide into the door lock and the deadbolt shoot back.

"Nola?" Nathan's voice called out. "I'm back from Sheboygan."

I unchained the door and opened it to find him grinning at me. He was holding two sets of keys and a white paper bag. He handed me my set of keys on their familiar ring and put the second set into his trousers pocket.

"How did you get these?" I said.

"I took them out of your bag." He walked in, then turned to shut the door and chain it again. "I wanted to lock you in from the outside, just in case you had the urge to go wander around where Johnson could find you. I made copies, so I can get in and out of the office on my own."

"You arrogant son of a bitch."

He laughed and handed me the paper bag. "I'm not sure what you call this, but it looked good."

Since it smelled good, too, I opened the bag and looked in. "A blueberry Danish," I said. "I'm tempted to shove it into your face, but I'll admit to being hungry by now."

He grinned at me with his big-eyed boyish smile. It dawned on me that he enjoyed making me angry, perhaps as payback for the frustration I was putting him through. I suspected that very few women—if any—had

ever told Nathan no. He reached inside his jacket and
brought out a folded sheet of paper.

"A photocopy of Johnson's letter to the newspaper,"
Nathan said.

"Thanks." I put it down beside my multifunction
printer. "I'll get this off to the Agency expert."

While I ate my breakfast, Nathan told me what he'd
learned from the homicide detective in charge of the
Romero case.

"He's convinced that Romero must have known
the killer," Nathan said, "because she was shot at close
range. I didn't bother to tell him your theory that she'd
been the one stalking him."

"Oh? You think I'm wrong?"

"Of course not! He wouldn't believe a word of it,
is all. So, the police suspect a man from her group of
college friends, most likely her boyfriend, Lawrence
Grampian."

"Fr. LG, aka Lupus Gubbionis."

"Yes, but I didn't tell him that, either. Most murders
are committed by someone the victim knows, and when
a woman's killed, the murderer generally does turn
out to be her husband or boyfriend. So I understand
Lieutenant Sanchez's line of reasoning."

"Even with the resemblance to the Israeli cases?"

"Sanchez had something new to tell me about that."
Nathan paused for a grim smile. "Grampian visited
Israel on one of those Christian pilgrimage group tours,
although it was some while before the murders were
committed. He could easily have gone back at some
point."

"Was this after my brother died?"

"Some months after, yes. Sanchez doesn't know
about your brother's death, of course, but I did bring
Patrick officially into the investigation as a missing
person. What happened to him is part of the pattern,

although 'missing' is far as I could go under the circumstances. Sanchez also knows that Pat had a connection to Grampian. He brought up the records of the missing person reports your mother filed at the time. Grampian was interviewed then."

"So Sanchez thinks he has a case again Frater LG?"

"He's too good an officer to think so at this stage of the investigation. He does see Grampian as a person of interest, especially since Grampian has no alibi for the night of the Romero murder."

"Of course he doesn't. It was a full moon night, which is why we can rule him out as a suspect, even with the Israel visit thrown into the mix."

Nathan looked puzzled.

"He couldn't have shot her." I spelled it out for him. "He had paws, not hands. Even if he'd gone back to Israel later, those murders happened at the full moon, too. No way he could have used a gun."

"All perfectly logical." Nathan paused for an aggrieved sigh. "That's probably why Romero's family won't hear a word against Grampian but can't explain why they feel that way to the police. They must know about his lycanthropy—and hers, for that matter."

"You can't keep it hidden from the people you live with."

"I can well believe that. Sanchez does want me to attend the funeral. I told him that my girlfriend would come with me."

I merely smiled.

"Well," he said, "I didn't want to expose your cover."

"That's fine."

He looked so aggravated that I laughed.

"Are you sure you're not a werewolf, too, Nathan?" I said. "You look like you're going to snarl."

He wiped the look away. "I do wish," he said, "that you'd call me by my first name."

"Yeah?" I got up and started for the kitchen. "Want more coffee?"

"No. We should get down to the office, but I'll drive."

"I'll take the streetcar and meet you there."

Nathan did snarl, though he reminded me more of a tiger than a wolf. The sight of flashing teeth reminded me once again of the scaly little spy. I disliked the idea of letting another such get a snoutful of my scent. Besides, when I glanced out the window I saw rain clouds gathering. The idea of dealing with a damp and crabby Nathan did not appeal.

"To be honest, though," I said. "There's a lot of stuff I can do right here, like finish the journals."

"I don't want to leave you alone."

"Do you really think Johnson's going to attack me in broad daylight?"

"I don't know what Johnson's going to do." Nathan turned grim again. "Neither do the police. It's just not the papers—the police themselves are afraid they have another Zodiac killer on their hands, because of the occult element. Sanchez had always considered the silver bullets an occult element, but now they have the letters, as well. They never caught the Zodiac, did they?"

"No, that's very true. But he killed at random for fun. There's a pattern to our case, and I suspect there's a motive, too. We just haven't found it yet."

"Of course, but we can't tell the police when we do."

"That does make life difficult, yeah."

"I'll admit that it's not likely that Johnson would come after you during the day, not unless he's willing to risk being seen, but why take chances?" He shrugged to emphasize the point. "I'll go down to the office, pick up a few things, and then come back. Don't leave."

"I won't. One last thing. Keep your eyes open when you're crossing the lobby. If you think you see something moving, like out of the corner of your eye, you're not imagining things. You may not be able to see it, but something could be there."

"Something?"

"Something it takes special training to see, yeah. I'm not joking or teasing you, Nathan. Chaotic forces generate some strange phenomena. At times they produce things that look like little animals. They're not alive, strictly speaking, but they can carry information back and forth."

Nathan stared at me. Since teaching him how to throw a Chaos ward would have taken weeks, I fell back on ancient lore.

"You don't have anything with you that has a Star of David on it, do you?" I said. "A tie clasp, maybe?"

"No, I don't. What are you talking about?"

"Wards. Things that repel Chaotic forces and beings." I considered for a moment. "If I drew a Star of David on a piece of paper, would you keep it in your breast pocket?"

Nathan sighed and looked upon me with the reproachful stare. "Oh, very well," he said at last. "If it'll make you feel better."

"It would. Definitely. And watch your back."

"That's always good advice."

Once Nathan had his improvised ward, he left, and I settled down with Pat's last two journals. These I read carefully and slowly. I even took notes on a scratch pad as a number of things began to fall into place. Once I finished, I went to my computer and logged on to the Agency to file a thorough report via TranceWeb. By the time Nathan returned, I had plenty to tell him.

Thanks to the first splatter of rain, he arrived damp, crabby, and lugging his sample case and a brown paper sack of groceries. Apparently black lettuce didn't appeal to him. While I put away the high calorie stuff he'd bought, he hung up his wet jacket on the shower rail, then returned to sit at the kitchen table and watched me.

"While I was at the office," he said, "I didn't see anything invisible."

"Good." I ignored the sneer in his voice. "You're lucky."

"Did you find anything new in the journals?"

"Yeah, a motive for Pat's murder."

He leaned back in his chair and smiled the tiger's smile, not his boyish grin. "Brilliant!" he said. "Tell me."

What I'd pieced together revolved around this mysterious DD, initials for a pseudonym, I assumed. At first he'd been all flattery as he tried to interest the Hounds in whatever his "something big" amounted to. Despite his protestations of piety and spiritual longing, they'd been wary and refused to take the bait. He'd withdrawn, leaving them all feeling "unclean" as Pat put it, as well as in danger. How had he known what they were and where to find them? DD never divulged that answer.

My poor brother had decided to try to find out. With the blessing of the group he pretended to be interested in DD's hints. They fenced back and forth for a while, with Pat fishing for information and DD doling out scraps. Finally DD admitted that he belonged to another secret organization, one devoted to a personage he called "the ruler of this world." All of Pat's well-trained Christian alarms went off. DD tried to convince him that this ruler operated as an agent of God, but Pat heard "Satan" loud and clear. He broke off all contact with DD, or so he thought.

"By then," I finished up, "DD must have figured that Pat knew too much about his secret group, not that he could have gone to the police about it."

"Why not? For that matter, doesn't your church have ways of dealing with such things?"

"It's not my church anymore, but Satanism's not illegal in the United States. DD didn't have to worry about the police on that score."

Nathan looked honestly surprised. "After all I've heard about your preachers and their television shows, I'd assumed something quite different."

"Oh, they'd love to start a crusade, but they can't, thanks to the Constitution. There was an openly Satanist group in San Francisco for years. My aunt told me that when she was a girl, their high priest used to drive around in a beat-up station wagon with an elderly lion in the back, behind one of those dog grates like Kathleen has in her SUV."

Nathan blinked, opened his mouth, stared at me for a moment, then finally spoke. "You're not joking, are you?"

"No."

"I was afraid of that. Very well, then. This group DD belonged to—they must have something else to hide."

"Yeah, something that can get them into trouble so big that it's worth killing for. Pat hinted about it in his journals. He was going to go to the police, but the full moon intervened. It gave Johnson three days, is my guess, to shut him up permanently."

"Which he did."

"Yeah, but Pat must have told the other Hounds. If we can make contact with them, we might be able to answer a lot of questions. If this Grampian has a brain in his head, he should be scared enough to tell us what he knows. He's probably next."

"Quite so. He knows that the police suspect him, so you're the one who has to make the contact."

"At least at first, yeah."

Nathan looked away and thought something through. "Another thing that troubles me," he said at last. "How did DD discover the Hounds in the first place? Did your brother ever find that out?"

"No, but I can make a guess. Chaos calls to Chaos. Werewolves are essentially Chaotic. The Hounds are rowing upstream against a torrent, trying to control that side of their natures. Pat's journals make that very clear. DD—or maybe even Johnson—could practically smell them out on the aura field."

"You're assuming there's two of them?"

"Well, of course. DD couldn't have shot the Romero girl."

"Why not?"

"Because he has to be a werewolf, too. Why else would he have tried to join the Hounds?"

Once, thanks to a variety of odd circumstances, I'd been forced to break a bottle of beer over a man's head. He had looked at me with the same expression of aggrieved surprise as Nathan did, but unlike the other guy, Nathan did not fall forward onto his face. He merely said something in Hebrew in a tone of voice that told me it wasn't a phrase from the Bible.

"What's wrong?" I said.

"Is everyone in this sodding case a sodding werewolf?"

"They run in packs, Nathan. They find each other and revert to type. So, yeah, I'd expect the major players in this game to suffer from lycanthropy or be involved with someone who does."

I waited for him to answer. He fixed me with the reproachful stare but kept quiet.

"Okay," I continued. "We also have Jerry's evidence about the Chaos lights and the well-dressed guy by the windmill. Jerry was convinced he was a Chaotic."

"By saying that he gave him the creeps, you think it was?"

"Yeah. It certainly suggests Chaos on the move." Something struck me. "And this may be why the forces of Harmony saddled me with you. It could be that Johnson and company are responsible for the Chaos breaches.

My handler thought there had to be a connection, and he may have been right."

"Saddled you with me? That's insulting."

I couldn't help it. I laughed.

"Oh, very well," Nathan said. "I suppose I deserve that."

"You do, yeah. Now, I want to go talk with the Agency's other stringer. Annie, her name is. She lives out in the Sunset district, that is, about twenty blocks west of here and then ten or so south. Think that'll be safe enough?"

"If I'm with you."

"Okay. We'll take a cab."

"No, we won't. It's too dangerous. But I'm driving." He looked as if he were hiding a smile. The secrecy intrigued me enough to keep me from arguing.

"Will you try to drive like a sane person instead of James Bond?" I said instead.

"I do not drive like someone in those wretched movies."

"No, you're worse. In the movies they use highly trained stunt drivers."

He set his hands on his hips and glared at me.

"I'll call Annie and make sure she's there." I decided I might as well give in. "It might be one of her Senior Center days."

Annie answered the phone and told me to come right over. I relayed the information to Nathan.

"Good," he said. "I was hoping she'd be willing to see us right away."

"The Agency owes her money, and she needs it."

I got my burgundy trench coat and umbrella from the bedroom. I figured that I might as well be well-dressed if I was going to die in a car accident. When I came out, I noticed that Nathan had put on a gray V-neck sweater over his shirt and under a shabby khaki raincoat that looked like old Army issue with all the insignia removed, which, as he admitted when asked, it was.

He needed that extra layer, too, when we left the apartment. The rain pelted down, unusually heavily for the beginning of March, but then, we'd had an unusual amount of rain already this year. As we walked, I was looking around for the Audi, but I never saw it. Nathan led me around the corner to a squarish black sedan. When I looked in I saw a red, white, and blue light bar on the dashboard and what appeared to be a full radio-phone as well.

"This is a squad car," I said.

"Unmarked, but yes." He was grinning at me. "Which is why I can't let you drive it."

"Okay, but where did you get it? I can't believe the cops would just let you have one."

"Connections. That's all."

I decided that forcing the issue would be out of line and got myself and my trepidation into the car. The drive over rattled my nerves, but not quite as much as I'd been dreading. Whenever we got into any kind of traffic, Nathan flipped on the car's siren, and other drivers got out of our way, thus saving themselves as well as us from death or dismemberment.

Annie lived in a quiet neighborhood where the streets stayed empty all day, which meant we could park without one of Nathan's tire screeching flourishes. Annie's studio apartment, if you could call that cheap and illegal rathole a studio, had originally been a garage. Like most garages in the Sunset district, this one stood underneath the square-built Thirties stucco house it belonged to. Similar Art Deco cubical houses, painted in various dull colors, mostly grays and whites, lined both sides of the street. The only color came from the tiny squares of green lawn beside each driveway.

"Bleak neighborhood," Nathan said.

"Very," I said. "Especially when it's foggy, and it usually is out here. Today's rain counts as fog relief."

I opened a narrow wooden door that led to an equally narrow concrete walk down the side of the house. Barking greeted us.

"That's Duncan," I told Nathan. "Kathleen gave him to Annie. He does a good job on watch."

Annie had seen us coming from her tiny side window. With the fox terrier at her side, she stood in her doorway, a gray-haired woman with thick glasses. She wore faded jeans rolled up around her ankles and a blue sweatshirt so baggy you could have hidden a watermelon under it. A battle with breast cancer had cost her thirty pounds and her life savings.

"Come in, come in!" she said with a glance at Nathan.

I introduced her, and we followed her and Duncan inside. First thing, she took my umbrella and put it into the kitchen sink to drip. She kept her one long room as spotless as Aunt Eileen's house. It reeked of the same cleaning products. At the back end, by the window that looked out into a halfhearted garden, she sat us down at the round oak table and chairs that she'd owned since her better days. We squeezed ourselves in between the table and the tiny refrigerator and stove.

"Can I offer you some tea?" she said.

"None for me, thanks," I said.

I didn't want her spending any of her food money on us, and Nathan either didn't like tea or had caught my mood, because he said no as well. Fortunately the Agency had put plenty of cash into my bank account, thanks to the State Department dumping Nathan onto us. When I handed Annie five twenties, she looked as if she might cry, just for a moment, before she put on a brave little smile.

"I only invoiced you for eighty." She peeled off one of the twenties and held it out.

"I invoiced the Agency for more on your behalf." I grinned at her. "Keep it, and I've got more work for you."

"About those Chaos lights?"

"You saw them, then."

"Yes, I certainly did." She paused to put the money away in her jeans pocket. "I was trying to clear out some of the weeds in back when they floated over, heading north. They were on the TV news last night, too. Someone driving by took pictures of them with his cell phone. It really is amazing, what you can do with a phone these days."

"That's for sure. Did you pick up anything about them?"

"They were here because of someone. That's all."

"Jerry told me the same thing."

"You know, I had the oddest feeling about Jerry last night." Annie frowned and looked away. "That he knows something you need, but he doesn't know you need it, and so, of course, he didn't tell you."

"That could be real important. Thank you. He's probably up in the stratosphere by now, though. I paid him the money the Agency owed him. You can guess what he did with it."

"Oh, yes, his drug problem. It's really too bad—"

Annie's face stiffened into a mask. She half-rose from her chair, propped herself palms down on the table, and stared down the length of the room into the shadows at the far end. I slewed around in my chair but saw nothing but her neatly made daybed and her collection of framed prints and posters.

"What is it?" I made my voice as soft as I could.

"Persian white." Annie sat back down with a little sigh. "Do you know what that means? Some breed of cat, maybe?"

"No," I said. "It's a top grade of heroin."

Nathan made a small choking noise of agreement.

"Well, I think," Annie said, "that Jerry either just bought some, or found out where to get it, or some such thing. I think that's what he has to tell you, but I'm not sure." She turned to Nathan. "I'm sorry to be so vague, but you know how these things work."

"I'm beginning to," he said.

"You're new to the Agency?"

"No, he's with Interpol," I broke in. "We're just assisting."

"Interpol? Oh, like that TV show, the one on the BBC channel." Annie gave him a bright smile. "That's nice. Well, probably Jerry can tell you a lot more than I can about this sort of thing. Drugs, I mean. It really is too bad that he's so addicted to cocaine."

"Yeah," I said, "but he can't see it that way. Yet." I took another twenty out of my jeans and slid it across the table. "I'll invoice the Agency later, but you might as well have this now."

"Well, thank you!" Annie beamed at the twenty, then tucked it away with the others. "Such a help!"

Nathan had tactfully looked away during this exchange of cold cash. Annie noticed him studying the framed posters on the wall down at the other end of the room. The lithographs portrayed a woman in a flowing black dress and red turban; she stared out at the viewer with a crazed expression on her face.

"My grandmother was a vaudeville performer," Annie said. "She had a very successful mind-reader act. Most of the so-called psychics on the circuit were nothing but tricksters and cheats, of course, but she really could read minds and see into the future and the like. I suppose that's where I get it from."

"Seems reasonable," Nathan said. "As reasonable as any of this is."

"We must be quite a trial for you." Annie patted his hand in a grandmotherly gesture. "Policemen are usually so rational." She lifted her hand, smiled, and held up his Interpol ID. "My grandmother knew so many little tricks. Vaudeville must have been so very interesting."

Nathan stared at her, started to speak, then merely laughed. He slipped the ID back into his pants pocket. "Must have been," he said. "I'm just glad you're on our side."

I decided that I might as well try calling Jerry, but he never answered his phone. He was either asleep, with a client, or too loaded to answer. After a good many rings, I did get a tasteful message via an answering service, announcing that Mr. Jerome had left his salon for the day but would return calls during business hours. Annie and I got a good laugh out of this cover story.

"After all," she said, "the things he does would curl my hair, certainly!"

Nathan smiled politely, and we left.

As we walked back out to the street, I was considering Annie's flash of insight. I knew only the basics of the drug trade, but even the network news talked about heroin from Afghanistan and how it reached American markets. I waited till we were clear of the house before I said anything to Nathan.

"Persian white, huh? You think?"

"I do. It comes through Kurdistan, where Johnson was spotted."

Spotted. The word caught my attention and refused to let go. I was standing in an enormous library, miles of pale gray shelves in all directions. In a flurry of white wings the angel came to me and showed me an open book. "Sister Peter Mary," the angel said. "Heresies."

I was sitting in the backseat of the unmarked squad car. Nathan sat next to me with his arm around my shoulders. Rain pounded on the metal roof with the sound of machine guns. When Nathan leaned close to study my face, I caught the faint scent of witch hazel.

"Why don't you use a real aftershave?" I said.

"I suppose that means you're back," he said. "Do you remember me putting you into the car?"

"No, now that you mention it. Why do you look so frightened?"

"You might have warned me that you go into walking trance states."

"I didn't know I did."

Since Nathan's arm felt heavy and warm, I could assume that he was real, and the angel had been the illusion. The scent of his painful idea of aftershave lotion underscored my conviction. Otherwise, I might have doubted it. I wanted to rest my head on his shoulder and sleep, but he slid over to the open door and got out of the car.

"Come sit in the front." He held out his hand.

I needed his help to change seats. During the ride I fought off the clouds gathering inside my head. If the angels wanted to tell me something, I figured, they could damn well wait till I got home. They must have been assisting, however, because Nathan actually drove in a halfway sane manner, and we got a parking spot right near my apartment—a sure sign of divine intervention.

Nathan helped me out of the car and held the open umbrella over us both. Once I got my feet on the solid sidewalk, I took a deep breath of wet air and felt my head beginning to clear.

"How do you know what a walking trance is?" I asked him.

"It's something I learned in my miserable childhood. Here's the door to your apartment building. Mind the step up."

"I'm okay now, thanks."

I shook myself free of his arm, an ungrateful action in a way, but I was determined to stay unmelted. Getting inside my own space made me feel almost normal again.

I hung up my wet coat on the shower rail and dumped the umbrella into the bathtub. The effort of returning to the living room made me flop ungracefully onto the couch. I realized too late that I'd left myself open to his sitting next to me. He took off his raincoat and tossed it over the back of the computer chair.

"You need something to eat," he said.

"I don't think I could keep it down."

"If you don't eat, you're going to keep slipping into trance."

"How do you know—oh, right, the spiritual retro kibbutz."

He looked at me and smiled. "I should have known your agency would do a workup on me."

"Of course. Yours probably did one on me."

"It didn't find much."

"Neither did mine. What happened to that kibbutz, by the way? Is it still there?"

"No. A year after my father and I left, Reb Ezekiel had a heart attack in a whorehouse and died in the embrace of impurity. The remaining faithful lost their faith and fled."

"I can see why."

"There's no doubt, though, that odd things happened under his regime." He let his voice trail away for a moment, then shook himself. "So, yes, I know what fasting can do to someone."

"Okay, I'll eat. Just for you."

Since I'd left the heat on, the apartment was hot. He pulled his sweater over his head and tossed it onto the coffee table before he trotted into the kitchen and began bustling around. I rested my head on the back of the couch and considered my vision. The gray library, I realized, probably stood for my brain, and the angel symbol had been pointing out something that I knew or had known at one time and forgotten. Heresies: Asia

Minor, and the entire Mediterranean world, for that matter, had spawned a hell of a lot of them. Sister Peter Mary had confined her lessons to a few of the important "enemies of the true faith," as she'd called them. Arians, Nestorians, the iota controversy, Gnostics—empty words, jumbled together, rose in answer to the call of memory. One term, however—Gnostics—did ring in my mind as a subject that I'd once found interesting.

Nathan reappeared with a cheese sandwich, made with green lettuce and a lot of mayonnaise, and a mug of cold coffee, heavily spiked with milk. I'd never been waited on by a guy wearing a gun before. It had a certain charm.

"Thanks," I said. "I appreciate this."

"You're welcome."

He handed me the plate and mug, then disappeared into the kitchen again. He reemerged a moment later with a plate of his own, then sat down next to me.

"Good sandwich," I mumbled, then swallowed before I went on. "I'm surprised you know how to make one."

"Why? I live alone. The bachelor's best friend, sandwiches. Usually I stuff things into pita bread, but English style will do."

"Yeah. I'm a lousy cook myself."

For some minutes we ate in silence. I tried to figure out why the word "spotted" had seemed so important, what it might signify in conjunction with heresies. I dimly remembered a college history lecture about a cult where leopards loomed large, drawing a chariot of some kind. Dionysus, yes, but something even older. They had some kind of peculiar ritual—

"Castration," I said. "That's it!"

"I beg your pardon!" Nathan snapped.

"Nothing personal! I'm trying to remember what cult had leopards and the priests castrated themselves."

"Oh. Cybele, the Great Mother."

"That's it, yeah, thanks."

Nathan took another bite of his sandwich, ate it, then wiped his mouth on his shirtsleeve. "Would it be intruding," he said, "to ask why you were trying to remember that?"

"Just an everyday thought around here." I drank some of my coffee. "Seriously, though, it was the word 'spotted' that sent me off into that trance. I saw an angel who talked about heresies. Cybele goes back too far to be considered a Christian heresy or any other kind of heresy. The ancient world didn't think like that."

"Quite so, every god welcome in the pantheon and all that. Are there any Christian cults that leopards figure in?"

"No, not that I ever heard. It's time to hit the Internet, I think. I'll see what I can Google up."

Nothing, as it turned out. I found thousands of pages about Gnostic heresy and heresies in general, and even more about Satanism, but no cults that featured leopards or anything spotted. I had reached the point of giving up when Nathan had a brilliant thought.

"Wait," he said. "We were discussing Kurdistan. Any heretical beliefs would have to fall away from Islam, not Christianity."

"Of course! How dumb can I get?"

After a few muddled minutes of trying various search terms, and quite a few more of link surfing, I finally hit the target, or to be precise, my web browser did.

"Peacocks, not leopards," I said. "Ever hear of the cult of Tawsi Melek?"

"Melek? A king, is it?" Nathan said.

"That's what this article calls him, yeah. The Peacock Angel or the Peacock King."

"No, I haven't."

"Neither have I, and apparently we're not alone in our ignorance. It's pretty obscure. There are some remote tribes in Kurdistan who worship this guy as the ruler of this world and the universe." I skimmed down the screen. "The believers say he's a holy emanation of the supreme god, the first emanation in fact. He went on to create the physical world following the supreme god's instructions, with a lot of lesser emanations to help."

"Ah. Sort of a divine foreman."

"Yeah, but the Islamic clerics brand him as Satan. I'll bet the Christian ones would agree."

The angel appeared beside my computer desk. He smiled at me and raised both hands in blessing. "Coat of many colors," he said.

"Why couldn't you just say peacock?" I said. "It would have saved me a lot of time."

"There are no peacocks in our holy book."

And with that lovely bit of chop logic, he disappeared.

CHAPTER 6

"I SUPPOSE," Nathan said in a profoundly weary tone of voice, "I'm going to have to get used to you speaking to things that aren't there."

"It would help you maintain peace of mind, yeah," I said. "An angel just confirmed my guess about the peacock king cult."

"Brilliant. How I am going to tell that to Sanchez?"

"No need for sarcasm." I considered the legitimate question behind the tone of voice. "For one thing, we can't be sure that Johnson and DD belong to it. These angels I see aren't real, you know. They're just visualized symbols from my own mind, so they're not particularly reliable."

"You can't know how glad I am to hear you say that."

"What?" I said. "You didn't think they were real, did you?"

"No, I thought you thought they were."

I swiveled around in the computer chair. He was looking at me without the slightest hint of a smile.

"I've never met anyone like you in my life," Nathan continued, "not even when I was a child among the nutters. How am I supposed to know what you believe?"

"That's a reasonable question, actually. You can always just ask."

"There are times when I don't even know how to frame the question." He crossed his arms over his chest and glared.

I glanced around fast, but no Sister Peter Mary materialized. She must have missed her cue.

"I don't know what to tell you," I said, "except I'm sorry. If it weren't for the State Department, you wouldn't have to deal with any of this. They're the ones who put your agency in touch with mine."

"Fine!" His voice climbed a couple of notes up the register. "Blame the sodding government!"

"Who else am I supposed to blame?"

"Oh, I don't know. Blame is a stupid word to use, anyway."

"You're the one who introduced the concept into this discussion."

Nathan growled at me, very tigerlike, then caught himself. I could see his face change as he made himself relax. He stopped hugging himself to keep the rage in, sighed, looked away, swallowed heavily, all of the little techniques they teach people in anger management classes. I could practically check them off a list, which made me realize that he must have taken a course of those classes. What would he be like in a real rage? Though it might have been an interesting scientific experiment to provoke him and see, I decided to play it safe.

"I really am sorry," I said. "It must be hard, working with someone as weird as I am."

"You're not weird," he said. "That's the problem. You look and act completely normal about everything except for these—these things."

"Things like Image Objectification of Insight and then the LDRS, you mean?"

"And walking trances." He glared at me. "You implied you'd never fallen into one before."

"I haven't, no. I don't know what caused it, either."

I had a theory about that trance, but I refused to share it with him because of the direction it might lead us—lust, again, or more accurately—peace, Sister Peter Mary—Qi. Nathan extruded Qi every time he looked at me. I picked it up, responded with Qi of my own, and ended up with far too much energy. Some of it automatically sublimated into various odd states of consciousness, including walking trance.

"I'll try to avoid them in the future," I said. "You're right about eating now and then. Fasting does do weird things to the mind."

"Yes, I saw a lot of that when I was a boy."

I caught something in his voice that I'd never heard there before: sadness. I longed to say, "Tell me about your mother, Nathan," then decided I'd been foolhardy enough for one day. He ended the conversation by standing up and taking our empty plates into the kitchen.

"I've got to check in with Sanchez." He reappeared briefly in the doorway. "Forensics should have reported back to him by now."

Sure, I thought. And you want to bury the whole subject of your childhood, too. By now it should be obvious that I majored in psychology in college. I went on for a master's in the vain hope of understanding myself and my family better. Although I learned a lot about normal people, psychic traits and the like lay way beyond mainstream research. I could hear Nathan talking in the kitchen. In a few minutes he returned and sat down next to me on the couch.

"How's the police hunt going?" I said.

"At a fairly brisk pace. They're putting his photo on all the TV news stations and their Internet sites." Nathan looked relieved at the change of subject. "Running the usual computer checks. Searching for Romero's clothes, which would have been blood-soaked had she been wearing any. They couldn't find them at the scene, so they're assuming Johnson took them as a fetish object."

"That's a disgusting thought."

"Serial killers do disgusting things. In the two cases back home, the police found the corpses naked, too, don't forget. So it looks like a behavioral pattern if you don't understand what actually happened."

"Yeah. She wouldn't have been wearing anything but a wolfskin that night."

"Shall I tell Sanchez that?" He made an attempt to smile. "At any rate, while I was on the phone just now, the report on that television truck did come in. Forensics found a fingerprint inside the TV repair truck's door that matched the print they'd taken from Romero's body."

"So that's a confirmed link."

"Yes, with both William Johnsons."

"They're absolutely sure the other one's still in the slam?"

"If you mean in prison, yes. Sanchez actually went so far as to call the warden at the Soledad State Prison to make sure."

"So much for my hope that he'd escaped and no one had noticed. But this means either our William or the mysterious DD killed that poor guy just to have a cover story when they went hunting for Pat's journals. Not nice boys, these."

"Quite so, assuming they knew about the journals."

"Well, true. They obviously didn't know that I had them over here."

"Yes, but I meant, did they know that the journals existed?"

"Gotcha. Yeah, all the Hounds kept journals. They read aloud from them at their meetings."

"So DD would have known Pat kept them. He'd suspect that Pat had written about him and his 'something big.' Very good."

"It's possible that Johnson had finally traced them to Michael just before I took them. I put wards on them, so the trail would have stopped there."

Nathan considered this for a moment, then shrugged. "It makes as much sense as anything does in this situation," he said. "What we have to concentrate on now is finding Johnson and his wolfish friend."

"I should do another LDRS."

"Is that really—" He broke off. "Yes, good idea."

What had he been about to say—is that really safe? Of course it wasn't, but I still needed to do it. I considered building myself a Shield Persona first, but doing so would have drained a part of my energy. The loss, coupled with the difficulties that Nathan's presence caused, would have left me too off-balance to be effective, especially against a strong opponent like Johnson.

After last night's adventure I'd left my supplies in the kitchen. I sat down at the table, focused on a blank piece of paper, and sent my mind out to Johnson. Nothing. Absolutely nothing came to me. I looked up to find Nathan hovering in the doorway.

"He seems to have left the planet," I said. "And yeah, that's a joke. I can't pick him up."

"Do you think he's dead?"

"No such luck. No, he's just very good at hiding would be my analysis. You know, if we went to his last sensed location, I might be able to pick up his trail again. No guarantees, but it's worth a try." I stood up and began gathering my crayons. "I'd better take the tools of the trade with us. Let me just get a plastic bag."

"It's stopped raining. Didn't you notice?"

"Uh, no. Sometimes I forget about things like that. Weather, you know. And outside."

"Outside your mind, you mean."

He'd nailed that. I turned and looked out the kitchen

window. The clouds above were pulling apart off to the west. Shafts of late afternoon sunlight broke through like pillars of light among the distant houses.

Most people think of Golden Gate Park as the home of museums, the Japanese Tea Garden, and other such tourist attractions. To the west, though, lies the real park, the one we locals use, a string of meadows with artificial lakes tucked among trees, some planted to look wild, others walled in concrete to give children a safe place to sail toy boats. "Portals of the Past," the doorway to nowhere, that is, stood on a strip of grass beside a sort of shallow bay on one of the smaller lakes. Behind it trees and shrubs screened it from the busy street just a few yards away.

That far west Nathan found parking easily, right in front of the lake. We walked around on a dirt path to the newly restored pillars, part old marble, part new concrete carefully painted to mimic marble. I noticed that the shallow water of the little bay had turned green and thick with algae, though the main part of the lake looked clean enough. By then the sun was doing its best to drive away the rest of the rain clouds. Dappled light fell across the grass, then faded back to cold gray as the atmosphere won a round. Out on the lake a flotilla of ducks swam toward us.

"Sorry," I said and waved my empty hands. "No food, guys."

They turned and quacked off, muttering about misers in Duckish, I assumed. We'd just reached the Portals when my cell phone beeped: Michael.

"Hey, bro," I said, "what's up?"

"Lots." He sounded triumphant.

Briefly, I feared that he'd managed the wolf transformation after all, then I remembered that the moon was waning. "I take it you've got something to tell me," I said.

"I wanted to thank you. How's that, huh? I read one, and now she's going out with me."

It took me a moment to supply the antecedents: girl who liked vampire novels, my advice that he read one of them, her decision to date my little brother.

"That's really cool," I said. "When?"

"Tonight. I did a lot of work in the yard with Uncle Jim, and he paid me for it."

"That's double cool. Is he over his snit?"

"Oh yeah. He always gets over it sooner or later."

"Good. I—damn." The phone cut out.

Michael redialed immediately. "That was weird," he said. "Where are you?"

"In the park by one of the lakes. The Portals of the Past. Know what that is?"

"The—oh, yeah, the weird doorway."

"It is weird, yeah, seeing it just standing in the shrubbery."

"No, I mean really weird. The energy—"

The phone cut out again. I'd just recharged it that morning. Michael got through one more time.

"Maybe that's what wrong with our phones," he said. "The energy there. Can't you see it?"

"No, I sure can't."

"That's really weird, then. I know I didn't just imagine it." He paused for a long moment. "Look, I've got to go get cleaned up and stuff. Call me tomorrow, will you?"

"For sure," I said. "Have fun tonight!"

"I will. Bye."

I clicked off and put the phone back into my jacket pocket. Nathan was leaning against a convenient tree and watching me with a slight smile. I couldn't call it a fond smile, but it came close enough to make me uneasy.

"My brother," I said, then remembered that I have a

couple of them to differentiate. "Michael, the youngest one."

"The one who wants to be a werewolf?"

"Yeah, but he's over that, thank God and the little fishes. I think he wanted it more to feel like part of the family than anything, although he did talk about impressing his girlfriend."

Nathan's expression changed to the reproachful stare.

"What's wrong?" I said.

"He wanted to be a werewolf so he'd feel like part of the family."

"Um, well, yeah, I guess that would strike you as kind of odd."

"Just slightly." He peeled himself off the tree. "I suppose I'm getting used to them."

The family, I assumed he meant, and let it lie. Michael's comment about weird energies concerned me more at the moment than Nathan's feelings. The space between the pillars appeared perfectly ordinary, as did the weathered marble lintel above them, which at the moment dripped stray drops.

"That's strange," I said.

"Strange how?" Nathan used his long-suffering voice.

"You can't feel it either, huh?"

"Feel what?"

"Something between the pillars. A weird energy, Michael called it."

"No, I can't. Can you?"

"No, and that's what's so strange."

Nathan muttered something under his breath, then climbed the marble steps and walked through the pillars before I could stop him. Nothing happened, other than his reaching the other side. He held one hand up near his hidden shoulder holster and peered along the path into the shrubbery, then shrugged and walked back through and down.

"I don't suppose you felt anything strange," I said, "when you walked through the doorway."

"Nothing, no."

"All right. I guess you've got to be attuned to it or some such thing, which makes me wonder about Michael. He may be developing a talent."

"There was a time," Nathan said wistfully, "when I would have heaped scorn on everything you're saying. No more. Ah, the good old days and all that."

Although I was tempted to try walking between the pillars myself, I decided on discretion, not valor.

"Rats," I said, "it's too wet to sit on the ground, and I want to do an LDRS."

"Then let's go back to the car."

Once I settled myself in the backseat, where I had more room to draw, I got my pad and my crayons out of the tote bag. A voice in my head told me, "He's come back."

I saw. I drew lines of gold along the moldings of what seemed to be a huge room, oblong splashes of dark red, furniture with slender bowed legs—pictures on the wall, beautiful pictures. The view moved and swirled. I felt someone else's mind reaching for mine. With a shake of my head I broke away and concentrated on tearing the sketch off the pad. When I handed it to Nathan in the front seat, he frowned as he studied it.

"A posh hotel lobby?" Nathan said.

"Maybe. Or a living room in some mansion? You mentioned that Johnson had plenty of money to show around. He must have either money of his own or a well-off backer of some kind."

"If they're dealing Persian white, of course they have money."

I collected my crayons and stuffed everything back into the canvas tote. Briefly, I sensed the wall again and one of the paintings—a Watteau, nothing an individual would own.

"Art museum." The Collective Data Stream rose up and bit me. "Like the Palace of the Legion of Honor. It used to have stuff like that in its galleries anyway. They changed things around before I got back, so I don't know how much of the old stuff is still there. But I've picked up Johnson in that area before. Land's End, it's called."

"Is that where the Holocaust Memorial is?"

"Yeah."

"Get in the front seat. We're leaving."

I changed places as fast as I could while he grabbed the phone. I heard him say, "Nathan from Interpol," and then, "I've had a tip on Johnson." He hung up the phone again.

"Safety harness," he said. "We're going to make some speed." He grinned at me. "Sanchez and some uniformed officers will meet us there."

I would prefer to forget the next couple of minutes of my life, but they'll always live on in my nightmares. Nathan hit the lights and the siren, and we went howling down JFK Drive, which was crowded with cars on this weekend afternoon. Some people might find it exciting, racing through traffic in a police car driven by a crazed Israeli secret agent. I found myself trying to remember childhood prayers. At least Nathan knew where we were going. I could never have given him coherent directions.

At the Twenty-fifth Avenue exit he wrenched the wheel around. We skidded into a right turn, burst through the red light on Fulton, and raced up the hill toward Geary as if all the devils in hell were after us. They may have been, come to think of it. Driving like that should be a sin, police or no police. A frenzied left onto California—against the light, of course—I slid down as

far as the safety belt would let me in the muddled idea
that when we crashed, the dashboard might protect my
vital organs.

I could hear other sirens rushing our way as we
wrenched around onto Lincoln Drive and started up the
hill through the greens of the civic golf course. I began
praying that the usual crowd of golfers had all stayed
away because of the rain. At the top of the hill we burst
out into the parking area across from the museum itself,
which sat a good distance back from the street behind
a lawn framed by colonnades on either side. Nathan
slammed the car to a stop. He'd slid out and started running toward the museum before I could thank the saints
for our safe arrival.

One black-and-white cop car sat by the sidewalk. Two
others joined it just as I staggered out of Nathan's car.
Uniformed police piled out and ran, guns drawn, across
the grass and past the enormous Rodin statue that sat in
the middle of the long lawn. I leaned against the car and
gasped for breath until it dawned on me that Johnson
could be right at hand. I returned to the car, shut both
doors, and slid down in my seat again, praying this time
for invisibility.

Another unmarked car came howling up the drive
and slid to a stop not far from ours. A dark-haired fellow
in a navy blue suit that screamed "police officer" despite
its civilian cut flung open a door and emerged. I caught a
glimpse of his face, pale brown skin, dark mustache, eyes
with the look of an eagle, before he too dashed for the
museum. Lieutenant Sanchez, I figured.

The placid dowager of a building, very Beaux Arts,
was having the excitement of its life. People began
streaming out, frightened tourists from the look of them,
huddling together under umbrellas or in their hooded
parkas. As they trotted past to the cars parked in the lot
behind me, I could hear them gabbling to each other.

Locals, dressed warmly though properly, followed with stately dignity. When you live in fear of an 8.0 on the Richter scale, you can accept a mere police raid with a certain calm.

I was acting like a coward, I realized, not a San Franciscan born and bred. I got out of the car again and let my mind range toward the museum in Search Mode. I received only a dim impression of Nathan standing on a marble floor just inside the entrance. I could pick up not the slightest trace of Johnson. Damn! I thought. He gave them the slip. Since he'd felt my attempt to locate him, I could guess that he'd decided to take no chances and simply left the scene.

Although I had to wait close to an hour, Nathan and Sanchez eventually confirmed my insight. I saw them striding across the lawn by *The Thinker* and hurried over to meet them on the sidewalk.

"He was there, all right," Nathan said. "The clerk at the entrance desk confirmed it from the photo. Unfortunately, he managed to get out and was gone by the time we arrived."

With Sanchez standing beside him, I said nothing about knowing it already. Sanchez was looking me over with one eyebrow quirked, as if wondering what I was doing there. I match Nathan's predilection for using cross-agency ID, which I carry for such occasions. I took it out of my inner coat pocket and handed it over. Sanchez looked at it, whistled under his breath, and handed it back.

"You didn't tell me," he said to Nathan, "that your girlfriend was—well, let's just say, government."

"She doesn't like it advertised," Nathan said. "Don't forget, that agency doesn't really exist."

"Right." Sanchez sent a grin my way. "I've forgotten already."

I figured I could always kick Nathan later and merely

smiled. "The question I have," I said, "is what was Johnson doing here? Art lovers don't generally go in for serial killing."

"Good question," Sanchez said. "Meeting someone—"

"That would be my supposition, too," Nathan broke in. "It's a public place. No one would think twice about two people walking through the galleries talking to each other."

"Yep," Sanchez said. "We—"

"You'd best follow that up," Nathan said.

"We intend to." Sanchez glanced at me. "The museum's shutting up early. My partner and I are going to be asking the staff some questions. I'll fill you in, Nathan, if we get any relevant answers."

"Thanks," Nathan said. "I'd appreciate it."

Sanchez continued to look my way. "I don't suppose," he said at last, "that you can tell me why your people are interested in this case."

"I can't, no. Sorry."

"You're as closemouthed as he is." Sanchez nodded at Nathan.

"We make a good pair," Nathan said.

I kept smiling out of sheer willpower and let Nathan say the good-byes. As soon as we'd gotten into the car, I kicked him in the nearer shin as hard as I could. He winced and reached down to rub the rising bruise.

"What's that for?" he said.

"Don't even try to tell me you don't know."

He laughed and started the car.

As we left the museum grounds, I was thinking about my real mission, investigating the cause of the Chaos breach that Annie and Jerry had reported to the Agency. Although I'd seen the hunt for Johnson as a distraction, I realized that the two lines of inquiry were beginning to converge. What if Johnson or DD or both and their mysterious cult lay behind the uprush of Chaos forces? It seemed plausible, perhaps even likely.

"Nathan," I said, "where are we going?"

"I was waiting for you to tell me."

He took his eyes off the road to look at me, then swore in Hebrew. With a squeal of tires he swerved around an improvident golf cart. My heart pounded briefly.

"Back to my apartment," I said. "Can you find it?"

"Yes, and would you calm down? You're making me nervous."

"I'm making you—" I gave it up. Words could not express.

I did, however, live to see my apartment again. Who could ask for more? Nathan escorted me up the stairs and inside, then left to stash the car. He'd found somewhere to garage it, he told me. Leaving a cop car out on the street at night did strike me as a bad idea. He returned with a huge vegetarian pizza, which smelled too good for me to resist, though I limited myself to one slice and a sliver. While we ate, we watched the TV news. Although the broadcast featured the excitement out at the Legion, it focused on Sanchez and never mentioned us, for which I thanked the powers that be.

"What now?" Nathan turned the set off.

"It's time to test our assumptions about this Peacock Angel cult. If it's really satanic, then it qualifies as a Chaos force, and I should be able to pick it up. If it's just a cover story for smack dealers, then I won't."

"I'd call selling heroin chaotic."

"To a lot of dealers it's just a business. They approach it the same way as our Mr. Morrison imports prayer shawls."

"The end result, however—"

"Well, yeah. It derails a lot of lives. Which reminds me, I wonder if Jerry's come down enough to talk to me."

Jerry answered his phone, but he sounded coked-out wired and made very little sense. When I mentioned Persian white, he did admit that you could find a lot of it on the street, but he declined to supply details over a wireless connection. I told him I'd check with him later and punched off.

"Well, it's out there," I told Nathan. "Once he has a mind again, Jerry may or may not have some idea of who's dealing it."

"I see. I told Sanchez to follow up on the narcotics angle, by the way, while we were waiting around in the museum. He's got the resources."

"Good. That's not in my usual line of work at all. The cult, however, might be."

"Do you have any idea of how to find out?"

"Of course. By working a little sympathetic magic."

"Killing a black cock and peering at the entrails?"

"Yuck! No, going into a full trance, on purpose this time. It's a good thing you're here, though. Sometimes I flop around, and I don't want to set the place on fire."

"On fire—Nola, what exactly do you have in mind?"

"You'll see. Hold on while I get the black candles."

"You're joking!"

I merely smiled and trotted into the bedroom. I kept the tools for the Chaos Diagnostic Emergency Procedure, as the Agency calls it, under my bed in a suitcase. I pulled it out and returned to the living room to find Nathan standing by the window and peering out at the street. I put the suitcase down on the floor and knelt to open it.

"Er," I said, "something wrong?"

"No, just making sure nothing is." He let the curtain fall and turned back into the room. "What's all that paraphernalia?"

"More tools of the trade." I took out the black velvet cloth and shook it out to display the white pentagram painted on it. "I lie on this with the votive lights set around it."

"They *are* black." He knelt and picked up one of the small candle glasses. "Where does one find black votive candles?" He titled the glass to get a good view of the wax filler.

"In the Mission district, in candle shops. You can get all sorts of herbs and stuff there."

Nathan set the glass down fast, as if he thought it might contain bugs.

"The point, you see," I continued, "is to perform a fake black magic ritual. 'Without intent' is the technical term for fake. We're back to the principle of like calling unto like. I'll pretend to align myself with Chaos and then see what comes up to sniff the bait. Let's hope it doesn't bite, is all."

"You've been thinking too much about wolves lately."

"That could be, yeah."

After I moved the coffee table out of the way, I spread out the cloth between couch and computer chair. I arranged the candles, then got a box of kitchen matches and lit the array. I turned off the lamps and lay down—carefully, avoiding the candle flames—on the pentagram with my head between two points. Theoretically I should have been naked, but for obvious reasons I kept my clothes on.

Nathan stayed kneeling by the couch. In the flickering candle-thrown shadows, I had trouble seeing his face, which at moments looked angry, at others utterly incredulous. I decided that he was probably feeling both ways at once. I actually felt some sympathy for him, a technological weapons expert, a special agent used to seeing the world in terms of life-and-death politics, faced at the moment with some of the oldest superstitions in the world.

And to make things worse, they worked.

"Now look," I said. "Sometimes I roll around, so if I get too close to the flames, grab the candle in question, will you?"

"Very well." He sounded deeply weary, as if perhaps he'd just heard that he was going to face a firing squad on the morrow. "Whatever you say."

I stretched out my arms to either side and closed my eyes. Knowing that someone waited close at hand to make sure I didn't catch my hair on fire made sinking into the trance easier than usual. I muttered the names of a few demons, just for local color, and let myself drift off.

At first I saw the usual hypnopompic images, flashes of the day, odd visual flickers of people I knew, a shot of Kathleen's old gray Persian cat. They vanished, and I floated, conscious in a black void. I thought of Johnson and the mysterious DD. As soon as I pictured the face I'd seen in the photographs, I heard chanting, a dissonant wailing in the dark. Color exploded, electric blues and greens—yes, peacock colors, but these danced on the backs of reptilian creatures, flying and wheeling like a flock of birds, all claws and beaks.

A voice cried out, *"Vide! Adest daemona!"*

Bad Latin, I thought, an attempt at "See, the demoness is present!" Then I realized that whoever had called out meant me. I had the dim perception of a room filled with candlelight. Shadowy figures, seven in all, sat in a circle. They peered out of the hoods of their black robes and stared up in my direction, but thanks to the hoods, to say nothing of the dim light and the whirling reptiles, I could see none of their faces clearly.

One of the figures strewed a handful of resin incense onto the charcoal in an overly large brass brazier. Gray smoke swirled up and dimmed the scene still further. Still, I could grasp an image of their circle and file it away in my memory. I picked up their mind-sets, too, mostly a sweaty excitement, in some cases tinged with sexual tension. I found Johnson's mind oddly at peace and oozing confidence, but he'd shielded the deeper layers beyond my ability to reach them.

One of the hooded figures began to cough as the smoke swirled her way. She pulled a tissue out of the sleeve of her robe and sneezed into it a couple of times. The other coven members turned to glare at her. I caught a glimpse of her face inside the hood—pale eyes and blonde eyebrows—before she sneezed into the tissue again. I heard a man's voice snarl and her answering whine, but my trance vision began to break up as the smoke grew thicker and another coven member began to cough. I suddenly wondered if I'd managed to set my apartment on fire. The thought broke the vision and the trance state both.

I woke up on the floor just as Nathan turned on the lamp. He'd snuffed out the candles. The last wisps of smoke from their wicks floated around me.

"I'm sorry." Nathan's voice shook. "I couldn't stand it anymore. You were writhing around and gabbling."

"Ah." I sat up. "Demonic possession."

He stared at me openmouthed.

"That's a joke," I said as fast as I could. "That kind of noise is just the response of the autonomic nervous system to the trance state. So is the body motion. It's like you're trying to wake yourself up. Honest."

Nathan sat down on the edge of the couch and took a deep breath. "I've never thought of myself as a religious Jew," he said at last. "A member of the tribe, certainly. It's my identity. But religion?" He shrugged the idea away. "But I'm surprised by just how abhorrent I found that—that—whatever it was. Display, I suppose I mean."

"Just a technique, honestly." I stood up, stepped off the cloth, then picked it up to shake it out. "I'm sorry if it offended you."

He leaned back against the cushions and looked up at me without a trace of emotion on his face. "Offended?" he said at last. "That's not the word."

"Repelled?" I said. "Disgusted?"

He shook his head no and looked away. I concentrated on folding up the cloth, then put it back in the suitcase. The votive glasses would have to wait until they cooled down.

"Frightened, to be honest about it," Nathan said abruptly. "I was seeing something unclean on the Sabbath—that's the thought that came to me—and I was frightened. I was shocked at my own reaction."

"I'm genuinely sorry. I wouldn't have done it if I'd known it would take you that way."

"How could you have known?" He paused to run both hands through his hair and push it back from his face. The soft curls twined around his fingers. "It surprised me, didn't it?"

"Okay." I stood between the computer chair and the couch and dithered. He'd taken a risk, shown me something of himself that baffled him, and I found the openness much sexier than mere muscle, though he had plenty of that, too. Watch it, O'Grady! I told myself. Think of the complications! Think of the danger! Think of what Aunt Eileen would say! I sat down on the computer chair.

"Uh," I said. "Do you want to know the results?"

"Yes, of course." He gave me an oddly grateful smile, maybe at the change of subject. "I gather there were some."

"Oh yeah. We have a full-blown Chaos cult on our hands. Johnson's part of it, all right, but I'm ninety-five percent certain that the others have no idea how dangerous he is."

"Those are good odds. What made you think that?"

"They struck me as rank amateurs. They didn't even

know how to use incense properly. One of them sneezed at the smoke and broke the mood for everyone."

Nathan grinned.

"You actually do believe me," I said, "that I saw all this, I mean."

"You told me that Johnson was in the museum, and yes, he'd been there. From now on, I believe you."

A welcome change, that.

"I say a cult," I continued, "because there were seven people at the scene. They'd suited up for some kind of ritual. I saw a flock of Chaos critters, too."

"Brilliant. What do these people want, anyway? The ones that join cults like this?"

I shrugged. I'd often wondered the same thing. "I can only guess," I said. "Excitement, you know, the old antinomian thrill. Money, sometimes. The Peacock Angel's supposed to supply the goods of this world. I've run across that attitude before, people who want to be filthy rich and don't mind the filthy part. They don't realize that they're setting themselves up to be tools of the Chaos forces."

"Do you realize you talk about Chaos in two different ways? Sometimes it's a force—like gravity, I suppose—and others, a personality."

"It partakes of both is why. Like light being both a wave and a particle—it all depends on how you look at it. In the Middle Ages, they personified the forces as demons with Satan in charge. Today we tend to think of electricity or some universal principle—the opposite of gravity, I'd say. Chaos makes things break up and fly apart. Gravity sticks them together, the universal principle of Order. Harmony goes beyond gravity to make everything work together. Too much gravity, and birds couldn't fly. Not enough, and the air the birds fly in disperses into outer space."

"In a mad sort of way that makes sense." Nathan glared at me again. "But only in a mad sort of way."

The only answer I could give to that was a shrug.

Thinking of demons made me remember the bad Latin—*Vide, daemona adest!*—instead of the idiomatic *ecce daemona*, and, of course, *vide* was singular, not plural. Perhaps the group I'd contacted had been playing around with some invocation ritual, one that was supposed to call up a female demon. Or had Johnson been asking his Peacock King for a glimpse of the woman who was trying to track him down? Maybe *vide* referred only to one person after all: him. I turned cold all over. If so, I'd just tipped him off. The flying reptiles had gotten a good look at me even if no one else had.

"What's wrong?" Nathan said. "You've gone quite pale."

"Have I? Just tired, I guess. This stuff isn't easy to pull off." I could have kicked myself. I'd slammed a mental door in his face after he'd taken the risk of showing me something of himself.

"No, I don't suppose it is. You should get some sleep."

"Yeah. I should." I got up and realized that I ached all over. "The procedure worked, all right. You know what they say, no pain, no gain."

Although I considered myself somewhere between a coward and a worm, I gathered up the candles, shoved them back into the suitcase, and started to take the whole mess into my bedroom. I'd just put my hand on the door when Nathan got up from the couch.

"Nola," he said, "do you like having these talents?"

"No." Here at least I could be honest. "I used to hate them, in fact, but they're not going to go away, and so I might as well use them. I try to do so in ways that benefit everyone involved, but that doesn't mean I have to like them."

"I see. That's how you stay sane, isn't it? Not glorying in them, I mean."

"Yeah. You hit it in one."

His smile caught me, not the boyish grin, not the tiger, but just a smile. I felt myself starting to melt from the inside out.

"See you in the morning."

I nipped into the bedroom before I liquefied right into his arms. Yet I have to admit I regretted my solid state for the first time in years.

CHAPTER 7

I WOKE TO A GRAY MORNING and the sound of Nathan's voice, speaking English in short bursts. I sat up in bed and realized from the pauses that he was talking on the phone. A break in the case, maybe? I rolled out of bed, grabbed a pair of jeans from the floor, and put them on. I'd just finished pulling on a V-necked teal sweater when Nathan pounded on the door.

"Nola, are you awake?" he said. "I've had a call from Sanchez."

"I am, yeah." I opened the door and found him shivering just beyond, dressed in nothing but his jeans and a nice patch of curly brown hair on his chest. "You're going to catch cold if you're not careful."

"I wouldn't be surprised. I thought California was going to be warm."

"Not in March. What did Sanchez have to say?"

"There's been another silver bullet murder."

I felt as sick as if I'd bitten into spoiled fruit.

"This one's all wrong, though," Nathan continued. "Here, let me get dressed."

"Please do. I'll be right out."

I put on socks and running shoes, used the bathroom, then trotted out to the living room and the smell of fresh coffee. Nathan, dressed in a gray sweater over jeans and a white shirt, emerged from the kitchen with two full mugs. I took one gratefully.

"Why is it all wrong?" I said.

"The victim was an obstetrics nurse at a hospital out on Geary Boulevard. She was coming home from the night shift, her usual shift."

"She couldn't possibly have kept that job if she'd been a werewolf."

"Exactly, but of course I couldn't tell Sanchez that." Nathan paused for a sip of coffee. "I begin to see the difficulties you must have in your line of work. It must be nearly impossible to link up with the local authorities."

"Fortunately we don't have to do it very often. Do you think this murder is a copycat?"

"It could be, though casting silver bullets doesn't strike me as an everyday skill. It could also be Johnson trying to throw your agency off the track."

"By making himself look like a common or garden variety serial killer? I can buy that. Does Sanchez want you to go down to the station?"

"Not yet. I think he's beginning to feel crowded out of his own territory."

"Gosh, I wonder why?"

"So do I." Nathan sounded honestly puzzled.

I made a mental note to stop wasting my time on irony.

"But at any rate," Nathan continued, "we'll hear later." He rubbed his stubbled chin with one hand. "I need to shower and shave."

"You know, I'm still curious. Why do you use witch hazel instead of aftershave? Doesn't it sting?"

"They all sting. I've never seen any reason to stink of scent." He made a face at me. "Flowers and all that."

"There are some musk and ginger ones."

"It's still scent."

I let the subject drop.

After he cleaned up, Nathan tried to push breakfast upon me. I held him off. It was bad enough watching him eat cold pizza. When he was finished, he paced back and forth in the apartment making various phone calls to mysterious non-English-speaking locations. He also received a lot of calls, which meant I got heartily sick of his phone's more or less musical ring. It sounded so strange, played in the thin high electronic notes, that it took me a while to recognize the first few bars of Bach's Toccata and Fugue in D Minor. Once I realized what it was meant to be, it sounded even worse. I did my best to ignore it and him and logged onto the TranceWeb open board.

Three of the four replies I'd gotten about the two William Johnsons stated what I already knew, that the situation I'd described was impossible. The fourth jerk thought I was posting a hoax "just to waste our time." I left him a vicious reply and turned to e-mail. The code expert had picked up the scans of Johnson's letters and promised he'd analyze them as soon as possible.

In our archives I found what seemed at first to be plenty of information about Satanic groups in the San Francisco Bay Area, but most of the reports dated back twenty years or more. The original Church of Satan had pretty much folded its tents and moved out of town once Anton LaVey, the founder, had passed to the other side. Various of our stringers and agents had picked up traces of other covens, although they tended to confuse modern pagan and Wicca groups with Satanists. By the time I finished weeding out all those false leads, I had precious little hard information left, and not one mention of the Peacock Angel. I sent a sharp note to Y about educating our staff on the difference between Satanism and Wicca. I ended the session by posting my report on the previous night's CDEP run.

After he finished his phone calls, Nathan flopped

onto the couch and grabbed the remote to channel surf. He found a soccer game, flipped on the sound, listened to the Spanish language commentary for a few seconds, then flipped the sound off again. He kept watching, though, utterly absorbed in the back and forth of the little white ball. I began indulging in domestic fantasies, pretending we were normal people, sitting around relaxing on a foggy Sunday morning.

Except of course, I had work to do. I decided to concentrate on the coven member I was mentally calling Sneezy, as in one of the seven dwarfs from the Disney movie. Not only had I gotten a definite impression of her mind, but her reaction to the overdose of resinous incense had given her a human touch, a point of empathy. Frankincense and myrrh—I'd always hated those sickly scents when I went to church with my mother, who favored a regressive Tridentine Mass community. The Magi probably brought the resins to the infant Jesus, or so I believed back then, to fumigate that crummy stable and drive out the bugs.

Be that as it may, I took my pad and crayons into the kitchen to work. Before I did the LDRS, I decided to run a Search Mode: Personnel on Sneezy. I pictured her pale blue eyes looking out from the black hood, then let my mind range out in a light trance. Immediately I registered a cluster of emotions, sexual longing, confusion, fear, all of them floating around the blurred image of a man. When I focused down, I realized that the image existed as a memory in her mind. I broke the contact because I had no way of finding out if the male figure in the memories came from recent experience or from her past.

Since Sneezy had no mental defenses, I felt some guilt about probing into her life, but not enough to stop me. The LDRS went splendidly. Even with my usual scrawled excuses for drawings I received clear glimpses of an expensive house: a large living room decorated in pink and white, heavy on the rose prints and gold accents, with bay windows that looked out onto a long lawn bordered with flowers. Sunday papers lay scattered on the floor beside her chair.

The data began to flow faster. I started a new drawing with the scribbled figure of a man in the doorway. He seemed to match the blurry memory image I'd seen early. He also knew I was spying. I felt shoved away, snarled at, turned upon, but this time I ended the session myself before he could send the wave of pain my way.

Johnson? I found it hard to believe that any woman could long for the man I'd seen in the photos and experienced in Search Mode. The mysterious DD maybe? I'd gotten a vague impression that he was young and had dark hair, just like Jerry had described, but those two details fit at least a million men in the Bay Area. If indeed it was DD, then Sneezy was fooling around with a dangerous toy. I sealed my mind from both of them.

I took the drawings out into the living room and found Nathan still engrossed in his game. A glance at the screen told me that they were playing in the seventy-eighth minute, almost finished, not counting whatever penalty minutes had accrued. I set the LDRS sketches down by my computer and went into the bedroom to call my little brother.

I tried to reach Michael's cell phone—nothing. His phone must have malfunctioned again, I supposed. I checked the time, just past eleven, and tried Aunt Eileen's landline. She answered on the second ring.

"You must have gone to the early service Mass," I said.

"We did for a change, yes," Aunt Eileen said. "It's actually sunny over here, and Jim said he wanted to get church over with so he could work in the yard."

"Ah, that's my uncle! Can I talk to Michael?"

"He's not here. He borrowed Jim's truck and drove over to the park. At least, he said he was going to the park to look at something. That new girlfriend of his lives over on Anza, I think it is, so I'll bet that's where he really went." She paused for a maternal chuckle. "It's close enough to the park so he wasn't technically lying."

"Hah! That's probably why he turned off his phone."

"Very likely, yes. Anyway, he promised to be back by noon. He and Jim were going to go buy some more annuals for the floral borders."

"Okay, I'll call later, or have him call me."

"I will. Have a good day off."

I ended the call and wondered why I felt dread like a knife between my shoulders. I remembered what Michael had told me about the "weird energy" in the doorway to nowhere. He'd gone to the park to "look at something." The dread doubled. I went back to the living room.

"Nathan?" I said.

He made a sound like "wha urmph?" —the normal response of a guy interrupted while watching a game on TV.

"I've got to get over to the park. Michael's in trouble."

Unlike a normal guy, Nathan straightened up and switched off the box. "All right," he said. "I'll go get the car."

The dread kept me company the entire way over to the lake and the portal. I wanted to be wrong, prayed that Michael was hanging out at his girlfriend's house, but I knew better deep inside. Sure enough, when we drove up to the lake, I saw Uncle Jim's old red Chevy pickup parked on the side of the road. As Nathan pulled up behind it, I was unbuckling the safety belt and unlocking the door. The second he turned off the engine I got out and ran for the monument.

"Michael!" I called out. "Mike, it's me, Nola!"

No answer, just the quacking of ducks and the rustle of the long streamers of willow leaves in the wind. I
pulled out my phone and hit his number on the speed
dial. Nothing, not one ring—I gave it up and put the
phone away. By then Nathan had caught up with me.

"He might have left the truck here and walked somewhere," Nathan said.

"A teen who's just gotten his driver's license? Walk?"

"Improbable, yes."

I trotted up to the portal and gave it a good looking
over. Although I felt nothing unusual, it struck me as
somehow different than the day before. When I climbed
up a step to examine the pillars, I saw a faint scratch
running from top to bottom along the inside of the left
column, as if a vandal had scraped a car key down it—an
eight-foot-tall vandal, maybe. The right pillar bore
a similar mark. When I pointed it out, Nathan leaned
close to peer at it.

"It almost looks burnt," he said. "Just the scratch
mark, though, nothing on the rest of the pillar, and there
are no smoke stains."

I stepped through and back again without experienc-
ing the slightest sensation of an energy field. Either the
thing Michael had noticed had disappeared, or I simply
wasn't attuned to it.

"Your pad and crayons are still in the car," Nathan
said. "Shall I get them?"

"Please," I said. "Or wait, I'll come with you. I can sit
in the backseat to draw."

As we started back along the path at a normal pace, I
noticed the shallow bay, its water calm even though the
wind rippled the deeper parts of the lake. I saw a change
I'd missed on my frantic run to the doorway.

"Look at the water right here," I said. "It's clear, no
green scum. Even if the gardeners spread herbicide, it
wouldn't work that fast."

"They wouldn't be working on the weekend anyway, would they?" Nathan said. "To skim it with nets, for instance."

"Not when they'd get double overtime, no."

In the trees beside the path a creature scuttled away with the snap of a twig. I caught a glimpse of a skinny blue tail, no fur, just scales. I turned fast and charged after it. One of the reptilian meerkats, all right—it tried to scamper up a tree, but I sketched a ward and flung the energy straight for its ugly little back. It squealed, then vaporized with a puff of yellow smoke.

Chaos breach. Something had happened here that should never have happened in our part of the multiverse. Nathan was waiting on the path with his hands on his hips and his head cocked to one side, watching me. I ignored him and walked to the edge of the pond. I took a deep breath and opened myself to the vibrations. Ducks came quacking softly toward me, then scattered, flew up in a frenzy of terrified honking and the flapping of wings as a blue crackle of sheet lightning skittered over the bay.

I shook my head and looked around. Ducks paddled calmly in the burned-clean shallows. The scene that I'd just perceived had occurred some while earlier in response to the Chaotic discharge, which had left a scar on the time stream. No ordinary electricity, whether natural or man-made, would have had that lingering effect. Nathan walked over to join me.

"Some sort of energy release happened here," I said. "I can't tell you any more than that, except my little brother probably got caught in the middle of it." I could hear my voice shake. "He looks a lot like me, and there's a goddamn serial killer out there who might not be able to tell the difference between us, not from a distance, not with Mike's long hair."

Nathan took a step toward me and held out his hand.

I was tempted to take the offered comfort, but I turned away instead.

"You can't mean an ordinary explosive," he said. "A pipe bomb or such. It would have destroyed the monument."

"Very true." I breathed deeply and got myself under control. "No, this wasn't anything ordinary like those—what do they call them? IEDs?"

"Yes, improvised explosive devices." He reached inside his jacket and took out his phone. "I'm going to call Sanchez."

"Are the police even going to take this seriously? If it weren't for the circumstances, he could maybe have just wandered away somewhere into the park. Usually they don't pay much attention to missing teens until it's too late."

"Usually I'm not involved with the case."

"That's true." I managed to smile. "Let me try an LDRS first, okay? If he did just walk down to the men's room it could be real embarrassing."

The LDRS turned up nothing. I tried for a solid fifteen minutes—nothing at all, just the same cold emptiness I'd felt on occasion when looking for Johnson. I sat half-crouched in the backseat of the car while Nathan paced back and forth on the grass outside and called Sanchez. I only heard snatches of what he said. I didn't really want to hear more.

An image rose in my mind, what the Agency calls a PI, a Possibility Image, something that might have happened, might happen, or maybe would never happen but could. Michael lay facedown on a pavement and bled from the mouth and nose. I tried to work with the image, but it refused to show me context. Only blood, a trickle of blood running across a dirty sidewalk—I killed the image before I screamed aloud. A cold rage filled my mind and heart. If these people, Johnson and DD, had harmed my family, I would make them pay. They would never regret anything in their lives the way they were going to regret harming Michael.

Chaos watch, O'Grady! I told myself. *You're slipping toward Chaos!*

The universe has evolved forces of Order to counter those of Chaos and keep the balance. No matter how imperfect we are and how badly we employ them, human beings have created institutions of Order that mimic those evolved energies. Justice instead of revenge, for example: I reminded myself that I'd sworn to serve the balance, and with a Chaos breach to solve, that meant serving Order in the hope of Harmony. In this situation I had to trust in the principle of justice instead of seeking revenge.

At the moment Nathan was talking with a representative of the force of justice, who probably already had his hands full of Chaotic problems on what should have been a quiet Sunday afternoon. I thought of the family of that nurse, her life of helping other women ended by Johnson's silver bullets, and of the driver of the carjacked truck, as well. I swore to myself that they too would have justice. I took one more deep breath and let my rage dissipate, which enabled me to leave the car as a civilized human being instead of a vengeance-crazed creature.

Nathan clicked off his phone with a satisfied little nod.

"How did Sanchez respond?" I said.

"He's taking it seriously because I pointed out that our psychopath might have mistaken Michael for you," Nathan said. "He wants me to go interview your aunt's family and then report back to him. A squad car's on its way here to take photos and dust down the truck for fingerprints, all that sort of thing."

"Are we waiting for them?"

"It would be best if we did. I don't want evidence disappearing before they get here."

"Okay. That'll give me time to call Aunt Eileen."

"I don't envy you the task." He spoke quietly but sincerely. "Do you want me to call—"

"No. But I think it's time to tell her who you really are."

"Go ahead, but I'd prefer it if you left the situation at my working for Interpol."

Aunt Eileen took the news that Michael had gone missing surprisingly calmly, though the calm sounded to me like the kind of shock that keeps a person from truly understanding a bad situation.

"I had such a strange dream about him last night," Aunt Eileen said. "He was standing on a street that ran through sand dunes. What was odd was that there were streetcar tracks down the middle of the street, but nothing else around. He was trying to call you, but his phone wouldn't work."

I hoped he still existed in a place where he could find another phone, but I didn't say that, of course. "That sounds prescient."

"I hate those. I never know what they mean until it's too late for me to do anything about it. I'd rather not know anything about the future. The present's usually quite messy enough."

"I've got to agree with that. Which reminds me in a weird sort of way: I don't know when the police will be finished with Uncle Jim's truck."

"Well, when they are, I'll drive him over to fetch it." Her voice weakened as the shock wore off and left her half in tears. "Nola, I hope and pray Michael's all right."

"So do I." I had to snivel back my own sudden stab of fear. "Look, I'll be coming over with a police officer. You've already met him, though I never gave you his real name."

"Morrison?"

"Yeah, but his real name is Ari Nathan. He's an Israeli officer from Interpol. I'll tell you more later."

"All right, dear. Israeli?" Her voice brightened. "At least he's not a Protestant or something worse." She hung up before I could say anything further.

I turned around to speak to Nathan and saw that he'd opened the trunk of the unmarked squad car. He retrieved a roll of bright yellow DO NOT CROSS — CRIME SCENE tape, then stood looking around him.

"What's wrong?" I said.

"This area's too big to close off with one roll of tape," Nathan said. "Well, I can at least block the path behind the thing."

Seeing the tape made me feel like vomiting. My brother, my little brother, the youngest of us all, was the subject of a police investigation into what might turn out to be murder. Nathan strode off around the lake. When he began stringing the tape from tree to tree, I couldn't bring myself to help him. I leaned against the hood of the squad car and watched from a distance.

Nathan had used up all the tape by the time the San Francisco police finally arrived, a patrol car first, then a van. A cop wearing only a pair of blue swim trunks got out of the van. He began pulling on a wet suit. The sickness in my stomach intensified.

"He's a police diver, isn't he?" I said. "He's going to look for Michael's body in the lake."

"They have to rule out every possibility," Nathan said. "It doesn't mean they expect to find him there."

I nodded, unable to speak. This time, when Nathan held out his hand, I took it, just for a brief clasp, but it helped. A police sergeant, the driver of the van, strolled over to ask who I was.

"The sister of the missing boy," Nathan spoke for me. "She's the one who reported that he hadn't come home on schedule. Now, when your man does the underwater search, tell him not to ignore any recently dead animals."

"Okay." The sergeant nodded, then trotted back to the van. I realized that to him, the situation was just business as usual.

By that time passing cars had begun to slow down to allow their passengers to rubberneck. I turned my back on them and propped myself against the hood of Nathan's car. The police diver pulled on a mask and waddled, awkward on his swim fins, into the lake. In the shallow water, he didn't need scuba gear. With a splash he dove. Like a seal he surfaced, sucked in some air, and dove a second time.

Eventually he waddled out, dripping pond weeds and water, carrying a very dead duck. The few feathers it had left were singed black. The blue lightning had caught one member of the flock. With his free hand he pulled off his mask.

"This was the only thing I found." He held up the duck. "God only knows what killed it, huh? I thought it was worth a look."

"Yes," Nathan said. "Save it for Forensics."

Again, I found it impossible to speak. I could comfort myself by thinking that if the blue lightning had caught Michael, he'd be lying dead on the marble steps. It must, therefore, have missed him. Not much comfort, I admit, but all I had.

Just as the diver began stripping off his wet suit, another unmarked car drove up. Sanchez got out and strode over to consult with Nathan. I returned to the front seat of our car to give my wobbly legs a rest. After a few minutes Nathan slid in behind the wheel and pulled his door shut.

"Sanchez has taken over," he said. "It's his territory, after all. He'll call when he has something to tell your family."

"Whatever," I said. "Do you remember how to get to Aunt Eileen's?"

"Not very well. I'll drive more slowly if you really want me to."

"Please. I've had enough shocks for one day."

We managed to arrive at Aunt Eileen's without causing any accidents. As we climbed the stairs to the front porch, Uncle Jim opened the front door to greet us. He's a tall, hulking man, not fat exactly, just large all over, and at that time his gray hair still sported a wide streak of its original red. He threw one arm around me and squeezed out a hug to half-drag me inside.

"Glad you're here," Uncle Jim said. "I think he's run away. First the trouble with your damn mother, and then I never should have yelled at the kid over that damn TV. Jeezus H, he's a good kid under all the crap, and I—"

I could smell whiskey. "Uncle Jim, it's not you. Don't blame yourself, okay? I talked to Michael yesterday, and he told me you'd worked things out."

"Oh." Uncle Jim pondered this in a sudden calm. "Then why the hell did he leave my truck in the park?"

"That's what the police are trying to figure out." Aunt Eileen hurried into the room. She was wearing a pink playsuit from the early Fifties, shorts and a short-sleeved blouse all in one ugly button-up piece. The color almost matched her fuzzy slippers. "Jim, darling, why don't you go rest in your study? I put the old TV in there so you could watch the ball game."

"Watch the ball game when my nephew's gone missing?" Jim pulled himself up to the full height of indignation.

"Well, there's nothing you can do." Aunt Eileen turned to Nathan. "Or do you need to talk with him?"

"Probably not, Mrs. Houlihan." Nathan had most likely smelled the whiskey cloud.

Grumbling to himself, Uncle Jim shuffled off down

the hall, heading for the study and the Giants game. Eileen led me and Nathan over to the family side of the room, where she hovered in front of the brown armchair. Heat blasted out of the wall unit. I shed my jacket in a hurry. Nathan hesitated, then left his on.

"Where's Brian?" I said.

"Upstairs in his room," Eileen said. "He's horribly frightened and can't admit it. He's blaming himself for not going with Michael this morning, but that would only mean they'd both be missing, I suppose. I just don't know what to think."

"I'd like to talk with your son," Nathan said. "If I may."

"Of course. I'm sure he knows more than I do. You know how boys are, keeping things to themselves. Should I call him?"

"I think it would be better," I broke in, "if Nathan talked with him without us girls right there." I was remembering the scent of marijuana in my brother's hair.

"Good idea," Nathan said, then turned to Aunt Eileen. "If you could show me up?"

"Yes, I'd better. It takes a while to learn your way around this house. It's all the add-ons, I suppose."

"Very well. Another thing—can you give me a good, clear photo of Michael? The police need one for the television news. We need a description of what he was wearing when you last saw him as well."

She started for the hallway with him right behind. I flopped into the blue armchair, which had been moved around to take up the empty place left by the stolen television. In a few minutes Aunt Eileen returned and sat down heavily in the brown chair, which faced mine.

"When they're done upstairs," she said, "would you go talk with Brian? He needs reassuring."

"Sure. I'll be glad to."

"Thank you, dear. He's been so upset, first Jim ranting and raving at him, and now this. I keep thinking of the poor driver of that truck the thieves used."

"Yeah, so do I. It's not a happy thought."

"Losing the TV seems so trivial now. We've heard nothing about the burglary, by the way. I don't suppose the police have the time to worry about little things like that."

"They should. It's a felony," I said. "That system must have cost a couple of thousand at least."

"Three thousand plus, as Jim reminds me several times a day. Not that it seems to matter much now. This is so awful! Nola, be honest. Do you think Michael's dead?"

"No. As far as I can tell, he's still alive. I just don't have any idea where he is."

"I see. Do you think the burglary had anything to do with this?"

"It could, yeah. But then again, it might just be a co-incidence." Chaos, I thought, reaching a grimy claw toward my family. "It's probably got something to do with Pat's journals, the ones Michael gave me. Pat had gotten himself into trouble, and he wrote about it."

Aunt Eileen leaned her head back against the chair and closed her eyes. "What kind of trouble?" she said. "I hope he didn't bite someone again. Or did he get some girl pregnant?"

"No, no, nothing like that. As far as I know, he never did anything wrong himself. Someone approached him about getting involved with drugs, serious drugs. He turned them down. He was planning on going to the police about it."

"If he wrote all that down, no wonder they wanted the journals." She sat up straight again and fished a tissue out of the pocket of her playsuit to wipe her eyes. "But why take the television?"

"To make it look like an ordinary robbery."

"Oh. Yes, I can see that." She sighed and shoved the tissue back into her pocket. "I still don't understand why Michael's disappeared."

"Neither do I, but I'm wondering if that Sam Spade guy from your dreams thought he was me."

Eileen grimaced and looked away for a long silent minute. "Well," she said at last, "I hope your Mr. Morri—I mean Nathan can find him. Nathan's his last name?"

"Yeah, and he's just a colleague. Honest."

Aunt Eileen raised a skeptical eyebrow. I was saved from the gimlet eye when Nathan came clattering down the stairs. He stood hesitating in the doorway. I got up and went over to talk with him.

"Brian didn't know much." Nathan spoke in a soft voice. "He did tell me that he and Michael were riding bikes in the park when they saw that doorway. This was a month or so ago. They liked to pedal up to the top of Twin Peaks and then coast down O'Shaughnessy all the way to Seventh and the park."

"I don't even want to think about how fast they'd be going when they hit level ground."

"Quite so. I told him to stop doing it, not, I suppose, that he will. At any rate, they left the house every chance they had, he told me, because your uncle was raging about the property taxes."

"As he does twice a year every year," I said. "Huh, this is interesting, if it's not a coincidence. Jerry and Annie noticed the first Chaos symptoms in late January."

"Yes, very interesting. Sanchez tells me that Persian white began showing up at around that time, too. They had an uptick in street arrests involving it."

"No coincidence, then. But about Michael—"

"Michael was convinced that some kind of energy curtain was hanging inside the pillars. Brian says he couldn't see anything. I gather that Brian then teased him about it. Told him he was seeing things because he smoked too much dope, that kind of silly stuff."

"Which is probably why Mike went back when I told him I couldn't see it, either," I said.

"Good guess. He took it like a dare, I'd say. I would have, at his age."

I could see him doing just that. "Look," I said, "I'm going to go talk with Brian, too. Let's hope Aunt Eileen doesn't drag out the family photos again."

"It's fine with me if she does. The police will need a picture of Michael, something they can ID him from if necessary."

Necessary, I thought. Like if they find his body some-where. I winced and headed for the front stairway, the one close to the living room. Like so much of the house, it never would have passed an inspection, which was doubtless why the Houlihans never bothered to get building permits. Some Houlihan who thought he knew carpentry had put these stairs in way back before World War Two, and they creaked, complained, and bounced under my feet as I climbed.

Brian kept his room far neater than many teens, cer-tainly neater than I'd kept my half of the room when I was his age. He had a black pressboard desk overflowing with papers and schoolbooks, and rock posters littered the white walls, but the only thing on the floor of the narrow room was the blue and gray striped rug. When I came in, Brian himself was lying on his bed looking miserable. He sat up and swung his legs over the side. I took the only chair.

"I'm sorry," he blurted. "I never should have ragged on him like that."

"It's okay, Bri! You couldn't know."

"That something was really there, you mean?"

I started to explain, but he kept talking in a burst of self-deprecation.

"I know I don't know shit about anything," he said. "I'm not like the rest of you. I know I don't have any talent—"

"Whoa!" I held up one hand for a silence. "That's not what I meant at all."

He did stop and for the first time looked at me, really looked, that is, instead of keeping his gaze somewhere near me. It had never occurred to me before that Brian might envy the family members with wild talents. Those of us who had them usually considered them a damn nuisance at best and a hindrance to our long-term survival at worst.

"I meant that you couldn't know that Michael would stop there at the pillars," I said. "I bet he didn't know it himself until he drove by."

"Oh." Brian considered this briefly. "Maybe not. I figured he was really going to see Lisa, and the pillar thing was just an excuse."

"Lisa? That's the new girlfriend?"

"Yeah. I told Inspector Nathan about her, too." He paused and looked to a poster of U2 as if he were contemplating an icon. "Was that cool?"

"Sure. The police have to know everything. You never know what might be important."

"Okay. But what happened to Mike? I don't understand."

"Nobody does at the moment. I'm working on the theory that someone saw him there and didn't like the idea for some reason." I could hear the doubt in my own voice.

"Did they kidnap him, you mean?"

"I don't know. I really don't. I just know that he's gone somewhere where he shouldn't be. Which reminds me. From now on, be careful, will you? You and Mike look a lot alike. Don't go out at night alone. You know what happens to those guys in the horror movies who ignore all the warnings."

"Yeah." He tried to smile, but his voice quavered, and he swallowed hard. "They didn't kill him, did they?"

"I doubt it. I'd know if he were dead. You can trust me on that."

"Okay." He paused for a long moment. "I just feel like shit for teasing him."

"Don't. It's not your fault. Whatever happened to Mike, you didn't do it."

"Okay." His voice dropped to a whisper.

I left before my presence brought him to tears. He didn't need embarrassment on top of everything else.

I'd just come back downstairs when a phone began ringing in the kitchen. Aunt Eileen got up and hurried to answer it, but the ringing stopped when she was only halfway down the hall. Uncle Jim had picked it up in his study.

"It's your sister," he called out. "It would be."

"I'll take it in the kitchen," Eileen called back.

I gathered that Mother still had her habit of phoning everyone in the family on Sunday in order, usually, to berate them about their various failings. I sat down in the chair Aunt Eileen had just vacated, opposite Nathan, who was just closing a photo album.

"I've found several clear images of your brother." Nathan tapped his shirt pocket. "Your aunt told me to take whatever the police needed."

Uncle Jim wandered back out into the living room to join us. He stood aimlessly between our two chairs, his hands shoved in the pockets of his gray trousers. "Can I offer you a drink—" he began.

"No, no thanks," Nathan said. "I'm on duty."

"Oh, right. Jeezus H, I never realized how much waiting there is, when something like this happens." He

turned and looked down the long white room to the
portrait of Father Keith. "It would happen on a Sunday!
Well, I'll give Keith a call when Eileen's off the damn
phone. See if he's done with business yet."

I smiled at another family joke, Father Keith's "business day." Uncle Jim shifted his weight from one foot
to the other and back again. Nathan looked at me, I
looked at him, we both looked away, because we could
do nothing, sure enough, but wait for Sanchez to call. I
had the grim feeling that when he did, he'd have nothing
to report anyway. With the slap of fuzzy slippers on a
polished floor, Aunt Eileen bustled into the living room
and broke the ugly mood with an uglier one.

"Nola, I'm sorry, but I had to tell your mother. She's
on her way here."

"Oh, Jeezus H God in heaven!" Jim muttered. "That's
all we need, that old dragon!"

"Now, Jim darling." Aunt Eileen laid a hand on his
arm. "Michael's her son, and she's really upset."

I got up fast and motioned to Nathan to join me.

"Please, try to remember." Eileen was looking ear-
nestly into Jim's eyes. "We haven't heard from Nola in
weeks. She hasn't come back into town. Can you remember that? She isn't here."

"Of course I can. Why the hell do you think I
couldn't?"

With a dignified toss of his head, Uncle Jim stalked
off, heading for his study, where, or so I devoutly hoped,
he'd fall asleep in front of the old TV. I turned to Nathan.

"We need to leave," I said. "Now."

"Very well." He looked and sounded utterly puzzled.
"Mrs. Houlihan, try to stay calm. The police are doing
their best."

"For all the good that's going to do," Aunt Eileen
said. "But thank you anyway."

I steered Nathan out of the house and down to the car as fast as I could. For a change I appreciated his predilection for high speeds on city streets. Once we'd made the turn onto O'Shaughnessy, I could relax despite the occasional screech of brakes and the way he laid on the horn. Mother would never have recognized me in this unfamiliar car if we zipped past her on the road.

"What is it about your mother?" Nathan said abruptly.

"Just what Uncle Jim said. There are times when she really is an old dragon, and you don't want to be around her when she is. Today she'll actually have a good reason for some full-scale histrionics."

For a welcome few minutes he concentrated on his driving.

"Is that like lycanthropy?" he said eventually.

"What? No! Just a metaphor for her awful temper."

"That's a relief."

"Oh, come on, did you think she actually turned into a dragon now and then?"

"I told you, I don't know what to believe anymore."

He sounded perfectly serious. I clung to the hope that he was teasing me.

"Well, I have to admit," I went on, "that she has her reasons. One of the things that drove her around the bend was having seven kids in just under sixteen years."

"That would unbalance anyone, I should think. And then, I take it, your father deserted the family?"

"I don't know if you can call it that. He may have. He may not have. One Friday night he drove down to the store to buy a six-pack of beer and never came back."

"Good God! Did the police—"

"They found the car and the six-pack not all that far from home, but they never found a trace of him." I paused—should I lie outright or just skip the truth? I decided on the latter. "They called it a carjacking and murder, eventually, but there wasn't any actual evidence for that. They wanted to make it possible for my mother to declare him legally dead and get on with her life."

"I'm so sorry." He looked sincerely saddened. "That must have been very difficult for all of you."

"Yeah. You could say that. You can imagine how upset she's going to be with Michael gone missing. A rerun."

Nathan made a sympathetic noise and ran a red light. I said nothing more about the family tragedy. I hoped, in fact, that he'd forget to ask again.

We returned to the apartment to wait for our phones to ring. When neither did, after an hour of watching Nathan watch soccer on TV, I realized that I had to do something about Michael's disappearance or I'd go crazy. I decided to try a particular procedure that the Agency called Mind Penetration. Although it hovers on the edge of being unethical, the Agency has never outright banned it, merely designated it as "use only in extreme circumstances." With six people confirmed dead, counting Pat, and now a seventh gone missing, these were just that.

"Those pictures of Johnson," I said. "Do you still have them, or are they at the police station?"

"They made copies." He switched off the TV. "Why?"

"I need them. I'm going to try to get a fix on Johnson's actual mind. I might be able to sense if he knows anything about Michael."

Nathan brought out the envelope. I retreated to the kitchen table to work. I put the passport picture on top of the pad of paper I used for LDRS to give it a neutral background, then laid my hands on either side of the picture. I leaned forward, stared into Johnson's eyes, and let my mind range out.

Immediately I felt his presence, carried to me on a wave of fear tinged with physical pain. He'd been cut on

his arm, somehow, and the cut terrified him far beyond
its severity. He was fussing over it, taking a bandage
off, putting it back on, over and over, while in the background of his consciousness he was listening to someone
taunt him for worrying. He began to get angry, then en-
raged, at the constant taunting. With him occupied with
his anger, I could probe a little deeper. I picked up fleet-
ing images: dry grass, trees, a sudden lupine face loom-
ing over him. Mary Rose in wolf-form.

Johnson's mind swirled and tipped—I can't think of
any other way to describe it—as if he were a boat caught
in a vortex in a sea of terror. Rage and terror—no coherent thoughts could penetrate that storm. I shut down
and withdrew.

I ran my fingers along the table edge to remind myself
I had a body, then looked around at the familiar kitchen
to make sure I knew where I was. I found the sight of
Nathan standing in the kitchen doorway oddly reassuring. No matter what I thought of his complete lack of
good manners, he was solid, real, and a good shot. With
Johnson in his current mood, the "good shot" loomed
large in my favorable appraisal.

"Mary Rose bit Johnson, all right," I said. "And boy is
he pissed about it."

Nathan laughed, one short sound. "What do they call
that?" he said. "Karma?"

"That'll do, for sure. The trouble is, I couldn't pick up
anything about Michael—or anyone else, for that matter, except Mary Rose." I shuddered from a sudden cold
insight. "He's glad he killed her. He enjoyed it entirely
too much."

"We always knew that he was a psychopath. Try not
to dwell on him. Can you put him out of your thoughts?"

"I'll try."

I managed to perform a Conscious Evasion Procedure
by giving Nathan back Johnson's photo and then ripping

up the piece of paper that it had touched. Although I'd planned on scanning for Sneezy and other members of the coven, the effort from the MP followed by the CEP left me exhausted.

Nathan insisted that I rest on the couch while he went out to hunt up some dinner. I found an animé serial on TV and watched that to occupy my thoughts until he returned. He brought a massive amount of take-out food from the deli down the street, enough little white cardboard boxes to half-cover the coffee table. Nathan sat at one end of the couch; I sat decorously at the other. I ate some marinated artichoke hearts, the only vegetable among his purchases, and sampled a few bites of the other stuff despite Nathan hectoring me to eat more.

"Are you really that afraid of me slipping into trance again?" I said.

"No, I'm afraid you'll starve to death. Look at your sodding collarbones! They stick out."

"They're supposed to." I shielded them with one hand. "It's the in look."

He rolled his eyes heavenward and opened another white box. "Baklava." He grinned as he held it out. "Want some?"

You bastard! I thought. Of course I did. He shoved the box into my hand.

"Have it all," he said. "I got it for you. I don't care much for sweets."

Box or plate, fingers or fork—I find it impossible to eat anything that's both sticky and flakey without making a mess. By the time I finished I ended up with drips of honey and bits of phyllo on my sweater as well as my hands. I went through a couple of napkins getting it off.

"There's some on your face, too." He slid over next to me. "Shall I wipe it off?"

He leaned close, his lips half-parted, his eyes so soft and warm that I realized he was planning on licking the honey away. I should have pushed him away, I should have moved, but my own raw desire caught and held me.

The phone in his shirt pocket rang with a burst of Bach. I yelped, he swore, I got up from the couch.

"I'll just wash my face," I said and ran for the bathroom.

When I came back, Nathan was still talking on the phone. I collected the boxes of leftovers and stowed them in the fridge, a nice mundane task that kept me in my reality. I returned to the living room just as he was putting the phone into his shirt pocket.

"That was Sanchez," he said. "They've put out an all-points missing persons for Michael. Forensics tells him that yes, that dead duck was electrocuted. They're freezing the autopsied remains on the off chance they'll need it for evidence later."

That bit of news destroyed the last remnant of my romantic mood.

"I'm glad they're doing something." I took my own phone out of my pocket. "I'll just call Aunt Eileen and tell her."

"Yes." With a long sigh Nathan picked up the TV remote. "You might as well."

CHAPTER 8

MARY ROSE ROMERO'S FUNERAL SERVICE was scheduled for one o'clock Monday afternoon. I was surprised to hear that it would take place in a mortuary chapel rather than an actual church. I wondered if her parents blamed themselves for her lycanthropy, a pity if so, and were keeping her funeral simple out of shame. I could imagine my mother doing that. Since Nathan and I would probably have to go to the grave site afterward, I was relieved when the day turned out sunny if cold.

For this kind of event I had a black wool challis dress with an A-line skirt and a short-sleeved jewel-neck bodice—plain, appropriate, and let's face it, ugly. I wore it with black high heels and a black jacket that was actually part of a dinner suit. Since he'd stay outside for the service with Lieutenant Sanchez, Nathan dressed like a cop—the navy blue pinstripe suit with a white shirt and, of course, the gun in the shoulder holster under the jacket, an appropriate enough accessory.

The squat stucco mortuary sat behind a parking lot well back from Junipero Serra Boulevard in Daly City. At the moment, cars filled about half the lot, including the long gray hearse that would take the casket to the cemetery, a few miles farther south in the little town that functions as San Francisco's land of the dead. *Gaudeamus igitur,* I thought, because *nos habebit Colma.* We timed our arrival to the edge of being late, so I could slip into the chapel without an invitation. I made a point of signing the guest book, though, as "Nola O'Grady (Pat's sister)."

In the chapel, recorded organ music fell softly from speakers high on the blue-gray walls. A white casket, barely visible under garlands and sprays of red and yellow flowers, stood on a bier in front of the altar, where a priest in full vestments knelt in prayer while an altar boy stood guard. Behind him on the wall hung an enormous crucifix. *In spe resurrectionis,* I thought. Or is it *expectatione,* not just hope, of the resurrection? I could no longer remember which.

I took a seat in an empty pew at the very back, right by the door, and looked over the sparse gathering. Since morticians usually reserve the front rows for the family, I assumed that Romero's people sat there. A middle-aged woman wearing a black skirt suit, whom I pegged as the mother, leaned against a gray-haired man, most likely the father. At times they'd turn their heads and look around them with dazed eyes. The mother's slack mouth and slumped posture indicated she'd been given a tranquilizer of some kind.

Behind them sat a gaggle of young women, Mary Rose's friends from college, I figured, judging from their ages and their cobbled-together attempts at appropriate clothes—tight black sweaters, mostly, and short black skirts better suited to clubbing. They huddled together, frightened, whispering among themselves, still disbelieving that murder had touched them through a friend's death. Behind them sat three young men, who'd also scrounged together black clothing including, in one case, a black jacket with the Giants' logo on the back. They sat close together and neither moved nor spoke. I

wondered at first if one of them was Frater LG. Pat had
never described his fellow pack members except in the
most general of terms, but they seemed unlikely candi-
dates for the alpha male.

Just as the priest rose from his kneel, a young man
dressed in a black suit entered the chapel. I realized
that he had to be Lawrence Grampian, young, blond,
tall, and utterly stricken, his eyes puffy, his face streaked
red and raw from weeping. He stopped in the chapel
door and looked around with a toss of his head, then
slunk in and sat down at the other end of the pew I was
occupying. He glanced my way and stiffened, staring at
me for a long minute, then looked away with a swing of
his head as if in fear. Pat had resembled me, just as we
O'Gradys all resembled each other, what was left of my
family. When four young men in suits entered the chapel, Grampian got up and joined them in another pew.

Since I had work to do, I paid as little attention to the
actual service as possible, which skipped serving Mass,
no doubt at the parents' request. They both stared at
their daughter's casket through the entire thing without
a tear or a sound, as if they'd already poured out every
last bitter drop of their grief. While the priest spoke, I
was testing the atmosphere in the chapel, opening myself to whatever forces might have been present.

Overwhelming grief flooded my mind, dull grief on
the part of the friends, the drugged miasma surrounding the parents, and the wild animal rage of Lawrence
Grampian. I wrenched my mind away and began to
scrutinize the chapel itself. As I considered the floral
cascade over the coffin, I saw a tiny face peering out
from among red roses, all long snout and teeth. It disappeared so quickly that I thought the grief might have
objectified itself into an image. I refrained from throwing a ward just because my talents do sometimes get in
their own way.

The bell began to toll, a prerecorded death knell sounding over speakers. Mortuary attendants slithered forward with a peculiar silent, please-ignore-us walk and began to remove the flowers from the casket. Underneath lay a white pall marked with a purple cross. Grampian, his four friends, and Romero's father stood up and strode forward. They hoisted the coffin and carried it up the aisle behind the priest and the altar boy, who led the procession with a silver crucifer. While the bell tolled on, the mourners followed, and I fell into line at the very end.

Outside the sunlight made me blink and squint. I stood off to one side as the pallbearers slid the coffin into the waiting hearse. It stuck halfway, an awkward moment that made Romero's mother collapse in tears. The father left the ghastly juggling act to the young men and the mortician and rushed to help her up from the sidewalk. I heard him say, "We don't have to go," and her murmured answer, "I want to."

I stepped back into the doorway and sketched a Chaos ward, then flung it at the coffin. I heard a high-pitched squeal, inaudible to anyone else, apparently, since no one reacted to it. The coffin slid safely forward into the hearse. You filthy bastard, I thought. Had to add one last measure of misery!

The mortician hurried over to the parents and guided them into the limo waiting behind the hearse. As the funeral party dispersed into various cars, Nathan jogged over to join me.

"We're going to the cemetery," he said. "Sanchez and a squad car are driving at the head of the procession. We bring up the rear along with another squad car."

"Good. Johnson's nearby. I haven't seen him, but I know for sure he's prowling around."

"Very well, then. Stay on your guard. One good thing, he won't be able to hide a long gun in broad daylight."

On this happy thought we joined the cortege.

The grave site lay on the side of a grassy hill, a smooth slope of perfect lawn running down to a small artificial stream shaded by an ancient willow tree. The grave itself, a slash of dark brown earth, opened like a mouth waiting to devour Mary Rose's mortal remains. I refused to climb that slope in heels and found a place to stand on the flat near the artificial stream, out of the way of the police presence.

At the crest of the slope, well above and behind the funeral party, Nathan and Sanchez took up a position. Every now and then they turned to look behind them, just a casual gesture, or so an observer might think. I doubted if it would fool Johnson. Downhill, a couple of uniformed police officers were strolling back and forth on guard. Police at the funeral—a dismal addition to the more usual miseries of death.

The pallbearers had just turned the coffin over to the sexton when Grampian broke. He threw back his head and howled, a long drawn-out wolf cry, then slumped over the coffin and wept. Everyone stared openmouthed, but no one moved toward him, not even the useless priest. Grampian lifted his head and howled again and again, always the wolf cry, a raw animal grief, begging his slain mate to return as if he'd managed to forget for that moment that she could never return. Mary Rose's mother began to sob. I kicked off the heels, ran up the hill, and grabbed Grampian's elbow.

"Stop it!" I said. "Remember where you are!"

He fell silent and looked up at me with half-blind eyes.

"Come on," I said. "You don't have to watch them bury her."

He staggered to his feet and let me lead him away. We walked some ten yards downhill and stood by the artificial stream with our backs to the service. I retrieved my shoes and put them on.

"You've got to be Nola," he said. "Pat's sister."

"That's me, yeah." I fished in my little black bag and brought out a couple of tissues. "Here. Wipe your face."

He followed orders with shaking hands, then shoved the soggy tissues into the pocket of his suit jacket. "Thanks," he said. "That was pretty damn stupid of me."

"I'm not blaming you. If anyone asks you what the noise was, tell them it's keening. They won't know the difference."

His mouth twitched in a minuscule smile. His eyes stayed hollow and distant.

"I need to talk with you," I went on, "but obviously now isn't the time. Can you give me your phone number?"

He nodded and pulled his wallet out of his trouser pocket. He took out a business card and handed it to me. I glanced at it and saw that he created professional Web sites on a freelance basis, then tucked it safely away in my bag.

"Okay, good," I said. "I'll call you tomorrow. In the meantime, for God's sake, be careful! Don't go out at night alone. Don't go walking in the wilderness. Come to think of it, don't go out at all. You're being hunted."

"I figured that." His eyes flared wide with rage. "But he's not the only one who knows how to shoot a rifle."

"Don't do anything stupid! What are you planning, Grampian? A little revenge?"

He glared at me. His eyes were a pale blue, glittering like ice.

"You'll be playing right into Satan's hand if you do," I said. "Is that what the Hounds are all about? Giving in to the urge to rip and tear?"

He closed his eyes and half turned away, but not

before I saw tears run. He wiped them off onto his jacket sleeve.

"No," he whispered. "It's not."

"Good. Remember that and play it safe." I turned and looked past him to the grave site. The priest was scattering a handful of dirt onto the coffin, which is, generally speaking, the worst moment of the graveside service for the mourners. "Did Pat ever introduce you to Father Keith?"

"Yeah." He opened his eyes again.

"If you need to talk to a priest, call him. He understands everything. Get it? Everything. He'll even shelter you at the full moon if you need him to."

"Okay. Thanks. Thanks a lot, I—" He let his voice trail away. "I'd better go back. Mrs. Romero's in worse shape than I am."

"Yeah, you should. She needs all the support she can get."

I watched him walk uphill, slump shouldered, hands shoved deep in his pockets, to rejoin the gathering at the grave site. He caught Mrs. Romero's hand, and they knelt together to pray as the priest continued reading the service.

I decided to risk using Search Mode: Individual and let my mind range out to Johnson. I received a quick flash, a contact, a feeling of nearness, then broke the link fast before he could focus in on me. I heard a raspy little chortle up in the branches of the willow. A green lizard-thing, more possum than meerkat, crouched under the curtain of leaves. Gray drool dripped from the corners of its stubby, toothy mouth. I flung a ward straight at its head and caught it just as it tried to dematerialize. Half a shriveled body fell to the ground and crystallized before it broke up and disappeared. I have no idea where the other half landed.

Up on the hilltop Nathan suddenly shouted, an oddly

soft sound drifting down on the breeze. I looked up
and saw him and Sanchez take off running, disappearing from the crest down the other side. One of the uniformed cops trotted up to me with a small black box in
his hand.

"The inspectors have seen him," he said. "I'm supposed to stay with you."

"Okay," I said. "Thanks."

He nodded and muttered a few words into the black
box.

The mourners began to leave, trickling away a few
at a time, while the gravediggers finished filling in the
grave. It was an awful moment, a last farewell marred by
police yelling back and forth, by the businesslike click of
shovels and the dust rising from the falling earth. It took
both Grampian and Mr. Romero to get Mrs. Romero to
leave her daughter. They were carrying more than leading her as they made their slow way past. You will have
justice, I thought in their direction. Fat lot of good it will
do to ease your grief, but you'll have it.

Now and then my police protection spoke into his
black box or listened to its cryptic announcements.
Finally he turned to me. "They've lost him," he said.
"But we've put out an all points on the car."

"Good," I said. "Thanks. Let's hope."

"Yeah. This guy is a real nutcase."

"It sure looks that way, yeah."

Most devotees of Chaos do go insane eventually, but
most in ways harmless to others. They sink into a pro-
found depression or a state that mimics the symptoms
of obsessive-compulsive disorder. Some, however, like
Johnson, take it out on the rest of the world.

In about fifteen minutes Nathan came jogging down
the hill. He released the officer guarding me, then waited
for him to get well away before he spoke.

"Just as we thought," he said. "Johnson was wandering around, pretending to look at gravestones. He ran the minute he saw me and Sanchez. There was a black Jaguar waiting for him on the road back there." He jerked his thumb in the general direction of over the hill. "With a driver."

"DD?"

"Possibly. Very possibly. The front door was open, and the car started moving the moment Johnson got in, before he could even shut the door. Still, we have the license number. Sanchez had a check run on the car. It was reported stolen last night."

"From where? Did he say?"

"Yes, San Francisco. A neighborhood he called Pacific Heights. The owner had been visiting friends there and came out to find his car gone."

"It's a neighborhood where you'd find an expensive car like a Jag, all right. A thief who wanted one would know where to look." I glanced uphill to the grave, where the priest had finished his prayers. "Can we get out of here?"

"Yes, certainly. Sanchez will be just as glad to be rid of me." He sighed. "No doubt you feel the same way."

"No," I said, because he'd caught me off guard. "Not necessarily."

He grinned at me. I turned away and headed for the car. He followed and caught up with me.

"While we were standing around," Nathan continued, "Sanchez told me that the narcotics division is starting a crackdown. They're going to pull in everyone and anyone they suspect of dealing heroin and ask tough questions. In among the small fry in this operation is someone who's going to tell them everything he knows. There always is. It's probably an underling who's been sent to prison twice before and doesn't want to fall under that—what is it? The three strikes and you're in for life program?"

"Yeah, that's basically it. Good. Let's hope they turn up a solid lead before Johnson kills someone else."

The sun had finally decided to shine and burn back the fog. Under a blue sky we returned to my apartment, where I changed out of the funeral garb as fast as I could. Jeans and a bright print blouse, this time, white with little red roses on it—I wanted something cheerful. I opened the drapes in the front room, too, to let in the light.

"Johnson's not going to come calling in broad daylight," I said.

Nathan went into the kitchen and dragged out the leftover deli food. To make him shut up about my not eating, I finished off some potato salad and a cold piroshki while I gave him my impressions of the funeral.

"Creatures?" he said. "You saw creatures?"

"Yeah. Every now and then I see a creature that's just my image objectification, but these, damn it all, were the real deal."

Nathan absorbed this along with some pastrami.

"What I'm wondering," he said after he'd swallowed the mouthful, "is how Al Qaeda fits into this."

"It doesn't. By now that should be clear. Unless your agency held back a lot of information, here in my territory at least it's a domestic Chaos case, spiced up with a little drug-running. International terrorists need not apply."

"I can't believe my superiors would hold back data I need to get the job done."

"Neither can I. No one has ever accused your government of being careless when it comes to outside enemies."

"Or internal ones, either."

"True enough. The driver of that getaway car, did he look anything like the guy Jerry described?"

"It was hard to see him, but he could have been young

and he could have had dark hair." Nathan frowned down at the floor. "Not a very precise description, I'll admit."

"I want to try an LDRS on this DD guy, but I don't have a lot to work on. Tomorrow I'm going to try calling Grampian. If he's put the pieces of his mind back together—"

I stopped talking and let my mind focus on a sudden threat. Johnson—I knew the greasy touch of his mind, now—a tendril of feeling, a Search Mode force field hunting for me—I hoisted a barrage of imagery, walls, stones, a knight's flaming sword. The tendril caught fire and disappeared. It took me a few seconds to focus back on the real world. Nathan was holding a handful of olives halfway to his mouth and staring at me.

"Johnson's figured out who I am," I said. "He must have gotten a good look at me during the funeral."

"He was down on the other side of that hill. Or do you mean during the service in the chapel?"

"Not that kind of look. He didn't have to use his physical eyes. One of his creatures probably relayed an image before I destroyed it."

Nathan muttered a few Hebrew words under his breath and funneled the olives back into their container.

"What are we going to do about this?" he said. "I could get Sanchez to give you twenty-four-hour police protection."

"And advertise where I am?"

"Any other ideas?"

"Catch him before he catches me? That's the ideal solution, but so far we're not doing a real good job of it."

Nathan sighed and picked up the olives again. He ate them meditatively, one at a time, spitting each pit back into the cardboard box. I decided I didn't want to watch and began to clear away the remains of the meal.

"What about this afternoon?" Nathan said.

"I'd been thinking of going back to Aunt Eileen's, but

now I don't know. If there's going to be trouble, I want it happening away from the family."

"That would be best, yes. I don't suppose you can do that LSD thing for Johnson safely now that he recognizes you."

"LDRS, not LSD. This has nothing to do with drugs."

"I was trying to make a joke. You know, lighten the mood."

"That's probably impossible, but thanks anyway."

I dumped all the containers into the garbage pail I kept in the kitchen. The plastic liner bag had gotten full to overflowing, thanks to Nathan's habit of actually eating at mealtimes. I pulled it out, knotted it, and started for the back door. Nathan trotted over and stopped me.

"Where are you going with that?" he said.

"The garbage chute. It's just outside."

"I'll take it." He held out his hand. "There's an alley out there leading up to the back steps. Anyone could get through that flimsy gate. He could wait there for you to come out."

I handed him the bag. My SAWM was going off like a fire alarm. Although I wondered—well, all right, I desperately wanted to know if Johnson lurked nearby, I decided against doing an LDRS. He'd already shown he could swat me away, at least when he wasn't drowning in his fear of developing lycanthropy. I doubted if I could be lucky enough to find him in the middle of a fit for a second time. Threatening him again meant giving him another link right back to me. DD, however, presented a different target. Nathan came back in and began washing his hands at the sink.

"I'm going to try scanning for the driver of that car," I said. "If nothing else, I'll find out how dangerous he is."

"Do you have enough information to work from?"

"Probably not. I was thinking we could drive down to the windmill in the park where Jerry detected a Chaos force. His scent might be stronger there—if it's the same guy, of course."

"Worth a try, certainly. Let me get out of this suit."

While he changed into jeans, I called Aunt Eileen. She'd had no word from the police about Michael.

"Your mother," Aunt Eileen told me, "is hysterical, but for a change no one can blame her."

"I can't, either," I said. "Any dreams?"

"I saw Michael standing on Mission Street near Thirtieth, where the big Safeway is, except it wasn't a Safeway at all. It was some kind of farmer's market, and some of the people selling vegetables looked like goblins. Well, like some kind of deformed creature, anyway."

"That's really strange."

"So strange that I doubt if it was really Michael I was seeing. Just my anxieties, I'd say, except it was so vivid."

Ambiguity, again. "Well, if you have any more dreams," I said, "call me and let me know."

"This is all so awful." Eileen paused for a deep breath to calm herself down. "I had to call Michael's school today and tell them why he was absent. There's only a week or two left before spring vacation, thank heavens, so he won't have a ton of make-up work if we get him back soon enough."

If we get him back at all, I thought. Aloud I murmured something reassuring and ended the call. That Michael's schoolwork might present a problem had never occurred to me. On such small details of everyday life, though, does the balance between Order and Chaos depend. My aunt and women like her serve Harmony in their own way.

Nathan, dressed in jeans and a shirt, came out of the bathroom. He was carrying his suit, which he then proceeded to drape haphazardly over my computer chair.

"Were you talking with your aunt?" he said. "I suppose she's quite upset still."

"I'm afraid so, yeah. Uncle Jim will help her calm down in a while, though."

"Really? I should have thought he'd make things worse."

"No. The Houlihans have their good qualities."

"Don't tell me they have talents like—"

"Some of them do, yeah. The older generation had more than Uncle Jim does or his son. Clarice is pretty sharp, though. I don't know about Brian yet. He thinks he doesn't have any talents, but neither did I until I was sixteen. Then they hit in force."

"Interesting." Nathan paused as if waiting for me to say more.

I merely smiled. That period of my life still had the power to depress me if I thought about it in any detail.

"Ready to go?" Nathan said eventually. "Do you have anything you can do to protect yourself from these, um, mental attacks, I suppose you could call them?"

"They're just that, and I do, yeah."

"Very well, but I need to make a few phone calls before we go to look at this windmill."

I started to agree, then caught myself. "No," I said. "Sorry. We need to go now, and we need to get there fast."

Which, though true, was a stupid thing to say to Nathan. During the resulting wild ride down to the west end of the park I managed to raise a Shield Persona by sheer force of will. Even when I'm not in a car driven by a maniac, I hate doing it, because it cuts off the flow of information from all of my extra sensing mechanisms, learned and natural. On the other hand, it would also cut Johnson off from me. If I needed to, I could drop it in a couple of seconds.

Golden Gate Park contains a lot of odd things tucked away in glades and dells and little gardens. The Dutch windmill has to be one of the most spectacular of these oddments, a fully restored wooden windmill like a souvenir of the eighteenth century, set to one side of a sunken garden. A thick hedge surrounds a roughly circular area of lawn, and in the middle of the green lie geometrical flower beds which define a segmented circle.

We came screaming down Kennedy Drive and pulled to a stop near the windmill. By then my feeling of urgency had swelled to a near-physical ache. I staggered out of the car and stood hyperventilating for a moment while I waited for Nathan, then led the way down the shallow stone steps through the trees. In the flower beds tulips bloomed, a gorgeous display in various reds, purples, and golds, nodding in the breeze. The sight of the garden allowed me to relax. We'd gotten there in time—whatever that meant.

I sat down on the damp grass on the far side of the garden and took out my pad of paper and crayons. If anyone saw me, they'd assume I was drawing the windmill, which certainly would have inspired a real artist. Covered in dark wood shingles, it stood at least four stories high, crowned by the huge wooden vanes, tip-tilted into the wind. In the cool sea breeze the blades creaked like a ship under full sail. Nathan stood staring at it while I got settled.

Before I started the LDRS procedure, I dropped the Shield Persona and did a Search Mode: Chaos scan of the area as far as I could reach. The windmill itself gave me an uneasy feeling, nothing urgent, more like a drifting scent of Chaos on the wind. I picked up a stronger sensation nearby, but I couldn't refine it into an image or a presence. I hoped the LDRS would give me more information.

Before I could start, Nathan stepped forward and considered the windmill with narrowed eyes. When I followed his gaze, I noticed a vertical row of little unglazed windows, one for each story, I assumed. On the ground floor I could see a closed door.

"Could someone get inside there?" Nathan said.

"Only with one of the Parks Department people along. They keep it locked."

"Good, but locks can be picked."

"You should know."

He smiled his tiger's smile and began prowling around behind me, his suede jacket unzipped, his hands always close to the shoulder holster.

I assembled in my mind the few things I knew about Johnson's confederate. I had only the information from Jerry, my trance contact with the *adest daemona* ritual, Nathan's quick glimpse of Johnson's getaway driver at the funeral, and my deduction about his lycanthropy from Pat's journals. I wasn't expecting much from the scan, but I hit pay dirt, or rather, pay dirt hit me.

As soon as I started, I realized I was drawing the vanes of the windmill, poking up from a sea of surrounding trees.

"Nathan?" I said as quietly as I could. "They're right around here somewhere. To the east, I think. Back toward the main body of the park. Maybe on the road."

Nathan turned in that direction with a slow, casual motion and peered into the thick foliage surrounding the east end of the sunken garden. I started a new drawing. The windmill loomed over the scene and the trees. My hand began superimposing a sleek black shape—a car—on the view.

"They're parking on Kennedy Drive," I said. "Right near here."

We heard a car door creak open. A figure, male, appeared at the entrance to the garden.

Nathan spun around fast, and the pistol seemed to leap into his hand. I jumped up, scattering crayons, just in time to see a youngish, dark-haired man in dark slacks and a cream-colored shirt standing on the steps and staring our way. The way that the shirt caught the light said "raw silk" to me, an expensive little number, all right. I could feel DD's shock at seeing us. I also picked up his wave of sheer terror as he turned and ran.

"Stop!" Nathan yelled. "Police!"

Nathan took off after him, yelling, "Police!" all the way. I focused my mind and got a clear image of DD's back and head. More to the point I could feel him gasping on the point of panic as he raced up Kennedy Drive. For a few seconds I could see out of his eyes: the black Jag, its door open—I heard a shot and the squeal of brakes. I glimpsed Johnson, bent over the steering wheel as the Jag sped off with DD safely in the passenger seat. I heard another shot before Nathan came back, out of breath and furious.

"The bastard knows how to drive, all right," he said between quick gasps for breath. "I was aiming for his tires or gas tank. He took evasive action. Professionally trained, I'd say."

"If it's any comfort," I said, "I locked onto DD's mind. I'll know him from now on."

"Good." Nathan put the gun away and took his cell phone out of his pocket with a quick flip of his wrist. He punched a speed dial key. "Nathan from Interpol here."

I left calling Sanchez to Nathan and knelt down on the grass to pick up my crayons. I'd just gotten everything back in my tote bag when I heard a siren wailing. Someone had reported those shots to the police, I assumed, and sure enough, two uniformed cops came running down the steps toward us. Nathan held his Interpol ID up where they could see it and trotted over to meet them.

I sat back down on the lawn and let my mind roam after DD and Johnson. By then they both had raised

Shield Personas. Still, I received quick little flashes of the minds behind the shields, because they were distracted by an argument. I could pick up a constant natter of recrimination and general nastiness as they traveled farther and farther away, but their shields remained strong enough to turn aside any deep probe. I could tell that they were heading more or less south but nothing more. Ordinary reason told me that they'd probably turned onto the nearby Great Highway as they fled a possible police chase.

I returned my mind to the present location just as Nathan strode up. "They're putting an all-points out for the Jag again," he said. "Including the Highway Patrol. One of the officers told me that there's some kind of major road—"

"The Great Highway, so called," I said, pointing west. "A couple of blocks that way. And we're close to the county line, so I'm real glad the Chips are involved."

"The who?"

"Slang for the California Highway Patrol, sorry."

Nathan acknowledged the explanation with a nod, then set his hands on his hips and stared off to the south for a moment. With a shrug he turned back to me.

"What did Sanchez say?" I asked.

"That he'd have the windmill searched. The two officers on scene are going to stay until he and his team can get here."

"Do they want us to stay?"

"No." The word sounded more like a snarl.

Sanchez, I assumed, had grown tired of Nathan telling him how to do his job. Nathan shoved his hands into his pockets and glared at the windmill.

"What now?" Nathan said. "There's nothing more I can do here."

"Well," I said, "I'd like to go back to the Portals of the Past. We can be sure our perps won't be lurking there."

The sun hung low in the sky when we reached the doorway to nowhere. Shadows striped the lake, and the ducks had settled down for the evening among the weeds at the water's edge. Uncle Jim had taken his truck away the night before. A short length of yellow police tape still flapped from one tree. Nathan took a jackknife out of his jeans pocket and cut it off, then crumpled the tape up and stuffed it into my tote bag.

As I walked up to the marble pillars, I dropped the Shield Persona. I sent my mind out in Search Mode: Chaos again and mounted the steps to stand between them. This time I felt an odd twinge of energy, not a field, more like a stray wisp. I grabbed it—mentally, of course—and twisted it into a loop. I was hoping to track down DD. Instead I found myself thinking of Michael. I switched the Search Mode over to Personnel.

Michael! I sent the thought into the loop. Mike, can you hear me?

I felt a twitch of recognition, nothing so definite as an answer, but a twitch, as if Michael, wherever he was, had suddenly thought of me and wondered why.

"Mike's alive, all right," I said. "I thought so. We O'Gradys can usually tell when one of us leaves for good."

Nathan had been watching me with his head cocked a little to one side. "When Pat was shot," he said, "did you—"

"Yeah." I remembered the frantic couple of hours I'd spent, calling around the family, desperate for news. "I was in Mexico at the time, but I knew. I finally got hold of Kathleen, and she confirmed."

"I see. Mexico?"

"None of your business. But anyway, I'd know if Michael were dead."

"You're certain of that?"

"As certain as I can be. What worries me is how long he'll stay alive. I don't know where in hell he is."

"Let's hope it's not hell."

I managed to laugh. "Yeah, let's hope."

I spent another ten minutes or so on the steps, trying to renew the contact with Michael. Nothing. As the loop I'd made out of the energy trace slowly dissipated, I received the impression that Michael had moved beyond my range. The portal and Michael's disappearance baffled me so badly that I realized I'd better consult with Y.

"Nathan?" I said. "I need to go into trance."

"Very well, but do it in the car. I won't drive off till you're done."

He slid in behind the wheel while I settled myself in the backseat. Since in D.C. office hours were long over, I used our emergency frequency to send out a trance message to Y. In a few minutes he responded. His blond movie-star image popped into visibility beside me in the backseat.

"What's all this?" he said.

"I've got a major Chaos breach on my hands here," I said. "And my brother Michael's been caught up in it."

The blond eyebrows over the perfect blue eyes shot up in surprise. When I finished telling him about my brother's disappearance through the portal, he thought about my recital for so long that I began to have trouble holding the trance state.

"I do have an idea," he said at last. "From what I know about your family, your brother's bound to have some sort of wild talent. Have you considered parallel worlds? What you describe could be a gate of some sort. Michael may have the ability to sense gates and lock into their energies."

"I know about parallel world theory, sure, but a gate? Are those real?"

"Theoretically, thus possibly so. Our database is inconclusive on that point. Unreliable, even."

"That's what I was afraid of."

"Now, I'll admit that Michael being a world-walker sounds far-fetched, but it does fit what few facts you have about this thing in the park. Look, I'll consult with a couple of our people and get back to you on that."

"A world-walker? There's a name for it?"

"Oh, yes. They show up every now and then, or I should say, they claim to."

"Suppose that he is in a parallel or deviant level of the multiverse. Do you think he'll ever find his way back?"

"I really don't know. I need to research the whole subject."

"Okay. I'm worried sick."

"I assumed that. I'll treat this as a top priority fact search."

Y disappeared without another thought.

I woke myself up, stretched, and got out of the backseat. I was yawning as I slid back into the front seat next to Nathan.

"I'm tired, I guess," I said.

"You haven't had a proper meal all day. We're going out to dinner."

We went to the pizzeria near the apartment, where I could get a salad while he ate the heavy stuff. Thanks to the Shield Persona, I began to feel drunk. My normal senses, the standard issue five, worked perfectly well. The others had dulled down and almost vanished, leaving me feeling half-alive, confused, wobbly, all the things that alcohol in excess does to you.

We returned to the apartment just as the night was rolling in with the fog. Before I opened the front door, I dropped the SP and went into Search Mode to scan the apartment—as safe as I'd left it. I raised the SP again immediately. Nathan insisted on going in first. I followed him and stood by my computer desk while he looked around. Streetlights and shop lights cast odd patches of glare and shadow across the furniture and the floor.

"We left the drapes open," he said. "I'll just close them."

I started to make some trivial remark. Nathan lunged, grabbed me, and dragged me to the floor just as the bay window shattered. Glass sprayed. The bullet slammed into the opposite wall. Another followed through the break in the window. I could hear screaming from the street outside, a staccato of shots, and the crash of more breaking glass. A car alarm began honking in a hysterical sob. Nathan rolled away from me, slithered across the floor and around to the side of the couch, then stood up, gun in hand, and peered out the side window.

"Stay down," he said. "I think he's gone, but that sodding sign keeps blinking, and it's hard to see the roof behind it."

"Is that where he was?" I found it hard to speak.

"Only place he could have been."

A pair of sirens, coming from opposite directions, cut through the yelling and the honking car horns on the street. Footsteps pounded up the stairs outside my apartment. Someone hammered on the door. "Police! Open up!"

"Yes, officer!" Nathan called out. "I'm on my way."

As he strode across the room, he put the gun back into the shoulder holster, then zipped up his jacket. I decided that greeting the cops while lying sprawled on the carpet was too déclassé for words and sat up, but I made sure that the bulk of the couch stayed between me and the window. Nathan opened the door first a bare crack, then wide enough for a uniformed officer to push his way in.

"Lady, get back!" The cop shouted at Mrs. Zukovski, who was dithering behind him in a floor-length flowered bathrobe, then looked at Nathan. "Is everyone all right in here?"

"Yes," Nathan said. "Fortunately, we were rolling around on the floor at the time."

If he hadn't just saved my life, I would have thrown something at him, preferably something sharp and heavy. The cop sputtered, then arranged a straight face. Nathan switched on the overhead light. Mrs. Zukovski dithered herself through the door. A hairnet covered her purple hair.

"Oh, my gawd!" She stared at the broken window. "Look at all that glass! It's going to cost me a bundle to fix that bay."

"Lady," the cop said, "your tenant could have been killed. This sniper is a real nutcase. It's just a damned good thing her boyfriend was here, or you'd have a real mess to clean up."

Mrs. Z pulled a crumpled tissue from a bathrobe pocket and snuffled into it.

"I heard more shots," Nathan said.

"That was him," the cop said, "taking potshots at a couple of pedestrians, but he missed them, thank God for that."

"Good." Nathan reached inside his jacket and took out his Interpol ID. The cop's eyes widened. For a moment he looked like a small boy meeting a famous football player.

"Thanks, Inspector," he said. "I remember hearing about you. You're here on official business, aren't you?"

"Yes, related to the Romero murder."

"I've called in a SWAT team. I need to get a forensics team up here to dig those bullets out of the wall."

"Very good. Carry on."

The cop pulled out a cell phone to call for his backup personnel. Nathan unzipped his jacket and stowed the

ID. When she caught sight of the shoulder holster, Mrs. Z came out with another, "Oh, my gawd!"

"It's all right," I said. "He's a police officer, too."

"Oh, oh, well, I suppose, oh . . ." She let the last "oh" turn into a sigh. "I'll have to call George. I don't know where he's going to get some plywood or something this time of night."

George was the minimally skilled handyman she hired for odd jobs.

"Well, I can't use the apartment with no window," I said.

"Oh, oh well, I suppose not, oh . . ."

I let it drop. I had worse things to worry about than street noise and cold drafts. I could hear bullhorns outside as the SWAT team cleared the street. Sirens came and went. I found myself remembering Uncle Jim's complaint about all the waiting involved in disasters. Finally, after about ten minutes, more police came pounding up the stairs to join us.

The forensics people took photographs of the wall and the window, close-ups of the bullets in the wall, and then of the bullets once they dug them out, leaving a pile of plaster and paint chips on the floor. Mrs. Z collapsed onto a kitchen chair and sniveled into her tissue while she watched that part of the operation. I figured that she was doing a cost analysis on the repair.

The forensics expert, wearing plastic gloves, showed the bullets to Nathan before he sealed them into a manila paper envelope.

"They appear to match the others," Nathan said. "The two murders in Israel, that is, but I can't be sure without putting them under the microscope."

"Any idea of what kind of gun?" Forensics said.

"Yes, as far as we could tell, he was using a Dragunov SVD."

Forensics blinked at him.

"It was originally a Soviet sniper's rifle," Nathan went on. "They show up all over the Middle East thanks to Soviet arms sales, but the Iranian DIO still manufactures them."

"No shit?" Forensics turned to an assistant, who had a pad of paper and a pen. "You writing this down?"

"Of course," she said. "What's the DIO?"

"Domestic Industries Organization," Nathan said. "Do you want the name in Farsi?"

"No, no, I don't know how to spell those Arabic names."

Nathan winced. "Farsi isn't Arabic. It's not even related to Arabic. Never make that mistake if you ever go to the Middle East. That kind of ignorance is what marks an American as a possible victim."

The forensics tech cringed, but she kept writing.

While Forensics worked, the original cop on the scene interviewed all three of us, though all he really wanted from Mrs. Z was the time when she heard the glass break. Since she could remember the commercial she'd been viewing at that moment, he could confirm the time later with the TV station. During Nathan's part of the interview he admitted that we hadn't been rolling around on the floor, which seemed to relieve Mrs. Z's feelings to some extent.

"I was looking out the window at the moment," Nathan said. "I saw movement on the roof, and then what appeared to be someone lifting a rifle, and I reacted. Knocked her out of the way. Army training, you know. We have to worry about snipers and the like back home."

The cop nodded.

"I'm glad it didn't turn out to be someone on the roof with a broom." Nathan looked my way. "I hope you're not bruised."

"Don't worry about it," I said. "Not a problem."

The SWAT team called in at that point. Johnson had gotten clean away. He was good at what he did.

When the police team left, Mrs. Zukovski followed, mumbling down the stairs behind them. I shut the door and switched off the overhead glare. The blinking purple light from the restaurant sign filled the room and glittered on the broken glass lying all over the couch.

"Is it going to be safe to stay here tonight?" I said.

"Of course not," Nathan snapped. "Nola, he knows where you live. Think!"

"I'm trying. For some reason I feel oddly scattered."

"Go pack a suitcase. We're leaving."

"Where are we going to go?"

"I'm not going to tell you." He smiled in a tight-lipped kind of way. "If I tell you, Johnson might pull the information out of the air or your mind or whatever that is."

"Unfortunately, that could happen."

"So I thought. But you're going to have to trust my driving."

"I think I'd rather trust Johnson. The end result will be the same, but the bullet will be quicker."

"Look, I promise you that I'll try to slow down and all that, since you want me to drive like a sodding—oh, never mind. I'll try."

I threw together some clothing and necessities, then retrieved Pat's journals from the hamper. Nathan took some of his luggage as well, including the sample case that, theoretically, held prayer shawls. Before we left, I started to put up the Shield Persona, then damned the danger and took it down. I needed all of my wits about me, even the weird ones. If the police couldn't keep Johnson too busy to worry about me, I figured, then why were we paying taxes?

As we hurried downstairs, we met George coming up, wrestling an enormous sheet of plywood. Mrs. Z followed and gabbled instructions while she carried his tool box.

"Will you be back in the morning?" she said to me.

"Maybe, maybe not," I said. "If not, I'll call."

Ambiguity, I thought. That's what I need to project. As we drove off, I let my mind run through a hundred possibilities for our destination, our direction, and every other factor I could think of. If nothing else, it kept my mind off Nathan's driving.

On our way to the cemetery in Colma, Nathan had noticed a franchise-type hotel on the frontage road beside the freeway. A tan stucco building with a Spanish Baroque false front, it took up most of a block, the better to confuse a stalker. The young man working the desk seemed indifferent to who we were and whether we had reservations just so long as Nathan had a credit card. The Interpol ID, however, woke him up fast.

"If anyone comes in and wants the room number," Nathan said, "or phones and wants to be connected, do not do it without checking with me first. Do you understand? That's very important."

"Yes sir," the clerk said. "Understood. I'll leave a note for the day shift, too."

I wandered away and stared at a blank spot on the wall while they finished the transaction. I wanted to avoid knowing the room number. When we went upstairs with the luggage, I also avoided looking at the door. I filled my mind with thoughts of a hotel in Lake Tahoe where I'd stayed some years before and visualized the view of the lake at night from its windows. If Johnson was working a Mind Penetration or scan on me, he'd end up thoroughly confused.

The window of the room that I actually stood in looked downhill to the street in back of the hotel. Since the queen sized bed sat near the window, Nathan pulled the drapes shut as soon as we got in. The room as a whole, decorated mostly in golds and browns, contained a sofa as well as the bed, but it looked much too short for Nathan to stretch out on.

"In the morning, we should be able to see the local police station from here," Nathan said. "Down the hill and over a little."

"That should give Johnson something interesting to think about."

"So I thought, yes."

I was having interesting thoughts of my own. Suppose Johnson had made his shot, I asked myself. In those last few seconds you would have had the conventional regrets about never seeing your family again and dying young, but be honest, O'Grady, one of those regrets would have been that you turned Nathan down.

Johnson, of course, had missed.

I sat down on the edge of the bed and watched Nathan, who had taken off his jacket and the shoulder holster, while he stowed the luggage out of the way at one end of the narrow room. He put the sample case near the window, then reached inside it. I heard a click as he turned on some device, the interference generator, I assumed. I liked the way he moved, no theatrics, no fuss, just the quiet self-control of a man who knew he was a man. He turned around and gave me a look of the sort that's usually described as smoldering. I could feel the Qi rising, swirling around us both like a thrown net.

"I'll sleep on the floor if you'd like," he said.

"Not necessary." I smoldered right back at him. "Ari."

I was expecting him to grin or make some triumphant wisecrack. Instead, he merely walked over and sat down next to me, close enough for me to feel his warmth and to smell him. I'd never realized before that the way a man smelled could be so erotic. His warmth blended with the rising Qi. I felt a trickle of sweat run down between my breasts. He breathed as deeply as if he'd just smelled perfume and leaned closer.

"You don't feel like you owe me something, do you?" he said.

"Why? Just because you saved my miserable life?"

"Yes, exactly that."

"No. It's sheer unbridled lust."

"Oh, well, then." He grinned at me. "I can do something about that."

And he did. Oh, my God, did he ever. For half the night.

CHAPTER 9

SINCE ARI WANTED TO KEEP MOVING, he kissed me awake at eleven A.M., an hour before the hotel's checkout time. I finished waking up in the shower, then dried off and got dressed in jeans and the rose print blouse again. He'd already packed everything else. When I glanced out of the window, I felt all my senses come on-line for the first time in days. The return gave me an energy rush that made me feel profoundly alive. Because I wanted to stay that way, I risked deploying Search Mode: General. A danger warning touched my mind, but softly. I placed the threat some ten miles away to the north and west.

"I don't suppose you'll want breakfast," Ari said.

"This morning I do. I'm starving."

"Good." He grinned at me. "Well, now I know what to do when you need to eat a proper meal."

I puffed up with false dignity and turned my back on him, but I could hear him laughing.

For breakfast we went to the Cafe Boulevard over on John Daly, which is as close to a main street as the "other D.C." has, as my sister Kathleen used to call this oddly disjointed small town when we were teenagers. I figured Ari would enjoy a real American breakfast in an American restaurant that's a kind of upscale tribute to the Fifties. We sat in a maroon vinyl booth, where he proceeded to order an amazing amount of food. I asked the waitress if I could have a single scrambled egg and a half-order of hash browns. I was waiting for Ari to tell me to eat more, but he merely smiled.

I found out why when the food arrived. He began piling stuff from his plate onto mine—a chunk of an omelet stuffed with cheese and mushrooms and a piece of toast with butter, for starters.

"You're going to eat that," he said. "No more of those walking trances."

"Well, I ordered a perfectly adequate breakfast."

"No, you didn't." He glowered at me. "Last night I was half-afraid I'd break your sodding ribs. I could have counted them in pitch darkness."

I glowered right back and picked up my fork. I was planning on eating only a few bites of everything, but after all the exercise of the past night, I succumbed. For some minutes neither of us spoke.

"A question," Ari said eventually. "The members of your family each have individual odd talents, but you've got quite a range of them. Is that unusual?"

"We vary, yeah, but most of us who have any gifts at all have more than one. It's just that I've undergone training with mine, so I can use them more efficiently. If you've got a proclivity, the right kind of training can expand it."

"That makes sense."

"And some of our talents overlap within the family, too. Mostly among the O'Gradys, though."

"Overlap?"

"Some of us have a small gift for something that someone else has in spades. Like Kathleen and Pat—she has a really deep empathy with animals, but she could never assume the wolf-form, not that she'd want to. And like them, I've got a sharp sense of smell."

"Somewhat wolflike?"

"Only somewhat, though Pat used to tease me about it. But that's probably why I could feel the little bit of energy left in the portal, but I couldn't really do anything with it. Michael and I must overlap, too."

Ari nodded and put a chicken-apple sausage on my plate.

"I've had enough," I snapped.

"No, you haven't. Eat it, and here's another slice of toast, too. You don't have to have jam on it."

"Gee, thanks! You're just lucky we're in public at the moment, or you'd be wearing the jam."

He laughed at me.

"But this is all," I went on. "Enough. Basta. The end."

"Yes, you mustn't eat too much at once after a long period of starvation."

"I wasn't starving."

"Those ribs of yours, and then your hip bones—I rest my case."

I snarled but let the subject drop. If the food hadn't been so damned good, especially the hash browns, I would have continued refusing to eat it, just on general principle, but as it was I finished everything. I had to admit, though only to myself, that the sensation of having eaten as much as my body demanded felt wonderful.

When we finished eating, I phoned Lawrence Grampian, who had followed my advice and stayed holed up in the apartment he shared with three of the other Hounds. We could come over any time, he told me. The roommates had all gone to work or class.

Grampian lived not all that far from Aunt Eileen, it turned out, in a bleak modern apartment building close to McLaren Park, a convenient location for full moon nights. Unlike the much-tended Golden Gate Park in its middle class neighborhood, McLaren contains one children's playground and a lot of unkempt grass and

trees still in the natural state of a California hilltop.
Though the neglect does benefit the local werewolves,
the working-class people who live nearby rightfully
complain about the lack of money spent on their green
space.

When he answered the door, Frater LG stared at
us as if he'd forgotten who we were. His face was unshaven, his eyes still red and swollen, his pale hair filthy.
His cheeks were so chapped from tears that they appeared sunburned. He wore a white T-shirt and a pair
of plaid flannel pants that resembled pajamas but did
mercifully zip up at the front. He showed us into a living
room containing one sagging couch, two old armchairs,
and an enormous TV, bigger even than the one my aunt
and uncle had lost to the fake burglary, flanked by wall-
mounted speakers. In one corner a wastepaper basket
overflowed with crushed beer cans.

"Want something to drink?" he said. "We've got
some beer in the fridge."

"No, thanks," Ari said. "Did Nola tell you who I am?"

"A cop—I mean police officer, right?"

"Yes, but I'm one who understands your condition."

Grampian started to speak, then wept, just a scatter of tears that he wiped off with the hem of his shirt.
"Sorry," he mumbled. "I'm way broken up. Every damn
thing makes me cry." He snuffled loudly. "But it's a relief, hearing you say that."

"I can well imagine," Ari said. "Look, I'm operating
on the assumption that you had nothing to do with your
fiancée's death. What I need is information so we—the
San Francisco police and I—can find the actual killer."

I thought Grampian might cry again, but he gulped
for breath, closed his eyes for a moment, and forestalled
another breakdown. "Let me get a roll of TP," he said.
"I've used up all the Kleenex we had."

As well as fetching a toilet roll, Grampian combed

his hair in the bathroom. He returned looking a little more kempt and flopped down on the battered brown sofa, leaving the chairs for us. Ari got out the envelope of Johnson photos and handed them over.

"This man is wanted for two similar murders in Israel," Ari said. "He's the prime suspect in the Romero killing. Have you seen him before?"

Lawrence studied each one, then shook his head and handed them back. "No, never," he said. "He's a Dodger fan, huh? Figures."

"Do you know or have you ever met a man named Arnold Jacoby?"

"Yeah." Lawrence abruptly looked away. "He was killed, too, wasn't he?"

"In Israel, yes. We already know that he suffered from lycanthropy."

"Okay." Lawrence looked at Ari again and tried to smile. "I don't have to protect his rep anymore, then."

"No, you don't. Was he a friend of yours?"

"A good friend, yeah. He's the one who made me see you could be half wolf and still be a decent human being. I visited him when I went to Israel. I never thought it'd be the last time I'd see him."

"I'm sorry you've lost him." Ari turned slightly and nodded at me to take over.

"I've been reading Pat's journals," I said. "He talks about a guy he calls DD. Do you know who that is?"

"David Doyle, but I bet that's not his real name. That's what he called himself when he came sniffing around our—" he hesitated briefly "—pack. We all started saying that DD stood for Devil's Disciple after a while. He thought that was way cool."

"Did he? Pat thought he was a member of a Satanic cult."

"That's right, yeah. Pat told me it came from somewhere really weird, like the Middle East."

Ari raised an eyebrow at that but said nothing.

"Did Pat tell you anything more about it?" I continued.

"No." Grampian thought for a moment. "Pat wouldn't listen when Doyle tried to tell him more. I do remember that. It was Satanic, and that was all he needed to know."

Yeah, that's Pat, all right, I thought. Aloud, I said, "What does Doyle look like?"

"He's a little older than me, dark hair, kind of good-looking, I guess. Soror JE called him cute, anyway. He must have money from somewhere, because he always had flashy clothes, name labels, that kind of shit."

Ari and I exchanged significant looks.

"In the journals," I continued, "Pat hinted that Doyle was engaged in some kind of illegal activity. Did Pat ever tell you what it was?"

"Drugs, yeah," Grampian said. "Hard drugs, too, like heroin."

Ari smiled in satisfaction. "Good," he said. "That confirms what we suspected. The police are going to be very interested in your evidence. They now have every right to issue a warrant for Doyle's arrest."

Even though I kept priming Grampian with questions, he would have talked without them, unburdening himself of over a year of pent-up guilt and secrets. One thing became immediately clear: he blamed himself for Pat's death.

"I never should have let your brother try to get information out of that rotten son of a bitch," Grampian said at one point. "I'm sorry, Nola. I can't tell you how bad I feel that I didn't just tell Pat to leave trouble alone."

"Would he have obeyed you?" I said.

"Sure." He spoke with an innocent certainty. "I'm the alpha in our pack."

When the family realized that Pat suffered from lycanthropy, we'd all read up on wolf behavior. The knowledge came in handy now. "Tell me something," I said, "do you think Doyle was an aggressive beta male?"

"Damn right he was! He ran with us a couple of times, and I could tell right away what was on his mind." He made a noise uncomfortably close to growling. "Join up and get the other betas on his side and then challenge me."

"More likely," Ari broke in, "he would have just had you shot outright. The man whose pictures I showed you? We think he's working with this Doyle."

Grampian went white around the mouth, but not from fear. "Like he did with Mary Rose, you mean. He was sniffing around her. That's the first step, get the alpha female interested." He smiled but his ice-blue eyes stayed cold. "She bit him. I thought it was great when she did it, but now I wish she never had."

"Why?" I said.

"She kept at it and made him roll over and piss on his stomach. It made him furious. She'd humiliated him in front of the whole pack."

"Furious enough to want her dead?"

I waited, sure he was going to weep again, but he collected himself with a couple of deep breaths.

"Yeah," Grampian said. "It was the full moon, or I'd think he was the one who shot her. He was always bragging about how good he was with guns. He was good at everything, if you believed him, anyway."

"Not good enough to shoot a gun with paws," I said.

Grampian nodded his agreement.

"We have a fingerprint, anyway," Ari said. "It was Johnson, not Doyle."

Grampian thought this over, then shrugged. "But I bet that fucking swine put him up to it. I want to tell the cops, but how? I don't know his real name, I don't know where he lived."

"Hold on a sec," I put in. "You don't know where he lived?"

"No. I asked a couple of times, but he was always real vague. In the old Haight, he'd say, or near the park." He paused briefly, then continued. "He wouldn't tell us anything about himself, and there's another big problem. Suppose I did go to the police. God help me, how can I get into it without ratting out our pack?"

Ari took the recorder out of his jacket pocket.

"Here's how," Ari said. "Tell me everything you can about Doyle without mentioning the wolves. The smallest detail might be important, even down to his brand of wristwatch, did he wash his car or leave it dirty. Everything you can think of, but especially Pat's testimony about the drug dealing. Just remember, this will all be on the record."

Grampian talked for a good fifteen minutes. He rambled around, backtracked, paused at times when he'd been about to slip up and mention the wolf pack, which he instead referred to simply as "our Bible club." We had a lot of solid information by the time he finished. Ari clicked off the recorder and pocketed it.

"One more thing," I said. "Why didn't you go running with Mary Rose that night?"

"I did." His voice trembled as he held up a shaking hand. A fresh pink scar slashed across the middle of his palm. "I stepped on a piece of broken glass. So she went on ahead while I tried to chew it out. I heard the shot. I ran on three legs, but the killer was already gone." His entire body began to shake as badly as his voice. "She was already dead. I couldn't do anything. I couldn't call the police. I couldn't do anything." Tears began to run down his face again. "Can't you see what that's like? I couldn't do one goddamn thing." He threw back his head and howled.

"Stop it!" I got up and practically dove for the couch.

"Lawrence, listen to me!" I sat down next to him and grabbed him by the shoulders.

The howling stopped, but he continued to tremble.

"You've got to call Father Keith," I said. "Ari, do you have anything I can write the number on?"

Ari did, the back of the receipt from breakfast. He handed me a ballpoint pen as well. I wrote down the number, then glanced around. On top of one of the wall speakers lay a cell phone. I got up, grabbed it, and brought it back to Grampian.

"Call him right now," I said. "Don't worry. He'll be expecting you. And remember, you're in danger. Don't go out at night, not even in a crowd. Warn the rest of your pack, too."

We left Grampian talking on the phone to Father Keith and showed ourselves out. As we went down the stairs, Ari shot a puzzled glance my way. "When did you call your uncle?"

"Hmm? I didn't."

"Well, how did you know that Keith was expecting Grampian to call?"

"Ari, after all this time—"

He actually blushed. "More fool me," he said. "Never mind."

We got into the car, but instead of starting the engine, Ari sat looking out the windshield and drumming his fingers on the steering wheel. I followed his glance and saw nothing but a sagging gray house behind a concrete lawn, spotted with puddles from the recent rain.

"What is it?" I said.

"Just thinking about something Grampian said. He believed that Pat would have obeyed him, the alpha male. Do you think that's true? What if a new alpha male, Doyle, say, had asked him to do something illegal?"

"Like dealing Persian white?"

"Exactly."

"I can't speak for the other guys in the pack, but Pat would have said no. That's probably what got him killed. Doyle could tell that he'd never come around."

"That makes a certain sense, yes."

He started the car, made an entirely too flamboyant U-turn, and we headed off downhill. I caught myself just before I asked him where we were going.

"The trouble with all of this," Ari said abruptly, "is not being able to tell Sanchez the whole truth."

"Yeah, unfortunately. Some of the information you have on tape should help them work the narcotics angle, though."

"That's true. I'll call him once we've reached a stopping place."

Sanchez, however, contacted Ari while we were still in transit. Out of consideration for my feelings Ari pulled over to the side of Alemany Boulevard before he took the call. Watching him trying to drive while talking on the phone would have been too much for me to bear. For a few brief minutes he merely listened, then gave Sanchez a summary of what we'd learned from Grampian about Doyle. When he finished, he told me Sanchez's news.

"They've found the Jaguar. It was abandoned just south of San Francisco on the Great Highway. He's got a team going over it for evidence."

"Think they'll find any?"

"You never know. Criminals have careless moments just like everyone else, now and then."

"True. They must have had another car stashed somewhere, maybe that blue sedan, the one I saw in the first scan I did."

"I assume so, probably near where they abandoned the Jaguar. Sanchez also gave me the report on the windmill. It's not what we expected at all. The lock had been picked, all right. The police found stacks of consumer goods inside."

"Say what? No drugs?"

"Not unless you count coffee and chocolate as drugs. The raid turned up hundreds of pounds of those, plus watches, old-fashioned cameras and film, electric batteries of various sizes, and baseball gear, shirts and caps for a team called the Dodgers, mostly." He frowned, puzzled. "And the oddest thing of all is that they found receipts with everything. It had all been paid for with cash. Everything but the baseball gear came from Costco. I didn't realize you had those in America."

"We sure do, and that explains the quantities." I don't mind admitting that the news baffled me. "So it's not contraband at all."

"Apparently not, though it had no right to be there, so they confiscated it anyway." Ari shrugged. "They'll stake out the place in case the trespasser returns. Do you think it could be Doyle or Johnson?"

"I really don't know. That's the last kind of stuff I expected to be in there. On the other hand, they've been spotted there twice now."

"And who else would have left all those goods there?"

"Well, yeah. Wait—those receipts must have had dates on them."

"Everything had been purchased over the weekend, Sunday morning at the latest."

"Just before Michael disappeared. That's ominous."

"I'm afraid so, yes."

I made a mental note to file a report on this development as soon as I could log on. Ari started the car again.

"Let's go," he said cheerfully and pulled right out into traffic without a backward glance. Horns blared, but we lived.

Our destination turned out to be the Morrison

Marketing office. I had to agree when Ari remarked that Johnson most likely would stay away from somewhere so obvious and so public, at least during the day. I took the book bag of Pat's journals from the car, but we left the luggage in the trunk.

When we arrived, Ari insisted on changing offices with me. The inner office window looked out on a straight drop six stories down to asphalt. I'd never seen any evidence that Johnson counted "human fly" among his accomplishments. Ari took my desk in the outer room with its view of the Bay Bridge approach. He fired up the computer in order, he said, to "file reports."

"Do you have an encryption system?" I said. "The one on there won't work for you."

"We have our own, don't worry."

On my old desk, the landline phone was blinking. The message came from Y's secretary, worried again about the publicity for the new line of dog food. The code word made me laugh, not a pleasant sound, but technically a laugh.

"What?" Ari said.

"My handler has talents of his own. The code word he picked turned out to be pretty damn appropriate. Dog food. Wolf chow, more like it."

I took a notepad and pen out of the desk drawer, then went into the inner office. I settled into the comfortable leather chair to go into trance. As soon as I signaled to Y, his image appeared in the chair next to mine.

"I'm damn glad you've gotten in touch," Y said. "I've been worried sick. Annie reported that you were shot at last night."

"Yeah, I was, but he missed. How did she know?"

"It's all over the news. Serial killer nearly claims new victim. It's the kind of story they love."

"I suppose it would be. Anyway, let me fill you in."

I gave him a full report on everything—well, excluding my love life—that had happened since I'd last filed a report via TranceWeb. He listened solemnly, nodding now and then.

"I got your report on the coven question," he said when I was done. "I checked the archive, and you're quite correct. The state of the information there is appalling. Very outdated."

"I'm glad to hear you say that. Could you have a researcher set up a background file?"

"I certainly will."

"Good. I'll continue investigating the coven I found. I did get a clear mind print of one of the individuals in it. She strikes me as victim more than perp, bored and lonely and looking for some excitement, that kind of person. But Johnson was there, and I bet that means more excitement than any of them want."

"No doubt! I'm beginning to understand why the I Ching wanted you back in San Francisco. The place is Chaos-prone."

"At times, yeah, but now and then, we strike a blow for Harmony."

"I suppose so, historically speaking. Still, the Agency had better put some thought into the general situation there."

Had I been awake, I would have groaned aloud. I suspected that some kind of meddling supervisor was going to descend upon me in the near future.

"Now, however, about the case in hand." Y's image froze while his body consulted his notes. The image revived. "It's beginning to sound like things are falling into place."

"Yeah, except for two things, Doyle and Johnson. Where are they? The local police are busy trying to hunt them down, but so far no luck."

"Shouldn't you leave that to them? You're too valuable an agent to go on putting yourself in danger. Our policy is simple—stay away from police matters if at all possible."

It was time we changed that policy, or so I felt, but I knew better than to push until I got a direct order to back off.

"Right," I said instead. "They're the experts."

"Speaking of which, I talked to a few of our experts about your missing brother."

In my physical body, my heart pounded a couple of times. I calmed myself before it woke me up.

"One of them has military contacts," Y continued. "He was allowed to look at a report from a satellite system that you and I don't know about. Right?"

"Right."

"It picked up the energy flash you described. The military is very interested in just what that might have been. Our expert thinks that the Army is sending someone to San Francisco to take a look at it. Maybe they'll find out more than we can, now that they know about it. If they do, our operative will get the pass-through."

"That sounds real good."

"Yes. Now, as to where your brother is, the one resource person I have in that area agrees that the deviant level theory is possible. She doesn't like the term parallel worlds, because they aren't really parallel. They apparently shoot off in all directions." His image looked utterly confused. "She showed me a lot of math, but I can't remember much of it."

"Don't worry about it," I said. "If you showed it to me, I wouldn't understand it, either. The only math I studied in college was statistics. Our talents are more reliable than that."

"Well, probabilities do come into this. She remarked that there must be an explanation for what happened. Since every explanation is extremely unlikely, even the most improbable of the explanations could be true. It came in at—" again the pause to consult notes "—a point one percent for all causes except for the deviant level theory, which came in at point zero nine percent."

"Statistically speaking, that's not a big deviation."

"That's what she said, too. If the world-walker theory is correct, then the gate deposited Mike somewhere. He must have some sort of natural attunement to such things. You're sure he's still alive?"

I ran a quick mental check. "Yeah," I said, "I am."

"Good. I've uploaded her contact information to TranceWeb. She goes by the name of NumbersGrrl. She spells it gee ar ar el, for some reason."

"If that's her handle, she must be a geek."

Y looked confused again. "No, not Greek," he said after a moment, "she's African American."

"Oh. Sorry." I suppressed my emotional reaction, that is, the trance equivalent of laughter. "I really appreciate the effort you've put into this."

"Well, I've always had hopes of recruiting more members of your family one day. Michael sounds like he could be a very valuable addition to our crew."

I was surprised at how much I wanted to argue the point. I refused to have my little brother working such a dangerous job—until I remembered that he'd already found the danger on his own.

"He's still underage," I said. "And he needs to get an education first."

"I do realize that. Oh, I have a bit of gossip-level data that you might want to know. About Nathan? It seems that his superior officers were glad of the excuse to get him out of the country and their hair for a while. He's too good to fire, but apparently he's unusually—well, the word my source used was blunt."

"Yeah, as in blunt instrument. I can understand that."

"I see. Well, over and out."

He disappeared.

I came out of the trance and made some notes on the things Y had told me. One detail stuck out, that the shooting had made the TV news. Aunt Eileen had doubtless seen the segment. When I called her, she greeted me with a: "Thank heaven you called."

"I'm sorry I didn't get in touch sooner," I said. "I've been really busy with the police and all of that."

"Particularly busy with one policeman, I should think! Nola, honestly!"

I was several miles away, but I blushed. I should have known.

"If you're going to do things like that," Aunt Eileen went on, "I hope you're using birth control. I don't care what the pope thinks, him and all those old cardinals. What would they know about sex, anyway, or if they do know, shame on them!"

"I'm using that new ring." I decided to change the subject. "But have you heard anything more about Michael?"

"No." She paused, and sadness welled up. "I was hoping that Lieutenant Sanchez would call again, but he didn't. I don't suppose he has anything to tell us."

"Probably not. But I want you to know that I'm as sure as I can be that Mike's still alive. I'd know if he'd gone on to the other side."

"Well, dear, that's a real comfort. I actually think I would, too. I did have another dream. Do you remember me telling you about the farmer's market and the goblins?"

"Yeah, sure do."

"In this dream I saw one of them close up. It wasn't a goblin at all. It was a man with a really horrible tumor growing inside his face. His cheek was swollen so badly that he couldn't open one eye. I still don't know if the dream means anything, but somehow that made it seem more real."

"I see what you mean." I wrote down a few quick notes. "I'm not sure what it signifies, either, but it strikes me as important."

"It did me, too. Now, I'll call you if the police tell me anything more."

I ended the call, then leaned back in the leather chair to think. Y was probably right, I decided, about leaving Doyle and Johnson to the police—well, mostly to the police. I saw nothing wrong with passing them information through Ari. Thanks to our interview with Grampian, the cops could issue a search warrant for Doyle and maybe bring him in first. A little persuasion, plus his fear of being in custody with the full moon only a couple of weeks away—he'd probably spill everything he knew about Johnson in the hopes of getting out on bail before the wolf-change began.

And if he didn't get out in time? If he couldn't post bail? What were the police going to do if they had a werewolf on their hands? Send him to the SPCA for custody? I made a note to ask Y how we'd handle such an occurrence, then put the matter to one side.

The agency had supplied a laptop for the office. I was just powering it up to contact NumbersGrrl when I heard a rustle behind me. I spun the chair around and saw a blue lizard-meerkat thing crouched behind the wastepaper basket. I raised my hand to execute the ward and the Chaos creature with one gesture, but it whined and rose up on its hind legs to beg. Its slimy green eyes stared at me in terror.

"Listen, you," I said. "Get out of here now, and I won't blast you to hell."

It whined, pissed green slime, and vanished. So did the puddle, I'm glad to say. Johnson and Doyle already knew who I was and where I lived. Since they'd found

the office, too, I had very little left to hide. I saw no reason to destroy a thing that so obviously felt fear whether
it truly lived or not.

When I logged onto TranceWeb I went straight to e-
mail. Our code expert had taken a look at Johnson's two
letters. I transferred the information into a regular file,
then got up and opened the door to the outer office. Ari
was sitting at my old desk and looking at a computer
screen full of Hebrew letters. Just as good as TranceWeb,
I thought, when it comes to keeping secrets from me, at
least.

"Ari?" I said. "The Agency guy thinks the symbols on
Johnson's two letters represent a stage of the alchemical
process. He calls it the nigredo."

"Which means?" Ari swiveled the chair around and
looked up at me.

"Dissolution, basically. The old alchemists summed
things up in the formula *solve et coagula*—dissolve and
congeal, in English. The nigredo's part of the *solve*, the
dissolving of the *prima materia* so it can be reconstituted
in the *coagula* part of the formula."

Ari blinked, stricken.

"I've got all this in a file," I said. "I'll print it out for
you."

"Thank you. But why did Johnson put those symbols
on the letters?"

"The expert doesn't know. Finding out is our job, he
says."

I got the reproachful stare.

"But I'll make a guess," I went on. "I think Johnson's
telling us his state of mind, but he doesn't know that's
what he's doing. Consciously, he probably figured those
symbols would scare people, is all."

"That makes sense." He paused for a sigh. "In the
usual mad way."

I returned to the office and TranceWeb to check the

FAQ on Chaos critters. I read through all the entries just in case I needed the information later—not that it was terribly helpful. For example, no one knew how the Chaos masters had managed to make artificial constructs that digested actual food as an energy source. Our R and D people were working on the problem, or so the FAQ said, but the comment was two years old.

Before I filed my official report, I paused to run a quick SM: Personnel on Sneezy. The contact came so easily that I knew she had to be distracted by some strong emotion. As I focused in, the light dawned. I'd caught her in the middle of having sex—with Doyle. Busy though he was, I could pick up the print of his ugly little mind. I shut off the contact immediately. I'd learned something new about Sneezy, all right. She had terrible taste in men. I wondered if he were living in her elegant house, wherever that was. If so, Johnson had to be off on his own somewhere, as I'd never felt his presence in that location. I would have, too, since he left the psychic equivalent of the stench of secondhand garlic everywhere he went.

I had just finished filing my report when Ari opened the door and stepped in.

"Time to leave," he said. "I hope you don't mind, but for some reason I'm quite tired."

"Gosh, I can't imagine why."

"Neither can I." He looked and sounded perfectly serious.

I'd forgotten about Ari and irony. I smiled and took the laptop with me.

Our next mystery destination turned out to be a big hotel down on Fisherman's Wharf, right in the middle of a decent sampling of off-season tourists who, I figured, would muddle the aura field better than any electronic scrambler. The room was a definite step up from the bargain hotel of the night before, all decorated in creams and blues, with a sitting area and a good television as well as the usual sleeping arrangements. Ari had an amazing expense account.

Since I technically still served on Chaos watch, we left the hotel so I could take a look around. I led the way through the tourist area, all gray concrete, sleazy shops, and cheap attractions. The aimless mob of sightseers drifting through could have hidden fifty Chaotics, because I never could have sensed them there. The crowd pulsed with a muddle of thoughts and half-heard conversations, the crying of exhausted children, and the ramblings of men who'd had too much to drink.

We walked to the silence of one of the oldest wharves, where actual fishing boats still docked. The sun was setting out beyond the Golden Gate, turning the dead-calm water into patches of rainbow, thanks to the flecks of engine oil and gasoline floating among the boats. Ari put his arm around my shoulders and pulled me close while we looked north across the bay to the Marin hills, dark and tranquil in the twilight mist.

"Nola," he said, "do you think you'll like living in Israel?"

"Say what?"

"Well, it's very different from California."

"Ari, what exactly are you—"

"Do you think I'm going to just walk out of your life? When we get this bit of work taken care of, I mean."

I pulled away and looked up at his puzzled frown.

"A warning," I said, "I'm not going to marry anyone, not even you."

"Well, all right. We can just live together, then."

"I am not moving to Israel with you."

"Why not?"

"What do you mean, why not?" I wanted to say, "We've just met and I hardly know you," but when I considered my behavior of the night before, those sentiments rang hollow. "My family's all here, my job's here, and that's enough of a reason."

"No, it isn't. We can always visit." Ari grinned at me. "But we can discuss this later if you'd like. We do have other things to tend to."

"Yeah, we certainly do. Like finding my brother."

I turned and started back to the hotel. He caught up with me and took my hand, a comfortable fit in his. As we returned to the room, I thought about telling him the truth, that all my other—well, boyfriends for want of a better word—had all wanted to marry me as long as we were together, right together, that is, within a couple of miles of each other. Once they went farther away than that, on a business trip or vacation or whatever, they began to remember how strange I was.

Just like Kathleen, I saw no reason to lie to them about my talents or my family. When they were with me, none of that mattered. But once we'd separated, it only took a few days for the truth to sink in. They had ended our relationship every single time.

The first few hurt. Now I knew what to expect. I reminded myself that I had no reason to worry about Ari's long-term plans. Let him go back to Israel to report to his superiors, and that would be that.

While he took a shower, I distracted myself by seeing if I could find a show worth watching on TV. If Johnson were trying to see through my eyes with an MP or SM: P, maybe a dose of Looney Tunes or *Star Trek* would make him sign off on the attempt. The limited hotel cable offered no cartoons at all, not even animé. The only *Trek* episode I could find was "Spock's Brain." I don't know why I was surprised. It had been that kind of week.

The hotel, however, did offer free wireless access. I set up the laptop, which of course lacked the listing of all my usual search sites. I could remember most of them—a good thing, too, because I realized I could look for events that might be considered evidence of those deviant world levels. Since the Agency laptop had TranceWeb installed, I logged on and left an e-mail for NumbersGrrl. After I logged off, I got a temporary Yahoo address and hit the surf. I was just taking notes on one interesting "haunted" hotel in the Midwest when I heard Ari come out of the bathroom.

"Find anything?" he said from behind me.

"Yeah, actually, I did." I turned on my chair and forgot what I was going to say.

Ari was wearing only a towel, wrapped and knotted around his waist. Lamplight glistened on the patches of damp on his chest and back. He picked up a pair of his briefs from the chair by the bed, then looked at me with his head tilted to one side.

"Is something wrong?" he said.

"Oh, no."

"All right, then. Start thinking about where you want to go for dinner."

"I'm not hungry yet."

All at once he caught the drift and grinned at me. "We can always have room service," he said, "later."

Fortunately the hotel's room service stayed available till eleven. Ari fell asleep almost as soon as we'd finished eating. As I was putting the dirty dishes out in the hall, I saw the Chaos critter again. It sidled up to the remains of my salad and whined at me.

"Go ahead," I said. "You can eat that."

I'd hidden a half-eaten roll in a napkin just so Ari wouldn't insist on me finishing it. I unwrapped it and put it out for the creature next to the salad bowl. I left it chowing down and returned to the laptop and my research.

Hauntings have a great many explanations, simple fraud in a lot of cases, brought on by the perpetrator's desire to be famous or to get money for their story out of the junk press. Memory combined with sincere longing produces "ghosts," too, when a person sees their dead partner sitting in his favorite chair or hears her voice in the other room. In my early days with the Agency, I'd researched three cases that really did appear to be actual ghosts, all of them violently dead, but even those might have been time-stream scars rather than visitations.

The so-called hauntings that interested me at the moment fell into a different, very rare category. Glimpses and voices, we can call them, of different worlds—the sound of someone walking in the room above, or a glance out the window into a different seeming view, an argument dimly heard on the other side of a bedroom wall. A woman reported standing in a shopping mall and seeing a man walk straight toward her, as if she were invisible; at the last moment she stepped aside and saw him vanish. A teacher and her entire class heard a child crying in the cloakroom of her schoolroom, but when she looked, no one was there.

I gathered a handful of these events, if we can call them events. They all had one thing in common. They'd happened in complicated spaces, a convoluted mall, an old school building bristling with new construction, a sports stadium, a hotel. The locations might have been analogs, in a sense, for those deviant levels that "shot off in all directions," as Y's expert had told him.

The role of the portal and its energy field in the case I had in hand puzzled me. The only theory I could come up with was that Doyle and Johnson had somehow invented an artificial way to skip from one deviant level to another and back again. They must have had some sort of talent or access to information about the process to even think of the idea in the first place. If they could control the skips, they could bring their drugs from Kurdistan to the United States without ever going

through Customs simply by going into their own world
and then out again into ours.

I managed to convert all these observations to reasonable prose and e-mailed them off to NumbersGrrl to
get her opinion. By then the clock read one in the morning. I turned off the laptop and crawled back into bed. In
his sleep Ari rolled over and reached for me. I cuddled
close and drowsed off to the sound of his heart beating.

Morning light and the noise of a busy hotel woke me
early. Ari had already gotten up and dressed; he was sitting on the other side of the room talking on his cell
phone. I staggered past him to go take a shower. When
I was done, I put on the glen plaid trousers and a dark
blue wrap top.

Ari was talking on the phone in Hebrew by the time
I left the bathroom. Though he never shouted or even
raised his voice, I could feel his SPP: pure anger poured
out of him. Finally he clicked off with a snarl.

"What's wrong?" I said.

"Nothing." He paused for a couple of seconds.
"Procedural difficulties." Another pause. "But I had a
good talk with Sanchez earlier. They're holding a news
conference in a couple of hours to ask for citizen help
in finding the Silver Bullet Killer. They're going to flood
the TV news services with pictures of Johnson and a description of Doyle, offer a reward, that kind of thing. A
friend of the Romeros has persuaded the bank he works
for to donate thirty-five thousand. The mayor's fund is
putting in ten thousand more."

"That should bring in a few tips."

"Let's hope." He stood up and stretched. "They want
me to appear at the press event."

"Saying what?"

"That the suspects are also wanted in Israel for
murder."

"Both suspects?"

"I doubt it, but it could be true." Ari shrugged. "Sanchez has the right idea. He wants to stress that these men are too dangerous for anyone but the police to approach."

"Now there I agree one hundred percent."

I decided to try an LDRS for Johnson before we checked out. If he tracked me to the hotel, we'd be long gone before he arrived. As soon as I started to draw, my hand sketched out the view from the backseat of a small car. I picked up the sensation of eating greasy food, too, some kind of fast food eggy horror, and the definite stink of an unwashed human.

"I think Johnson's living in a car," I told Ari. "But damn it, I can't focus on what it looks like. He's too busy stuffing his face."

"Well, can you try again later? That's very significant."

"Yeah, I will, but we'd better get on the road."

They held the press conference in a bleak wood-paneled room at the Hall of Justice, a concrete slab of a building down near the Morrison office. I sat well away from the clustered cameras and microphones and watched while Sanchez spoke at length, announcing the reward. Ari added a few sentences about the murders on his home turf, then mentioned Michael and displayed his picture as another possible victim.

In that building, with cops swarming all around, I felt safe enough to run a full Search Mode for Johnson. I picked up danger loud and clear to the west-northwest on the inner compass. When I tried to refine the sensation, I felt the greasy anxiety I'd come to associate with the murdering bastard. While I should have stopped the scan immediately, I had picked up something so interesting that I let it run for a brief few moments more.

The anxiety I felt was coming from Johnson, not me. He was so intensely preoccupied with something that I risked probing a little deeper. His thoughts circled around and around the bite Mary Rose had given him. Soon, in less than three weeks, the moon would return to full. He would know, then, if he'd been infected or not.

Next I searched for Doyle, only to run into a solid Shield Persona. I tried every trick I knew, but I never managed to break it down. I did receive a faint impression of gloating, a childish satisfaction that Johnson might be going to suffer what he himself had had to suffer for years. I broke off the attempt rather than subject myself to that twisted sentiment any longer.

As soon as the conference ended, a uniformed officer trotted up to Sanchez and Ari, who listened intently to what he had to say. Ari filled me in as we walked back to the car, parked in an underground garage.

"Forensics came through," Ari said. "They found some prints on the windmill goods that match Johnson's. He—and probably Doyle—put those things inside it."

"That's weird. That's totally weird."

"Everything about this case is. Why are you surprised?"

"You have a point. Unfortunately."

I made another stab at finding Johnson as soon as we reached the car. I sat in the backseat with my pad and crayons. Johnson seemed to be on his guard by then, but I did see a few faint images—a steering wheel, a misty view framed by a metal rim, glimpses of a dashboard. I tore off the sheet of paper and tried again with Doyle, only to get the same kind of scribbles minus the steering wheel but plus a stretch of blue metal. Wherever they were, they were sitting in the blue sedan together.

"This is not real helpful." I put my supplies back in the tote bag. "I'm just surprised they haven't left town."

"So am I," Ari said. "Arrogant little sods, aren't they?"

"Yeah, apparently so. Unless they can't leave for some reason."

I changed seats to the front, buckled on the seat belt, and realized what I'd just said.

"Ari, I need to get back to the doorway in the park."

"Are they there?"

"No. I just need another look at it."

Although downtown the sun shone, out by the Portals of the Past the fog lingered. The gray sky reflected on gray water. The ducks quacked as they glided back and forth out in the pond. The marble pillars and lintel stood unchanged. As I walked up the steps, I perceived no energy field whatsoever, but when I stood directly under the lintel and held my hands out to the sides like antennae, I felt the barest trace of a very faint wisp of energy.

"Hah! I thought so."

I returned to solid ground and a puzzled, shivering Ari.

"You should have worn that sweater," I said. "Or jumper. Whatever you call it."

"It's in the boot. I'll fetch it in a moment. What did you pick up in there?"

"The energy field's gone. If it's regenerating, it's doing so really slowly." I realized that I'd never told Ari about Y's theory. "The Agency thinks this thing leads into deviant levels of the multiverse, aka parallel worlds. Do you know what those are?"

"I've seen them referred to in science fiction films." His voice turned weary. "Don't tell me those are real along with everything else."

"I don't know if they are or not. No one at the Agency's sure about any of this. But just suppose for a minute that they are real. Now, suppose Johnson or Doyle comes from such a level. He could have turned this portal into some kind of device that lets them go back and forth."

"Very well. I'm supposing. Carry on."

"Michael may have the ability to move between

levels on his own, on the natch, as it were. If Michael walked through the gate, he'd give the energy field a double blast of psychic power—Qi, as we call it. He'd short the thing out. Now the portal's nonfunctional, just as if that had happened."

Ari blinked, looked briefly distressed, then smiled his tiger's smile. "Which leaves Johnson and Doyle trapped here without their escape route."

"If our suppositions hold, it's no wonder they haven't left the Bay Area. They need this gate, and they must be hoping to fix it, or maybe they're hoping it will regenerate the field on its own."

"Do you think it will?"

"I don't know. I hope so, because this theory means that Michael's trapped on the other side of it."

"I thought you said he could come through on his own."

"*Maybe* he can. Even if he can, does he know it? Can a person with his talent just come back anywhere, or do they need another gate of some kind? No one knows. This is all new territory for the Agency."

Ari frowned down at the ground. He absently kicked a stray eucalyptus pod, then looked up.

"I remember now," Ari said. *"Kefitzat haderach."*

"Say what?"

"It's a term from a midrash. It means "a shortening of the way," a shortcut, I suppose you'd call it. It's one of the things that Reb Ezekiel claimed he could teach. Teleportation of a sort, my father told me. But now I wonder." He nodded at the portal. "It could easily have meant something like this."

"If you could pop into a gate and pop out somewhere else, yeah, that would shorten the journey, all right. That's fascinating. I just wish I knew more. If Sanchez can round them up, maybe we can make Johnson and his lupine pal give us some answers."

LICENSE TO ENSORCELL   223

"True. The police might be able to make some sort of bargain."

"I was thinking of a more direct method."

"Nola!" Ari's voice turned sharp. "I know you love your brother, but I'm not going to do anything unethical."

"Not beating them up or anything. Sheer psychic talent."

"Oh. Very well, then."

He didn't realize that if I used my talents to force a confession, I'd be doing something as unethical in my little world as physical torture would be in his. You're slipping into Chaos thinking again, O'Grady, I told myself. Watch it!

"There's one thing that makes me doubt our suppositions," I said, "and that's how public this place is. You'd think they'd rent a house and build their device inside out of sight."

"This portal might have some particular property they need," Ari said.

"Could be." I wondered if Y could figure out a way to analyze the portal without attracting the wrong kind of attention. "Either that, or the theory's not valid."

"Well, that's always a possibility." Ari glowered at the lintel for a moment. "Vitrified marble."

"Say what?"

"Marble is limestone transformed by high heat, usually volcanic action. This particular bit's been through a second vitrification, thanks to the fire in 1906. There might be some sort of crystallization that transformed the stone into something they could work with."

"I'm impressed," I said. "Science isn't my strong point."

"I've noticed. But then again, it's not mine, either. I suppose it would be unethical to nick a bit off a pillar and send it to a lab back home."

"Not a good idea, no. The citizenry just raised a lot of money to repair the thing."

"Oh, very well." He paused, glancing around. "Let's go. There's too much cover around here. I don't want anyone taking another shot at you."

"I'd just as soon avoid it myself."

"That's why you need me for a minder."

"A what?"

"Sorry. A keeper, I believe the American word is."

"Very funny. Ha-ha. Let's get out of here."

He grinned at me and caught my hand as we walked together back to the car.

CHAPTER 10

ALTHOUGH ARI REFRAINED FROM telling me where we were going, he'd driven only two blocks before I realized that we were heading for my apartment. I concentrated on images of the hotel in Daly City where we'd spent Monday night, just in case Johnson came snooping around the aura field, but I never felt his greasy touch upon my mind.

We found a place to park up from Judah. I took one piece of luggage, the suitcase containing Pat's journals, with me, and Ari brought along the sample case. When we came around the corner, I saw that plywood still filled in the bay window. Ari opened the street door leading to the stairs, then stepped sharply to one side. Since no hail of bullets greeted him, we went in. We'd just gotten to the landing when Mrs. Z opened her door with a blare of TV noise. She was wearing the orange muumuu that clashed with her purple hair.

"You back?" she said.

"Yeah, but I don't know if I'll stay," I said. "I see that George hasn't finished the repair."

"Well, he was supposed to show up today, but you know how he is. What was all that noise last night?"

"Noise? I wasn't here."

"You weren't?" She let her mouth hang open. "Oh, oh, well, I suppose, oh . . ."

I could feel Ari go tense in sudden alarm. He laid a heavy hand on my shoulder.

"Let me just take a look." He set his sample case down on a step. "Give me that suitcase."

I did, then waited on the landing with Mrs. Z while he went upstairs. He put his key in the lock, turned it, then swung up the suitcase like a shield before his face and kicked the door open. Nothing blew up except his temper. He swore so violently that Mrs. Z began to dither even though neither of us understood a word he was saying. I ignored her, snagged the sample case, and trotted halfway up the stairs.

"You can come up," he said. "They're gone."

They? I hurried up the rest of the way and looked into the apartment. All my worldly goods lay strewn across the floor, the couch cushions, the books, the china cat figurines, some of my clothes from the bedroom, even. When we went inside, I put the heavy sample case down and stood there staring at the mess. I could see that every kitchen drawer had been emptied out, and the fridge, too. I was expecting that they would have taken my computer and the TV, but the electronics all sat where I'd left them. I pointed them out to Ari.

"They were in a hurry," he said. "Too much of one to even stage a proper burglary."

The searchers had hit the bedroom as well, stripped down the bed, tipped up the mattress, emptied the drawers of my dresser, thrown the clothes out of my closet. I had two pieces of good jewelry—some diamond earrings and a gold and opal brooch that had belonged to my grandmother. They sat in their little velvet boxes in a corner with the dust bunnies. I picked them up and put them back onto the dresser.

"What a mess!" I said. "Doyle must have been looking for Pat's journals."

"Which you took with us. Good."

From behind us I heard an "Oh, my gawd!" We returned to the living room to find Mrs. Z staring horrified at the disarray.

"Why didn't you call the police?" Ari said. "When you heard the noises."

"Well, I didn't think it was, oh, I suppose I should have, oh, er, it wasn't that loud. I just thought it was you two doing, oh, well, I don't know, something."

Ari smacked his right fist into the palm of his left hand and snarled as if he were thinking murderous thoughts. She stepped back fast and pulled herself up to her full height, such as it was.

"And here I thought you'd be a nice quiet tenant." Mrs. Z shot me a dirty look, then turned and shuffled away. At the door she paused. "First the window and now this."

I heard her going down the stairs; her TV blared and cats meowed as she entered her apartment. The door slammed, the lock clicked, the noise dimmed.

"What do you bet she raises the rent?" I said. "But Jeezus H, as Uncle Jim would say. We could have had the bastards if she'd only called the cops."

"Maybe." Ari took a deep, calming breath. "We might have had a dead police officer, too, if a patrolman had come up those stairs alone."

"That's true. We should call them now, I guess."

"Yes. I'll just get Sanchez on the phone."

More police, more forensics techs, this time to strew fingerprint powder around and make the mess worse. The police interviewed Mrs. Z, who gave them no useful information. She did whine about tenants who disrespected her property. Once the police left, Ari and I stood in the living room and looked at the disaster zone.

"It's going to take a while to clean all this up," I said.

"We've got to be out of here before dark," Ari said. "Here, I'll put the spoiled food into the garbage. Why don't you find the things you want from the bedroom, and then we'll leave."

I did pick up the broken pieces of the various cat figurines that Kathleen had given me over the years. I hummed "Taps" while I dropped them, one at a time, into the wastepaper basket. In the bedroom I tipped the mattress back onto the box spring, then began throwing clothes back into drawers. Mostly I needed clean underwear. As I was searching through the heaps, I found the black album about Pat's murder. I put that aside to take with me just as Ari walked in.

"I'm surprised they left it." Ari nodded at the album.

"I put a Chaos ward on it a long time ago," I said. "They probably never even saw it."

"What?"

"If you put a Chaos ward on something, a dedicated follower of Chaos will have trouble seeing it. It's not that the thing's invisible. It's just hard to notice. The problem is that the wards only work on small items. Small non-living items, that is. A dedicated Harmony person has a kind of built-in ward."

"I'll have to take your word for that." Ari scowled at the album as if it had just betrayed him.

"This particular ward tells us a lot, though. Johnson and Doyle are dedicated Chaos people, all right, but at a pretty low level. The wards wouldn't deflect an ordinary rip-off artist or a Chaos master."

I returned to scrounging for underwear. I heard Ari whistle under his breath and turned to see him holding a pair of black thigh-high stockings, the kind with built-in garters at the top, so you can leave them on.

"Would you like to see those modeled?" I said.

Ari looked at me and blushed scarlet.

I took that as a yes and tucked them into the suitcase.

We ended up at another franchise motor inn that night, this one out on Van Ness Avenue, all beiges and browns and comfortable enough. Once we had a room, Ari went back down to the lobby to flash his Interpol ID around and show the staff the pictures of Johnson. I used the Agency laptop to log into TranceWeb. First I filed a brief report on the contents of the windmill. I had a pair of long e-mails from NumbersGrrl that began to make the entire concept of the multiverse a lot clearer, even without the math. Once I answered those, I returned to searching the net for hauntings of the correct type. In about twenty minutes Ari came back.

"No luck," he remarked. "But sooner or later, if the police keep showing these pictures around, we'll find someone who's seen Johnson."

"I hope it's sooner, before our scumbag kills someone else."

My cell phone chimed. Aunt Eileen again, I figured, and I answered. No one spoke in return.

"Hello?" I said again.

Nothing but silence at first, and then a whisper-faint trace of a word that I couldn't quite make out—yet it seemed that I should know it.

"Hello?" I snapped. "Who is this?"

The whisper again, slightly louder—was it "help" that the person was saying? The call went dead. I clicked off my phone and looked up to find Ari staring at me.

"Do you think that was Johnson?" he said.

"No. I don't feel slimed. I don't know who it was. It was a terrible connection, and then the call got dropped." Michael, I thought. Oh, my God, could that have been Michael?

The phone chimed again. I grabbed it and opened the line.

"Hello?"

"Nola? It's Kathleen."

"Say, did you try to call me just now?"

"Yeah, but the call got dropped."

So much for the Michael theory. Obviously I had ghostly glimpses on the brain.

Since Jack always watched the TV news, Kathleen had learned the hard way that Michael had disappeared. I was surprised that Aunt Eileen or Mother hadn't called her; she was angry about the same thing.

"It's not fair," Kathleen snapped. "Just because I don't live in the city anymore, I'm out of the loop."

"Come on," I said. "Did you really want Mother to call you? She's in full cry havoc and let slip the dogs of war mode."

Silence, then: "No, oh, okay, but Aunt Eileen—"

"— is worried sick." I broke in. "Look, why don't you take over? E-mail everyone else and make sure they know."

"Good idea. I want to feel like I'm doing something."

I could understand that.

When we finished talking, I found myself thinking of Sneezy. Had she seen the nightly news, too? I visualized her face, peering out of that ridiculous black hood, and tried an SM: Personnel. I picked her up immediately, because she was terrified. Although I couldn't be sure, I got the impression that she was pacing back and forth in her elegant living room while she trembled on the verge of tears. I started to withdraw the search; then on an impulse I sent her words: *Don't confront him. Just don't confront him. Pretend it's okay.*

I had never had the slightest success with the various telepathy experiments the Agency researchers have tried, and I still haven't to this day, but that night I could have sworn she heard me, because I felt her surprise.

I returned to being aware of the hotel room and realized that Ari was staring at me.

"Uh," I said, "was I talking aloud?"

"Yes. I should be used to it by now, I suppose." He returned to stuffing a hotel laundry bag full of dirty clothes while he talked. "When I finish this, you need to eat something. Think about what you'd like."

Although I started to argue, I realized that he was right, because I felt as if I might float out of my body at any minute. He put the bag outside the door just as the maid came by to pick it up. When I heard him ensure that the laundry would be done by morning by tipping her extravagantly, I wished I had his kind of expense account instead of mine, which involved monthly haggling with the Agency's accounting department. When he came back in, he locked the door and put on the chain.

"They do have room service here," Ari said. "Shall I order some dinner?"

"Oh, I don't know. How hungry are you?"

Ari smiled and ran a hand over his chin. "I need to shave," he said.

"Okay. You do that while I change."

"Change?"

"I brought those stockings."

By the time we finished dinner, somewhere around ten o'clock, the late evening news shows had begun on the local TV stations. We sybaritically lay in bed while Ari flipped channels to see how much coverage the morning's press conference was getting. Plenty, as it turned out, and several anchormen used phrases like "as we told you earlier" to indicate coverage on the all-important dinner hour broadcasts. Pictures of Johnson and speculations about Doyle showed up on every channel.

"I figured they'd take this seriously," I remarked during a commercial. "But I'm glad to see it."

"So am I." Ari started to turn the set off, then hesitated as video of the marble portal appeared on the screen.

"Put on the sound, okay?" I said.

Vic Yee, a local investigative reporter and one of the best, stood in front of the gate to nowhere. "A secret meeting with the mayor today," he was saying. "A reliable witness who asked to remain anonymous told me that the group of military officers met with the mayor for several hours. The fate of this San Francisco landmark hangs in the balance. No one could come up with a reasonable theory of why the Army would want to impound the Portals of the Past, but there was general agreement that the talks were heading in that direction."

The anchorman chimed in with a question or two about financial compensation, which, Yee guessed, would be forthcoming. The news show cut to commercial. Ari doused the sound again.

"Impound it?" I said. "They must mean dig it up and carry it away."

"I'd say so, yes. I take it that your military has heard about this gate theory."

I hesitated, wondering how honest I could be, but after all, Israel was a military ally of the United States. If Ari passed along what little I knew, I'd hardly be betraying my country.

"I'd say that's likely." I compromised on half-truths. "Why else would they want the portal? It's really obscure. I'll bet that half the people in San Francisco don't even know it exists."

"It's not a brilliant public monument, no. Ugly, really."

Ari switched off the television, set the remote on the nightstand beside the bed, and reached for me. Tempted though I was, I rolled away and sat up.

"I've got to check one more thing," I said. "Be right back."

He shrugged and lay down again.

I wandered into the middle of the room away from the distractions he offered. I took a deep breath and tried another SM: P for Sneezy. I picked her up on the inner radar right away. Her signal came in so strongly that I tried overlaying it with an SM: Location. She lived straight west of my current location at a distance of a couple miles, nearly to the ocean. Sea Cliff, I thought. A fancy house in the Sea Cliff neighborhood would fit the glimpses that the LDRS had given me.

Although I continued to pick up Sneezy herself, the impression of place dimmed and faded out. A man came into her view, a man who frightened her. He'd shielded himself from me so successfully that I knew it had to be Doyle.

I broke off the SM: P and turned around to see that Ari had fallen asleep. His travel clock on the nightstand read midnight. I retrieved my cell phone from the pile of clothing on the floor beside the bed and took it into the bathroom where I could talk without waking him. The police had set up an automated anonymous tip line, which I used to leave the information that "the dark-haired dope dealer" had been seen driving around Sea Cliff with a blonde woman. I threw in the blue late-model sedan while I was at it. If they picked up Johnson by "mistake," so much the better.

Although I considered filing a quick report to the Agency, I was yawning too hard to think. I turned off the lights and went back to bed.

In the morning, I tried scanning again for both our perps only to be blocked in all directions. From Sneezy I did pick up a trace of fear but nothing more.

"They're really on to me," I told Ari. "They've thrown up some kind of shield that I just can't get through. That's one of the hazards of my job, I'm afraid. We're generally dealing with people or things that have the same talents we do. Otherwise we could just leave them to the cops."

"Things?" Ari said. "What do you mean, things?"

"You don't want to know. Let's just say werewolves are the least of them, okay?"

Ari opened his mouth to argue, then thought better of it. "Very well," he said. "What about breakfast?"

"I'm not—well, yeah, I am hungry. I have to admit it."

I was expecting him to make some smart crack, but he contented himself with a smug smile.

After we ate, I decided to increase my chances of getting a successful LDRS on Johnson and Doyle by returning to the Portals of the Past. Even though the pillars no longer functioned as a gate, they seemed to lend their trace energy to my talents. We entered the park at Tenth Avenue on the north side and drove down Kennedy toward the lake where the pillars stood. For a Thursday morning the traffic seemed oddly heavy, and the closer we got to the lake, the worse it became. Ari finally pulled over some distance from the monument and parked just east of Transverse Drive.

"We'll make better time if we walk," he said.

As soon as I got out of the car, I heard a distant voice speaking over some sort of amplification equipment—a cheap one, whatever it was. The echo and reverb distorted the words beyond decipherment.

"Don't tell me someone's giving a free concert!" I said. "I won't be able to concentrate with rock music blaring."

"It's a peculiar time of day for a concert," Ari said.

As we headed west toward the lake, the voice from the loudspeaker gradually came into focus. "Say no to imperialism on a local level" was the first full sentence I heard. My heart sank. "The arrogance of the military needs to be reined in," the speaker continued. "Are we going to let them rip off part of our history?"

"No!" A crowd answered, a pretty good-sized crowd from the sound of it. "Army out!"

"Crud," I said. "A demonstration."

At that point the sidewalk rounded a curve and led us to the lakeshore. Across the rippling water I could see the crowd clustering around the pillars and spilling onto the paths beside the lake. Ari raised his hands in front of his face and peered between them to isolate portions of the view, then began counting the demonstrators in groups of ten. He'd been trained in crowd control some-where along the way, I supposed.

"About three hundred," he said at last. "Not bad for this time of day and such short notice."

"That's my hometown for you. Need a political rally? We provide express service."

"Everyone looks so respectable." Ari sounded disap-pointed. "I'm surprised."

True enough, most of the people in attendance wore casual but clean and up-to-date clothing. I noticed that a lot of them had gray hair, and among the men were a sizable number of gray beards, too, but on the whole the crowd could have been waiting to get into a day base-ball game. I glanced around and saw a TV news truck parked across the street from the lake. The reporter and the cameraman were leaning against the truck and sip-ping coffee with a disappointed air.

"Those reports of crazed hippies in San Francisco have been greatly exaggerated," I said. "That all ended thirty years ago."

Signs there were in profusion, though, most of them carrying some version of the message: "Keep our por-tals in the park." I even spotted a couple of retro peace symbols. A youngish woman in a gray tweed skirt and turquoise silk blouse trotted up to us and held out a flyer printed on pink paper.

"Would you like one?" she said politely.

"Yes, thanks." I took it and noted the headline, "MILI-TARY SPENDING OUT OF CONTROL."

"You know, I never even knew this pillar thing was

here," she said. "But I don't see why the army should get
to have it."

She trotted off again. Just when I was about to pro-
nounce the demonstration boring, four beaten-up old
cars drove up and parked right out in the middle of
the street, where they blocked the westbound traffic. A
swarm of young men dressed in black, with their faces
half-covered with bandannas and ski masks, emerged
and headed for the lake. As they walked, they chanted,
"No army no," at the top of their lungs.

"Time to leave, Ari," I shouted over the noise. "The
anarchists have arrived."

The speaker with the portable bullhorn asked the lads
in black to be quiet, but they drowned him out with random catcalls and began to push their way into the crowd.
The TV reporter and cameraman put down their coffee
and grabbed their equipment. Ari tapped my arm to get
my attention, then jerked his head in the direction of
Transverse and our car. I let him lead me away just as the
demonstrators started booing the anarchists. The formerly
peaceful crowd started to seethe like a pot of boiling water. Out in the street car horns blared as the two-way traffic tried to make its way around the abandoned cars.

We'd gone maybe a hundred yards when the chanting died away. I paused and looked back. A phalanx of
gray-haired men had surrounded the anarchists and
were marching in lockstep toward the sidewalk, slowly,
deliberately, and smiling all the while. One step at a time
they backed the lads in black right up to the edge of the
street. Inside this human corral the anarchists pushed
this way and that, but they were too disorganized to
mount an effective countermove. On the lake side of the
human clot, other people hurried to join the grays, as I
began calling them. They all stood quietly, saying nothing, merely thickening the lines around the disruption so
that none of the anarchists could break through.

I glanced at Ari and saw him watching with a half-smile, partly surprise, partly admiration.

"Years of practice!" I told him.

In the distance off to the west I heard police sirens coming. The anarchists made a break for their cars, pushing toward the street side of the human corral. The demonstrators stepped away and let them go. By the time the police arrived, the lads in black had taken refuge inside their cars. They might have just driven away if the police had only left well enough alone.

Four squad cars in all pulled up. The police had a bullhorn of their own, and they used it to demand the crowd disperse. Apparently the organizers hadn't bothered to get a permit. Most of the demonstrators did as they were asked, fading into the shrubbery or striding around the lake to the sidewalk. The anarchists clambered out of their cars and began shouting at the cops.

As we hurried away down Kennedy Drive, I glanced back again to see the cops shoving a couple of the guys in black up against a squad car while the other anarchists jeered and swore. A shower of rocks sailed through the air. I stopped looking. I knew that I'd see the violence on the TV news, while the peaceful demonstration would go unremarked. We reached our car safely, but even though we'd left the trouble behind, Ari insisted I roll up the window and lock the door on my side. We could still hear shouting, horns honking, and the police bullhorn.

"I've never seen anything like that," Ari said. "Those older men, that is. I've seen far too many of the other sort."

"I'll bet. Those guys were good, all right. Old hippies, probably. Aunt Eileen told me that there used to be people called monitors for the big marches. They knew how to keep things under control."

"I can't imagine your aunt marching in the streets."

"She was just a kid at the time, but the older O'Briens

were all involved in the peace movement. A lot of Catholic families were."

More sirens wailed, these coming from the east. We watched a shiny black police van rush by, most likely crammed with cops in riot gear. The anarchists had gotten what they wanted: a full-scale incident.

"Once this current case is over," I said to Ari, "I'll have to investigate those guys in black. I wonder if they've got full-blown Chaos affiliations."

"I should think it's obvious they do. They are anarchists, after all."

"Yeah, but the question of who's affiliated with what is never that simple. Look at those cops. They're part of an institution that's just as obviously aligned with Order, right? So what did they do? Waded right in and ended up causing a Chaotic situation."

"Well, you have a point in this particular case. An excess of zeal on their part. But the police have the right to break up an illegal demonstration."

"Illegal? In the States we have the right to peaceful assembly. We also pay for this park with taxes. You could argue that the demand for a permit is what's illegal here."

Ari drummed his fingers on the steering wheel while he considered. For a moment I thought he was going to argue further, but he shrugged and glanced my way with a carefully neutral expression.

"Where to?" Ari said. "You can't work here."

"That's for sure. Okay, take Transverse out of the park. I've got an idea."

I gave Ari directions to the Sea Cliff neighborhood, which borders on Land's End at the northwestern edge of the city. If I could pinpoint where Sneezy lived, I figured, the police could lay a trap for Doyle.

We drove out Thirtieth Avenue to Lake, then wound along the twisting, terraced stretch of that street, lined with big homes on thick green lawns that must have cost a small fortune in water bills. This little enclave caters to the well-heeled bourgeoisie, successful orthodontists and the like, rather than the really rich. If ostentation can be quiet, then Sea Cliff has quiet ostentation down pat. We ended up on Sea Cliff Avenue itself, which marked the edge of things urban. Ari parked in a small lot the city had provided for those who came for the view.

Since I'd run into Doyle's shield earlier, I decided to get out of the car. The metal frame would impede me enough, I figured, to make breaking through his defenses more difficult. I walked over to a chain-link safety fence that blocked access to the dangerously uneven cliff top and the straight drop down to the ocean. Even the weeds on the other side of the fence looked trimmed and well-watered.

The big houses, some starkly modern, some a vaguely Mediterranean style, all of them smooth with stucco walls and big flat windows, sprawled up the hill behind us. Ari joined me and stood gaping at the view. We'd come west beyond the Golden Gate Bridge and were overlooking an inlet of the ocean, a dark winter blue, not the bay, although the Marin headlands lay shadowed by fog to the north. I pointed out the bridge itself off to the east, wreathed in sea mist. A pair of brown pelicans flew by, skimming the water far below our man-made perch.

"This really is an amazing city," Ari said. "You turn the corner of a city block, and you're faced with raw nature."

"California's all like that," I said. "It grew out of the wilderness, and one of these days it'll fade back into it, too. Human things do that. We're all only temporary, humans and our cities both."

"Oh, yes. Not that we like thinking about it, but living in the Middle East you can't escape it. Jerusalem may be five thousand years old, but all around it are the ruins of places that would be even older—if they still existed."

While I got ready to work, he leaned against the hood of the car and looked back at the view of the bridge and the misty bay beyond. I steadied my mind and did SM: I—first for Doyle, then Johnson. I picked them up easily because they were distracted, arguing again, nattering back and forth like whiny children.

"Ari," I said. "They're not far from here."

He pulled his phone out of his pocket. "Can you give me a direction?"

"Let me try for Sneezy."

As soon as I started the Search Mode: Personnel, I knew. I picked up nothing, not fear, not nerves, not her mind, nothing. My throat suddenly ached like the worst case of strep in the world.

"The bastard!" I croaked. "He strangled her."

Ari swore in Hebrew and clicked on his phone. As soon as I broke off my attempt to reach her, the pain in my throat disappeared. I'd picked up a time-stream scar, but most likely a very short-lived one. Although Ari still held his phone, he'd not dialed it. He stood with his head cocked, listening to some distant sound. In a moment I heard it too: police sirens, coming closer. His phone rang with mangled Bach.

"Nathan here," Ari said, then paused, listening. "What's the location on that?" Another long pause. "I'll meet you there." He put the phone away, then turned to me. "A dead woman in a house on Lake Street. Strangled in her bed. Her housecleaner found her when she came to work."

"Why does Sanchez think this murder's related to the others? I mean, I know it is, but how does he know?"

"The killer left a silver bullet on the pillow beside her."

"The bastard!" I would have said more, but fury made it impossible.

We drove over to the house that had formerly belonged to Sneezy, a two story pale pink stucco number on the flat just at the edge of the neighborhood. It sat behind the long lawn I'd seen in my earlier scan. Even without the address we would have known it by the bevy of squad cars parked in front. As I looked around at the other houses on the street, all of them two and three stories of smoothly painted stucco, with heavy doors and gated entranceways, I thought of fortresses, but I saw women behind windows, half-hidden by drapes, peering out at this disruption in their privileged midst. I could feel their fear without even trying.

We found a parking spot about halfway down the block. I stayed in the car and let Ari go alone to speak with Sanchez. I was remembering Y's casual remark about our policy, to leave criminals to the local police if at all possible. Well, it wasn't possible, not anymore. I had wanted to obey the policy, to leave Johnson and Doyle to the police—I included Ari in that category—and put all my energy into finding my brother. But Doyle and Johnson had just added another of my fellow citizens to their list of victims: first Mary Rose, then the driver of the carjacked truck, next the obstetrics nurse, and now Sneezy, who had taken Doyle into her home and her bed only to end up strangled.

Although I couldn't have given a rational reason, I knew that Doyle had killed her. Sometimes, like Jerry, I do just "know" things, usually things I wish I didn't. Johnson also remained dangerous. He might decide he needed to lay down another false clue by killing someone equally innocent. Since I'd tested the strength of his talents, I knew that the police alone would never catch him—not without me.

Ari returned in about fifteen minutes. Sanchez had everything well in hand, he told me.

"The housecleaner's hysterical, of course," Ari said.

"She apparently had been in the house for some time before she discovered the body."

"Poor woman! That would creep most people out, all right, to find out you'd been busily cleaning away with a corpse in another room. Did Sanchez tell you anything about the victim?"

"A divorcee in her late forties with plenty of money, apparently. The housecleaner told him that the dead woman had been lonely but recently had found a boyfriend."

"Doyle," I said. "I wish I could prove that for a court of law."

"The fingerprints will, eventually. Forensics is dusting down the room. They'll match up with those they obtained from the windmill." Ari leaned forward and put the car key in the ignition. "Shall we go?"

"In a minute. I want to risk an LDRS first."

Even if Johnson or Doyle did pinpoint my location, the knowledge would do them no good, because we'd be leaving. I sat in the backseat with my pad and crayons and thought about our pair of killers. Johnson came in loud and clear.

Fear—not mine, his—a stomach-wrenching panic slammed into my mind. My hand grabbed a crayon and swept a gray line halfway across the page. A black scribble, next, and rage poured over me, a waterfall torrent so strong that my hand spasmed. He hated Doyle, raged and hated because his former partner had brought him to the place where the terror lived.

I turned the page and went on drawing, lots of green, tangled branches, the blue car speeding off. All at once I felt Johnson sense my probe. I wrested away my end of the connection, but he tried to follow. I began to count down from a hundred in threes. By the time I reached thirty-seven, he'd given up.

I got into the front seat and handed the drawings to Ari.

"I think Doyle's driving away in this one," I said. "The picture represents something Johnson saw, not something Johnson did."

Ari looked at it, then punched in a number on the car's phone.

"Nathan from Interpol," Ari said. "Our government contact has given us a partial license plate on the blue sedan." He paused. "Right. That's the first car Johnson was spotted driving, but we think Doyle has it now."

Ari continued talking, pausing often to let his auditor take notes. I looked at the second drawing and saw two letters and a number scrawled across the blue shape. When I turned back to the first page, I realized that the gray line and the black scribble defined, roughly of course, a rifle. When thieves fall out, it's bad, I thought. When Chaos thieves do, it's worse.

"Armed and dangerous, yes," Ari said. "I'll check in with you later." He hung up.

"That was clever." I laid a fingertip on my scribble of the blue car's license plate. "Letting Sanchez think this came from a satellite or whatever they use these days."

"You don't know?"

"Of course not. Ari, I know what I know real well. Beyond that—" I shrugged and spread empty hands.

"And your agency lets you out on your own?"

"Out of what?"

"The asylum, of course." He was smiling at me.

"Oh," I said. "You're joking with me for a change."

"Trying, anyway. You were looking rather grim."

"I'm feeling rather grim. If it weren't against my principles, I'd say I'm in the mood for revenge, and I don't care if it's served warm or cold."

He looked at me with his gorgeous dark eyes narrowed in puzzlement.

"It's a *Star Trek* reference," I said. "A Klingon proverb."

"A Klingon—" Ari paused for a deep breath. "If you're done here, I'll drive on."

"Please do."

Whether it was a case of revenge or justice, I'd done enough probing for the moment. If the police could bring them in, so much the better. They had until tomorrow morning, I decided, before I ran out of patience.

"Has Sanchez told you anything about the Persian white angle?" I said.

"No," he said. "Only that they're still pursuing it."

"Okay, then I'll call Jerry again." I glanced at my watch. "It's only two o'clock. He should be awake in another hour or so."

Ari knew where he wanted to go next; he started the car and drove off without asking for directions. I realized that once he'd visited a given area, he could remember it without prompting. We ended up back in Daly City, at the same motor inn we'd stayed in before, though we did get a different, somewhat larger room. While Ari stowed the luggage in the closet, I looked out of the window at the long downhill view to the police station.

"Why here again?" I said.

"I wanted to get you away from that corner of the city and somewhere close to the police if we needed them." Ari walked over and leaned on the windowsill next to me. "I don't want those killers near you, Nola. Our fine pair must be getting desperate by now. They know that the police have thrown a net over the city. They can't leave, they can't stay—and they're both armed."

"Yeah. So? It's my job to—"

"It's the police force's job. Leave it to them."

"If I thought they could bring our maniacs in, I would. They haven't so far."

"These things take time."

"Yeah, and while they take time, people get killed."

Ari crossed his arms over his chest and glared at me.

I decided that arguing would only waste our time and my energy, since I had every intention of doing what I wanted no matter what he thought.

"I'm going to call Jerry," I said. "Okay?"

"Of course." The glare softened. "No harm in that, is there? I don't mean to act like a tyrant."

"Of course you do. You love acting like a tyrant. It's kind of cute, really."

He growled under his breath and turned his back on me. There's more than one kind of revenge in this world.

By then, around three in the afternoon, Jerry had woken up enough to answer his phone, though the first thing I heard on his end of the line was a yawn.

"It's Nola," I said. "Are you conscious?"

"Unfortunately, yes," Jerry said. "What's up?"

"I need information about that matter we discussed a couple of days ago, about the availability of a certain item."

He said nothing for a couple of minutes. Since both of us have talents, I could pick up a few fragments of his mental processes, a kind of shuffling through the files in his brain.

"Oh, that," he said at last. "The white lipstick from Iran."

"Yeah. Do you still have any of it left down at the salon?"

"No, and I don't know where to get any, either, not right now. It's odd about that, darling. The suppliers show up in the city only now and then. You can't count on them at all. I suppose that's the way they do business over in those faraway places or something. The cosmetics vendors had a lot of it just recently, but they've sold out. They don't know when they'll get any more."

"That's too bad. Well, so it goes."

"Yep." He paused for a long yawn. "Sorry. I've been

having trouble sleeping lately, but last night I finally did get to beddy-bye at a reasonable hour."

"Reasonable, huh? When?"

"Four A.M. I'm shocked, shocked, I tell you, at how late it is now. I feel like someone hit me on the head with a padded mallet."

"Go have some coffee," I said. "And don't forget the orange juice."

Jerry laughed and hung up.

Ari had flopped down on the small brown sofa at one end of the room—in front of the TV, of course. He put the remote down and quirked at eyebrow at me.

"Apparently our boys have sold everything they had to sell," I told him. "You know, something just occurred to me about those receipts for the goods in the windmill. They made their last buy just before Michael blew out their transportation. What do you bet they were planning on taking it all back home that night?"

"That seems reasonable," Ari said. "Huh, do you suppose they'd spent most of their profits?"

"I just bet they did. That would explain why they aren't hiding out in some motel somewhere or taking a plane back to some other gate. They're broke. Well, assuming the deviant level theory is true."

I sat down next to him on the sofa. We both stared at the gray blank face of the TV as if we were expecting visions to appear onscreen. To be honest, I was expecting just that, but the angels refused to show up.

"It occurs to me," Ari said eventually, "that we've missed the key to their operation. The point isn't selling heroin in and of itself. The point is getting American money to buy the sort of goods the police found in the windmill. It would be next to impossible to burglarize the stores that stock that kind of merchandise."

"Not and get away cleanly with so much heavy loot,

no. Too many alarms, security guards, and all the rest of it."

"Just so." Ari's smile turned tigerish. "Now, if they do come from some sort of deviant world, then we can assume that batteries and chocolate and the rest of it are valuable there, enough so to make the risks of gate-hopping or whatever you want to call it worth taking."

I turned cold all over. "Oh, God, just what kind of a place is Michael stuck in?"

"Not a very pleasant one, I should think." He frowned in thought. "I wonder if odd talents like your family's are well-known there. Judging from Johnson and Doyle's little business venture, criminal gangs recruit the people who have them."

"If so, we've got to get Michael out of there fast."

"Yes, he'd be entirely too valuable to whomever's behind this operation."

I thought of Aunt Eileen's recent dreams about Michael, standing on a street in the midst of sand dunes, or going to a farmer's market at the place where a supermarket stood in our world. And one of the farmers had a tumor that was eating his face—what had happened there, wherever it was? Some kind of plague, maybe? I shuddered. Ari put his arm around my shoulder and pulled me close.

"Cold?" he said.

"No. Frightened for Mike's sake."

"I can't say I blame you. And here we are again, waiting for news."

"Yeah. For a little while, anyway."

I looked at Ari's watch. It read a few minutes past four. The police had about eighteen hours to deliver, and I had the same amount of time to come up with my next move.

CHAPTER II

WE ENDED UP WAITING FOR THE REST of that afternoon. I did some hard thinking and some more research in the Agency files. I also sent NumbersGrrl e-mail about a nagging problem and received a fast reply. It was consistent with the theories, she told me, that there could be two William Johnsons, one in our world, the other in the deviant level. Doppelgängers.

"Fascinating, Captain." The opening line of her e-mail branded her a geek, all right. "I just wish I could write it up into a paper for *Nature.* Can't you just *see* the editorial faces when they read it? LOL! But there's that little matter of the Agency contract."

I commiserated. Another Agency policy comes down to "silence is golden, because it keeps Congress off our backs."

We went out to dinner at the Boulevard again, where Ari graciously allowed me to have a salad instead of some calorie-crammed full meal. Even though he laughed at me, I was convinced that my jeans were tighter than they'd been the week before.

"I don't see how you can tell," Ari said. "You wear them a size too big."

"I don't see any reason to wear clothes that look painted on. Besides, this way they hide my figure flaws."

"You haven't got any figure flaws." He waved his coffee spoon at me. "What you do have is an eating disorder."

I scowled at him and speared a piece of tomato with my fork. He let the subject drop, or I might have speared him.

As soon as we returned to the hotel, I called Aunt Eileen, just to check in with her. Things had been quiet at the house, oddly quiet, she said, without Michael around. She'd dreamed about him again.

"He was talking with a dark-haired girl named Lisa," Eileen told me. "A very pretty girl, but she had a club foot. Lisa's the name of Michael's new girlfriend, but Brian told me that her feet are perfectly normal, as far as he could see, anyway."

"Could you see where Mike was?" I said.

"In a very shabby room. It almost looked like the walls were covered with pieces of cardboard cartons. But I only got a few glimpses of them."

I wondered if the Lisa she'd seen was another doppelgänger, but I decided against mentioning that to Aunt Eileen.

"The girlfriend, by the way," she went on, "has called here twice to see if we've had any news about Michael. She sounds genuinely worried, poor girl."

"I don't suppose she knows anything that could be useful."

"I did ask her. All she knew is that Michael called her Sunday morning. He was going to stop by the park to see 'something,' he told her, then go on to her house."

"Which he never reached."

"She was really angry until she heard the news at school. After I called them, the principal announced that he'd disappeared in the hopes that one of his friends would know something helpful, or so she told me." Aunt Eileen paused for a sad sigh. "In my day we wouldn't have dreamed of calling a boy's house, though I have to admit that the circumstances probably give her a good excuse."

"I'd say so, yeah."

After we ended the call I got out the Agency laptop again and tried to do some more research on the Web. I found nothing new and finally gave up in disgust. As usual Ari was watching soccer on TV with the sound off. I was about to suggest a better way to spend the evening when his phone rang: Lieutenant Sanchez.

For some minutes Ari paced around, listening more than talking, then signed off. He sat down on the edge of the bed and smiled his tiger's smile.

"They found the car, the blue Toyota," he said. "Parked on Geary Boulevard. Someone's been living in it, Sanchez told me. Dirty clothes, blankets, food scraps, the usual."

"Yeah, that was Johnson. Was it listed as stolen?"

"Yes. The officers who found it were looking it over when they saw a man who more or less answered Doyle's description come out of a shop. He took one look at them and went back in. The shop owner told them he'd run out the rear door."

"So he knows the cops have it."

"Yes, unfortunately. He won't be going back to it. They've towed it."

"He's going to be real desperate now. Did they find any weapons?"

"No, which worries me. It's possible our pair found a place to hide at least the long guns."

"To say nothing of a place to make silver bullets, unless they cast them back home in the deviant level."

"True. I was hoping it would be the windmill, but obviously not." Ari paused, thinking. "So, what now? I can't do much more on my own without stepping on Sanchez's toes. I hate waiting around doing nothing, but he's mobilized his resources well. They should pay off eventually."

"Eventually could be too late for the rest of the Hounds. Don't forget, Doyle knows who they are. I'll bet he even knows where Grampian lives. As long as those two are on the loose, Grampian's in danger, to say nothing of the occasional innocent bystander."

"That's very true." He got up and began pacing again. "If I could only tell Sanchez the truth, we could get Grampian police protection."

"Until the full moon, anyway."

"That's what I mean, *if* I could tell Sanchez. I agree that Grampian's probably marked as their next victim. Do you think he has the sense to stay inside?"

"Not during the full moon. As long as he's thinking like a man, he'll do the right thing. Once he starts thinking like a wolf, all bets are off. The rest of the pack won't be able to stay away from their run, either."

"And Johnson could be waiting for them. Not my idea of a good outcome."

"It isn't mine, either. Sanchez has resources, sure, but so do I. It's time I mobilized mine. I want to go discuss things with Annie tomorrow, unless of course the cops catch Doyle and Johnson tonight."

They didn't. We woke in the morning to thick fog and no news from Sanchez. Before we checked out, I called Annie to make sure she'd be home. On the way to her converted garage we stopped at a bakery. I bought more bread and pastry than we could eat in order to make sure we'd have leftovers to leave with her.

When we arrived, she insisted on making tea and sat us down at the round table to wait for the kettle to boil. Duncan joined us and kept a worshipful canine eye on Annie while we talked.

"Here's the plan," I told her. "I keep making LDRS scans and passing the tips to you. You get to be the

neighborhood busybody who sees things and relay the
tips to the cops. They have an anonymous tip line as well
as a regular one. Use a couple of different names."

"Yes, I copied down the numbers from last night's
news," Annie said. "What about Jerry?"

"He won't call the police, not even for Agency money.
Not even with a fake name."

"You're right, aren't you?" Annie considered for a
moment. "You know, I could do a few scans, too."

"No, it's too dangerous. Johnson already knows who
I am. He doesn't know you, and let's leave it that way."

"Yes, he does know who you are." Annie fixed me
with a gimlet eye that would have done Aunt Eileen
credit. "That's why I'm worried about him shooting
you."

"You have a point," I said. "But I'm not real keen on
him shooting you, either."

"I think we can avoid that if we're very careful. You
see, I've been thinking about that reward. It's up to fifty
thousand according to the morning paper."

"It could come in handy, huh?"

Annie smiled, but the lines around her eyes seemed
to get deeper, and the eyes themselves, behind their
thick glasses, wearier.

"Well," I said, "that's another good point, but only
if you live to spend it. Let's see what we can come up
with."

We drank tea, they ate pastry, and I nibbled at half
a bear claw while we tossed ideas back and forth.
Eventually we arrived at a few conclusions I could live
with. Duncan got the rest of the bear claw, then Ari
drove Annie and the dog to somewhere a good distance
away from her studio. I deliberately avoided knowing
the location, just in case Johnson could read it from my
mind. Ari came back for me in about twenty minutes.

So far most of the scans I'd done for Johnson and

Doyle had placed them in the northwest quadrant of the city or by the portal. We drove to the park and the pond by the doorway to nowhere that might have led to somewhere. The demonstrators had done a good job of cleaning up after themselves. Although the grassy areas looked trampled and worn, I saw only one piece of trash lying on the ground. I picked that up myself, an orange handbill reading "STOP THE MILITARY MACHINE!" Ari stayed in the front seat, ready to contact the police should Johnson or Doyle drop by to test the moribund energy field. I got in back with the pad of paper and the crayons. Sometimes low tech really is the way to go.

First I tried to locate Doyle. I could pick up enough of an impression to know that he was still alive and not all that far away, but his shielding held. He seemed perfectly calm, the bastard, for a man who'd just murdered a woman who'd trusted him.

Johnson was a different matter. As soon as I started the LDRS, my hand began to move. The images came so fast that I was scribbling rather than drawing, laying in big areas of color. After three pieces of paper I made myself stop and examined what I'd done. A lot of blue-green water, a lot of gray lines, either concrete or stone, a lot of dark green shrubs. In one picture gray tree trunks rose out of the shrubs to the oddly flat caps of dark leaves that top California cypress trees. I made an unladylike remark.

"What?" Ari said.

"This could be anywhere along the California coast."

"But you placed him in the city earlier."

"Right, and thanks." I paused to stare at the pictures and let my mind roam around the memory rooms inside my brain. "Land's End."

"Has Johnson realized you're spying on him?" Ari said.

"No, which is puzzling. He must be asleep. Safer for him to sleep during the day and only go out at night."

"Sleeping where?"

"Good question. There are motels down by the beach not far from there, but none of them up on the point itself. It's part of a national park. Yet everything I'm seeing is outdoors." An earlier bit of evidence occurred to me. "The windmill isn't all that far from Land's End."

"You'd better come sit up front. We need to be ready to move. I'll figure out a way to tell Sanchez without mentioning all the psychic—" He paused briefly. "—talents."

I had just settled myself in the front seat, though, when Sanchez called Ari. I could hear the conversation over the car phone's scratchy speaker.

"We just got a solid tip," Sanchez said. "A old woman walking her dog out at Land's End saw someone who looks a hell of a lot like Johnson. He's made himself a shelter in the underbrush. I'm proceeding to the location with a SWAT team."

"On my way." Ari flipped on the siren.

I refuse to relive the details of that drive out to Land's End. Let's just say I became intimately acquainted with the fear of death that's the lot of every human being. Well, every sane human being. Ari seemed to lack it. At any rate, eventually the car slid screeching and wailing into the parking lot above the ruins of Sutro Baths.

Way down at the foot of the hill the Pacific stretched out, wrinkled and silver. A thick fog wreathed around Seal Rock and spread long tendrils toward the land. The incoming tide crashed over the long concrete foundations that had once supported swimming pools and glass buildings. In them I recognized the gray lines that I'd been drawing in the LDRS scans. The hill rose sharply, cut with a flight of wooden stairs, up to the terraced parking lots.

In the lots police cars sat at odd angles. Officers

with bullhorns swarmed around the ruins below and cleared the area of vulnerable innocents. In the damp, cold weather few people would have been down on the beach in the first place, I figured. Overhead a police helicopter beat the air with a *thwack thwack thwack* like a crazy drummer in a heavy metal band. To my left, the parking lot ended in a strip of ornamental plantings. Just beyond lay Point Lobos Avenue, running from the Great Highway up to the hill. Across the avenue lay the unkempt green mass of Sutro Gardens, a welter of shrubbery and weathered sculptures.

When I turned to my right, I saw the cypresses of my vision, standing tall at the crest of another hill, this one a gentle curve rising from the parking lot. Beds of native plants, carefully tended to look wild, covered the lower slopes, but higher up thick swaths of brush, weeds, and shrubs, spiky junipers, mostly, grew under and around the trees. A dirt path wound down toward the parking lot.

"There's Sanchez," Ari said. "Stay with the car."

He slid out and ran off, leaving the door open behind him. I saw him draw his handgun as he ran. I got out more slowly and shut the car doors. Sanchez, also armed, was standing and talking with Ari two terraces down. The SWAT team, or so Sanchez had told Ari in the original call, was working its way over from the other side of Land's End, a couple of miles from the parking lot, in the hopes of getting Johnson to surrender or, at least, of flushing him out of cover. I had the grotesque thought that he was in the same trap as a grouse or partridge in those old-time hunting parties, when British lords perched on shooting sticks and let underlings chase the game right to them for the slaughter. Unlike the birds, however, Johnson had a gun of his own.

Distantly I heard shots. The police in the parking lot ran to crouch down and take cover behind their cars, but

they had drawn handguns at the ready. I realized that
they formed a cordon all the way up to the street above.
I also realized that I'd be dead meat if I continued standing out in the middle of the open lot. I ran around to the
other side of the car and followed the police example.

Someone fluttered down from the sky and crouched
next to me—St. Maurice, I figured, judging by his
Roman-style breastplate over a tunic. In one hand he
carried a gladius, the short stabbing sword of the legions.
His wings spread hugely to either side like the white
spray of the sea breaking over the rocks.

"Ave," I said. *"Si vales, valeo."*

"Bene," he said. *"Valeo, sed maxime obstat tibi peri-
culum."*

I could have told him that. Danger stood in everyone's way, not just mine. I risked a glance over the hood
of the car. Ari and Sanchez had moved behind Sanchez's
unmarked squad car, but they stood tall rather than
crouched as they looked up toward the top of the hill.
When I followed their glance, I could see something
moving through the underbrush.

"Non!" St. Maurice said. *"A tergo, stulta!"*

I swung around in my crouch and saw a dark-haired
man, who might have been considered good-looking if
he hadn't been so unshaven and filthy, emerging from
the thickets of Sutro Gardens across the avenue. Doyle's
expensive clothes had not stood up well to sleeping in
the underbrush. The cream-colored silk shirt had acquired a lot of tears and stains. He still, however, had a
gun with him, a rifle of some sort. I took a deep breath
and began to gather Qi.

Doyle dodged across the street. At the edge of the
parking lot he paused right out in the open. He must
have been trusting that the police would be looking in
the other direction, toward Land's End, but the helicopter hovered above. Suicide by blue, I thought. Chaotic

that he was, he never noticed me, the warded agent of Harmony, crouched by the car. I gathered Qi, spun Qi around on itself until it formed the nucleus of a sphere, hot between my hands—fast, ever faster, felt it glowing and pulsing, pushing against my fingers. Slowly, as if he had nothing to fear in the world, Doyle raised the rifle and took aim at Ari.

I stood up fast and flung up my hands.

"Doyle!" I yelled. "Game over!"

He swung around just as I sent the energy sphere flying. It transferred with the speed of light and slammed into his face. For a brief moment an ovoid of silver light surrounded him like an aura; then the force of it knocked him sideways and off-balance. He dropped the rifle and fell twitching to the ground. His face hit the asphalt so hard that his nose spurted blood. I heard Ari yell and running footsteps.

"Bene fecis," St. Maurice said. *"Vale."*

The apparition disappeared just as Ari reached me. He holstered his handgun, then knelt down beside Doyle, who raised his head and smiled, an utterly mindless gape, just as if blood wasn't flowing over his lip and dribbling onto his chin. His dark eyes looked more like a cow's than a human's, placid, unthinking, bizarrely happy, really.

"He'll be that way for a couple of hours," I said.

Ari stared at me, then stood up. When I snapped my fingers, Doyle clambered to his feet. When I put my hands behind me, so did Doyle. Ari had him cuffed before Doyle realized what had happened, but again, he showed not the slightest distress, just leaned against the hood of the squad car and smiled. Ari picked up the fallen rifle.

"This is what ensorcellment does?" Ari said.

"Yeah," I said. "It's not pretty, is it?"

"No." He swallowed heavily. "I'm beginning to understand about that license."

Up on the hill shots rang out, these near, too near.
I flinched. Doyle laughed, the gurgling sort of laugh a
baby makes.

"The team's firing into the ground," Ari said.

"The ground?"

"Any bullets shot into the air will come down again,
possibly on you, possibly on the person you're trying
to capture." Ari gave me a look of faint disgust that reminded me of St. Maurice, calling me stupid. "The idea
is to take him alive. We need information."

"Well, we've got one of them, anyway." The moment
I spoke I knew I lied. The full force of a SAWM hit me
like a blow. I spun around, looked behind us—nothing—
spun back, looked up on the hill just as Johnson burst
out between two trees. I heard shouting as Johnson
stopped on the dirt path, the rifle irresolute in his hands.

"Surrender!" Sanchez grabbed a bullhorn and yelled
at him. "You've got no hope, Johnson! Drop the damn
gun, and put your hands in the air!"

"Tawsi Melek!" Johnson screamed the name, then
raised the rifle and turned our way.

Ari grabbed me and dragged me to the ground a
split second before Johnson fired. Doyle jerked around
and took one step away from the car. He smiled out at
eternity, then buckled to his knees. Blood spread across
his cream-colored silk shirt as he pitched forward to lie
crumpled on the asphalt.

Ari rose to one knee, swung up the rifle with an oddly
casual gesture, and fired a single shot. Up on the hill
Johnson flung himself—no, he fell over backward. I realized that he was dead just as the SWAT team crested
the hill behind him. Ari stood up, tucked the rifle under
one arm as casually as if it were an umbrella, and trotted
off to join Sanchez. I had just seen him kill a man with
less emotion than he showed when he kissed me.

The cold sunlight behind the fog turned much

brighter, as if it were molten silver pouring down over the scene. I got up, looked at Doyle's body and decided that I really wanted to vomit. I staggered over to the ornamental planting and did so. The crazy thought in my head was to make sure and miss the yellow tansy, an endangered species.

I wiped my mouth on an old tissue I found in my jacket pocket and tried to consider what to do next. Returning to the car meant seeing what was left of Doyle again. A second crazy thought joined the first, that I could just walk downhill and buy myself a drink at the Cliff House. I stayed where I was, of course, waiting at the scene of disaster once again as police swarmed around the parking lot.

Sanchez and Ari hurried up the hill to take a look at Doyle's body. I heard Sanchez say, "I don't understand what made him hold his fire."

"Neither do I," Ari said. "He did trip and fall, though."

Liar, I thought. But technically, I suppose, ensorcellment did lie beyond his understanding.

More sirens wailed toward us. The police helicopter sank out of the sky and landed on the lowest terrace downhill in a gust of rotors that spun to a stop. The sudden silence made my ears ring. I decided that I needed to sit down and walked back to the car. Sanchez turned to me and frowned in concern.

"I'm glad you're all right," Sanchez said. "It's too damn bad you had to be here and see all this."

"Yeah?" I said. "That's just the way it worked out."

"Your partner is one hell of a shot," Sanchez went on. "He tells me it's all in a day's work."

I smiled. I had nothing more to say.

The day's work dragged on for a couple more hours. Forensics, an ambulance, and then the inevitable TV cameras arrived. I sat in the car while Ari stood around talking with Sanchez and making phone calls, some in

Hebrew, some in English. Once my stomach calmed down I took out my phone and called Annie. As I suspected, she'd been the "old woman walking her dog" who'd phoned in the tip to the police. Although she'd done a couple of scans to pinpoint Johnson, she hadn't gone anywhere near Land's End. What I hadn't suspected was that she'd be so upset at hearing both men were dead.

"I feel terrible," Annie told me, "just terrible. I don't know what I thought would happen, but I never thought they'd be killed. I'm a silly old woman, Nola. That's all I can say." Her voice wavered on the edge of tears.

"No, not silly." I remembered St. Maurice. "But it's a war we're fighting. Shit happens when Chaos gets belligerent."

"I suppose so."

"Think of Sneezy. Doyle murdered her. I can't shed any tears over him."

"Well, true enough."

Annie fell silent for a long couple of minutes. I could hear Duncan whining in the background. Eventually she said, "there, there, good dog" to him, then spoke to me. "I'm going to lie down, I think," Annie said. "I've had too much excitement."

"Good idea," I said. "So have I."

Next I called Aunt Eileen and left a message on her answering machine, simply saying that I was safe and not to worry when she watched the evening news. Just as I clicked off Ari came back to the car. He slid into the front seat and turned to me.

"Thank you," he said. "One of the officers down below told me that Doyle was aiming at me just before you did whatever that was."

"Yeah, he was," I said. "You're welcome."

"I'm going to drive you back to your apartment, and

then I have to go down to the Hall of Justice. There's no
need for you to wait around there."

"More paperwork?"

"Of a sort." He cocked his head to one side and considered me for a moment. "Because of Johnson. I have
the legal right to use armed force, but not carelessly. He's
dead, and we can't just shrug and say well, that's that.
I need to sign a statement and make sure they know
where I'll be and that sort of thing. Interpol will put me
on paid leave while the review of the incident proceeds.
Since there were rather a lot of witnesses, it shouldn't
take long. He shot Doyle with one of his silver bullets.
There's no doubt that he's the man we were hunting."

"Right. I'll have to file something like that myself, jus-
tifying the use of ensorcellment."

"You look exhausted. Let's get you home." He put
the key in the ignition, then hesitated. "I forgot about
the state of your apartment. Would you rather go somewhere else?"

"No. I'll start cleaning things up."

"Very well." He started the car. "I'll try to drive more
carefully."

He did, too, stopped at all the stop signs, signaled before changing lanes, drove in short like a Californian—no,
far better than that. I watched him and wondered what
he really felt about Johnson. Anything? His SPP read
as perfectly calm, weary, yes, but calm and certainly not
remorseful. We stopped at a red light on Twenty-fifth at
Fulton. Ahead lay the park, a green billow of tranquillity
under the silver fog.

"You've killed someone before, haven't you?" I said.

"Yes. I don't like thinking about them. I won't like
thinking about this incident, either."

That answer eased my mind considerably. "I feel like
I had something to do with killing Doyle," I went on. "If

I hadn't ensorcelled him, he would have dropped when he saw Johnson."

"Johnson would have shot him anyway. I assumed he was aiming at you, but Sanchez saw it from a better angle. Doyle was the target all along."

The light changed, and we drove on, curving into the trees at a reasonable speed. I was pondering St. Maurice, another one of my image objectifications, I supposed. I must have heard Doyle behind me and—heard what? A man leaving a garden some thirty yards away? With a helicopter banging the air overhead? Not possible, O'Grady, I told myself. *No, stupid, from the rear!* The saint-image had pointed out the direction of the attack when I could have had absolutely no idea of what lay behind me.

I refused to draw the only logical conclusion.

Chapter 12

SINCE I NO LONGER HAD TO WORRY about Johnson, Ari dropped me off in front of the apartment, then drove on. As I crept up the stairs, Mrs. Z's TV covered the sound, and she stayed in her lair. The sight of my apartment made my stomach twist. Dirty plywood, pocked with old nail holes, blocked the main panel of the bay window. Shards of glass lay scattered on the carpet in front of the disassembled couch. About half of my worldly possessions cluttered the floor.

"What did you expect?" I said aloud. "The good fairies would come while you were gone?"

Getting everything back in order took me a couple of hours of hard work, good, honest, tiring work that I appreciated for the way it filled my mind. By the time I finished making my space mine again, the sky was growing dark, and the streetlights were glimmering outside. I stood by the kitchen window and watched the purple sign over the Persian restaurant start blinking. A streetcar rumbled by, its windows lighted against the night, crammed with people coming home from work. I thought of contacting Y, but I was quite simply too tired to file the ensorcellment report. I promised myself that I'd do it first thing in the morning.

I wandered back into the living room and turned on

the floor lamp. With the dirty tan plywood reflecting it back, the quality of the light struck me as unpleasant, but the overhead would have been worse. I was considering moving the lamp away from the window when I heard keys in the door.

"Ari?" I called out.

"Sheboygan." He sounded exhausted. "Is the chain on?"

"No, I forgot." It didn't matter anymore. No one was trying to kill me. For the first time that day I felt relieved, a deep, animal relief. I was alive, and the predators were dead. Our ape ancestors must have experienced the same feeling when they lured a hyena into running headfirst into a rock.

Ari came in, carrying a pizza. Somehow the sight of that utterly mundane cardboard box made me laugh. He smiled at me, the ordinary smile, not the tiger, not the boyish seducer. I took the box from him and carried it into the kitchen while he took off his jacket.

"Did it go okay down at the hall?" I said.

"Oh, yes, all routine." He sat down in a kitchen chair and stretched out his legs with a sigh. "Grim, but routine. I'll be on admin leave until everything's settled. Annie's going to get the reward, by the way. I made sure to ask. It'll take a while, bureaucrats, you know, but it's hers."

"Good." I took a couple of the plates that I'd washed earlier and put them on the table. "Forks?"

"Why? It's probably not very hot." He opened the box and contemplated the pizza within. "Vegetarian again. I thought you'd prefer that."

"I do. Thanks."

I put a stack of paper napkins on the table, then sat down opposite him. He picked up a piece and laid it onto his plate, then looked up.

"I'm going to have nightmares tonight." His voice

was so calm that he might have been commenting on the food. "Do you want me to sleep on the couch? I'll probably wake you up otherwise."

"No, the bed will be fine. I'd rather be right there if you need me."

He did have nightmares. Somewhere around three in the morning he started thrashing around. I woke up and heard him speaking in Hebrew, a few sharp short words that he repeated over and over. I got the impression that he was ordering someone to do something. I sat up and turned on the bedside light. According to the counseling courses I took for my master's, I should have let him work through the nightmare on his own, but he was shaking and sweating.

I ran my fingers through his hair and kissed his face until he woke up. He propped himself up on one elbow and stared at me in utter incomprehension, then smiled when he recognized me.

"The usual dream again," he said.

"What is it?"

"I'm back in the army on guard duty, and the boy starts walking up to the gate. I see him reach under his shirt, and I shoot him."

"Suicide bomber?"

"He was, yes." He lay back down with a long sigh. "They gave me a medal for it, but all I could think of was that he was sixteen years old, and I killed him."

"You didn't. The men who sent him did."

"That's what the commanding officer told me, too. But don't you see, I didn't know he was wearing the vest when I fired. He could have been scratching an itch." He stared at the ceiling for a moment. "I panicked, Nola. I killed him because I was frightened, not because I knew he was a threat."

"How old were you then?"

"Nineteen. Why?"

"Old men set boys up to do their dirty work for them, that's why."

I left the light on and lay down next to him. He rolled into my arms. I held him for a long time, that night, just held him, until we both drifted off to sleep and ordinary dreams.

In the morning I woke much too early to a barrage of messages on my landline answering machine. Aunt Eileen three times, Maureen once, Kathleen once, Sean twice, and—the call I regretted missing—one from Dan, who'd been allowed to phone by his commander in Iraq, where he was stationed at the time. Kathleen had sent him an e-mail with the news. The subject was always the same: getting Michael home.

I returned calls while Ari made coffee and finished the pizza for breakfast. I had no way to call Dan back, but Aunt Eileen told me that he'd been given compassionate family leave because of Michael's disappearance and would be returning home as soon as possible.

"It'll be so good to see him," I said.

"Yes, especially now." She sounded tired for so early in the day. "I'd better hang up, dear. I need to call your mother."

"You're a braver woman than I am."

"I'm older than she is. It makes it easier."

"Still—good luck!" On that note I clicked off.

Ari brought me coffee and sat down next to me on the couch.

"I take it," he said, "that Kathleen's forgiven you for not telling her about your brother."

"Yeah, she has. I don't blame her for being upset about it. The politics in my family are almost as complicated as the situation in the Middle East."

"Not quite as deadly, I should hope."

"Well, no. Though there have been a couple of Christmas parties that came close. Usually some of the

older men had too much to drink and then started arguing about politics." I suddenly laughed at one of those
memories that's only funny in retrospect. "I remember
one party at Aunt Eileen's when Harry O'Brien, the
family's token Republican, got into it with Uncle Jim
over some local election. I forget the issue, but Uncle
Jim was whipping the cream for the pie while they argued. And all at once he lifted the electric mixer and just
sprayed Uncle Harry up and down with whipped cream.
From the spinning blades, you know."

"What did Harry do?"

"Yelled bloody murder and picked up the bowl and
dumped the whole batch over Jim's head. He looked
like Santa Claus."

We shared a good laugh.

"But Michael and Brian were watching, and they got
scared. They were what? About six. They went howling
out of the kitchen and ran upstairs and hid somewhere.
It took me an hour to find them."

"I'm not surprised. I've never seen a house like your
aunt's. That day I questioned Brian? I nearly couldn't
find my way downstairs again."

"Yeah, I'll bet. I—" The words that I'd been meaning
to say disappeared. "Oh, my God."

"What?"

I put my coffee down, then stood up and walked a
few steps, as stiff as a zombie.

"Nola, what?"

"I just thought of something obvious."

I heard Ari get up. I took one more step and walked
into a section of the gray library where the shelves shot
off in all directions. None of the books slid or tumbled
off, not even on the shelves that went straight up. The
angel was standing behind a dark oak lectern. When
it turned to look at me, I noticed it wore pince-nez. It
opened a book and shoved it in my direction.

"Family history," it said. "Family future."

I was propped up on the couch next to Ari, who had his arm tight around my shoulders. I leaned my head against his chest—yes, he smelled like Ari, all right, witch hazel and all. I reminded myself that he was real and the angel only an image.

"I've done that again," I said.

"Yes." He sounded annoyed. "I told you that you needed to eat something."

"You were right, okay? Don't get mad at me, Ari. I don't have the energy for a good satisfying fight."

"I'm not angry," he snapped. "It's frightening, seeing you drift off and fall like that."

"Fall?"

"Yes, fall! This time, I'm glad to say, you weren't standing on a sidewalk when you went down."

I pulled away, then turned a little so I could see his expression: dead serious. "I didn't realize I fell before," I said. "Why didn't you tell me?"

"I thought you knew. What would happen if you were crossing the sodding street, and you dropped like this?"

"Nothing good." I considered the situation for a minute or so. "I'd probably take up permanent residence in the Beyond."

He growled under his breath. "I saved you a piece of that pizza. You're going to shut up and eat it."

I shut up, then got up and followed him into the kitchen. While he put the pizza onto a plate, I contemplated the vision. The meaning seemed clear.

"If there's another gate in San Francisco to these deviant levels, what do you bet it's in the Houlihan house? It was built by generations of people like me."

"A good bet, then," Ari said. "Assuming these levels exist."

"Always assuming that, yeah. What I wonder is why our two perps didn't find it when they burgled the place."

"Good question."

"They might have been looking in the wrong rooms. Uncle Jim mentioned that they tore the boys' rooms apart. A gate wouldn't be up there."

"Why not?"

"I don't know, now that you mention it. I need to go take a look." I reached for my phone. "I'll just call Aunt Eileen—"

"Eat first."

I ate. I put milk in my coffee, too. I was beginning to wonder how important being a size four really was, compared to, say, avoiding a fall into trance in front of moving streetcars. Once I'd finished my breakfast, I called Aunt Eileen and asked if she'd be home.

"So Ari and I can drop by," I said.

"I'm always glad to see you," she said, "but why?"

"For reasons too strange to say over the phone. I'll tell you when I see you. Will it bother you if Ari comes along?"

"No, dear, of course not." She sounded resigned. "I've always liked your boyfriends, you know. It's just that I wish you'd wait to sleep with them until you're engaged at least. At least!"

"Every girl needs a hobby."

When Aunt Eileen sighed in deep martyrdom, I decided I owed her some kind of explanation.

"You see," I said, "sex is real important to me. With all my talents and training, I could end up floating around my inner world if I wasn't careful and never making contact with reality again. Sex keeps me in my body."

I waited while she thought about my remark.

"But don't you think," Aunt Eileen said eventually, "that taking up modern dance would work as well?"

"Er, no. Sorry. Uh, see you soon."

I signed off fast.

My current impetus toward sinful behavior was

running hot water in the bathroom sink so he could
shave. For a moment I sat on the couch and stared out at
nothing; then I remembered that I had to file an ensorcellment report. I'd put it off long enough.

I logged onto TranceWeb. First I procrastinated by
reading the latest from NumbersGrrl; then I got down to
it. I found the correct form and began to fill out the routine heading. The image of Doyle's face, grinning mind-
lessly as the blood soaked through his shirt, rose up in my
mind and made it hard to type. I forced myself to write
simple clear sentences, as I filled in one little box at a
time. Place where ensorcellment occurred. Others present at site. Person ensorcelled. Reason for ensorcellment.
I could see him raise the rifle and sight downhill at the
two police officers. Outcome of ensorcellment attempt.

That was the hard one, the outcome. I found myself
thinking of Pat, who must have bled as much as Doyle.
More, maybe, as he struggled to drag himself to the road
and safety.

"Nola?" Ari walked out of the bathroom. "Are you
all right?"

"No," I said and started to cry. "My poor brother!"

He strode over, took my hands, swept me up, and
pulled me into his arms. I clung to him while he stroked
my hair and murmured a few words in Hebrew. What
they meant didn't really matter. I managed to stop crying. He pulled up his T-shirt so he could wipe my face
with the hem.

"We're a fine pair," he said. "Walking wounded."

"Yeah, you're right about that, aren't you?"

He pulled the shirt back down, then kissed me.
"Better now? We need to get over to your aunt's."

"Yeah, we do. I've got to log off first. It's this damn
ensorcellment report."

He turned and looked at the computer screen.
"There's nothing there."

"Well, actually there is. You just can't see it." I took a look myself to make sure. The form still filled the screen. "Let me just get this over with."

While I typed in the last few statements he stood behind me with his hands resting on my shoulders. I figured that since he could read nothing onscreen, I wasn't giving away any Agency secrets. I finished, hit send, and logged off TranceWeb.

"That is the most peculiar thing I've ever seen," Ari remarked. "When you hit a key, I'd see a little spark on the screen, no letter, just a spark, and then it would disappear into what looked like thick fog."

"It's clever, isn't it? The pride of the Agency."

I shut down the computer before we left, though. No Agency operative keeps their computer always on. Chaos has its hackers.

In the chilly morning Aunt Eileen was wearing one of her favorite Fifties acquisitions, a navy blue and pink paisley patterned quilted skirt, mid-calf length, formed into a squishy sort of cone by the starched petticoats underneath. She'd topped it with the baby blue twinset she'd found at Goodwill the week before. For shoes she wore a pair of blue flats and not the fuzzy slippers. For such small favors we are thankful.

With Uncle Jim at work and Brian in school, the house sounded empty when we came in, as if every word echoed in some huge cavern. My mind was playing one of its usual tricks, I realized, objectifying my idea that a spot somewhere inside led to spaces larger than anyone had suspected. Aunt Eileen ushered us into the kitchen, where, she informed us, she was baking cookies.

"They smell good," I said to Aunt Eileen. "Thank you."

"You're welcome, dear," she said. "Now what's all this that's too peculiar to say over the phone?"

As best I could, I explained: deviant worlds, gates

between same, Michael's developing talent. Eileen listened carefully, asked questions now and then but looked not the least surprised or startled. It occurred to me that she'd heard stranger stories, over the years, about members of her family. Pat's lycanthropy, in particular, had staggered everyone.

"Well," she said when I'd finished. "That *is* interesting. I've always felt that this house had secrets. When I was first married, Jim's mother was still alive, you know, and she came to live here with us. She told me that she was sure the house had ghosts, but I never heard or saw them. Neither did Clarice or Jimmy, when they still lived at home, and certainly Brian's never said anything about them."

"Sean heard them, though."

"That's right, but I always thought that Sean had gotten the idea from Nanny Houlihan."

"I suspect he heard the same voices she did, is all," I said. "You know, I should call Sean."

"I would, dear, really. I'd be interested in what he has to say about all this." She glanced at Ari. "Sean is Nola's older brother. It's Daniel, Maureen, Sean, Nola, Kathleen, Patrick, and Michael." Her voice wavered on Pat's name. "I wanted Nola's mother to name Michael something else, because of all those awful jokes, Pat and Mike, you know, but she wouldn't."

"I gather," Ari said, "that she's a woman of strong opinions."

"How very tactful you are." Eileen favored him with a smile. "I should get out the photo album, and—"

Ari's phone rang and saved us both. He got up, answered, and wandered out into the hall to talk with Sanchez, I assumed, since he was speaking English. Aunt Eileen leaned across the table and whispered to me.

"He really is attractive, but, Nola, honestly! You don't have to sleep with every good-looking man you meet."

"I don't. Maybe one in a hundred. If that."

She rolled her eyes to invoke heaven. I could hear Ari talking out in the hall.

"You're not having a joke on me, are you?" he was saying.

A pause while Sanchez apparently reassured him that no, whatever it was was no joke.

"I'll bring O'Grady with me," Ari said next. "Her lot will want to know about this."

Another pause.

"Very well, then, we'll be right down." Ari clicked off his phone and returned to the kitchen. "Nola, this is one for your agency."

"I was beginning to get that impression," I said. "What is it?"

"I'll tell you in the car." Ari turned to Aunt Eileen. "I'm sorry, Mrs. Houlihan, but I've got to take Nola away. Police business. They need us to look at some evidence."

"I understand, dear. But why don't you just call me Aunt Eileen?" She smiled at him. "You might as well."

Every other boyfriend I'd ever brought around had turned icy cold at this suggestion—politely, mind, but icy all the same at the thought of being swept up into my family. Ari actually smiled. "Thank you," he said, "I will."

As soon as we got into the car, Ari turned toward me. He laid one arm along the back of the seat.

"Think back to yesterday," he said. "The two corpses went to the morgue at about what? Sixteen hundred hours? They were put in the usual cold storage drawers. This morning there's not much left of them. They're disintegrating."

My turn for the open mouth and sheer disbelief. "What do you mean, disintegrating?"

"Rotting flesh, crumbling bones. We'd best get on our way there, or there might not be much left to see."

"I can't go to the coroner's office in a pair of old jeans and a Giants T-shirt."

"Good point. Home first, then."

In honor of my supposed important job with the government security apparatus, I wore a gray skirt suit with a dark blue silk blouse and heels. By the time we reached the coroner's complex in City Hall, the two corpses had been moved to a special room. Sanchez waited for us in an antechamber, where the tech, a somber Asian woman, made us all don lab coats, surgical masks, little plastic shower caps, and plastic gloves. For a final fashion touch we slipped big blue slipper-things over our shoes.

"We've taken samples for lab work," she told us. "The coroner is pushing everything through as fast as he can. You know, I've worked here for twenty years, but I've never seen anything like this."

"Are you going to freeze the remains?" I said.

"If we can. We've been taking photos every fifteen minutes. You'll see why."

We did. She ushered us into an icy-cold examination room. Fluorescent lights gleamed and reflected off the pale green tile that covered the walls, floor, ceiling, and counters. The smell of disinfectant hung so strong in the air that it penetrated the pressed fiber masks we wore. Under that smell lurked another, a rich decay of dead meat. What was left of the two corpses lay naked on stainless steel tables, side by side.

All of their skin had vanished and most of the flesh to the point where I had no idea which was Johnson and which was Doyle. Gobbets of a sticky black substance stuck to the bones of hands and feet. Red lumps clotted the long bones. The rib cages had collapsed over the gooey remains of organs. The skulls had lost so much flesh that I could see exactly how the plates of bone were disintegrating. Rather than turning spongy or powdery, they had broken up into crystals, little sharp-edged cubes.

Sanchez made a gagging noise and left the room. Ari turned decidedly pale above the edge of his mask, but he stayed. I was too fascinated to feel disgust. The appearance of the bones resembled—what?

"Pixilation," I said aloud. "They look like a digital image that's breaking up, only in 3-D."

"That's it!" the tech said. "I knew it reminded me of something."

It also reminded me of the way Chaos creatures turned to smoke or powder when a ward touched them, but I kept that to myself. Another line of inquiry presented itself.

"Where are their clothes?" I said. "Doyle bled heavily when he was shot. I wonder if the blood's still on his shirt or if it's decayed away."

"I'll check that. Have you seen enough?"

"More than enough, thanks." I glanced at Ari.

"Yes, quite," he said.

We returned to the antechamber and stripped off the medical gear, which went into a special plastic bin for later destruction. The reigning theory at the moment was that both men had suffered from some sort of disease along the terrifying lines of Ebola.

"Have they identified any kind of virus?" I said.

"Not yet," she said. "The really odd thing is, they looked perfectly healthy when they came in. Well, aside from being dead."

On the off chance that a disease had indeed caused the rapid decay, I ran an SM: Danger check on the room behind us. It picked up nothing but a faint whisper of old peril averted. Unfortunately, I had to keep this good news quiet. The tech made a phone call and discovered that on coroner's orders, the dead men's clothing had been placed in isolation in sterile containers.

"I'll have to look into that for you," she told me. "I'll pass the information on to Homicide when I get it."

With that we could make our escape. I needed open air. While Ari fetched the car from the underground lot, I stood on the sidewalk in front of City Hall and luxuriated in pale sunlight. Across the street in Civic Center Plaza, the rows of plane trees lifted bare branches to the clearing sky. A few homeless men sat on one of the benches under the trees, merely sat, barely speaking, wrapped in odds and ends of torn sweaters and jackets. Immediately behind me rose the high gray steps that led up to the glass and gilded bronze facade of City Hall.

I walked back and forth and put some hard thought into what I'd just seen until a cab pulled up and distracted me. A Chinese-American man in a business suit got out, not very tall, with thinning gray hair, carrying a briefcase, absolutely nothing unusual about him except he looked extremely familiar. As he hurried up the steps toward the ornate doors of City Hall I realized that rather than being someone I personally knew, he was Vic Yee, the investigative reporter who'd broken the story about the Army's attempt to impound the Portals monument. If he'd come down to City Hall on the track of a story, it would be something more subtle and probably more important in the long run than the sensational death of the Silver Bullet Killer.

I wondered if he'd heard about the disintegrating corpses. It seemed unlikely, but I hoped he had. If the coroner was holding any information back, Yee would ferret it out. By the time Ari drove up, I had a theory of my own. I got into the front seat and buckled on the safety belt.

"Any ideas about the decay?" he said.

"Yeah," I said. "It looks like more evidence for the deviant level theory. I'll have to consult with the Agency expert before I can be sure."

"You've not been sure about any of this," Ari said. "Carry on."

"Okay, here's what I've learned so far, mostly from the expert's e-mails. If deviant levels exist, every one of them is going to have its own individual nature. Anything that exists within them will be part of that nature, not ours, and that includes human bodies. She told me that the atoms of our bodies are sort of woven into the structure of our universe. We don't exist like eggs in a basket, separated by shells from everything around us. We're actually one of the properties of space-time. It's kind of like a tapestry or embroidery. You can't just cut one motif out of it. It'll unravel. Okay?"

"I'm following you so far, yes."

"Our two Chaotics were in the wrong level, not the one they were born in. Here's my theory, and it hasn't been confirmed, okay? They were cutouts from the cloth, and so they could unravel. The matter in their bodies would be unstable while they're here, especially without the life force to sustain them."

"That last makes no sense at all. Life force?"

"Ever read Henri Bergson?"

"He's not that Swedish filmmaker, is he?"

"No, that's Ingmar Bergman."

"Sorry."

I waited to continue until Ari finished swerving around a sudden pedestrian.

"But anyway, I can't really explain what I mean by life force," I said. "I've got an intuitive grasp of it, but I can't put it any more clearly than that."

"Very well, then."

Ari laid on the horn and blasted the slow SUV ahead of us into the right lane. I decided that the secrets of the universe could wait till we got home alive, assuming we did.

But what would this effect mean for Michael, I

wondered, if it were true that his substance belonged in our part of the multiverse to the exclusion of all others? He was wandering somewhere out of place, out of touch, the most lost of all possible lost boys. If he got so much as a cut finger in that other world, would the rot set in and spread?

"We've got to get Mike back," I said. "Fast."

"Quite so," Ari said. "The question is how."

"I'm beginning to get an idea."

I brooded the idea all the way back to the apartment. Although I called Sean as soon as I got in, his line was busy. I changed out of the suit into a decent pair of jeans and a new top, pale gray with a green watercolor print and a deep V neck that I figured Ari would like. He did.

"A question," I said. "If you're on admin leave, why did Sanchez call you?"

"He pretended to forget. The leave's not from his department, after all." He smiled at me. "But he did it because of you, not me. He's out of his depth. He knows it, he can't admit it, but he's good enough at his job to do something about it. The coroner's already brought in the federal-level health people, but your agency's part of the security apparatus. You have need to know."

"Right. And I have need to file another report. Calling Sean can wait a few minutes."

I considered contacting Y directly, then decided that using TranceWeb to file an official paper, where others could see and read it, would be a more efficient way to get the word out. Composing this report went fast and easily, compared to the ensorcellment filing. When I finished, I marked it "TOP PRIORITY" and "URGENT." I also sent my theory about the life force—Bergson's élan vital—to NumbersGrrl, then checked my personnel file. A brief message waited for me. "Ensorcellment report taken under advisement." Nothing more.

"Well," I said, "I haven't been placed on leave yet."

"Good," Ari said. "At least one of us isn't in limbo."

"That's true. I need to act fast before they put me there."

Sean's phone persisted in being busy. I took the opportunity to check TranceWeb again and found two things, a terse confirmation that my report on the corpses had been received, and an e-mail from NumbersGrrl. I read it twice, then logged out again.

"Hope!" I said.

"What?" Ari said.

"If my speculation's right about the deviant levels and Michael and all that, then the most likely thing is that he's in some version of San Francisco, just one or two levels away, that is. I had a few dark fears, like maybe he'd been dumped into interstellar space or on some other planet."

"Do you watch a lot of science fiction films?"

"I've been known to, yeah. Why?"

Ari set his hands on his hips and scowled at me. I got the point.

"Well, all right, maybe the interstellar space idea was kind of far-fetched," I said. "Still, the news is good. My idea just might work, after all."

CHAPTER 13

WHEN I FINALLY GOT HOLD OF SEAN, about an hour past noon, he told me that Aunt Eileen had already called him. She'd invited him and his partner, Albert Wong, over to the Houlihan house. She'd included Ari and me in the invitation because she knew Sean and I would want to discuss finding Michael.

"I told her we'd bring some food," Sean said. "She feeds all of us too often as it is."

"Bless her heart!" I meant it sincerely. "Will Al be coming with you?"

"Sure. It's Uncle Jim's bowling night, so we'll only have to put up with Mister-I'm-Tolerant-I-Tell-You-Tolerant for a couple of hours."

"Ah, come on, Sean! He's trying. It's better than Al's dad, isn't it?"

"Well, yeah, I have to admit that. At least Al hasn't been consigned to the outer darkness of complete non-existence like I have."

"It'll be good to see you guys. Do you think Al could make one of his special lasagnas? I've love to have some of that again."

"Ohmigawd! The end of the world is upon us."

"Say what?"

In the background I could hear Al asking the same

thing. "Nola wants some of your special lasagna." Sean's voice became briefly fainter. "Yeah, the apocalypse is upon us, for sure."

"Oh, come off it," I said. "I'm not that bad."

"Yes, you are. The last time you were faced with Al's lasagna, you did a caloric analysis of it, layer by layer."

"Did I really?"

"Yes, you did. Complete with estimated fat grams."

"Tell Al I apologize."

Sean did so. I could hear Al speaking.

"He says in that case he'll make the lasagna," Sean said.

"Cool! How come he's not at work?"

"Furlough day. He's doing his share to keep the state of California from sinking slowly into the west."

"Well, then, when can you get over to the house? I need your help finding something."

"I think our esteemed aunt told me something about that, but it was garbled and really weird. Deviant levels of the multiverse? Michael's in one of them? You got to be kidding."

"I wish I was. I'll explain when I see you."

"Okay, we'll get there as soon as we can. Al can always make the lasagna over there. He and Aunt Eileen love to cook together anyway. What about your hunky new boyfriend?"

"I can't believe Aunt Eileen called him hunky."

"Of course not, but she made him sound hunky."

"Well, he kind of is, yeah. He'll be there, so you can see for yourself."

I ended the call to find Ari watching me with the reproachful stare. "What have I done now?" I said.

"What does hunky mean?"

"Sexy and good-looking, just like you are."

He made a sour face and snarled, but his SPP told me that he was flattered.

When we returned to Aunt Eileen's, Sean opened the door. He's the other natural beauty in our family, wavy black hair, brooding dark blue eyes, a full mouth and chiseled cheekbones, a slender body that he keeps reasonably well-muscled. He also trembles a lot, which detracts from the overall effect, though Al has told me that when Sean's asleep and still, he's almost too beautiful to be real. If I were still a believer, I'd thank God daily for Al, solid, loving Al who keeps my brother in one piece and reasonably sane.

I introduced Ari, who smiled and reached out to shake Sean's hand. Sean recoiled as if Ari had pulled a gun on him, then blushed scarlet at the gaffe.

"I'm sorry." Sean was looking at me with begging eyes. "I don't mean to be insulting."

"What?" Ari said in his typical subtle way. "Do you have a phobia about germs?"

"No." Sean swallowed heavily and took a step back. "You just shot someone, didn't you? I mean, not just now, but like, recently. He's dead, isn't he?"

Ari gaped at him.

"Sweetheart," I said, "why don't you go say hi to Aunt Eileen in the kitchen? And meet Al. You'll like Al. He's normal."

Like a good soldier Ari followed orders and marched off, though he did turn at the entrance to the hall and stare for a moment before going on. Sean continued trembling and rubbed his beautiful mouth with a perfect hand.

"I'm sorry," he whispered. "Nola, how can you sleep with that guy? He scares the hell out of me."

"I noticed. Come on, calm down." I slipped my arm through his in the hopes of steadying him. He leaned against me and quivered at a slightly lower register.

"Your boyfriend, he did just kill someone, didn't he?"

"He's a cop, Sean. He was part of the Silver Bullet

Killer task force. He's the one who brought down the guy who murdered Pat."

Sean took a deep breath, which slowed the trembling. "Okay, that's different," he said. "Aunt Eileen told me that you were shot at, too."

"Yeah, I sure was, but the creep missed." I decided against telling Sean that I would have been dead except for Ari's intervention. While the thought would have sweetened his opinion of Ari, he might have blacked out. He does that at times, when he hears overwhelming news.

Arm in arm we wandered outside to the backyard, Uncle Jim's great love in life, a long stretch of perfect lawn bordered by cottage-garden flower beds, in summer a welter of color and scent set off here and there by flagstone paths. A squirrel chattered in the maroon leaves of the Japanese maple. Sean and I sat down on a white bench under the bare branches of an ancient gnarled apple tree. Among the flowers and growing things, Sean took another deep breath and stopped trembling.

"I'm sorry I insulted your boyfriend," he said. "These things just jump out sometimes."

"Do you think I don't know that?"

"Yeah, okay. I'll apologize to him if you say so."

"No, I'll explain it to him later. He understands about the family. He's not a local police officer, by the way. He's from Interpol, and he'll be leaving the States soon, so it's not like you'll have to see him at every family gathering."

"Another guy who's going to leave you?"

"Yeah. I pick them for it, I think."

Sean cocked his head to one side and smiled at me. "You have the worst damn taste in men of anyone I know," he said. "And I know some guys who are really weird that way."

"I just bet you do. No, I don't want the details."

We shared a laugh.

"But look, about Michael." Sean began trembling again. "He's not dead, is he? I tried to see if I could find him, but I can't."

"He's not dead, no. He's in some other part of the multiverse. I'm working along that hypothesis, anyway. His talent just developed, and I think he's what the Agency calls a world-walker. That means he can access deviant levels at places where the level meets ours. At a gate, that is, between the two."

Sean tried to digest this pronouncement for a moment, then shrugged in the mental equivalent of a burp. "Whatever," he said. "What do you need me to find?"

"A way he can get back here. I'm betting there's one in this house. Do you remember the voices you used to hear?"

"The ghostwalk, yeah. And then in the other upstairs."

"The other upstairs?"

"Where Nanny Houlihan's rooms were. Nothing mystical."

"Right. I remember now."

The south end of the Houlihan house, two stories high, contains the kitchen, four bedrooms, and the master suite. The middle of the house, the living room section, is only a single story, but on the north side, there are two more stories' worth of rooms, all of them mostly rectangular though not precisely so. At the very northern end, three square little rooms sit one on top of the other like a tower. At one time Jim's mother lived in them.

"Let's look at the ghostwalk first," Sean said. "It used to scare the hell out of me when I was a kid."

We returned to the house and headed for the kitchen. When we turned into the hallway, I saw the blue meerkat-lizard thing. Just where the hall veered into its peculiar angle, the Chaos creature sat on its scaly little haunches and wagged its tail at me.

"What are you up to?" I said. "Spying for someone? Johnson's dead, you know."

At the name it squealed in terror. It jumped up, swung its head around, and ran toward the wall. Just before it rammed into the paneling, it vanished. I took that reaction as answering my question with a no.

"What did you see?" Sean said.

"Just a harmless critter."

"Okay. You still see those, huh?"

"Just now and then."

I squatted down and looked at the section of the wall that had been its apparent destination. To me it looked perfectly ordinary and perfectly solid. Sean knelt down beside me.

"That's spooky," he said.

"Yeah? Why?"

"I feel like I could put my hand through the wall right here."

He reached out, but I caught his wrist and held him back.

"Let's not take any chances," I said. "For all I know, your hand could stay over there while the rest of you stayed here."

He winced and flinched.

"How big is the spot?" I continued. "The spot that makes you feel you could go through it, I mean."

"Not very." With his hands he gestured out an area that was just about a foot on a side.

I muttered something unladylike and stood up. Michael was a skinny kid, but not that skinny. Sean followed my example.

"That's depressing," I said. "I was counting on a gate being here."

"There's still the other upstairs. I hated going in there

when I was a kid. Nanny Houlihan used to dare me to spend a night there, but I never could."

I had always remembered Nanny as a sadistic martinet of a woman. Apparently my memory was accurate.

"Well, it's daytime now," I said. "Let's take a look."

At the end of the north-running hallway stood a narrow staircase leading up into gloom. Some of the steps had a small pile of things on them—a stack of old books, some children's clothes, an ancient Mixmaster—things, I guessed, that Aunt Eileen had placed there to wait till the next time she had reason to go up. Sean and I each took a pile and climbed to the top. I pushed open the door and saw what appeared to be a well-organized, dust-free antique store. I flipped on the light switch.

"Eileen even cleans in here," Sean said. "Wow."

We placed our little heaps of once and future junk down by the door, then walked in. Sean stood with one hand on a treadle sewing machine and went into Find mode. His eyes narrowed and appeared to be focusing on some far distant place or time. His mouth went slack. I got a tissue out of my jeans pocket in case he drooled. He does, on occasion.

"I see a lot of comic books," he said eventually, "in plastic bags." He paused. "Baseball cards." He shook himself like a wet dog and came back to the moment. "I'll bet she saved everything Jimmy ever collected."

"So do I, but I'll also bet they're worth bucks by now. Next time Jimmy's in town, you might tell him they're here."

We searched the top room but found no stash of valuable paper products. None lurked in the next room down, either. Finally, at the bottom, where saner people than us would have started looking, we found them. A row of archival cardboard cartons, stacked four high, lined one wall. In Eileen's clear round hand they were labeled by content and year: comics, all right, and sports cards, football as well as baseball, plus Christmas cards, reusable Christmas wrap, and all the holiday decorations Eileen put out year after year, Easter, Fourth of July, and Halloween as well as Christmas.

We moved two stacks of cartons out into the middle of the room and contemplated the wall, papered in a delicate pattern of violets on a cream background, marred with a big oval stain about five feet off the floor. Ancient water damage, I assumed. The older Houlihans had had a very cavalier attitude to things like roof maintenance.

"This was Nanny's sitting room." Sean walked over to the window and pulled up the shade to let in a shaft of sunlight. "Toward the end Uncle Jim put a single bed in here, too, so she wouldn't have to go up and down the stairs."

"She used to talk about hearing voices," I said. "I thought she was nuts, frankly."

"I heard them, too, but then, I *am* nuts." Sean grinned at me. "So that might not count."

We fell silent to listen. I heard nothing, but at one point Sean frowned and tilted his head to one side.

"I thought I heard someone calling a dog," he said. "Did you?"

"No, not a thing."

"Whatever." He shrugged and spread his hands. "If there's a gate in this house, it's here. I'm not real sure, though, if there is or not. In the hallway I was sure, but not here."

I found solace in bad language. Sean agreed.

We returned to the kitchen, where as usual everyone had gathered. At the counter by the sink, Aunt Eileen and Al were chopping various kinds of food on matching cutting boards. She'd changed into turquoise capris with a white sleeveless snap-front blouse on top and the pink fuzzy slippers on the bottom. Al looked his usual normal self in jeans and a Giants T-shirt.

"It's good to have you back," Al said to me. "I'll have to hug you later, though. I'm chopping garlic."

"Later will be fine," I said. "It's good to see you, too."

Ari was sitting at the round maple table and drinking coffee out of a mug glazed with a view of Candlestick Park, one of the family mugs, not the porcelain ones with the flowers that my aunt saves for important company. I sat down next to him and snagged it for a sip. Sean took a chair across from us, but he turned Aunt Eileen down when she offered him coffee. He could get shaky on the natch.

Eileen took a plate of cookies from the top of the refrigerator, where she'd put them out of garlic and onion range, and placed them on the table. I picked up a wave of feeling from her. Her SPP confirmed a trace of fear but above all, apprehension.

"We'll get Mike back," I said. "Don't worry. Have you had any significant dreams?"

"Just a rerun of that one about him trying to call and his phone not working," Eileen said.

"Here's the crux of the problem. Suppose that there is a gate somewhere in this house, and suppose he could get through it. We've got no way to tell him that."

"The dreams told me he couldn't reach us, not that we couldn't reach him." Aunt Eileen frowned at the floor. "That doesn't sound helpful now that I say it aloud."

The angel appeared beside her. "Think!" It waggled its wings at me. "Messengers can go where angels fear to tread." It vanished.

"Actually, it's very helpful." I stood up. "These cookies are oatmeal-raisin, huh? Can I have one?"

"What? Of course!" She turned to Ari. "Any time that I can make her eat is a triumph. She won't, usually."

"I've noticed that," he said. "I've been coaxing her, but she's stubborn."

Sean and Al both laughed. I reminded myself that I

could kick Ari later and merely smiled. By her phone Aunt Eileen had a pad and pencil for messages. I took a piece of paper and wrote "Mike, go to the Houlihans'. Nola."

When Eileen handed me a cookie, I started to leave the kitchen. She hurried after me.

"Nola," she said, "you can eat in front of other people."

"Huh?"

Aunt Eileen frowned. "You don't have to hide when you eat something."

"Oh. This isn't really for me. There's this creature—"

I would have said more, but her frown disappeared. "I suppose," Aunt Eileen said, "you really do know what you're doing. After all, the government trusts you."

With a sigh she returned to the kitchen. As I continued down the hallway, I was thinking of Ari's smartass crack about my having an eating disorder. I shoved the thought away. I had something more important to attend to.

At the ghostwalk angle I crouched down and made the chirruping noise that Kathleen uses to call her cats at feeding time. With an answering chirp the lizard-meerkat thing walked out of the wall. Its long scaly nose twitched as it sat up to beg. I wrapped the cookie in the note and handed both over. With a snap of yellow claws it grabbed the bundle, then nibbled them together. When it finished, it licked its lips with a long green tongue, then dropped to all fours.

"Michael," I told it. "Find Michael. He looks like me." I pointed to my face. "Michael, my brother. Find him."

It trotted for the wall and vanished. I could only hope that the Agency's FAQ sheet on Chaos creatures was accurate. I'd followed the stated procedure for transferring information via lizard mail. Whether my ugly little friend could find Michael was another question entirely.

I stood up and realized that Ari was standing in the kitchen doorway, staring at me.

"What happened to that biscuit?" he said. "I saw you place it in midair, and then it disappeared bit by bit."

"I was feeding an invisible creature," I said, "just like the ones you didn't see that day you went to the office without me."

"I suppose you were talking to it, too."

"Yeah. You should be used to that by now."

"I'm trying."

He looked so woebegone that I walked over and reached up to kiss him, a very modest in-the-family-house kiss, and patted his arm. "You're heroic," I said and decided not to kick him later.

Back in the kitchen, Al was shredding grilled steak for the lasagna—no fatty hamburger meat for him— while Aunt Eileen had joined Sean at the table. When Ari and I sat down, she made her usual offer of getting out the photo albums. My first thought was to change the subject fast, but luckily the Collective Data Stream came to my aid. I had a second thought.

"Do you have any pictures of Nanny Houlihan?" I said. "Like in her sitting room?"

"I probably do," Aunt Eileen said. "I wonder where they are? I haven't thought about her in years."

"How nice for you," Sean said. "A blessing!"

We all laughed, except Ari, whom the Fates had spared from knowing her. While Eileen hunted for the pictures in her collection of albums, I explained about Nanny. She'd been a schoolteacher in her youth, and old habits die hard. She would suddenly turn to the nearest child and point while snarling out questions like "twice nine!" God help you if you got the wrong answer!

"She liked to rap small children on the head with one finger," I finished up, "a finger wearing a steel thimble, that is."

"The heavy china one with roses was worse," Sean put in.

"Oh, now, honestly!" Aunt Eileen returned, carrying an old-fashioned leather photo album. "When people get old, they lose their patience easily. Well, not that she ever had a lot to lose."

More laughter, and Aunt Eileen opened the album with a flourish. When she set it down in front of me, Ari turned a little in his chair to look. One photo, a faded black-and-white, showed Nanny in her sitting room, a thin, sour-faced woman with her hair done up in a messy bun on top of her head. She sat rigidly straight on an uncushioned chair, her hands folded tightly in her lap, and glared out at the camera. Behind her I could pick out the violets on the wallpaper, a fair bit darker than they currently were. A good-sized crucifix hung on the wall, the only other decoration, if you could call it that.

"That!" Sean pointed at the crucifix. "I remember that. The pope blessed it or something. She always said she wanted to be buried with it."

"She wasn't, though," Aunt Eileen said. "When she passed away, I looked for it, but I couldn't find it, not anywhere in the house."

"You should have called Sean." Al turned from his cooking and smiled at Sean.

"He was away at school, dear," Eileen said, "or I would have."

Sean returned the smile, then let it fade. He got up and stood looking out into space, his soft mouth slack.

"That's it," he said. "Come on, Nola. Aunt Eileen, can I borrow a good strong knife?"

"What are you going to do with it?" Eileen stood up and glanced at the counter.

"Make a cut on the wall of her old sitting room. I think the crucifix is in there. What do you bet she put it between the studs or something to scare the ghosts off?"

"Oh, good lord!" Eileen rolled her eyes heavenward. "She got so odd by the end, but Jim wouldn't hear of putting her in a home."

Aunt Eileen rummaged through kitchen drawers until she found an old but formidable looking carving knife. She handed it to Sean with her usual ritual reminder to be careful and not run with it. I followed him as he trotted out of the kitchen. At the ghostwalk angle I paused for a scan, but I picked up no trace of the Chaos critter.

In the erstwhile sitting room the sun still shone through the window, enough light for Sean to start digging at the wallpaper in the area I'd seen as water damage. I thought that getting through the wallboard underneath would be a chore, but the knife slit a double layer of paper and revealed a hollow space. Sean handed me the knife and pulled a long strip of wallpaper right off. We could see the mangled edge of what had once been wallboard and beyond that, the lumber forming the wall itself. Another slit, more pulled paper, and there it was, Nanny's crucifix, jammed into the wall between two studs.

"She must have cut this hole in the wallboard herself," Sean said. "With those old sewing shears of hers."

"Or else she gnawed it with her fangs," I said. "I'd guess she pasted a strip of leftover paper back over the hole, and that's why it was such an odd color."

I took the crucifix out and held it up to the light. Its years of incarceration had tarnished it black, turning it into an effective ward against both Chaos and Harmony.

"The gate's open now," Sean said quietly. "I can feel it."

My heart thudded once, then steadied itself.

"Let's hope Mike can find it, is all," I said.

"Yeah. What should we do with that?" He nodded at the crucifix.

"If we polish it up, I bet Uncle Jim will be glad to have it, a reminder of his mother and all."

"He probably will." His voice turned flat and cold. "For some odd reason."

"How's our mother treating you these days?"

"The same as always. I wish she'd lay off Al, is all. She keeps calling him 'that fag,' and then she cocks her little head and simpers like she's said something cute."

"Anger pretending to be just a joke, yeah. That's her MO. Or part of it."

Sean started trembling. I got a good grip on the crucifix with one hand and caught his arm with the other.

"Let's go back to the kitchen," I said. "I think I just heard Brian come in."

"Yeah, I heard him, too. He had basketball practice today."

In the kitchen Brian was standing by the table and stuffing cookies into his teenage metabolism. With his mouth full he mumbled a hello, then took a handful of cookies from the plate and bolted. I heard him pounding up the stairs.

"He still feels guilty about teasing Michael," Aunt Eileen said. "If it looks like Michael's really gone, I'll have to get him into counseling."

"That's a good idea," I said. "Do you have any silver polish?"

"Baking soda's better," Al put in. "I saw some in the cupboard by the fridge. Aunt Eileen, do you have an old aluminum pan?"

"Of course," Eileen said. "I save it for cleaning silver."

Trust them to know, I thought. While Al finished assembling the lasagna, Aunt Eileen took over cleaning up the crucifix. She agreed that Jim would be glad to have it. While she worked, she chattered along about Nanny, Nanny's husband, other Houlihans, old family stories that I'd heard a hundred times, yet hearing them again comforted me. Soon, I supposed, our grief over Pat would have receded enough for us to tell stories about him, whether rueful or humorous.

Every now and then I'd glance at Ari. I expected him to be bored halfway to tears, but he listened with what appeared to be real attention. A couple of times he even asked a question. Somewhere inside him, I thought, lurked a core of good manners if he could feign so much interest.

There were only a couple of cookies left on the plate when I heard a whine at the door into the hall. I looked and saw the Chaos creature, sitting up and staring at me. I took a cookie, grabbed another piece of paper and wrote, "bottom storage room." The creature followed me out to the ghostwalk angle, where I hunkered down. The creature stared at the cookie and licked its green lips.

"Find Michael?" I said.

It nodded a yes. I wondered if the nod truly meant it had found Michael or if it was lying in order to get the cookie. I handed over the loot anyway, just because it looked so hungry. It crunched the note and cookie down, drooled, then turned and darted back through the gate.

I'd gotten my plan underway. Now I had nothing to do but wait, hope, and try to think of another plan to use when this one failed. Optimistic I was not.

I'd just returned to the kitchen when the phone rang. Aunt Eileen left off simmering Nanny Houlihan's crucifix at the stove and answered, smiled, then turned to the rest of us.

"It's Dan!" she said. "He's in Chicago. He'll get here tonight. Late, but tonight."

Sean and I cheered, yelled, and called out greetings that Dan probably couldn't hear until Aunt Eileen told us, with great dignity, to pipe down.

"He's only got a few minutes till his plane leaves," she said. "I need to write the time and all of that down."

I got up and handed her the pad and pencil. Out of the corner of my eye I caught movement in the doorway: my Chaos creature had returned yet again. I took the last cookie from the plate and followed it into the hall. This time it trotted past the ghostwalk corner into the living room, where it stopped and looked back at me. I followed, and it trotted across the living room to the hall that led to the other upstairs.

At the door to Nanny's old sitting room it stopped and looked up at me with a wag of its scaly tail. I opened the door and realized that the room had changed. The cartons had disappeared, the wallpaper, too—painted yellow boards covered the walls. Instead of a shade, a dirty piece of old sheet hung drooping at the window. The creature sat on its haunches, paused to scratch under its chin with a hind paw, then whined at me. I threw it the cookie, which it snatched neatly from the air and gulped down.

The creature walked into the room, then paused to look at me over its shoulder. I considered following it in, but an attack of intelligence stopped me. It would do the family no good if I disappeared along with Michael. Besides, I could hear voices just outside the window. One of them sounded like an old man's, thick with a Hispanic accent and a hard, exhausted edge to every word. A shape appeared just beyond the filthy glass.

"Get your hands off that window," the old man said to the shape. "You no can go in there."

"What are you going to do about it?" Michael! But I'd never heard him snarl like that, never heard so much rage in his young voice. "Get out of my way."

The window slid up with a screech and a scatter of dried paint. Michael swung one leg in, then the other, and slithered through the window into the room. The moment his feet touched the floor, the room changed back. Violets on the wallpaper, a shade over the window, stacks of cardboard cartons—my brother stood in the midst of it all, staring at me.

Dirt streaked Michael's jeans and the Juan Marichal replica jersey he was wearing. He'd combed his oily hair straight back from his dirty face, which looked thinner, too, as if maybe he hadn't eaten in a while. The creature did a little four-legged dance and trotted over to him.

"Nola?" Michael said. "Is that really you?"

"It is," I said. "Come on, get out of there before the gate switches again."

Michael ran across the room and into the hallway. The creature skittered after him, then disappeared. I shut the door to the room, then turned to speak to him. He smiled at me, took one step, and passed out. I caught him, and although I staggered under his weight, I managed to lay him down before he hit the floor. The weight, and the way he stank of old sweat, reassured me that, yes, he had really returned.

"Ari!" I yelled across the living room. "Al!"

I heard them call back that they were on the way. I knelt down beside Michael and laid a hand on his cheek, which sported an ugly blue and purple bruise, though the skin looked unbroken. He lay so still that I grew terrified. Was he going to die right there in the hall?

"What?" Ari came running and stopped to stare. "That's your brother."

"It sure is, but something's wrong."

Between them Ari and Al picked Michael up and carried him into the living room while Sean hovered, mouthing useless advice. Brian shoved the brown armchair into a reclining position; then Al and Ari draped Michael into it. Aunt Eileen came in from the kitchen with a bowl of water and a wad of paper towels. When she began to wash Michael's face, he opened his eyes and stared at her.

"Am I really home?" he whispered.

"Yes, dear," Aunt Eileen said. "But I do think you need to see a doctor."

"Not right now. Please. I want to be home." He struggled to sit up, finally managed it, and swung the chair down so he could sit upright. "Nola?"

"I'm right here."

"I got your notes. That thing barfed them up on my shoes."

"I'd always wondered how they relayed information," I said. "Well, now we know."

Everyone else turned to look at me, a bristling hedge of questioning glances. I heard the back door open, then bang shut. I was saved from having to explain when Uncle Jim called out from the kitchen.

"I'm home! Where is everyone?"

"In the living room, darling," Aunt Eileen called back.

Uncle Jim came clomping down the hall and walked into the room. He glanced at the tenant of the brown armchair and stopped to stare, then took a few more steps, grinning all the while.

"Michael!" he said. "Thank God." He wiped the smile away and arranged a scowl. "Where the hell have you been?"

"Now I know I'm really home," Michael said. "Uncle J, I don't know where I was. I really honest to God don't, except it looked like San Francisco, but it wasn't. I don't want to talk about it."

"You're going to have to," I said, "but maybe not tonight. We had the police looking for you and everything."

"Dinner first," Aunt Eileen said. "Al, why don't you start that lasagna?" She glanced my way. "I'm going to have to call your mother."

"Not right now!" Michael sat up a little straighter. "She'll want to chew me out." He turned to me in appeal. "I bet she's not even worried. I bet she's just mad."

"Being angry is how she expresses her worry," I said.

"But you know, Aunt Eileen, you could wait a couple of hours to call. The saints will forgive you."

"Yeah," Uncle Jim put in, "wait until after I've had my dinner, at least, so I can digest the damn thing without having to listen to her."

When Al started for the kitchen to put the lasagna in the oven, Sean followed him. Aunt Eileen followed Sean because she wanted to start making the salad, and Uncle Jim drifted after her. I sent Ari into the kitchen to fetch Michael a glass of milk and some soda crackers to settle his stomach down.

Brian stood looking at his cousin for a moment. "Sorry," he whispered. "I never should have piled it on about that thing."

"It's okay," Michael said. "I might have done it anyway. I dunno. It kind of called to me."

Brian turned and bolted. I could hear him running up the stairs toward his room. Once we were alone, Michael leaned back to rest his head against the chair.

"What happened to me?" He looked up at me with eyes desperate to understand.

"I was hoping you could tell me. Let me make a guess, though. You walked through that portal in the park."

"Yeah. Big mistake."

"Do you remember what happened next?"

"Some kind of electric shock. After that I didn't remember much of anything for a while. I mean, like a couple of hours. I just sat there in the park and looked at the sand dunes where Fulton used to be." His eyes filled with tears. "I really don't want to talk about it."

"Well, eventually you'll have to, but tonight, yeah, I can cut you some slack." I heard footsteps and turned around to see Ari with the milk in one hand and a box of crackers in the other. "Have you called Sanchez?"

"Not yet." He handed the glass to Mike and the crackers to me. "Michael, for now you have amnesia. I think that's the best line to take with the police. You simply cannot remember anything much after you were hit on the head. That bruise looks quite convincing."

"I was hit on the head," Michael said. "But that was later."

"Brilliant! The police will want to know more, but we'll figure out something to tell them."

"Thanks." Michael drank half the milk in the glass straight off. "Okay, someone hit me on the head. I don't remember anything much. Got it." He finished the milk in one long glug and reached for the crackers. I handed them over. "Can I have some more milk?"

Ari took the glass and left to refill it.

"That's your boyfriend, huh?" Michael said. "Isn't his name Morrison?"

"No, it's Ari Nathan, and he's a cop from Interpol. Know what that is?"

"Yeah. You know what the worst thing was?"

"What?"

"There weren't any of us there. I mean, no O'Gradys, no O'Briens, no Houlihans. I looked us up in a phone book. There were phones there, but it was weird. They were all landlines." He paused to stuff his mouth with crackers.

"But you found this house okay."

"Yeah." The salty crackers made him mumble. "It looks different on the outside, though."

"Here's Ari with more milk. We can talk about all this later."

The Chaos critter was trotting after Ari like a pet dog. Michael grinned and held out a couple of crackers. The creature snatched them and crunched.

"Thanks," Michael said to it. "Good—well, boy or girl, I dunno."

Ari was watching the crackers disappear into what must have looked like thin air to him. A few bits fell onto the carpet. The creature picked them up with the tip of a green tongue, then slowly vanished.

After dinner, Uncle Jim headed off to bowling, and Aunt Eileen called my mother. When Ari and I left, Michael was feeling well enough to take a shower and change his clothes, a good thing, since we all knew that Mother would make some unnecessary remark about the dirt.

After we got into the car, Ari turned in his seat to look at me, or toward me, since it was getting dark by then.

"You're sure," he said, "that Michael wasn't just hiding near the house somewhere?"

"Very sure," I said. "I know it must all seem impossible to you."

"It does. I keep reminding myself that you said Johnson would be in the museum, and he was. And there's the windmill incident, where you were right again. I'm sorry, but this is all difficult for me."

"I know that. Not a problem."

Ari put the key in the ignition but didn't turn it. He looked at me again.

"It's just such an odd coincidence," he said, "one of those gates being here."

"Isn't it? I'm having trouble with that myself. There has to be a reason, besides, I mean, us being O'Briens and O'Gradys. Something keeps nagging at me. I should know why, the nag says. It must have something to do with Nanny Houlihan. It was her house before it was Uncle Jim's."

"Can you find out more?"

"I'm going to try. When Michael's back to normal, and she's not so distracted, maybe Aunt Eileen will remember something about her mother-in-law that will explain it."

"That will do to get on with, then." Ari started the car.

In the soft dark of early evening, Ari drove back to

the apartment without causing an accident or giving me an ulcer. We crept up the stairs and managed to avoid Mrs. Z, an omen that life had taken a turn for the better.

"There's still no glass in the window," Ari remarked as we walked in. "Just that sodding plywood. You need a better apartment."

"I need a raise first," I said. "Rents are high around here."

"Well, you may not be living in this city much longer." He grinned at me. "You'd find Tel Aviv interesting, I think, if you wanted to take a look at it. For a visit, a holiday, say."

I just smiled in answer. Yeah, sure, I thought. Just wait till you get home and start to think about things.

"I've got a report I have to file," I said. "The Agency will want to know that Michael's back."

"So will the police. I'll call Sanchez. They'll want to talk with Michael tomorrow, but I'll go with him."

"Will you?" I felt like I could cry out of sheer gratitude. "Thanks, Ari. I really appreciate it."

"Don't worry. If they try to get rough with the boy, I'll be right there."

And Sanchez will know it, too, I thought. Good.

After he finished the call, Ari settled himself on the couch and flipped on the TV. I sat down at my computer, but when I heard Vic Yee's voice, I swiveled around to listen to his story.

"A reliable source in the city attorney's office," Yee was saying, "has assured me that the city is going to fight the Army's attempt to confiscate the Portals of the Past. As a first step, they've arranged a judicial hearing tomorrow on the question of whether or not the Army must file an environmental impact report for the project. The hearing's likely result is that the Army officials will have to comply, resulting in a delay of some months if nothing else."

I laughed, but Ari looked utterly puzzled.

"What's wrong?" I said.

"I'm not used to seeing a military forced into compliance with local regulations."

"That's too bad. Life's saner that way."

I was waiting for him to ask if I was joking, but instead he gave me a dirty look and picked up the remote again. He began channel surfing with the sound off for soccer games. I got to work at the computer.

I found it much easier to write about Michael's return than the ensorcellment report of the morning. Still, I took a lot of care with the phrasing, since it did involve my brother. I was beginning to regret returning to San Francisco. I realized that as long as I lived in town, my family was going to get itself involved in my work, something I'd never wanted to happen. Yet at the same time, I hated the thought of leaving them again.

I finished the report, sent it off, and wrote NumbersGrrl a quick update on the situation along with my heartfelt thanks for all her help. Finally, even though it was late by then, I checked my personnel file. Much to my relief, the ensorcellment report had been accepted and marked "JUSTIFIED USE." I could thank Y for the speedy turnaround, I figured. I logged off in a better frame of mind than I'd been in for days.

I swiveled around on the computer chair. "You can turn up the sound," I said, "I'm done."

"It's all right," Ari said. "All the football matches are in Spanish, anyway." He clicked off the set and tossed the remote onto the coffee table. "I can think of better ways to spend the evening."

"Yeah?"

"Yeah." He imitated my accent. "Come sit down, and I'll show you."

So I did, and so did he.

Chapter 14

ABOUT MIDMORNING Dan drove Michael over to my apartment. Lucky Dan O'Grady, they called him in the Army, because he always knew if the enemy had laid an ambush or where the terrain could turn into a death trap for his men, like magic, they said, but of course, it's genetics, not magic. For an O'Grady he's tall, just a little over six feet, with the dark blue eyes and straight black hair of our clan, though he wore it in a buzz cut. The sight of gray hair at his temples shocked me. He'd just turned thirty-two, but he'd been through several years of hell in Afghanistan and Iraq since I'd last seen him.

Aunt Eileen had cut Michael's hair short, too, for the occasion, not in a crew cut, but to a respectable part at the side and comb over length, well above the collar. He'd put on a pair of slacks and a navy blue pullover sweater over a white shirt. Dan himself was wearing civvies for his leave, a pair of gray slacks, a rumpled blue shirt, both a little big for him, with an all-wrong white belt. He always looked uncomfortable out of uniform.

"Hey, bro," I said to Michael. "You're the very picture of teenage respectability. That's good styling for the cops."

Michael shrugged and continued looking around the

living room as if my collection of junk actually interested him. Although the bruise on his face had turned
to a bluish shade of purple, with the shorter hair it stood
out even more.

"Nervous?" Ari asked him.

"Yeah," Michael said and stared at the rug.

I introduced Dan and Ari to each other, then
watched as they shook hands and sized each other up,
both barely smiling, both pairs of eyes distant. Two of a
kind, I thought. After a couple of minutes they seemed
to realize it, too, and lapsed into affability.

"I hear you've been in the Middle East," Ari said.

"Yeah, taking a good look around your home turf,"
Dan said. "You know, Mike here's been telling me about
the portal he went through. I've seen things like that in
the ruins all over Iraq and Turkey, free-standing pillars
capped by a lintel. They all look worse for wear."

Ari's expression twitched, then smoothed into the
tiger's smile. "Yes," he said. "There certainly are a
good many of them, aren't there? In North Africa as
well."

And in Kurdistan, I thought. Light dawned inside my
own brain. No wonder Johnson and Doyle could travel
so easily without being traced. If even a fraction of those
ruined marble pillars had been altered by fires—and
from what I knew of ancient history, a lot of the now-
shattered cities in question had burned—our unlovely
pair had had a virtual freeway at their disposal. When
I glanced at Michael, I saw his eyes flare with sudden
curiosity.

"Ruined cities?" Michael said.

"You bet," Dan said. "Most of them died a couple of
thousand years ago. So far we've avoided adding to the
list, but we've come close in this last unpleasantness."

"Unpleasant—" Michael began, then grinned. "You
mean the war."

"Yeah," Dan said. "Unfortunately."

Michael's grin disappeared. As he stood there between Ari and Dan, I suddenly saw what he'd become one day, a man like them, tough and capable of violence, but smart as well. His talent would make him fundamentally an outsider, touched by strange things and fascinated by them.

Ari glanced at his watch. "Almost time for the appointment."

"Do you want me to go with you, too?" Dan asked Michael. "It'll go smoother if it's just you and Inspector Nathan."

"That'll be okay then," Michael said. "You don't have to come." He hesitated. "But you'll be here when we get back?"

"You bet," Dan said. "Remember, though, I promised Mom I'd have dinner with her, so I'll have to head over to her place." He glanced my way. "Could you guys take him back to Aunt Eileen's?"

"Sure," I said. "Not a problem."

I walked with Ari and Michael to the door. As they left, clattering down the stairs to the street outside, I could hear Michael asking Ari about the ruins in the Middle East. His life's work had just opened like the first page of a book. I shut the door and locked it, then turned back to find Dan settling himself at one end of the couch.

"Coffee?" he said. "Or that poisonous brew you call coffee."

"Always," I said. "I made a pot before you got here."

I got us both coffee and sat down at the other end of the couch. Dan sipped his and smiled in approval.

"Good and strong," he said.

"Thanks. How long will you be in town?"

"A couple more days. I got this leave because of Mike, but I'm also supposed to be thinking about OCS." He paused for another sip. "They want to kick me upstairs, but I dunno. I like being where I am."

A master sergeant, he was at that moment. "It's the responsibility of being an officer, isn't it?" I said. "That you don't want. For the decisions that could get someone killed, I mean."

Briefly he looked murderous, then laughed. "You always have my number, don't you? My kid sister with the X-ray vision."

I smiled.

"Mom came by Aunt Eileen's last night." Dan changed the subject to my own bête noire. "No one blew your cover."

"Thank God for that. I just hope I don't run into her on the street somewhere."

"San Francisco's small enough so you could. Do you think you'll ever end the feud?"

"I already have. You can't have a war if one party won't fight."

"Yeah, that's true, but I bet she won't drop it. That's just the way she is. She's pissed as hell that I'm staying at the Houlihans', even though they have the room and she doesn't."

"That's like her. While she was in the house, were there any phenomena?"

"Oh, Jesus!" Dan rolled his eyes heavenward. "Cracks, bangs, booms all over the house. You'd think we were launching fireworks from the roof. A vase shattered in the living room. Poor Al's T-shirt ripped up the back. She could only stay a hour, thank God, and it all stopped when she left."

"If she'd only admit she's got talents—"

"A cold day in hell when that happens."

"Yeah. Unfortunately."

We observed a moment of silence in honor of my mother's stubbornness.

"Uncle Jim told me," Dan said eventually, "that Nathan shot the guy who murdered Pat."

"He sure did."

"Good." Dan's expression turned solemn. "It's a crappy thing for me to say, maybe, but good."

"I'll admit to having thoughts that way myself, but I'd have preferred to see him get a fair trial."

"Yeah?" Dan shrugged. "Vermin are vermin. Why waste the money?"

We could have argued that one for hours. We'd done so before. Instead, I said, "Did Kathleen and Jack come over to Aunt Eileen's last night?"

"No, they'll be there tomorrow." He looked relieved at the change of subject. "I don't know about Maureen and the kids. They live too far away for a quick visit."

For hours, that day, we talked family gossip, Dan as eagerly as I. He'd gone into the Army at eighteen to get away from the role my mother had tried to impose on him, a sort of substitute father after Dad's disappearance. He'd been far too young to fulfill it, but over the years he'd drifted into that role, no matter how far away the Army took him.

Ari and Michael returned around five o'clock, just as Dan was getting ready to call Mother and tell her he'd be late. Mike flopped onto the couch, but the rest of us stood around in the middle of the room. Although Michael looked exhausted from the questioning, they had good news. Since Mike had bruises on his chest and shoulders, beyond the one on his face, Sanchez was willing to believe that he'd been mugged badly enough to spend his lost days in an amnesiac panic.

"Or at least," Ari told us, "he was willing to appear to have believed the boy."

"I don't think I get that," I said.

"Because of the Army team," Ari said. "Where did Michael disappear? At the portal. What does this Army team want from the city?"

"The portal." I smiled. "Okay, now I get it. Top secret stuff going on, and Sanchez figures he'll just keep his nose clean and out of it."

"Exactly. It worked out very well."

"Sounds like it." Dan glanced Michael's way. "So we don't need to get you a lawyer?"

"No," Michael said. "It's going to be okay."

"Good. I've got to go, Mike. I promised Mom we'd have dinner out somewhere. But I'll see you later." Dan strode to the door, then hesitated and turned back. "Say, Nathan. What about you and me and Mike go to a basketball game tomorrow night? The Warriors are home over in the Coliseum."

Michael sat up straight and beamed.

"Sounds good," Ari looked my way. "If you don't mind?"

"Not at all," I said. "I've got work to do."

"But can we take Brian, too?" Michael said.

"Definitely Brian, too." Dan grinned at him. "Good call."

The boys' night out turned out to be a great success, or so both Ari and Michael told me later. I only wished Dan could have stayed in town longer, but with Michael found, his first duty lay with his unit back in Iraq. Before Uncle Jim drove him down to the airport, they stopped at my place so I could say good-bye.

"Think about OCS, will you?" I said. "Military intelligence could use an O'Grady."

Dan blinked in surprise. "That never occurred to me," he said. "Okay, I'll think about it." Then he grinned. "You and your X-ray vision!"

Over the next few days, while we waited for Interpol and Ari's agency to decide what to do about Johnson's death, we spent as much time as possible with Michael. In bits and pieces he told me or tried to tell me, at least, what had happened to him. When I explained the concepts of the multiverse and its levels, he grasped the math and physics side of it better than I ever had. The social issues involved, however, baffled him.

"You know, at first I thought I'd ended up in the past," he told me, "but the dates all matched ours whenever I saw a calendar. They had paper calendars in windows and stuff. Weird."

"It was pretty low tech, huh?" I said.

"Yeah, because of some kind of war. Back when was that?" He frowned out at the air. "Someone told me. The 1930s, I guess. San Francisco never got bombed, but the radiation killed a whole lot of people."

"Wait a minute! Nuclear weapons in the 1930s?"

"Yeah, the Germans had them."

"Thank God we don't live there!"

"You bet! But the Germans lost anyway, and we bombed the Russians under—" He paused for a moment. "Under President Patton, yeah. That was his name."

"There must not have been a lot left of Europe after that."

"I got that impression. The States aren't much better off. Everyone wants to emigrate to Brazil and Argentina, but there are these long waiting lists to get visas and stuff. Even Mexico's real fussy about who they let in."

"So if you're born in California, you're going to stay there."

"Yeah. And so unless you're rich you join one of the gangs. If you're a Catholic guy, see, you're a Giants fan and belong to one of those gangs. And if you're Protestant, you root for the Dodgers. Things get pretty hairy. That's who beat me up, one of the Dodgers gangs, because I was wearing my Marichal shirt."

"I'm glad they didn't maim you."

"One of the Giants gangs heard the noise and came and pulled me out of it." He sighed. "Or they might have killed me. After that the BGs kind of took me in. That's the Bravos Gigantes, the gang that saved my butt. I told them that I came from a farm out in the valley and didn't know anything. It was kind of true."

Sports and religion, I thought, all mixed up into a Chaos cocktail, like the Blues and the Greens in Constantinople. Michael, it turned out, had never heard of Constantinople, so my analogy fell flat, but he understood the concept, all right, in a very reality-oriented way.

"Then later," Michael went on, "I realized that they knew about parallel worlds and gates, so I told them the truth."

"They knew?"

"Everyone knows about all kinds of talents there. I think it's the radiation. It scrambled a lot of genes."

Michael also confirmed Ari's theory about the consumer goods in the windmill. Our perps had dealt heroin to obtain American money to buy American luxury goods to take back and sell at home on the black market.

"The BGs told me that the Dodgers gangs were runners for the big dealers," Michael explained. "They took the orders and stuff like that. And if someone didn't pay fast enough, they collected the money."

"One way or the other, huh?"

"Yeah."

"I guess the Dodgers must have been in Los Angeles in that world, just like they are in ours."

"No, in Sacramento. They called it Sackamenna, but it's still the state capital. LA got bombed in a war with the Japanese. That was after America got nukes. No one would have bothered bombing Sacramento, though. It wasn't worth the trouble." He considered for a moment. "The BGs weren't a lot better than the Dodger gangs, just poorer, but they took me in, and I can't get too down on them. They dealt dope, just local weed, mostly." He looked away. "And then there were the girls."

"Ah. Hookers, and the guys were their pimps?"

He nodded and blushed. I got the distinct impression that my little brother was no longer a virgin. Aside from that crucial detail, I kept the Agency informed of everything Michael told me. Not only did I file constant reports, I had several trance sessions with Y.

"I've been consulting with the big boss," he told me in one of these. "We definitely have an interest in your brother, Nola. The Agency's prepared to offer him a college scholarship when he's ready to go, along the lines of the old ROTC programs. We pay most of the cost in return for a certain number of years of service."

"That would really help my family out," I said. "But you realize that you're going to have to negotiate with my mother."

Y's image went wide-eyed with fear—brown-eyed, too, and his hair darkened. The image of a small dragon materialized between our chairs and hissed.

"Unless our aunt manages to become Mike's legal guardian," I went on. "She's trying. Mother's considering it. She thinks Mike is an out-of-control juvenile."

Y's image relaxed with a small sigh of relief. The dragon disappeared. His eyes returned to blue.

"You know," I said, "your image changes when you get emotional. Do you really look like it?"

"No, I don't. I got in the habit of using this one, is all, back when you were new and working on a trial basis. I hide my real self with new recruits, in case they don't work out."

"Well, it would be cool to know what you're really like."

"I'll think about it. Keep those reports coming, will you? These glimpses of a deviant level are fascinating. The multiverse is like a chord played on a bevy of harps, but here and there, a discordant note is heard, adding piquancy."

"Which reminds me, what's the Agency going to do about that gate in my aunt's house? My uncle's nailed the door shut and put a padlock on it, but it worries them."

"I suppose it would. I'll talk to the big boss." The image winked at me. "Other changes are in the wind. Maybe some good ones."

"I hope that means I get a raise."

"It could, it could. But, Nola, these are dark and troubled times. We haven't forgotten your reports on the coven and the Peacock Angel. I fear that the masters of Chaos have looked our way."

"Have you been watching too much TV lately?"

"Perhaps I have." Y sighed again and disappeared.

That same day Ari finally heard from Interpol. They wanted him to come back to Israel to appear before some sort of commission before clearing his file of Johnson's death. They had a plane ticket waiting for him at SFO on a flight leaving that evening. I figured that some of the enemies he'd made at his agency saw their chance to rake him over the coals.

I helped him pack, then went with him down to the airport. With my cross-agency government ID I was allowed to skip all the usual security measures and go with him into the passenger waiting area even though I had no ticket. Two security guards escorted us, because Ari wore his beloved Beretta in its shoulder holster. I got the impression that he would be acting as something of an air marshal on the flight, in fact. He mentioned it briefly when we could be sure no one could overhear us. Just in case, he said.

"I hate to leave you," he said more publicly. "I was hoping we'd have another couple of days at least. But once I take care of this problem, I'll be back. I'm due some leave. We can discuss where we're going to live then."

For a moment I couldn't speak. The thought that I was seeing him for the last time hurt.

"Will you miss me?" Ari said.

"Yeah." I saw no reason to lie. "I will."

"I'll be back as soon as I can."

I smiled.

Ari gave me one last kiss, then ran for the gate just as the flight finished boarding. I wandered over to a window and leaned on the rail to watch as the El Al plane pulled slowly away from the boarding tunnel. I was wondering how he would send the final farewell, phone call or e-mail? I couldn't see him writing an actual letter on paper, the way that Josh Mitchell had. He had class, Josh, even if his desire for a normal life had gotten in the way of our relationship. But however Ari sent the good-bye, I knew I could trust him to be honest and straight out with it, no weaseling around about extra workload or sudden obligations, no postponing the inevitable.

The plane taxied out of sight to head for the runway. I left the window and walked away before I cried. I passed back through security on the strength of my cross-agency ID, then caught BART into town.

Ari sent me an e-mail the next morning, but only to say that he'd gotten back safely and that he missed me. I figured the spell hadn't worn off yet.

That afternoon Michael drove over to my place in Uncle Jim's old truck. He brought a big bag of fast food with him, hamburgers, fries, milkshakes—Aunt Eileen had given him the money, he told me, to make sure I ate. Although I suspected she'd had some healthier kind of food in mind, I kept my mouth shut about it. The Chaos critter trotted into the apartment with him and followed us into the kitchen. I put the food on plates and handed Michael one.

"Nola, there's something I've got to do," he said. "I bet you won't like it, though."

"Yeah?" I said. "Run it by me and see."

"I've got to get some stuff to José and the Bravos Gigantes. I mean, they saved my butt, and they took me in, and now I'm here where everything's okay, and they're not."

I had to admit that the sentiment gave him credit. "Stuff?" I said. "Define stuff."

"Nothing illegal."

"Okay, that's the first hurdle jumped."

Michael grinned at me. "I was thinking," he said, "stuff they could eat, like chocolate. Or maybe sell, like batteries. The problem is, I don't have much money, just about twenty bucks. That won't buy a lot."

He wanted, in short, the same kind of goods that Johnson and Doyle had collected for their gang's master. The Chaos critter rubbed up against him with a whine. They were both looking at me with big sad eyes.

"I suppose I could chip in a few bucks," I said, though I felt like a sucker. "But I don't want you wandering off away from the gate."

"This little guy can take José a note." Michael reached down and gave the critter a French fry. "José can see him. Or her. Or whatever."

"Oh, yeah?" I cut my hamburger in quarters and handed a portion to the critter, who grabbed it with greedy claws. "Tell me more about José."

Michael was watching the critter cramming the chunk of burger into its pointy mouth. He shrugged and looked up. "José's cool," he said. "I bet he's got talents like an O'Grady, but he doesn't want to talk about them. It's bad enough he got dumped by his mother. He doesn't want to get shot by the cops, too."

"Wait a minute. Back up here. Dumped by his mother?"

"Yeah, that's what happens to babies when they're born with defects. Their moms dump them in empty lots, and the gang girls take them in when they can find them in time. Before they die or the dogs get them."

"Dogs? You mean, like packs of feral dogs?"

"Yeah. The cops keep shooting them, but there's always more. A lot of them are deformed, too."

"Dogs or cops?"

"Just dogs. Deformed guys can't be cops."

"Okay. Well, I can chip in more than a few bucks. I'll see what I can squeeze out of the Agency accountant." I picked up another chunk of the hamburger and gave it to the Chaos critter.

"Nola, you're supposed to eat that, not give it away." Michael fixed me with an apprentice-level gimlet eye. "Inspector Nathan asked me to watch out for your eating disorder till he gets back."

"The miserable bastard!"

Yet Michael's innocent faith that Ari would be back touched me enough that I said nothing more. He'd have to learn the hard way, like I had, what happened to O'Gradys who got emotionally involved with normal people.

When we were done eating, Michael drove me down to a big warehouse store in San Bruno, where I spent a hundred bucks of Agency money and a bit more of my own on luxuries for the BGs. As well as chocolate, coffee, and a lot of over-the-counter medicines, Michael picked out shampoo and fancy soaps for the girls who belonged to the gang. Since Aunt Eileen had gone to her bridge club, and Brian was at basketball practice, we drove straight back to the Houlihan house.

Uncle Jim had nailed a board across the door into Nanny's old lair. Michael had already pried the nails out, very carefully, without bending them, he told me, and set them loosely back into the original holes. Sure enough, he could slip them out with his fingernails. He stowed them in his pockets, then leaned the board against the wall. While I watched, he deftly opened the padlock with a thin piece of wire.

"Where did you learn how to do that?" I said. "From the BGs?"

"Yeah. I figured it would come in handy someday."

The small square room smelled of mold and dust from the gash Sean had left in the flowered wallpaper. We carried the goods we'd bought inside and stacked them up by the window. Michael unwrapped a chocolate bar and used the paper to write a note, then fed the whole thing to the Chaos critter.

"Go find José," he said and tapped the left side of his face.

The critter whined once, then turned transparent and disappeared. We waited out in the living room for about twenty minutes before it returned. It trotted over to Michael, made a disgusting gurgling sound, and vomited an oddly clean note onto his shoes. Michael picked it up, read it, and grinned.

"They're on the way," he said.

We all hurried down to the storeroom, but the creature disappeared once we'd gotten well inside. As soon as it left, I felt the room shift. For a moment I could barely stay on my feet thanks to the nausea of seeing double. The violet wallpaper, the cartons of Jimmy's old collections, everything Aunt Eileen had put into the room existed as semitransparent shapes, as if they'd been made out of scratched-up plastic. Beyond them stood the solid presence of the bright yellow wallboard, the torn sheet at the window, and the boxes of goods that Mike and I had brought in.

"You'd better just wait in here," Michael told me. "You can look out the window, though."

He opened the window and climbed out. The last traces of Nanny's old room disappeared and left me standing in another world. I walked over to the window and leaned on the sill to see it.

The lot that this house sat on was roughly the same size and shape as that belonging to the Houlihan house, but instead of lawn and flowers, I saw row after row of vegetables, strangely distorted and misshapen vegetables. Morning glory plants as tall as trees grew in tangles of vines supported by wooden poles. The blue and purple flowers stood out vividly in the watery sunlight, huge flowers maybe six inches across. Out among big tomato plants studded with lumpy green fruit, two teen boys had grabbed a furious old man and were holding him by the arms. He was speaking Spanish so fast, spitting out the words, that I couldn't understand him, while the boys laughed and held on tighter every time he tried to wriggle free.

Michael stood by the window talking in slangy English with a blond boy of about his own age, who wore a pair of much-mended brown pants and a dirty Giants T-shirt. He was a good-looking kid, I thought, until he turned his head to say hello to me. I had the crazy thought at first that he'd plastered mushrooms on his face. Whether they were warts or tumors, I don't know, but growths crusted the entire left side of his face and neck, brown and scabby like layers of old mulch.

"This is José," Mike said. "That's my sister, Nola."

"Hey, hi," José said. "And hey, thanks. Mike told me you gave him the money for the stuff."

"Yeah," I said. "You're welcome. Thanks for saving his neck when he was here before."

"Sure. I knew he was one of us the minute we saw him." He grinned, exposing a gold front tooth. "Once we got the blood off him, anyway."

Michael laughed and returned the grin.

"Tell me something." I pointed to the enormous

tangles of flowering vines. "Why does he plant so many morning glories?"

"The seeds get you real high," José said. "We deal with the old dude here and then sell them."

"Got it," I said. "Thanks. I just wondered." I'd read somewhere that scientists thought morning glories might be one of the few plants that would flourish in high radiation conditions. I was seeing the theory confirmed.

José also had six fingers on each hand. I noticed it when he came into the room with Michael to haul the stuff we'd bought outside. When they were done, they stood outside the window and talked for a few minutes more, then shook hands. José whistled to the other boys, who let the old man go and came running to see what Michael had brought them. Other teens came out of the places where they'd been hiding among the plants and clustered around them. The old man recovered his dignity enough to creep up to the edge of the crowd. When Michael grabbed a two-pound bag of coffee beans and handed it to him, he grinned, his mouth wide and toothless.

While the BGs went through the boxes, I stared fascinated at this glimpse of a shattered and poisonous San Francisco. I could just see over the garden up the hill, where at home, nice looking houses sat in tidy rows. Not here—I saw a lot of unpruned trees and wild clusters of bushes. Among them stood the occasional shack or rambling wooden shelter. Distantly I heard dogs barking.

A few at a time, the gang members picked up boxes and drifted away until only José and a brown-haired girl with dark circles under her eyes stayed to talk with Michael. She wore a faded red tank top, a denim skirt way too short even for my taste in clothes, and a pair of heavy brown ugly shoes, one of which looked distinctly orthopedic—Lisa, I assumed. She said little, just stared at Michael while she ran one skinny finger up and down the glass bottle of perfume he'd given her. Looking at her arms, nearly fleshless, and prominent clavicle, I realized for the first time that, yeah, someone really could be too thin. Finally she turned and walked away with an odd rolling gait. The foot must have pained her. I'd never seen anyone with a club foot before. In my world, after all, babies had those problems corrected rather than being dumped in empty lots.

Michael shook hands with José one last time, then climbed back through the window. For a moment I saw double again, only this time the ghostly shapes belonged to José's world and the solid ones, to mine. When Michael shut the window, José's world disappeared. By the time we walked out into the hall, the gate had completely closed, and I saw nothing but Jimmy's old collections in their cartons, the proper shade at the window, and the violets on the torn wallpaper. Michael slammed the door behind us.

"Tell me something," I said, "do you think José and crew will try to use the gate?"

"They can't, not without me to open it." Michael picked up the board he'd left against the wall. "Nobody else in the BGs is a world-walker."

"Do you think you'll ever go back there again?"

"I dunno." He shrugged. "It's a pretty dangerous place."

"It's probably also radioactive. It takes a long time for the leftover death from a nuclear war to decay. I'd hate to have you lighting up Geiger counters for a hobby."

Michael shrugged again and fished in his jeans pockets. He brought out the nails he'd taken from the door and began sliding them back into the board. It took him several minutes to line the board and the nails up with the holes in the door, but eventually everything looked just like Uncle Jim had left it.

"The prospect of a long slow death from radiation

poisoning may not mean much to you." I took up my cheery little theme again. "But it's not exactly a cool way to go."

"Yeah."

"Mike—"

"Just shut up!" he snapped, then softened his voice. "You're right, okay? I just don't like thinking about it, what's going to happen to all of them." He turned around to look at me, and I could see tears in his eyes. "They'll be dead before they're thirty. If the cops don't get them, the rads will."

"I should have thought of that. I'm sorry."

"Well, maybe some of them will be okay. Some people do live a long time even with all the rads, like the old guy who owns the house. But no one knows why."

"Look, I'm real sorry I mouthed off."

"It's okay." He sighed and took the padlock out of his shirt pocket. "It's thinking about Lisa that really bums me out."

"I kind of wondered if that was the case."

He shrugged. I waited. He slipped the padlock back onto the staple, then closed it with a click.

"The Lisa here, you know?" Michael said at last. "I don't think I can see her again."

"She broke up with you already?"

"No, not what I meant. I don't think I can stand to see her again. I just don't know how to tell her." He turned around and looked at me with eyes full of real distress. "Hey, there's this other girl just like you, Lisa, but she's a cheap whore in another world, and she's gonna get real sick, too, one of these days, and here you are, okay and everything, but I can't look at you without seeing her, too. That's not going to go over real well."

"No, it isn't." I thought hard, but nothing came to me. "I don't know what to suggest, Mike, except to play for a little time. You were beaten up pretty bad. Tell her you're still kind of concussed, and you have to stay home and rest, doctor's orders, and then see what you feel like later."

"Okay. I'm beginning to see what you and Pat meant, when you talked about how fucking hard it is to be an O'Grady. I just didn't see it before."

"We all learn, and it's always lousy."

Michael said nothing more while we went outside. We got into the truck so he could drive me home, but rather than starting it, he leaned back in the seat and rested his hands on the steering wheel.

"Ah, hell," he said finally. "At least I got them some cool stuff. Thanks, Nola. I'll pay you back. Uncle Jim told me last night that he'll pay me for yard work. He wants to build some new back steps."

"Well, you don't have to."

"I want to." He managed a smile. "I don't want Inspector Nathan thinking I'm sponging off his girl-friend."

"He wouldn't approve of that, no."

If he ever finds out, I thought. If either of us ever see him again. Fat chance of that.

I was trying to reconcile myself to Ari being gone for-ever, but every time I logged on to my regular e-mail, I scanned down the list, dreading to see his final good-bye. I did get a second letter a couple of days later, announc-ing that Interpol had cleared him of any wrongdoing in his use of deadly force. He ended that one mysteriously, "further developments to come." I assumed he meant the news that our affair was dead and gone. As the days passed and I received no dismissal, I could put some dis-tance between us in my mind. After all, I'd only known the man for a couple of weeks. He couldn't matter that much to me.

I had a lot of work to keep me busy, reports to file about the Silver Bullet Affair, research into the Peacock

Angel cult, further discussions with Y about Michael
and his talents, and the problem of the Houlihan house.
Whether Washington would want to seal that gate, I
couldn't say, though Aunt Eileen worried about it daily.
I could see why, of course, even beyond the rational reasons against having a radioactive back door. Now that
I'd gotten a good look at it, I sensed a real peculiarity
about that deviant world level. Nothing about it added
up in my mind. Yet the thought of asking Mike to take
me there for a good look around made my stomach twist.

I took refuge in my other work. I also went back to
Morrison Marketing one last time to clear out my personal belongings. The Agency was shutting that cover
story down. I returned to Chaos watch and regular
dice walks, too, while I tried to decide if I should ask
for a transfer out of San Francisco. It would depend
on whether my family would be safer with me there or
elsewhere. Certainly my sister Kathleen expected me to
stay. We had lunch one day, and she mentioned that she
was giving a party soon that she wanted me to attend.
Aunt Eileen had no qualms about letting me know that
she wanted to keep me in San Francisco.

"Michael needs you," she told me one night on the
phone. "It's very nice of your agency to take an interest
in him, and heaven knows the scholarship money will
help with his college, but he needs a member of his family here with him. Sean can't help much."

"He needs help himself."

"It's not easy, being an O'Grady."

"Yeah. I should know."

"Well, that's very true, of course. Anyway, Michael
probably won't ask outright, but he really wants you to
stay."

That sealed the deal. "Okay, I'll put in for a permanent assignment tonight over the Internet. It's not a
hundred percent certain that I'll get it. Most likely I will,

but you never know what Washington will decide. I'll contact my handler tomorrow."

When I linked up with Y in the trance state, he had a surprise of his own for me. It's a good thing I recognize the touch of his mind, or I'd have been convinced that he was an impostor. Instead of a blue-eyed blond, his image appeared Japanese-American, with thick but heavily gray hair and glasses. In his youth, though, he must have been good-looking, and he still had a distinguished air.

"Wow," I said, "this is quite a change!"

"Yes," Y said, "I thought over what you said about appearances. It was time I showed you the truth. There really was no reason for me to look like Tab Hunter."

"Who?"

"A Fifties movie star. His career was over before you were born. Now, about this assignment request, I take it you want to stay close to your family."

"Yeah, that's part of the motivation."

"Well, it won't be a problem. I have news for you, good news, I hope. The Agency's decided to establish a San Francisco bureau." He rolled his eyes. "The higher-ups are calling it the Apocalypse Squad."

"Say what? Why?"

"The big boss thinks it's funny. Why else?"

"I thought maybe someone had a vision."

"No, nothing so sensible. At any rate, I'll start the paperwork for your new assignment and send it to you via TranceWeb. You're getting an offer to head up the new bureau. Don't be too flattered, though. No one else particularly wants the job."

I laughed. "I can see why," I said. "Does this mean a raise?"

"Yes, and a better expense account. I'll send you the details."

The details arrived that night at my home computer.

I looked them over while I ate a couple of cold-storage apples for dinner. The new salary, if everything went through, would allow me to move out of Mrs. Z's and find a decent apartment. Best of all, I'd be in charge with no supervisor to make my life miserable, though of course I'd continue to report to Y. I finalized my end of the agreement and sent it off right away, then called Aunt Eileen to share the good news.

"That's wonderful!" she said. "I'm so happy for you, as well as being glad you're staying. A promotion's always nice."

"Yeah, it sure is."

"Did your employer say anything more about the gate in the house? Closing it, I mean. It really is rather worrisome."

"He didn't, no, but I'll keep after him. I'm still wondering why it's there at all. I don't suppose Uncle Jim remembers anything about his mother opening it up or doing something that might have started it? Kind of as a back door to her lair."

"Lair is a good word for it." Eileen paused for a sigh. "We've talked about it, but no, we're both as baffled as you are. She did get awfully strange by the end, though."

"Well, we may never know." Yet I knew a thought was struggling to rise into consciousness. You do know. Think, O'Grady! Think!

The thought stayed hidden.

I stayed up late that night collating my notes on the deviant levels of the multiverse. We knew of one level that we could access. Could we find more? Did we want to? I had a feeling that the level we lived on presented enough trouble for the Agency without adding others, but I had no idea what the higher-ups would decide. I went to bed around two in the morning. As I was drifting off, I decided I'd sleep in.

At six in the morning, my phone chimed. I grabbed it

from the nightstand and opened the connection while I yawned.

"Hello, Nola?" Ari's voice. "Did I wake you?"

Here it comes, I thought, the brisk good-bye. "Yeah," I said. "Good morning."

"I was afraid of that, but I'm at the airport."

The words refused to make sense. "Say what?" I said.

"I'm at the airport, SFO. I'm waiting to get passed through customs by the security people. Will you come pick me up, or should I just rent a car?"

He'd come back to me. Maybe time stopped, maybe it didn't, but I stared at the phone until the universe started moving again.

"I'll pick you up," I said. "I want to see you again, not just identify your body in the morgue."

He chuckled, as close as Ari usually came to an actual laugh. "Take the underground down, and we'll rent a car here."

"Okay, but it better be one I can drive, not you. Where will you be?"

"Waiting for you at the underground station, assuming I'm through security by the time you get here. If I'm not there, wait for me."

He hung up, leaving me wide awake. If I hadn't still been holding my cell phone, I would have thought I'd dreamed the entire conversation. During the long ride down to the airport, I replayed it in my head with a running refrain of my own. He came back. And here I hadn't had a single premonition.

I got off the BART train and confirmed the reality. Rumpled from the long flight, unshaven, smelly, and just as gorgeous as I remembered him, Ari was waiting for me next to a huge mound of luggage. I tried to play it cool, but something gave way inside, and I ran to him. He threw his arms around me, pulled me close, and kissed me. Several times, in fact.

"Glad to see me?" he said at last.

"Hell, yeah," I said. "What is this, your vacation?"

"Didn't they tell you?" He let me go and stepped back. "About the new bureau?"

The pieces fell into place. "Yeah," I said when I could breathe again. "The Agency just didn't tell me you were part of it."

"I'm on an indefinite assignment via Interpol. I'm going to be your liaison with the local police. And your bodyguard."

"Indefinite, huh?"

"Well, my lot saw their chance to get me out of their sight, I think. I suppose I may have stepped on a few toes over the years."

"You? Really?"

Ari started to answer, then forced out a smile. "You're having a joke on me."

"Yeah, 'fraid so. Did you try to turn the assignment down?"

"Why would I have done that? Someone has to keep you from starving to death." He paused, glancing around us at the crowd of passengers, and dropped his voice. "I can't say much more here. But there are other reasons they sent me over."

"Let's go home, then, and you can tell me there."

"Over dinner. After I make sure you're hungry enough for a proper meal."

"Then maybe we should stop at the store on the way back. My apartment doesn't have room service, and who knows, it could be late by the time I work up an appetite."

"It could be." He grinned at me. "Let's go get that rental car. And this time, you can be on the insurance."

Agency Talents and Acronyms

ASTA Automatic Survival Threat Awareness

CDEP Chaos Diagnostic Emergency Procedure

CW Chaos wards

CDS Collective Data Stream

CEV Conscious Evasion Procedure

DEI Deliberately Extruded Images (visible only to psychics)

DW dice walk

E Ensorcellment

HC Heat Conservation

IOI Image Objectification of Insight

LDRS Long Distance Remote Sensing

MI Manifested Indicators (of Chaos forces)

PI Possibility Images

SAF Scanning the aura field

SM Search Mode

SM: G Search Mode: General

SM: P Search mode: Personnel

SAWM Semi-Automatic Warning Mechanism

SH Shield Persona

SPPP Subliminal Psychological Profile

UPC Unexplained Personnel Capabilities (occult powers)